Love's Labor Won

By

Emma Dorothy Eliza Nevitte Southworth

Love's labor won
by Emma Dorothy Eliza Nevitte Southworth

ISBN: 978-93-63055-85-8

Published by

DOUBLE 9 BOOKS

2/13-B, Ansari Road
Daryaganj, New Delhi – 110002
info@double9books.com
www.double9books.com
Tel. 011-40042856

ABOUT THE AUTHOR

Emma Dorothy Eliza Nevitte Southworth (December 26, 1819 - June 30, 1899) was an American novelist who wrote over 60 books in the late nineteenth century. She was the most popular American novelist of her day. In her works, her heroines frequently challenge modern ideas of Victorian feminine domesticity by demonstrating that virtue is naturally coupled with wit, adventure, and rebellion to fix any terrible situation. Though The Hidden Hand (1859) was her most popular novel, Southworth preferred Ishmael (1876). Emma Nevitte was born on December 26, 1819, in Washington, D.C., to Susannah Wailes and Charles LeCompte Nevitte, a trader from Virginia. Her father died in 1824, and she was given the name Emma Dorothy Eliza Nevitte at his final wish. She attended a school run by her stepfather, Joshua L. Henshaw. She later described her youth as lonely, with her best times spent exploring Maryland's Tidewater region on horseback. During such rides, she developed a deep interest in the area's history and mythology. After attending her stepfather's school, she finished her secondary education at the age of 15 in 1835.

CONTENTS

CHAPTER I
THE IMPROVVISATRICE

"Hers was the spell o'er hearts

That only genius gives;

The mother of the sister Arts,

Where all their beauty lives."

—Varied from Campbell.

"Beautiful."

"Glorious."

"Celestial!"

Such were the exclamations murmured through the room, in low but earnest tones.

"So fair and dark a creature I have never seen," said the French ambassador.

"The rarest and finest features of the blonde and the brunette combined; look at her hair and brow! It is as if the purple lustre of Italia's vines lay upon the snow of Switzerland's Alps," said a young English gentleman, of some twenty years of age, and from whom the air of the university had scarcely fallen.

"You are too enthusiastic, Lord William," gravely observed an elderly man, in the dress of a clergyman of the Church of England.

"Too enthusiastic, sir! Ah, now! do but see for yourself, if it be not profane to gaze at her. Is she not now—what is she? Queenly? Pshaw! I was, when a boy, at Versailles with my father; I saw Marie Antoinette and the beautiful princesses of her train; but never, no, never, have I seen beauty and dignity and grace like this. You have the honor of knowing the lady, sir?" he concluded, turning abruptly to a member of the French legation, standing near him.

"Oh, yes, monsieur, I have that distinction," said the affable Parisian, with a bow and smile.

"And her name is— —"

"Ah, pardon me, monsieur—Mademoiselle Marguerite De Lancie."

"Oh! a countrywoman of your own?"

"Excuse, monsieur—a Virginie."

"Ah, ha! Miss De Lancie, of Virginia," said the young Englishman, who, having thus ascertained all that he wished to know for the present, now, with the characteristic and irresponsible bluntness of his nature, turned his back upon the small Frenchman, and gave himself up to the contemplation of the lady seated at the harp.

This conversation occurred in a scene and upon an occasion long to be remembered. The scene was the saloon of the old Presidential mansion at Philadelphia. The occasion was that of Mrs. Washington's last reception, previous to the final retirement of General Washington from office. The beauty, talent, fashion and celebrity of the "Republican Court" were present—heroes of the Revolutionary struggle—warriors, whose mighty swords had cleft asunder the yoke of foreign despotism; sages, whose gigantic minds had framed the Constitution of the young Republic; men whose names were then, as now, of world-wide glory and time-enduring fame; foreign ministers and ambassadors, with their suites, all enthusiastic admirers, or politic flatterers of the glorious New Power that had arisen among the nations; wealthy, aristocratic or otherwise distinguished tourists, whom the fame of the young Commonwealth and the glory of her Father had attracted to her shores; women, also, whose beauty, grace and genius so dazzled the perceptions of even these late *habitues* of European courts that they avowed themselves unable to decide whether were the sons of Columbia the braver or her daughters the fairer!

And through them all, but greater than all, moved the Chief, arrayed simply, as a private gentleman, but wearing on his noble brow that royalty no crown could give.

But who is she, that even in this company of splendid magnificence, upon this occasion of supreme interest, can for an hour become the magnet of all eyes and ears!

Marguerite De Lancie was the only child of a Provençal gentleman and a Virginia lady, and combined in her person and in her character all the strongest attributes of the Northern and the Southern races; blending the passions, genius and enthusiasm of the one with the intellectual power, pride and independence of the other; and contrasting in her person the luxuriant purplish-black hair and glorious eyes of the Romaic nations, with the fair, clear complexion and roseate bloom of the Saxon. Gifted above most women by nature, she was also favored beyond most ladies by fortune. Having lost her mother in the tender age of childhood, she was reared and educated by her father, a gentleman of the most accomplished cultivation. He imbued the mind of Marguerite with all the purest and loftiest sentiments of liberty and humanity, that in his country somewhat redeemed the wickedness of the French Revolution. Monsieur De Lancie, dying when his daughter was but eighteen years of age, made her his sole heiress, and also, in accordance with his own liberal and independent principles, and his confidence in Marguerite's character and strength of mind, he left her the irresponsible mistress of her own property and person. Marguerite was not free from grave faults. A beautiful, gifted and idolized girl, left with the unrestrained disposal of her time and her ample fortune, it was impossible but that she must have become somewhat spoiled. Her defects exhibited themselves in excessive personal pride and extreme freedom of thought and speech, and some irradicable prejudices which she took no trouble to conceal. The worshiped of many suitors, she had remained, up to the age of twenty-two, with her hand unengaged and her heart untouched. Several American women had about this time married foreign noblemen; and those who envied this superb woman averred that the splendid Marguerite only waited for a coronet.

When at home, Miss De Lancie resided either at her elegant town house in the old city of Winchester, or upon one of her two plantations, situate, the upper among the wildest and most beautiful hills of the Blue Ridge, and the lower upon the banks of the broad Potomac, where she reigned mistress of her land and people, "queen o'er herself."

Marguerite was at present in Philadelphia, on a visit to her friend, Miss Compton, whose father occupied a "high official station" in the Administration. This was Miss De Lancie's first appearance in Philadelphia society. And now that she was there, Marguerite, with the constitutional enthusiasm of her nature, forgot herself in the deep interest of this assembly, where the father of his country met for the last time, socially, her sons and daughters.

In accordance with the elegant ease that characterized Mrs. Washington's drawing-rooms, several ladies of distinguished musical taste and talent had varied the entertainment of the evening by singing, to the accompaniment of the harp, or piano, the national odes and popular songs of that day.

Then ensued a short interval, at the close of which Miss De Lancie permitted herself to be led to the harp by Colonel Compton. She was a stranger to most persons in that saloon, and it was simply her appearance as she passed and took her place at the harp that had elicited that restrained burst of admiration with which this chapter opens.

She was, indeed, a woman of superb beauty, which never shone with richer lustre than upon this occasion that I present her to the reader.

Her figure was rather above the medium height, but elegantly proportioned. The stately head arose from a smoothly-rounded neck, whose every curve and bend was the very perfection of grace and dignity; lustrous black hair, with brilliant purple lights like the sheen on the wing of some Oriental bird, was rolled back from a queenly forehead, and turned over a jeweled comb in a luxuriant fall of ringlets at the back of her head; black eyebrows distinctly drawn, and delicately tapering toward the points, were arched above rich, deep eyes of purplish black, that languished or glowed, rocked or flashed, from beneath their long lashes with every change of mood; and all harmonized beautifully with a pure, rich complexion, where the clear crimson of the cheeks blended softly into the pearly whiteness of the blue-veined temples and broad forehead, while the full, curved lips glowed with the deepest, brightest flush of the ruby. She was arrayed in a royal purple velvet robe, open over a richly-embroidered white satin skirt; her neck and arms were veiled with fine point lace; and a single diamond star lighted up the midnight of her hair.

Having seated herself at the harp and essayed its strings, she paused, and seemingly unconscious of the many eyes riveted upon her, she raised her head, and gazing into the far-off distance, threw her white arm across the instrument, and swept its chords in a deep, soul-thrilling prelude—not to a national ode or popular song, but to a spirit-stirring, glorious improvisation! This prelude seemed a musical paraphrase of the great national struggle and victory. She struck a few deep, solitary notes, and then swept the harp in a low, mournful strain, like the first strokes of tyranny, followed by the earliest murmurs of discontent; then the music, with intervals of monotone, arose in fitful gusts like the occasional skirmishes that heralded the Revolution; then the calm was lost in general storm and devastation—the report of musketry, the tramp of steeds, the clashing of swords, the thunder of artillery, the fall of walls, the cries of the wounded, the groans of the dying, and the shouts of victory, were not only heard, but seen and felt in that magnificent tempest of harmony.

Then the voice of the *improvvisatrice* arose. Her subject was the retiring chief. I cannot hope to give any idea of the splendor of that improvisation—as easily might I catch and fix with pen, or pencil, the magnificent life of an equinoctial storm, the reverberation of its thunder, the conflagration of its lightning! Possessed of Apollo, the light glowed upon her cheeks, irradiated her brow, and streamed, as it were, in visible, living rays from her glorious eyes! The whole power of the god was upon the woman, and the whole soul of the woman in her theme. There was not a word spoken, there was scarcely a breath drawn in that room. She finished amid a charmed silence that lasted until Colonel Compton appeared and broke the spell by leading her from the harp.

Then arose low murmurs of enthusiastic admiration, restrained only by the deep respect due to the chief personage in that assembly.

"*La Marguerite des Marguerites!*" said the gallant French *attaché*.

"A Corinne! I must know her, sir. Will you do me the honor to present me?" inquired the English student, turning again to the Frenchman.

"Lord William!" interrupted the clerical companion, with an air of caution and admonition.

"Well, Mr. Murray! well! did not my father desire that I should make the acquaintance of all distinguished Americans?—and surely this lady must be one of their number."

"Humph," said the clergyman, stroking his chin, "the marquis did not, probably, include distinguished actresses, Lord William."

"Actresses! have you judgment, Mr. Murray? Do but look with what majesty she speaks and moves!"

"So I have heard does Mrs. Siddons. Let us withdraw, Lord William."

"Not yet, if you please, sir! I must first pay my respects to this lady. Will you favor me, monsieur?"

"Pardon! I will make you known to Colonel Compton, who will present you to the lady under his charge," said the Frenchman, bowing, and leading the way, while the clergyman left behind only vented his dissatisfaction in a few emphatic grunts.

"Miss De Lancie, permit me to present to you Lord William Daw, of England," said Colonel Compton, leading the youthful foreigner before the lady.

Miss De Lancie bowed and half arose. She received the young gentleman coldly, or rather absently, and to all that he advanced she replied abstractedly; for she had not yet freed herself from the trance that had lately bound her.

Nevertheless, Lord William found "grace and favor" in everything the enchantress said or did. He lingered near her until at last, with a *congé* of dismissal to her boyish admirer, she arose and signified her wish to retire from the saloon.

The next day but one was a memorable day in Philadelphia. It was the occasion of the public and final farewell of George Washington and the inauguration of his successor. From an early hour the city was thronged with visitors, who came, not so much to witness the installment of the new, as to take a tearful last look at the deeply-venerated, retiring President.

The profound public interest, however, did not prevent Lord William Daw from pursuing a quite private one. At an hour as early as the laxest etiquette would permit, he paid his respects to Miss De Lancie at the house of Colonel Compton, and procured himself to be invited by his host to join their party in witnessing the interesting ceremonies at the Hall of Representation.

The family, consisting of the colonel and Mrs. Compton and their daughter Cornelia, went in a handsome landeau, or open carriage.

Miss De Lancie rode a magnificent black charger, that she managed with the ease of a cavalry officer, and with a grace that was only her own.

Lord William, on a horse placed at his service by Colonel Compton, rode ever at her bridle rein; and if he admired her as a gifted *improvvisatrice*, he adored her as an accomplished *equestrienne*, an excellence that of the two his young lordship was the best fitted to appreciate.

Afterward, in the Hall of Representation, he was ever at her side; nor could the august ceremonies and the supreme interest of the scene passing before them, where the first President of the United States offered his valedictory, and the second President took his oath of office, win him for a moment from the contemplation of the queenly form and resplendent face of Marguerite De Lancie.

When the rites were all over, and their party had extricated themselves from the outrushing crowd, who were crushing each other nearly to death in their eagerness to behold the last of the retiring chief; when they had seen Washington enter his carriage and drive homeward; in fine, when at last they reached their own door, Lord William Daw manifested so little inclination to take leave, and even betrayed so great a desire to remain, that nothing was left Colonel Compton but to invite the enamored boy to stay and dine, an invitation that was unhesitatingly accepted.

Dinner over, and lights brought into the drawing-room, and Lord William Daw still lingering.

"Unquestionably, this young man, though a scion of nobility, is ignorant or regardless of the usages of good society," said Colonel Compton to himself. Then addressing the visitor, he said: "The ladies, sir, are going, this evening, to the new theatre, to see Fennel and Mrs. Whitlock in Romeo and Juliet. Will it please you to accompany us?"

"Most happy to do so," replied the youth, with an ingenuous blush and smile at what he must have considered a slight departure from the formal manners of the day, even while unable to resist the temptation and tear himself away.

In a few moments, the carriage was at the door, and the ladies ready.

Miss Compton and Miss De Lancie, Colonel Compton and Lord William Daw, filled the carriage, as well as they afterward filled the box at the theatre.

The play had already commenced when they entered, and the scene in progress was that of the ball at old Capulet's house. It seemed to confine the attention of the audience, but as for Lord William Daw, the mimic life upon the stage had no more power than had had the real drama of the morning to draw his attention from the magnificent Marguerite. He spoke but little; spellbound, his eyes never left her, except when, in turning her regal head, her eyes encountered his—when, blushing like a detected schoolboy, he would avert his face. So, for him; the play passed like a dream; nor did he know it was over until the general rising of the company informed him.

Every one was enthusiastic. Colonel Compton, who had been in London in an official capacity, and had seen Mrs. Siddons, averred it as his opinion that her sister, Mrs. Whitlock, was in every respect the equal of the great *tragedienne*. All seemed delighted with the performance they had just witnessed, excepting only Lord William Daw, who had seen nothing of it, and Marguerite De Lancie, who seemed perfectly indifferent.

"What is your opinion, Miss De Lancie?" inquired the youth, by way of relieving the awkwardness of his own silence.

"About what?" asked Marguerite, abstractedly.

"Ahem!—about—Shakespeare and—this performance."

"Oh! Can I be interested in anything of this kind, after what we have witnessed in the State House to-day? Least of all in this thing?"

"This thing?—what, Marguerite, do you not worship Shakespeare and Mrs. Whitlock, then?" exclaimed Cornelia Compton.

"Mrs. Whitlock? I do not know yet; let me see her in some other character. Shakespeare? Yes! but not traditionally, imitatively, blindly, wholly, as most of you worship, or profess to worship him; I admire his tragedies of Lear, Richard the Third, Macbeth, and perhaps one or two others; but this Romeo and Juliet, this lovesick boy and puling girl—bah! bah! let's go home."

"That's the way with Marguerite! Now I should not have dared to risk my reputation for intelligence by uttering that sentiment," said Cornelia Compton.

"Never fear, child; naught is never in danger," observed Colonel Compton, with good-humored, though severe raillery.

While Lord William Daw, with the morbid and sensitive egotism of a lover, inquired of himself: Does she intend that remark for me? Does she look upon me only in the light of a lovesick boy? Do I only disgust her, then? Thus tormenting himself until their party had entered the carriage, and driven back once more to Colonel Compton's hospitable mansion, and where his host, inwardly laughing, pressed him to come in and take a bed and breakfast.

But the youth, doubtful of the colonel's seriousness, piqued at his inamorata's scornfulness, and ashamed of his own devotedness, declined the invitation, bowed his adieus, and was about to retire, when Colonel Compton placed his carriage and servants at Lord William's disposal, and besought him to permit them to set him down at his own hotel, a service that the young gentleman, with some hesitation, accepted.

In a few days from this, General Washington left Philadelphia for Mount Vernon. And Colonel Compton, who went out of office with his chief, broke up his establishment in Philadelphia, and, with his family, set out for his home in Virginia.

CHAPTER II
"THE LOVE CHASE"

"— —When shines the sun aslant,
The sun may shine and we be cold;
Oh, listen, loving hearts and bold,
Unto my wild romaunt,
Margaret, Margaret!"
—E. B. Browning.

Colonel Compton and family, traveling at leisure in their private carriage, reached the Blue Ridge on the fifth, and Winchester on the seventh day of their journey, and went immediately to the fine old family mansion on the suburbs of the old town, which was comfortably prepared for the occupancy of the proprietor.

Miss De Lancie's elegant house on Loudoun street, under the charge of an exemplary matron, was also ready for the reception of its mistress; but Marguerite yielded to the solicitations of her friend Cornelia, and remained her guest for the present.

Compton Lodge was somewhat older than the town; it was a substantial building of gray sandstone, situated in a fine park, shaded with great forest trees, and inclosed by a stone wall; it had once been a famous hunting seat, where Lord Fairfax, General Morgan, Major Helphinstine and other votaries of St. Hubert, "most did congregate;" and even now it was rather noted for its superior breed of hounds and horses; and for the great foxhunts that were there got up.

Marguerite De Lancie liked the old place upon all these accounts, and sometimes, when the hunting company was very select, she did not hesitate to join their sylvan sports; and scarcely a hunter there, even old Lord Fairfax himself, who still, in his age, pursued with every youthful enthusiasm the pleasures of the chase—acquitted himself better than did this Diana.

But now, in March, the hunting season was over, and if Marguerite De Lancie preferred Compton Lodge to her own house, it was because, after a long winter in Philadelphia—with the monotony of straight streets and red brick walls, and the weariness of crowded rooms—the umbrageous shade of forest trees, the silence and the solitude of nature, with the company of her sole bosom friend, was most welcome.

The second morning after their settlement at home, Colonel Compton's family were seated around the breakfast table, discussing their coffee, buckwheat cakes and broiled venison.

Marguerite's attention was divided between the conversation at the table, and the view from the two open windows before her, where rolling waves of green hills, dappled over with the white and pink blossoms of peach and cherry trees, now in full bloom, wooed and refreshed the eye.

Colonel Compton was sipping his coffee and looking over the Winchester *Republican*, when suddenly he set down his cup and broke into a loud laugh.

All looked up.

"Well, what is the matter?" inquired the comfortable, motherly Mrs. Compton, without ceasing to butter her buckwheat.

"Oh! ha, ha, ha, ha," laughed the colonel.

"That is a very satisfactory reply, upon my word," commented the good woman, covering her cakes with honey.

"Don't—don't—that fellow will be the death of me!"

"Pleasant prospect to laugh at—that!" said his wife, twisting a luscious segment of her now well-sauced buckwheat around the fork, preparatory to lifting it to her lips.

"Oh! do let us have the joke, if there is a joke, papa," pleaded Cornelia.

"Hem! well, listen, then!" said Colonel Compton, reading:

"Distinguished arrival at McGuire's Hotel. Lord William Daw, the second son of the most noble, the Marquis of Eaglecliff, arrived at this place last evening. His lordship, accompanied by his tutor, the Rev. Henry Murray, is now on a tour of the United States, and visits Winchester for the purpose of becoming acquainted with the history and antiquities of the town!"

"That is exceedingly rich! that will quite do!" commented the colonel, laying down his newspaper, and turning with a comic expression toward Marguerite.

She was looking, by the by, in high beauty, though her morning costume was more picturesque than elegant, and more careless than either, and consisted simply of a dark chintz wrapper, over which, drawn closely around her shoulders, was a scarlet crape shawl, in fine contrast with the lustrous purple sheen of her black hair, one-half of which was rolled in a careless mass at the nape of her neck, and the other dropped in rich ringlets down each side of her glowing, brilliant face.

"Hem! the antiquities of Winchester. I rather suspect it is the juvenilities that our young antiquarian is in chase of. Pray, Miss De Lancie, are you one of the antiquities?"

Marguerite curled her proud lip, erected her head and deigned no other reply.

"Unquestionably you also have conquered a title, Marguerite; when you are married, will you place me on your visiting list, Lady William Daw?" asked Cornelia Compton, with an arch glance.

"Cease," said Marguerite, peremptorily, "if I were to be married, which is utterly out of the question, it would not be to a schoolboy, let me assure you!"

"If you 'were to be married, which is utterly out of the question'—why, you don't mean to tell us that you have forsworn matrimony, Marguerite? What do you intend to do? go into a cloister? Nonsense! in nine month you will marry," said Colonel Compton.

"I marry? ha! ha! ha! there must be a great improvement in the stock of men! Where is the unmarried son of Adam that I would deliberately vow to love, honor and obey? Why I should forswear myself at the altar! Of all the single men I meet, the refined ones are weak and effeminate, and the strong ones are coarse and brutal! I'll none of them!" said Marguerite, with a shrug of her shoulders.

"Thank you for making my husband a sort of presumptive exception," said Mrs. Compton.

"Will you call upon Lord William, this morning, papa?" inquired Miss Compton.

"My dear, believe me, the opportunity will scarcely be allowed. His lordship will not stand upon ceremony, I assure you. I expect to hear his name announced every moment."

And then, as in confirmation of Colonel Compton's predictions, a servant entered and handed a card.

"Humph! where have you shown the gentleman, John?"

"Into the front drawing-room, sir."

"Nonsense—bring him in here."

The servant bowed and left the room.

"Such a free and easy visitor is not to be treated with formality. It is as I foresaw, ladies! Lord William Daw waits to pay his respects."

At that moment the door was once more opened, and the visitor announced.

Lord William Daw was a pleasing, wholesome, rather than a handsome or distinguished-looking youth—with a short, stout figure, dark eyes and dark hair, a round rosy face, and white teeth, and an expression full of good-humor, frank and easy among his friends, and disembarrassed among strangers to whom he was indifferent, he was yet timid and bashful as a girl in presence of those whom he admired and honored; how much more so in the society of her—the beautiful and regal woman who had won his young heart's first and deepest worship. With all this the youngster possessed an indomitable will and power of perseverance, which, when aroused, few men, or things, could withstand, and which his messmates at Oxford denominated (your pardon, super-refined reader) an "English bull-dogish—hold-on-a-tiveness."

Lord William entered the breakfast-room, smiling and blushing between pleasure and embarrassment.

Colonel Compton arose and advanced, with a cordial smile and extended hand, to welcome him. "Heartily glad to see you, sir! And here are Mrs. Compton, and my daughter Cornelia, and my sweetheart, Marguerite, all waiting to shake hands with you."

The ladies arose, and Lord William, set at ease by this friendly greeting, paid his respects quite pleasingly.

"And now here is a chair and plate ready for you, for we hope that you have not breakfasted?" said the host.

Lord William had breakfasted; but would do so again. So he sat down at the table and spoiled a cup of coffee and a couple of buckwheat cakes without deriving much benefit from either. A lively conversation ensued.

"The history and antiquities of Winchester, sir," said Colonel Compton, with a half-suppressed smile, in reply to a question of the young tourist. "The history is scarcely a hundred years old, and the antiquities consist mainly of some vestiges of the Shawanee's occupancy, and of Washington's march in the old French and Indian War; but the society, sir—the society representing the old respectability of the State may not be unworthy of your attention."

Lord William was sure that the society was most worthy of cultivation, nevertheless, he would like to see those "vestiges" of which his host spoke.

"The ladies will take their usual morning ride within an hour or two, sir, and if you would like to attend them, they will take pleasure in showing you these monuments."

Lord William was again "most happy." And Colonel Compton rang and ordered "Ali," to be brought out saddled for his lordship's use.

Within an hour after rising from the table, the riding party, consisting of Miss Compton, Miss De Lancie, Lord William Daw, and a groom in attendance, set forth. The lions of Winchester and its environs were soon exhausted, and the party returned to Compton Lodge in time for an early dinner.

Lord William Daw sojourned at Winchester, and became a daily visitor at Compton Lodge. Colonel Compton, to break the exclusiveness of his visits to one house, introduced him at large among the gentry of the neighborhood. And numerous were the tea, card, and cotillion parties got up for the sole purpose of entertaining the young scion of nobility, where it was only necessary to secure Miss De Lancie's presence in order to ensure his lordship's dutiful attendance. Mr. Murray chafed and fretted at what he called his pupil's consummate infatuation, and talked of writing home to his father, "the marquis." Marguerite scorned, or seemed to scorn, his lordship's pretensions, until one morning at breakfast, Colonel Compton, half seriously, half jestingly, said:

"Sweetheart, you do not appear to join in the respect universally shown to this young stranger."

"If," said Marguerite, "the young man had any distinguished personal excellence, I should not be backward in recognizing it; but he is at best— Lord William Daw! Now who is Lord William Daw that I should bow down and worship him?"

"Lord William Daw, my dear, is the second son of the most noble, the Marquis of Eaglecliff, as you have already seen announced with a flourish of editorial trumpets, by our title-despising and very consistent democratic newspapers! He is heir presumptive, and as I learn from Mr. Murray, rather more than heir presumptive to his father's titles and estates; for it appears that the marquis has been twice married, and that his eldest son, by his first marchioness, derives a very feeble constitution from his mother; and it is not supposed that he will ever marry, or that he will survive his father; ergo, the hopes of the marquis for re-union rest with his second son, Lord William Daw; finis, that young nobleman's devoirs are not quite beneath the consideration even of a young lady of 'one of the first families of Virginia,' who is besides a belle, a blue, and a freeholder."

"Marguerite, future marchioness of Eaglecliff, when you are married will your ladyship please to remember one poor Cornelia Compton, who lived in an old country house near Winchester, and once enjoyed your favor?" said Miss Compton.

Marguerite shrugged her shoulders with an expression to the effect that the future succession of the Marquisate of Eaglecliff was a matter of no moment to her.

But from this time, Marguerite's friends accused her, with uncertain justice, of showing somewhat more favor to the boyish lover, who might one day set the coronet of a marchioness upon her brow. When rallied upon this point, she would reply:

"There are certainly qualities which I do like in the young man; he is frank, simple and intelligent, and above all, is perfectly free from affectation, or pretension of any sort. Upon individual worth alone he is entitled to polite consideration."

There was, perhaps, a slight discrepancy between this opinion and one formerly delivered by Miss De Lancie; but let that pass; the last-uttered judgment was probably the most righteous, as growing out of a longer acquaintance, and longer experience in the merits of the subject.

Thus—while Lord William Daw prolonged his stay, and Mr. Murray fumed and fretted, the months of April, May, and June went by. The first of July the family of Compton Lodge prepared to commence their summer tour among the watering, and other places of resort. They left Winchester about the seventh of the month.

Lord William Daw had not been invited to join their party, nor had he manifested inclination to obtrude himself upon their company, nor did he immediately follow in their train.

Nevertheless, a few days after their establishment at Berkeley Springs, Colonel Compton read in the list of arrivals the names of "Lord William Daw, Rev. Henry Murray, and two servants."

Enough! The intimacy between the young nobleman and the Comptons was renewed at Berkeley. And soon the devotion of his youthful lordship to the beautiful and gifted Marguerite De Lancie was the theme of every tongue. To escape this notice, Marguerite withdrew from her party, and attended by her maid and footman, proceeded to join some acquaintances at Saratoga.

In vain! for unluckily Saratoga was as free to one traveler as to another, provided he could pay. And within the same week of Marguerite's settlement at her lodgings, all the manœuvring mammas and marriageable daughters at the Springs were thrown into a state of excitement and speculation by the appearance among them of a young English nobleman, the heir presumptive of a marquisate.

But alas! it was soon perceived that Lord William had eyes and ears and heart for none other than the dazzling Miss De Lancie, "la Marguerite des Marguerites," as the French minister had called her.

Miss De Lancie's manner to her boyish worshiper was rather restraining and modifying than repulsing or discouraging. And there were those who did not hesitate to accuse the proud and queenly Marguerite of finished coquetry.

To avoid this, the lady next joined a party of friends who were going to Niagara.

And of course it was obvious to all that the young English tourist, traveling only for improvement, must see the great Falls. Consequently, upon the day after Miss De Lancie's arrival at the Niagara Hotel, Lord William Daw led her in to dinner. And once more the "infatuation," as they chose to call it, of that young gentleman, became the favorite subject of gossip.

A few weeks spent at the Falls brought the last of September, and Marguerite had promised, upon the first of October, to join her friends, the Comptons, in New York.

When Lord William Daw learned that she was soon to leave, half ashamed, perhaps, of forever following in the train of this disdainful beauty, he terminated his visit and preceded her eastward.

But when the stagecoach containing Miss De Lancie and her party drew up before the city hotel, Lord William, perhaps "to treat resolution," was the first person to step from the piazza and welcome her back.

Colonel Compton and his family were only waiting for Marguerite's arrival to proceed southward. The next day but one was fixed for their departure. But the intervening morning, while the family were alone in their private parlor, Lord William Daw entered, looking grave and troubled.

Colonel Compton arose in some anxiety to welcome him. When he had greeted the ladies and taken a seat, he said:

"I have come only to bid you good-by, friends."

"I am sorry to hear that! but—you are not going far, or to remain long, I hope," said Colonel Compton.

"I am going back to England, sir," replied the young man, with a sorrowful glance at Miss De Lancie, who seemed not quite unmoved.

"You astonish us, Lord William! Is this not a sudden resolution?" inquired Mrs. Compton.

"It is a sudden misfortune, my dear madam! Only this morning have I received a letter from my father, announcing the dangerous illness of my dear mother, and urging my instant return by the first homeward-bound vessel. The *Venture*, Captain Parke, sails for Liverpool at twelve to-day. I must be on board within two hours," replied the young man, in a mournful voice, turning the same deeply-appealing glance toward Marguerite, whose color slightly paled.

"We are very sorry to lose you, Lord William, and still sorrier for the occasion of your leaving us," said Cornelia Compton. And so said all the party except—Miss De Lancie.

Lord William then arose to shake hands with his friends.

"I wish you a pleasant voyage and a pleasant arrival," said the colonel.

"And that you may find your dear mother quite restored to health," added Mrs. Compton.

"Oh, yes, indeed! I hope you will, and that you will soon visit us again," said Cornelia.

Marguerite said nothing.

"Have you no parting word for me, Miss De Lancie?" inquired the young man, approaching her, and speaking in a low tone, and with a beseeching look.

Marguerite waved her hand. "A good voyage, my lord," she said.

He caught that hand and pressed it to his lips and heart, and after a long, deep gaze into her eyes, he recollected himself, snatched his hat, bowed to the party, and left the room.

Colonel Compton, in the true spirit of kindness, arose and followed with the purpose of attending him to his ship.

"There's a coronet slipped through your fingers! Oh, Marguerite! Marguerite! if I had been in your place I should have secured that match! For, once married, they couldn't unmarry us, or bar the succession, either, and so, in spite of all the reverend tutors and most noble papas in existence, I should, in time, have worn the coronet of a marchioness," said Miss Compton.

"And you would have done a very unprincipled thing, Cornelia," replied her mother, very gravely.

The blood rushed to Miss De Lancie's brow and crimsoned her face, as she arose in haste and withdrew to her own chamber.

"But, mamma, what do you suppose to have been the cause of Marguerite's rejection of Lord William's addresses?"

"I think that she had two reasons, either of which would have been all sufficient to govern her in declining the alliance. The first was, that Marguerite could never yield her affections to a man who has no other personal claims upon her esteem than the possession of a good heart and a fair share of intelligence; the second was, that Miss De Lancie had too high a sense of honor to bestow her hand on a young gentleman whose addresses were unsanctioned by his family."

The next day Colonel Compton and his party set out for Philadelphia, where, upon his arrival, he received from Mr. Adams an official appointment that required his residence in the city of Richmond. And thither, in the course of the month, he proceeded with his wife and daughter.

Miss De Lancie went down to pass the autumn at her own house in Winchester, where she remained until the first of December, when, according to promise, she went to Richmond to spend the winter with her friend Cornelia.

The Comptons had taken a very commodious house in a fashionable quarter of the city, and were in the habit of seeing a great deal of company. It was altogether a very brilliant winter in the new capital of Virginia. Quite a constellation of beauties and celebrities were there assembled, but the star of the ascendant was the splendid Marguerite De Lancie. She was even more beautiful and dazzling than ever; and she entered with spirit into all the gayeties of the season. Tea and card parties, dances and masked balls followed each other in quick succession.

It was just before Christmas that the belles of the metropolis were thrown into a state of delightful excitement by the issue of tickets from the gubernatorial mansion, to a grand ball to be given on the ensuing New Year's Eve. Great was the flutter of preparation, and great the accession of business that flowed in upon the milliners, mantua-makers and jewelers.

Miss De Lancie and Miss Compton went out together to select their dresses for the occasion. I mention this expedition merely to give you a clew to what I sometimes suspected to be the true motive that inspired Cornelia Compton's rather selfish nature, with that caressing affection she displayed for Marguerite De Lancie. As for Marguerite's devotion to Cornelia, it was one of those mysteries, or prophecies of the human heart, that only the future can explain. Upon this occasion, when Miss De Lancie ordered a rich, white brocade for her own dress, she selected a superb pink satin for her friend's; and when from the jeweler's Marguerite's hereditary diamonds came, set in a new form, they were accompanied by a pretty set of pearls to adorn the arms and bosom of Cornelia. Colonel Compton knew nothing of his guest's costly presents to his daughter. With a gentleman's inexperience in such matters, he supposed that the hundred dollars he had given "Nellie" for her outfit had covered all the expenses. And when Mrs. Compton, who better knew the cost of pearls and brocade, made any objection, Marguerite silenced her by delicately intimating the possibility, that, under some circumstances, for instance, that of her being treated as a stranger, she might be capable of withdrawing to a boarding-house.

The eventful evening of the governor's ball arrived. The entertainment was by all conceded to be, what it should have been, the most splendid affair of the kind that had come off that season. A suite of four spacious rooms, superbly furnished and adorned, and brilliantly lighted, were thrown open.

In the first, or dressing-room, the ladies left their cloaks and mantles, and rearranged their toilets. In the second, Governor Wood stood, surrounded by the most distinguished civil and military officers of the State, and with his unequaled, dignified courtesy received his guests. In the third, and most spacious saloon, where the floor was covered with canvas for dancing, the walls were lined with mirrors, and festooned with flowers that enriched the atmosphere with odoriferous perfumes, while from a vine-covered balcony a military band filled all the air with music. Beyond the saloon, the last, or supper-room, was elegantly set out. The supper table was quite a marvel of taste in that department; just above it hung an immensely large chandelier, with quite a forest of pendant brilliants; its light fell and was flashed back from a sheet mirror laid upon the center of a table, and surrounded by a wreath of box-vines and violets, like a fairy lake within its banks of flowers; on the outer edge of this ring was a circle of grapes with their leaves and tendrils; while filling up the other space were exotic flowers and tropical fruits, and every variety of delicate refreshment in the most beautiful designs.

The rooms were filled before the late arrival of Colonel Compton and his party. The ladies paused but a few minutes in the dressing-room to compose their toilets and draw on their gloves, and then they joined their escort at the inner door, went in, and were presented to Governor Wood, and then passed onward to the dancing-saloon, where the music was sounding and the waltz moving with great vivacity.

The *entrée* of our young ladies made quite a sensation. Both were dressed with exquisite taste.

Miss Compton wore a rich rose-colored satin robe, the short sleeves and low corsage of which were trimmed with fine lace, and the skirt open in front and looped away, with lilies of the valley, from a white sarsenet petticoat; a wreath of lilies crowned her brown hair, and a necklace and bracelet of pearls adorned her fair bosom and arms.

And as for Miss De Lancie, if ever her beauty, elegance and fascination reached a culminating point, it was upon this occasion. Though her dress was always perfect, it was not so much what she wore as her manner of wearing, that made her toilets so generally admired. Upon this evening her costume was as simple as it was elegant—a rich, white brocade robe open over a skirt of embroidered white satin, delicate falls of lace from the low bodice and flowing sleeves, and a light tiara of diamonds spanning like a rainbow the blackness of her hair.

As soon as the young ladies were seated, they were surrounded. Miss Compton accepted an invitation to join the waltzers.

Miss De Lancie, who never waltzed, remained the center of a charmed circle, formed of the most distinguished men present, until the waltzing was over, and the quadrilles were called, where she accepted the hand of Colonel Randolph for the first set, and yielded her seat to the wearied Cornelia, who was led thither by her partner to rest.

It chanced that Miss De Lancie was conducted to the head of the set, then forming, and that she stood at some little distance, immediately in front of, and facing the spot where Cornelia sat, so that the latter, while resting, could witness Marguerite. Now Cornelia very much admired Miss De Lancie, and thought it appeared graceful and disinterested to laud the excellencies of her friend, at she would not have done those of her sister, had she possessed one. So now she tapped her partner's hand with her fan, and said:

"Oh, do but look at Miss De Lancie! Is she not the most beautiful woman in the room?"

The gentleman followed the direction of her glance, where Marguerite was moving like a queen through the dance, and said:

"Miss De Lancie is certainly the most beautiful woman in the world — except one," with a glance, that the vanity of Nellie readily interpreted.

The eyes of both turned again upon Marguerite, who was now standing still in her place waiting for the next quadrille to be called. While they thus contemplated her in all her splendid beauty, set off by a toilet the most elegant in the room, Marguerite suddenly gave a violent start, shivered through all her frame and bent anxiously to listen to something that was passing between two gentlemen, who were conversing in a low tone, near her. She grew paler and paler as she listened, and then with a stifled shriek, she fell to the floor, ere any one could spring to save her.

Cornelia flew to her friend's relief. She was already raised in the arms of Colonel Randolph, and surrounded by ladies anxiously proffering vinaigrettes and fans, while their partners rushed after glasses of water.

"Bring her into the dressing-room, at once, Randolph," said Colonel Compton, as he joined the group.

Accordingly Miss De Lancie was conveyed thither, and laid upon a lounge, where every restorative at hand was used in succession, and in vain. More than an hour passed, while she lay in that deathlike swoon; and when at last the efforts of an experienced physician were crowned with thus much success, that she opened her dimmed eyes and unclosed her blanched lips, it was only to utter one word—"Lost"—and to relapse into insensibility.

She was put into the carriage and conveyed home, accompanied by her wondering friends and attended by the perplexed physician. She was immediately undressed and placed in bed, where she lay all night, vibrating between stupor and a low muttering delirium, in which some irreparable misfortune was indicated without being revealed—was it all delirium?

Next, a low, nervous fever supervened, and for six weeks Marguerite De Lancie swayed with a slow, pendulous uncertainty between life and death. The cause of her sudden indisposition remained a mystery. The few cautious inquiries made by Colonel Compton resulted in nothing satisfactory. The two gentlemen whose conversation was supposed by Miss Compton to have occasioned Miss De Lancie's swoon could not be identified—among the crowd then assembled at the governor's reception, and now dispersed all over the city—without urging investigation to an indiscreet extent.

"This is an inquiry that we cannot with propriety push, Nellie. We must await the issue of Miss De Lancie's illness. If she recovers she will doubtless explain," said Colonel Compton.

With the opening of the spring, Marguerite De Lancie's life-powers rallied and convalescence declared itself. In the first stages of her recovery, while yet body and mind were in that feeble state which sometimes leaves the spiritual vision so clear, she lay one day, contemplating her friend, who sat by her pillow, when suddenly she threw her arms around Cornelia's neck, lifted her eyes in an agony of supplication to her face, and cried:

"Oh, Nellie! do you truly love me? Oh, Nellie! love me! love me! lest I go mad!"

In reply, Cornelia half smothered the invalid with caresses and kisses, and assurances of unchanging affection.

"Oh, Nellie, Nellie! there was one who on the eve of the bitterest trial, said to his chosen friends, 'All ye shall be offended because of me.' And his chief friend said, 'Although all should be offended yet will not I,' and furthermore declared, 'if I should die with thee, I will not deny thee in any wise.' Oh! failing human strength! Oh! feeble human love! Nellie! you know how it ended. 'They all forsook him and fled.'"

"But I will be truer to my friend than Peter to his master," replied Cornelia.

Marguerite drew the girl's face down closer to her own, gazed wistfully, not into but upon those brilliant, superficial brown eyes, that because they had no depth repelled her confidence, and then with a deep groan and a mournful shake of the head, she released Nellie, and turned her own face to the wall. Did she deem Miss Compton's friendship less profound than pretentious? I do not know; but from that time Miss De Lancie maintained, upon one subject at least, a stern reserve. And when, at last, directly, though most kindly and respectfully, questioned as to the origin of her agitation and swoon in the ball-room, she declared it to have been a symptom of approaching illness, and discouraged further interrogation.

Slowly Marguerite De Lancie regained her strength. It was the middle of March before she left her bed, and the first of April before she went out of the house.

One day about this time, as the two friends were sitting together in Marguerite's chamber, Cornelia said:

"There is a circumstance that I think I ought to have told you before now, Marguerite. But we read of it only a few days after you were taken ill, and when you were not in a condition to be told of it."

"Well, what circumstance was that?" asked Miss De Lancie, indifferently.

"It was a fatal accident that happened to one of our friends. No, now! don't get alarmed—it was to no particular friend," said Cornelia, interrupting herself upon seeing Marguerite's very lips grow white.

"Well! what was it?" questioned the latter.

"Why, then, you must know that the *Venture*, in which Lord William Daw sailed, was wrecked off the coast of Cornwall, and Lord William and Mr. Murray were among the lost. We read the whole account of it, copied from an English paper into the Richmond *Standard*. Lord William's body was washed ashore, the same night of the wreck."

"Poor young man, he deserved a better fate," said Marguerite.

Miss De Lancie went no more into society that season; indeed, the season was well over before she was able to go out. She announced her intention, as soon as the state of her health should permit her to travel, to terminate her visit to Richmond, and go down to her plantation on the banks of the Potomac. Cornelia would gladly have attended her friend, and only waited permission to do so; but the waited invitation was not extended, and Marguerite prepared to set out alone.

"We shall meet you at Berkeley or at Saratoga, this summer?" said Cornelia.

"Perhaps—I do not yet know—my plans for the summer are not arranged," said Marguerite.

"But you will write as soon as you reach home?"

"Yes—certainly," pressing her parting kiss upon the lips of her friend.

The promised letter, announcing Marguerite's safe arrival at Plover's Point, was received; but it was the last that came thence; for though Cornelia promptly replied to it, she received no second one. And though Cornelia wrote again and again, her letters remained unanswered. Weeks passed into months and brought midsummer. Colonel Compton with his family went to Saratoga, but without meeting Miss De Lancie. About the middle of August they came to Berkeley; but failed to see, or to hear any tidings of their friend.

"Indeed, I am very much afraid that Marguerite may be lying ill at Plover's Point, surrounded only by ignorant servants who cannot write to inform us," said Cornelia, advancing a probability so striking and so alarming, that Colonel Compton, immediately after taking his family back to Richmond, set out for Plover's Point to ascertain the state of the case in question. But when he arrived at the plantation, great was his surprise to learn that Miss De Lancie had left home for New York, as early as the middle of April, and had not since been heard from. And this was the last of September. With this information, Colonel Compton returned to Richmond. Extreme was the astonishment of the family upon hearing this; and when month after month passed, and no tidings of the missing one arrived, and no clew to her retreat, or to her fate was gained, the grief and dismay of her friends could only be equaled by the wonder and conjecture of society at large, upon the strange subject of Marguerite De Lancie's disappearance.

CHAPTER III
THE FUGITIVE BELLE

"What's become of 'Marguerite'
Since she gave us all the slip—
Chose land travel, or sea faring,
Box and trunk, or staff and scrip,
Rather than pace up and down
Any longer this old town?
Who'd have guessed it from her lip,
Or her brow's accustomed bearing,
On the night she thus took ship,
Or started landward, little caring?"
—Browning.

Christmas approached, and the gay belles of Richmond were preparing for the festivities of that season.

Colonel Compton with his family and a few chosen friends went down to Compton Lodge to spend the holidays in country hospitalities, hunting, etc.

The party had been there but a few days, when, on Christmas morning, while the family and their guests were assembled in the old, oak-paneled, front parlor, before breakfast, and Colonel Compton was standing at a side table, presiding over an immense old family punch bowl, from which he ladled out goblets of frothy eggnog to the company, the door was quietly opened, and without announcement Marguerite De Lancie entered, saying, "A merry Christmas! friends."

"Marguerite! Marguerite!" exclaimed—first Cornelia, and then all the young ladies that were present, pressing forward to meet her, while the matrons and the gentlemen of the party, with less vehemence but equal cordiality, waited to welcome her.

"My lost sweetheart, by all that's amazing!" cried Colonel Compton, who, in his engrossment, was the very last to discover the arrival.

"Why, where upon the face of the earth did you come from?" inquired Cornelia, scarcely restrained by the presence of others from seizing and covering her friend with caresses.

"From Loudoun street," answered Miss De Lancie gayly, as she shook hands right and left.

"From Loudoun street? that will do! How long have you been in Loudoun street, sweetheart? You were not there when we passed through the town in coming hither." said Colonel Compton.

"I arrived only the day before yesterday, rested a day, and hearing that you were at the Lodge, came hither, this morning, to breakfast with you."

"Enchanted to see you, my dear! truly so! But—you arrived the day before yesterday—whence?"

"I may be mistaken, yet it seems to me that Colonel Compton's asking questions," said Marguerite, with good-humored sarcasm.

"Oh! ah! I beg pardon, ten thousand pardons, as the French say," replied Colonel Compton, bowing with much deprecation, and then raising a bumper of eggnog. "To our reconciliation, Miss De Lancie," he continued, offering to her first, and filling for himself a second goblet.

"*Paix à vous*," said Marguerite, pledging him.

"And now to breakfast—*sortez, sortez*!" exclaimed the Colonel, leading the way to the dining-room.

Cornelia was, to use her own expression, "dying" to be alone with Marguerite, to hear the history of the last seven months absence. Never before was she more impatient over the progress of a meal, never before seemed the epicureanism of old folks so tedious, or the appetites of young people so unbecoming; notwithstanding which the coffee, tea and chocolate, the waffles, rolls and corn pone, the fresh venison, ham, and partridges were enjoyed by the company with equal gusto and deliberation.

"At last!" exclaimed Cornelia, as rising from the table, she took Marguerite's hand and drew her stealthily away through the crowd, and up the back stairs to her own little bedchamber, where a cheerful fire was burning.

"Now, then, tell me all about it, Marguerite," she said, putting her friend into her easy-chair of state before the fire, and seating herself on a stool at her feet. "Where have you been?"

"Gypsying," answered Miss De Lancie.

"Gypsying; oh, nonsense, that is no answer. What have you been about?"

"Gypsying," repeated Marguerite.

"Gypsying!" exclaimed Cornelia, now in wonder.

"Aye! Did you never—or have you too little life ever to feel like spreading your wings and flying away, away from all human ken—to feel the perfect liberty of loneliness, as only an irresponsible stranger in a strange place can feel it!"

"No, no! I never did," said Cornelia, amazed; "but, tell me then where did you go from Plover's Point."

"To Tierra-del-Fuego, or the Land of Fire," said Marguerite, with a deep flush.

"Fiddlesticks! Where did you come from last to Winchester?"

"From Iceland," said Marguerite, with a shiver.

"Oh, pshaw! you are making fun of me, Marguerite!"

"My dear, if I felt obliged to give an account of my wanderings, their wild liberty would not seem half so sweet. Even my property agent shall not always know where to find me; it is enough that I know where to find him when he is wanted," said Miss De Lancie, with such a dash of hauteur that Cornelia dropped the subject. And then Marguerite, to compensate for her passing severity, tenderly embraced Nellie.

The Christmas party at Compton Lodge lasted until after New Year, and then the family and their friends returned to Richmond.

Miss De Lancie, yielding to a pressing invitation, accompanied them. And in town, Marguerite had again to run the gantlet of questions from her acquaintances, such as:

"Where have you been so long, Marguerite?" To which she would answer:

"To Obdorskoi on the sea of Obe," or some such absurdity, until at last all inquiry ceased.

Miss De Lancie resumed her high position in society, and was once more the bright, particular star of every saloon. Those who envied, or disliked her, thought the dazzling Marguerite somewhat changed; that the fine, oval face was thinned and sharpened; the brilliant and changeful complexion fixed and deepened with a flush that looked like fever; and the ever-varying graceful, glowing vivacity rather fitful and eccentric. However, envious criticism did not prevent the most desirable *partis* in the city becoming suitors for the hand of the belle, muse and heiress, as she was still called. But Marguerite, in her old spirit of sarcasm, laughed all these overtures to scorn, and remained faithful to her sole attachment, her inexplicable love for Cornelia.

"I am twenty-four, I shall never marry, Nellie. I wish I were sure that you would never do so either, that we might be sisters for life, and that when your dear parents are gathered to their fathers, you might come and live with me, and we might be all in all to each other, forever," said Marguerite, one day, to her friend.

"Oh, Marguerite, if that will make you happy, I will promise you faithfully never, never to marry, but to be your own dear, little Nellie forever and ever; for indeed why should I not? I love no one in the world but my parents and you!"

Will it be credited (even although we know that such compacts are sometimes made and always broken) that these two girls entered into a solemn engagement never to marry; but to live for each other only?

From the day of this singular treaty, Marguerite De Lancie grew fonder than ever of her friend, lavished endearments upon her, calling Cornelia her Consolation, her Hope, her Star, and many other pet or poetic names besides. Nevertheless, when the fashionable season was over, Miss De Lancie left town without taking her "Consolation" with her. And again for a few months Marguerite was among the missing. She was not one to disappear with impunity or without inquiry. Where was she? Not at either of her own seats, nor at either of the watering places, not, as far as her most intimate friends and acquaintances knew, at New York, Philadelphia or Richmond, for her arrival at either of these places would have been chronicled by some one interested. Where was she, then? No one could answer; even her bosom friend, Cornelia Compton, could only reply, "Gone gypsying, I suppose."

Again seven months rolled by, while the brightest star of fashion remained in eclipse.

Again a Christmas party was assembled at Compton Lodge, when the news of Miss De Lancie's arrival at her house on Loudoun street reached them.

Colonel and Mrs. Compton waited some days for her call, and then not having received it, they went to visit her at her home. They found Marguerite, as ever, gay, witty and sarcastic. She told them in answer to their friendly inquiries that she had been "at Seringapatam," and gave them no further satisfaction. She accepted the invitation to join the Christmas party at Compton Lodge, went thither the same day, and as always before, distinguished herself as the most brilliant conversationalist, the most accomplished musician, the most graceful dancer, and the most fearless rider of the set. At the breaking up of the company, however, though invited and pressed to return with the Comptons to Richmond, she steadily declined doing so, alleging the necessity of visiting her plantation.

Therefore the Comptons returned to Richmond without their usual guest, and Cornelia, for the first time in many years, spent the whole winter in town without Marguerite. But if Miss Compton was bereaved of her friend, she was also freed from her mistress, and entered with much more levity into all the gayeties of the season than she ever had done in the restraining companionship of Marguerite De Lancie.

Meantime Marguerite, in her wild and lonely home on the wooded banks of the great Potomac, lived a strange and dreamy life, taking long, solitary rides through the deep forests, and among the rocky hills and glens that rolled ruggedly westward of the river; or taking long walks up and down the lonely beach; wiled away to double some distant headland, or explore some unfrequented creek—or pausing lazily, dreamily to watch the flash and dip of the fish in the river, the dusky flight of the water fowl, or the course of a distant sail; getting home late in the afternoon to meet a respectful remonstrance from the elderly gentlewoman who officiated as her housekeeper, and a downright motherly scolding from her old black nurse, aunt Hapzibah, who never saw in the world's magnificent Marguerite any other than the beautiful, wayward child she had tended from babyhood; or giving audience to the overseer, who, spreading the farm book before her, would enter into long details of the purchase or sale of stock, crops, etc., not one word of which Marguerite heard or understood, yet which she would at the close of the interview indorse by saying, "All right, Mr. Hayhurst, you are an admirable manager"—leaving her friends only to hope that he might be an honest man.

But one circumstance seemed to have power to arouse Miss De Lancie's interest—the arrival of the weekly mail at Seaview, the nearest village. All day, from the moment the messenger departed in the morning until he came back at night, Marguerite lingered in the house, or mounted her horse and rode in the direction from which the messenger was expected—or returned if it were dark, and waited with ill-concealed anxiety for his arrival. Upon one occasion, the mail seemed to have brought her news as terrible as it was mysterious. Upon opening a certain letter she grew deathly pale, struggled visibly to sustain herself against an inclination to swoon, read the contents to the close, threw the letter into the fire, rang and ordered horses and a servant to attend her, and the same night set out from home, and never drew rein until she reached Bellevue, when sending her horses back by her servant, she took a packet for New York.

She was absent six weeks, at the end of which time she returned home, looking worn and exhausted, yet relieved and cheerful. She found two letters from Cornelia awaiting her; the first one, after much preface, apology and explanation, announced the fact that a suitor, Colonel Houston, of Northumberland, in all respects very acceptable to her parents, had presented himself to Cornelia, and that, but for the mutual pledge existing between herself and Marguerite, she might be induced to please her parents by listening to his addresses. Marguerite De Lancie pondered long and gravely over this letter; re-read it, and looked graver than before. Then she opened the second letter, which was dated three weeks later, and seemed to have been written under the impression that the first one, remaining unanswered, had been received, and had given offense to Marguerite. This last was a long, sentimental epistle, declaring firstly, that she, Cornelia, would not break her "rash" promise to Marguerite, but pleading the wishes of her parents, the approbation of her friends, the merits of her suitor, and in short everything except the true and governing motive, her own inclinations.

Miss De Lancie read this second letter with impatience; at the close threw it into the fire; drew her writing-desk toward her, took pen and paper, and answered both long epistles in one—a miracle of brevity—thus, "dear Nellie—tut—Marguerite," and sealed and sent it off.

Apparently, Cornelia did not find this answer as clear as it was brief. She wrote in reply a long, heroic epistle of eight pages, announcing her willingness to sacrifice her parents' wishes, her friends' approval, her lover's happiness, and her own peace of mind, all to fidelity and Marguerite, if the latter required the offering!

Marguerite read this letter with more impatience than the others, and drawing a sheet of paper before her, wrote, "Nellie! Do as you like, else I'll make you—Marguerite."

In two weeks back came the answer, a pleading, crying letter, of twelve pages, the pith of which was that Nellie would do only as Marguerite liked, and that she wanted more explicit directions.

"Pish! tush! pshaw!" exclaimed Miss De Lancie, tapping her foot with impatience, as she read page after page of all this twaddle, and finally casting the whole into the fire, she took her pen and wrote, "Cornelia! marry Colonel Houston forthwith before I compel you—Marguerite."

A few days from the dispatch of this letter arrived the answer, brought by an express-mounted messenger in advance of the mail. It was a thick packet of many closely-written pages, the concentrated essence of which was that Nellie would follow the advice of Marguerite, whom she loved and honored more than any one else in the world, yes, more than mother and father and lover together; that Marguerite must never wrong her by doubting this, or above all, by being jealous of the colonel, for indeed, after all, Nellie did not like him inordinately; how could she when he was a widower past thirty with two children? And finally, that she would not venture to ask Miss De Lancie to be her bridesmaid, for that would be like requesting a queen to attend her maid of honor in such a capacity; but would Marguerite, her dear Lady Marguerite, come and preside over the marriage of her poor little Nellie?

Miss De Lancie sat, for a long time, holding this letter open in her hand, moralizing upon its contents. "The little simpleton—is she only timid, or is she insincere? which after all means—is she weak or wicked? foolish or knavish? And above all, why am I fond of her? why have her brown eyes and her cut of countenance such power to draw and knit my heart to hers?—for indeed though to superficial eyes, hers may be a countenance resplendent with feeling, strong in thought, yet it is a cheat, without depth, without earnestness—let it be said!—without soul. Ay, truly! seeing all this, why do I love her? Because of the 'strong necessity of loving' somebody, or something, I suppose," thought Marguerite, sinking deeper into reverie. These sparks of light elicited by the strokes of Cornelia's steel-like policy upon the flint of Marguerite's sound integrity, thus revealed, by flashes, the true character of the former to the latter; but the effect was always transient, passing away with the cause.

Miss De Lancie took up the letter and re-read it, with comments as—
"I jealous of her lover! truly! I preside over her marriage! Come, I must answer that!" And drawing writing materials before her, she wrote, briefly as before.

"I would see you in Gehenna first, you little imbecile. Marguerite."

And sealed and dispatched the letter.

This brought Nellie down in person to Plover's Point, where by dint of caressing, and coaxing, and weeping, she prevailed with Marguerite, who at last exclaimed:

"Well, well! go home and prepare for your wedding, Nellie! I'll come and assist at the farce."

CHAPTER IV
LOVE

"——The soul that moment caught

A something it through life had sought."

—Moore.

"Forbear that dream! My lips are sworn apart

From tender words; mine ears from lover's vows;

Mine eyes from sights God made so beautiful;

My very heart from feelings which move soft."

—E. B. Browning.

The bridal of the only daughter of the Comptons was naturally an event of great importance, and consequently of much parade. The bride-elect was in favor of being married in the most approved modern style, having the ceremony performed at ten in the morning, and starting immediately upon a wedding tour. But Colonel and Mrs. Compton had some strong, old-fashioned predilections, and decided to have the time-honored, old style of marriage party in the evening. And accordingly preparations were made upon the grandest scale to do honor to the nuptials of their only child.

Marguerite De Lancie arrived upon the evening previous to the wedding, and was most cordially welcomed by the family. She was carried off immediately by Cornelia to her chamber for a *tête-à-tête*.

"Well, my little incapable!" Marguerite said, as soon as she was seated, "now tell me about your bridegroom! Long ago, you know, we divided the present generation of men into two classes—monsters and imbeciles; to which does your *fiancé* belong?"

"You shall see and judge for yourself, Marguerite! To neither, I think!"

"Oh! of course, you think! Well! who are to be your bridesmaids?"

"The Misses Davidge and—yourself, dear Marguerite, since you were so kind as to promise."

"So weak, you mean! And who are to be groomsmen?"

"Steve and Peyton Rutlidge are to lead out the Davidges."

"And who is to be my cavalier for the occasion?"

"There! that's just what I wanted to talk to you about, Marguerite! because you have the privilege of rejecting him as your proposed escort, and I hope you will. I am afraid of him; I always was! I cannot endure him; I never could! I hate him, and I always did! But the colonel proposed him, and papa and mamma would not permit me to object."

"But you have not yet told me who he is."

"Oh, you would not know if I were to tell you! though if you ever see him, you will never fail to know him thenceforth!"

"His name? You've raised my curiosity."

"Philip Helmstedt, my cousin! He is of those fierce and haughty Helmstedts of the Eastern Shore, whose forefathers, you know, claimed a prior right to the coast and the Isles of the Bay, from having made the place a sort of freebooting depot, long before the king's patent endowed Lord Baltimore with it, and who headed so many rebellions and caused so much bloodshed among the early colonists."

"Well, nearly two hundred years have rolled by. This fierce, arrogant nature must have been greatly modified by time and intermarriage."

"Must it. Well, now, it is my opinion that no one who knows the history can look upon Philip Helmstedt's bird-of-prey profile without remembering the fierce fights by sea and land of his freebooting forefathers."

"It is doubtless true that a strong and powerful race of men may have so impressed upon their descendants as to leave their own peculiar traits unmodified and predominant to the latest generations," said Marguerite, musing; and then, suddenly recollecting herself, she exclaimed: "Philip Helmstedt! surely I have heard that name in honorable association before, though I have never met the owner. Oh! by the way, is he not that gallant nephew, of whom I have heard your father speak, and who, though but thirteen years of age, followed him in the battle of Yorktown and performed such prodigies of youthful valor?"

"Oh, yes! he's fire-eater enough, and a terror in general, at least to me."

"But where has he been that I have never met him in society?"

"Oh! he has been for a number of years studying at Heidelburg, and traveling all over the Eastern Continent. I was sufficiently afraid of him before he went away, and I am twice as much in awe of him since he came back; so I want you to veto him, Marguerite; for you may do so, and then the colonel will get somebody else to stand up in his stead. Will you?"

"Certainly not. It would be a very great rudeness to all concerned," said Miss De Lancie.

The preparations for the marriage were, as I said, upon a magnificent scale. The *élite* of the city and county were invited to be present. Upon the important evening the house was illuminated and thrown open. At a comparatively early hour the company began to assemble.

At a quarter to eight o'clock precisely, the bride and her maids were ready to go down.

Nellie looked, as all brides are expected to look, "never before so lovely." A robe of embroidered white crape over white satin, a point lace veil, and a light wreath of orange blossoms, were the principal items of her costume.

The two younger bridesmaids were attired in harmony in white gauze over white silk, with wreaths of snowdrops around their hair.

The queenly form of Marguerite De Lancie was arrayed in a robe of the richest lace over white brocade; her superb black hair was crowned with a wreath of lilies, deep falls of the finest lace veiled her noble bust and arms, and the purest Oriental pearls adorned her neck and wrists; she looked as ever, a royal beauty.

Scarcely was the last fold of Cornelia's veil gracefully arranged by Marguerite, before the little bride, with a mixture of childish petulance and envy and genuine admiration, raised her eyes to the beautiful brow of her patroness, and said:

"Ah! how stately, how radiant you are, Marguerite! But how shall I look, poor, insignificant, little, fady pigmy! my very bridegroom will be ashamed of his choice, seen by the side of the magnificent Miss De Lancie!"

"Be silent! How dare you humble yourself, or flatter me so shamefully!" exclaimed Marguerite, flushing with indignation. "As for the 'magnificent,' that can be easily transferred; 'fine feathers make fine birds,' and queenly jewels go very far toward making queenly women," she continued, proceeding to unclasp the pearls from her own neck and arms, and to fasten them upon those of Cornelia.

"No, no, dear Marguerite, desist! I cannot, indeed. I cannot consent to shine in borrowed jewels," said Miss Compton, opposing this ornamental addition to her costume.

"They are your own; wear them for my sake, sweet Nellie," replied Miss De Lancie; clasping the necklace and kissing the bride with renewed tenderness.

"But your matchless set of pearls! a dower, a fortune in themselves! I cannot, Marguerite! Indeed, indeed, I dare not! Such a transfer would look as if you were not quite sane, nor myself quite honest," said Cornelia, with sincere earnestness.

"Ridiculous! I care not for them, or, I assure you, I should not give them away. Hush! don't put me to the trouble of pressing them upon you, for really I do not consider them worth the expenditure of so much breath. Stop! don't thank me, either, for I have no patience to listen. We are all ready, I believe? What are we waiting for?"

While she spoke, there came a gentle rap at the connecting door between Cornelia's and her parents' bedchambers. It was Colonel and Mrs. Compton, who were waiting there to embrace and bless their child before giving her up to the possession of another. Cornelia went in to them, and after a stay of five minutes, returned with her eyes suffused with tears, evanescent tears that quickly evaporated. And in another moment Colonel Compton came to the passage door and announced to the bevy of bridesmaids that the bishop had arrived, and that the bridegroom and his attendants were waiting downstairs.

"We are ready. But remember, colonel, that I have never met Mr. Helmstedt."

"I shall not fail to present him, Marguerite," replied the old gentleman, turning to go downstairs. The bride's party followed in due order; the third bridesmaid, leading the way, received the arm of her appointed escort, and advanced toward the saloon; the second did likewise; then Marguerite, in her turn, descended. She had never before seen the distinguished-looking personage, then waiting at the foot of the stairs to offer his arm and lead her on; but Colonel Compton stood ready to present him and all was well. Marguerite reached the last step, paused, and raised her eyes to look at the stranger, whom Cornelia's description had invested with a certain interest.

A tall, thin, muscular form, large, clearly cut aquiline features, raven-black hair, strongly marked black eyebrows, deep and piercing dark grey eyes, a stern and somewhat melancholy countenance, a stately, not to say haughty, carriage, a style of dress careful even to nicety, *a tout ensemble* indicating a forcible, fiery, high-toned, somewhat arrogant character, were the features impressed by first sight upon Marguerite's perceptions. She had scarcely made these observations and withdrawn her glance, when Colonel Compton, taking the stranger's hand and turning to her, said:

"Miss De Lancie, permit me to present to you Mr. Helmstedt, of Northumberland County."

Again Marguerite lifted her eyes.

A stately bow, a gracious smile, a mellifluous voice in addressing her, threw a charm, a warm, bright glow, like a sudden sunburst over those stern, dark features, clothing them with an indescribable beauty as fascinating as it was unexpected.

"I esteem myself most happy in meeting Miss De Lancie," he said.

Marguerite dropped her eyes, and blushed deeply beneath his fixed, though deferential gaze, curtseyed in silence, received his offered arm and followed the others, who were waiting at the door. The bride and groom brought up the rear. And the party entered the saloon.

The rooms were superbly adorned, brilliantly illuminated, and densely crowded by a splendid company.

The white-gowned bishop stood upon the rug in front of the fireplace, facing the assembly. A space had been left clear before him, upon which the bridal party formed. A hushed silence filled the room; the book was opened; the rites commenced, and in ten minutes after little Nellie Compton was transmogrified into Mrs. Colonel Houston.

When the congratulations were all over, and the bridal party seated, and the little embarrassments attendant upon all these movements well over, the programme for the remainder of the evening proceeded according to all the "rules and regulations in such cases made and provided"—with one memorable exception.

When the bride's cake (which was quite a miraculous *chef-d'œuvre* of the confectioner's art, being made in the form of the temple of Hymen, highly ornate, and containing besides a costly diamond ring, which it was supposed, according to the popular superstition, would indicate the happy finder as the next to be wedded of the party), was cut and served to all the single ladies present, it was soon discovered that none of them had drawn the token. Colonel Compton then declared that the unmarried gentlemen should try their fortune. And when they were all served, Mr. Helmstedt proved to be the fortunate possessor of the costly talisman.

When, with a courtly dignity, he had arrested the storm of badinage that was ready to burst upon him, he deliberately crossed the room to the quarter where the bride and her attendants remained seated, and pausing before Marguerite, said:

"Miss De Lancie, permit me," and offered the ring.

"Yes, yes, Marguerite! relieve him of it! He cannot wear it himself, you know, and to whom here could he properly offer it but to yourself," hastily whispered Cornelia.

Miss De Lancie hesitated, but unwilling to draw attention by making a scene out of such an apparent trifle, she smiled, drew off her glove, and held up her hand, saying,

"If Mr. Helmstedt will put it on."

Philip Helmstedt slipped the ring on her finger, turned and adjusted it with a slight pressure, when Marguerite, with a half-suppressed cry, snatched away her hand and applied her handkerchief to it.

"Have I been so awkward and unhappy as to hurt you, Miss De Lancie?" inquired Mr. Helmstedt.

"Oh, no, not at all! it is nothing to speak of; a sharp flaw in the setting of the stones pierced my finger; I think that is all," answered Marguerite, drawing off the ring that was stained with blood.

Mr. Helmstedt took the jewel, walked up to the fireplace, and threw it into the glowing coals.

"Well! if that is not the most wanton piece of destructiveness I ever saw in my life," said Cornelia, indignantly; "you know, Marguerite, when I saw Mr. Helmstedt draw the ring and come and put it on your finger, I thought it was a happy sign; but now see how it is? everything that man touches, turns—not to gold, but to blood or tears, that he thinks only can be dried in the fire!"

"Don't use such fearful words here on your bridal evening, dear Nellie, they are ill-omened. You are, besides, unjust to Mr. Helmstedt, I think," said Marguerite, who had now quite recovered her composure.

"They were false diamonds after all, Miss De Lancie," said Mr. Helmstedt, rejoining the ladies.

The bishop had retired from the room; the musicians had entered and taken their places, and were now playing a lively prelude to the quadrilles; partners were engaged, and were only waiting for the bride and groom to open the ball, as was then the custom. Nellie gave her hand to her colonel, and suffered herself to be led to the head of the set.

"Miss De Lancie, will you honor me?" inquired Mr. Helmstedt, and receiving a gracious inclination of the head in acquiescence, he conducted Marguerite to a position *vis-à-vis* with the bridal pair. Other couples immediately followed their example, and the dancing commenced in earnest. The lively quadrille was succeeded by the stately minuet, and that by the graceful waltz, and the time-honored and social Virginia reel. Then came an interval of repose, preceding the sumptuous supper. Then the outpouring of the whole company into the dining-room; and the eating, drinking, toasting, and jesting; then they adjourned to the saloon, when again quadrilles, minuets, reels and waltzes alternated with short-lived rest, refreshment, gossip, and flirtations, until a late hour, when the discovered disappearance of the bride and her attendants gave the usual warning for the company to break up. At the covert invitation of Colonel Compton, some of the gentlemen, who were without ladies, lingered after the departure of the other guests, and adjourned with himself and his son-in-law, to the dining-room, where, after drinking the health of the newly married pair, they took leave.

The next day Judge Houston, the uncle of the bridegroom, entertained the wedding party and a large company at dinner. And this was the signal for the commencement of a series of dinners, tea and card parties, and balls, given in honor of the bride, and which kept her and her coterie in a whirl of social dissipation for several weeks.

But from this brilliant entanglement let us draw out clearly the sombre thread of our own narrative.

Everywhere the resplendent beauty of Marguerite De Lancie was felt and celebrated. Every one declared that the star of fashion had emerged from her late eclipse with new and dazzling brilliancy. And ever, whether in repose or action; whether reclined upon some divan, she was the inspiration of a circle of conversationalists; or whether she led the dance, or, seated at the harpsichord, poured forth her soul in glorious song—she was ever the queen of all hearts and minds, who recognized in her magnificent personality a sovereignty no crown or sceptre could confer. All, in proportion to their depth and strength of capacity for appreciation, felt this. But none so much as one whose duty brought him ever to her side in zealous service, or deferential waiting.

Philip Helmstedt, almost from the first hour of his meeting with this imperial beauty, had felt her power. He watched her with the most reserved and respectful vigilance; he saw her ever the magnet of all hearts and eyes, the life of all social intercourse, the inspiration of poets, the model of painters, the worship of youth and love; shining for, warming, lighting, and enlivening all who approached her, yet with such impartiality that none ventured to aspire to especial notice. There was one exception, and not a favored one to his equanimity and that was Mr. Helmstedt himself; her manner toward him, at first affable, soon grew reserved, then distant, and at length repelling. Colonel Compton, who had taken it into his head that this haughty pair were well adapted to each other, watched with interest the progress of their acquaintance, noticed this, and despaired.

"It is useless," he said, "and I warn you, Philip Helmstedt, not to consume your heart in the blaze of Marguerite De Lancie's beauty! She is the invincible Diana of modern times. For seven years has Marguerite reigned in our saloons, with the absolute dominion of a beauty and genius that 'age cannot wither nor custom stale,' and her power remains undiminished as her beauty is undimmed. Year after year the most distinguished men of their time, men celebrated in the battles and in the councils of their country, men of history, have been suitors in her train, and have received their *congé* from her imperial nod. Can you hope for more than an Armstrong, a Bainbridge, a Cavendish?"

"I beseech you, sir, spare me the alphabetical list of Miss De Lancie's conquests! I can well believe their name is legion," interrupted Philip Helmstedt, with an air of scorn and arrogance that seemed to add, "and if it were so, I should enter the lists with full confidence against them all."

"I assure you it is sheer madness, Philip! A man may as well hope to monopolize the sun to light his own home as to win Marguerite De Lancie to his hearth! She belongs to society, I think, also, to history. She requires a nation for her field of action. I have known her from childhood and watched with wonder her development. It is the friction of marvelous and undirected energies that causes her to glow and radiate in society as you see her. It is sheer frenzy, your pursuit of her! I tell you, I have seen a love chase worth ten of yours—Lord William Daw——"

"Lord—William—Daw!" interrupted Philip Helmstedt, curling his lip with ineffable scorn.

"Well, now, I assure you, Philip, the heir presumptive of a marquisate is not to be sneered at. He was besides a good-looking and well-behaved young fellow, except that he followed Miss De Lancie up and down the country like a demented man, in direct opposition, both to the clucking of an old hen of a tutor, and the coldness of his Diana. He was drowned, poor youth! but I always suspected that he threw himself overboard in desperation!"

"Lord—William—Daw," said Mr. Helmstedt, with the same deliberate and scornful intonation, "may not have been personally the equal of the lady to whom he aspired. Very young men frequently raise their hopes to women 'who are, or ought to be, unattainable' by them. Miss De Lancie is not one to permit herself to be dazzled by the glitter of mere rank and title."

Yes. Philip Helmstedt hoped, believed, in more success for himself than had attended any among his predecessors or temporary rivals. True, indeed, his recommendations, personal as well as circumstantial, to the favor of this "fourth Grace and tenth Muse," were of the first order. The last male representative of an ancient, haughty, and wealthy family, their vast estates centered in his possession—he chose to devote many years to study and to travel. An accomplished scholar, he had read, observed and reflected, and was prepared, at his own pleasure, to confer the result upon the world. A tried and proved soldier, he might claim military rank and rapid promotion. Lastly, a pre-eminently fine looking person, he might aspire to the hand of almost any beauty in the city, with every probability of success. But Philip Helmstedt was fastidious and proud to a degree of scornful arrogance— that was his one great, yes, terrible sin. It was the bitter upas of his soul that poisoned every one of the many virtues of his character. But for scorn, truth, justice, prudence, temperance, generosity, fortitude, would have flourished in his nature. It was this trenchant arrogance that made him indifferent to accessory honors—that made him as a profound student, regardless of scholastic fame—as a brave soldier, careless of military glory—as an accomplished gentleman, negligent of beauty's allurements. It was this arrogance in fine, that entered very largely into his passion for the magnificent Marguerite. For here at last, in her, he found a princess quite worthy of his high devotion, and he resolved to win her.

God have mercy on any soul self-cursed with scorn.

And Marguerite? Almost from the first moment of their meeting, her eyes, her soul, had been strangely and irresistibly magnetized. I do not know that this was caused by the distinguished personal appearance of Philip Helmstedt. After all, it is not the beauty, but the peculiarity, individuality, uniqueness, in the beauty that attracts its destined mate. And Philip Helmstedt's presence was pre-eminently characteristic, individual, unique. At first Marguerite's eyes were attracted by a certain occult resemblance to his young cousin, her own beloved friend, Cornelia Compton. It was not only such a family likeness as might exist between brother and sister. It was something deeper than a similitude of features, complexion and expression. The same peculiar conformation of brow and eye, the same proud lines in the aquiline profile, the same disdainful curves in the expressive lips, the same distinctly individualized characteristics, that had long charmed and cheated her in Nellie's superficial face, was present, only more strongly marked and deeply toned, and truly representative of great force of character, in Philip Helmstedt's imposing countenance. But there was something more than this—there was identity in the uniqueness of each—faint and uncertain in the delicate face of Nellie, intense and ineffaceable in the sculptured features of Philip. As Marguerite studied this remarkable physiognomy, she felt that her strange attraction to Nellie had been but a faint prelude, though a prophecy of this wondrous magnetism.

Alarmed at the spell that was growing around her heart, she withdrew her eyes and thoughts, opposed to the attentions of her lover a cold, repellant manner, and treated his devotion with supreme disdain, which must have banished any man less strong in confidence than Philip Helmstedt, but which in his case only warded off the day of fate. Perseveringly he attended her, earnestly he sought an opportunity of explaining himself. In vain; for neither at home nor abroad, in parlor, saloon, thoroughfare or theatre, could he manage to secure a *tête-à-tête*. Whether sitting or standing, Miss De Lancie was always the brilliant center of a circle; and if she walked, like any other queen, she was attended by her suite. Only when he mingled with this train, could he speak to her. But then—the quick averting of that regal hand, the swift fall of the sweeping, dark eyelashes, the sudden, deep flush of the bright cheeks, the suppressed heave of the beautiful bosom, the subdued tremor of the thrilling voice, betrayed hidden emotions, that only he had power to arouse, or insight to detect, and read therein the confirmation of his dearest hopes. The castle walls might show a forbidding aspect, but the citadel was all his own, hence his determination, despite her icy coldness of manner, to pass all false shows, and come to an understanding with his Diana. Still Miss De Lancie successfully evaded his pursuit and defeated his object. What was the cause of her course of conduct, he could not satisfactorily decide. Was pride struggling with love in her bosom? If so, that pride should succumb.

Having failed in every delicate endeavor to effect a *tête-à-tête*, and the day of Marguerite's departure being near at hand, Mr. Helmstedt went one morning directly to the house of Colonel Compton, sent up his card to Miss De Lancie, and requested the favor of an interview. He received an answer that Miss De Lancie was particularly engaged and begged to be excused. Again and again he tried the same plan with the same ill-success. Miss De Lancie was never at leisure to receive Mr. Helmstedt. At length this determined suitor sent a note, requesting the lady to name some hour when she should be sufficiently disengaged to see him. The reply to this was that Miss De Lancie regretted to say that at no hour of her short remaining time should she be at liberty to entertain Mr. Helmstedt. This flattering message was delivered in the parlor, and in the presence of Colonel Compton. As soon as the servant had retired, the old gentleman raised his eyes to the darkened brow of Philip Helmstedt, and said: "I see how it is, Philip. Marguerite is a magnanimous creature. She would spare you the humiliation of a refusal. But you—you are resolved upon mortification. You will not be content without a decided rejection. Very well. You shall have an opportunity of receiving one. Listen. Houston and Nellie are dining with the judge to-day. Mrs. Compton is superintending the making of calf's-foot jelly; don't huff and sneer, Philip. I cannot help sometimes knowing the progress of such culinary mysteries; but I am not going to assist at them or to ask you to do so. I am going to ride. Thus, if you will remain here to-day, you will have the house to yourself, and Marguerite, who for some unaccountable reason, fate perhaps, chooses to stay home. Go into the library and wait. Miss De Lancie, according to her usual custom, will probably visit that or the adjoining music-room in the course of the forenoon, and there you have her. Make the best use of your opportunity, and the Lord speed you; for I, for my part, heartily wish this lioness fairly mated. Come; let me install you."

"There appears to be no other chance, and I must have an interview with her to-day," said Mr. Helmstedt, rising to accompany his host who led the way to the library. It was on the opposite side of the hall.

"Now be patient," said the colonel, as he took leave; "you may have to wait one or more hours, but you can find something here to read."

"Read!" ejaculated Philip Helmstedt, with the tone and energy of an oath; but the old gentleman was already gone, and the younger one threw himself into a chair to wait.

"'Be patient!' with the prospect of waiting here several hours, and the possibility of disappointment at the end," exclaimed Philip, rising, and walking in measured steps up and down the room, trying to control the eagerness of expectation that made moments seem like hours, while he would have compressed hours into moments.

How long he waited ought scarcely to be computed by the common measure of time. It might not have been; an hour—to him it seemed an indefinite duration—a considerable portion of eternity, when at length, while almost despairing of the presence of Marguerite, he heard from the adjoining music-room the notes of a harp.

He paused, for the harpist might be—must be Miss De Lancie.

He listened.

Soon the chords of the lyre were swept by a magic hand that belonged only to one enchantress, and the instrument responded in a low, deep moan, that presently swelled in a wild and thrilling strain. And then the voice of the *improvvisatrice* stole upon the ear—that wondrous voice, that ever, while it sounded, held captive all ears, silent and breathless all lips, spellbound all hearts!—it arose, first tremulous, melodious, liquid, as from a sea of tears, then took wing in a wild, mournful, despairing wail. It was a song of renunciation, in which some consecrated maiden bids adieu to her lover, renouncing happiness, bewailing fate, invoking death. Philip Helmstedt listened, magnetized by the voice of the sorceress, with its moans of sorrow, its sudden gushes of passion or tenderness, and its wails of anguish and despair. And when at last, like the receding waves of the heart's life tide, the thrilling notes ebbed away into silence and death, he remained standing like a statue. Then, with self-reflection and the returning faculty of combination, came the question:

"What did this song of renunciation mean?" And the next more practical inquiry, should he remain in the library, awaiting the doubtful event of her coming, or should he enter the music-room? A single moment of reflection decided his course.

He advanced softly, and opened the listed and silently-turning doors, and paused an instant to gaze upon a beautiful tableau!

Directly opposite to him, at the extremity of the thickly carpeted room, was a deep bay window, richly curtained with purple and gold, through which the noon-day sun shone with a subdued glory. Within the glowing shadows of this recess sat Marguerite beside the harp. A morning robe of amber-hued India silk fell in classic folds around her form. Her arms were still upon the harp, her inspired face was pale and half averted. Her rich, purplish tresses pushed off from her temples, revealed the breadth of brow between them in a new and royal aspect of beauty. Her eyes were raised and fixed upon the distance, as if following in spirit the muse that had just died from lips of fire. She was so completely absorbed, that she did not heed the soft and measured step of Philip Helmstedt, until he paused before her, bowed and spoke.

Then she started to her feet with a brow crimsoned by a sudden rush of emotion, and thrown completely off her guard, for the moment, she confronted him with a home question.

"Philip Helmstedt! what has brought you here?"

"My deep, my unconquerable, consuming love! It has broken down all the barriers of etiquette, and given me thus to your presence, Marguerite De Lancie," he replied, with a profound and deprecating inclination of the head.

She had recovered a degree of self-possession; but the tide of blood receding had left her brow cold and clammy, and her frame tremulous and faint; she leaned upon her harp for support, pushed the falling tresses from her pale, damp forehead, and said, in faltering tones:

"I would have saved you this! Why, in the name of all that is manly, delicate, honorable!—why have you in defiance of all opposition, ventured this?"

"Because I love you, Marguerite. Because I love you for time and for eternity with a love that must speak or slay."

"Ungenerous! unjust!"

"Be it so, Marguerite. I do not ask you to forgive me, for that must presuppose repentance, and I do not repent standing here, Miss De Lancie."

"Still I must ask you, sir," said Marguerite, who was gradually recovering the full measure of her natural dignity and self-possession, "what feature in all my conduct that has come under your observation has given you the courage to obtrude upon me a presence and a suit that you must know to be unwelcome and repulsive?"

"Shall I tell you? I will, with the truthfulness of spirit answering to spirit. I come because, despite all your apparent hauteur, disdain, coldness, such a love as this which burns within my heart for you, bears within itself the evidence of reciprocity," replied Philip Helmstedt, laying his hand upon his heart, and atoning by a profound reverence for the presumption of his words. "And I appeal to your own soul, Marguerite De Lancie, for the indorsement of my avowal."

"You are mad!" said Marguerite, trembling.

"No—not mad, lady, because loving you as never man loved woman yet, I also feel and know, with the deepest respect be it said, that I do not love in vain," he replied, sinking for an instant upon his knee, and bowing deeply over her hand that he pressed to his lips.

"In vain! in vain! you do! you do!" she exclaimed, almost distractedly, while trembling more than ever.

"Marguerite," he said, rising, yet retaining his hold upon her hand, "it may be that I love in vain, but I do not love alone. This hand that I clasp within my own throbs like a palpitating heart. I read, on your brow, in your eyes, in your trembling lip and heaving bosom, that my great love is not lost; that it is returned; that you are mine, as I am yours. Marguerite De Lancie, by a claim rooted in the deepest nature, you are my wife for time and for eternity!"

"Never! never! you know not what you say or seek!" she exclaimed, snatching her hand away and shuddering through every nerve.

"Miss De Lancie, your words and manner are inexplicable, are alarming! Tell me, for the love of Heaven, Marguerite, does any insurmountable obstacle stand in the way of our union?"

"Obstacle!" repeated Miss De Lancie, starting violently, and gazing with wild, dilated eyes upon the questioner, while every vestige of color fled from her face.

"Yes, that was the word I used, dearest Marguerite! Oh, if there be——"

"What obstacle should exist, except my own will? A very sufficient one, I should say," interrupted Marguerite, struggling hard for self-control.

"Say your decision against your will."

"What right have you to think so, sir?"

"Look in your own heart and read my right, Marguerite."

"I never look into that abyss!"

"Marguerite, you fill me with a terrible anxiety. Marguerite, for seven years you have reigned a queen over society; your hand has been sought by the most distinguished men of the country; you are as full of tenderness and enthusiasm as a harp is of music; it seems incredible that you have never married or betrothed yourself, or even loved, or fancied that you loved! Tell me, Marguerite, in the name of Heaven, tell me, have any of these events occurred to you?" He waited for an answer.

She remained silent, while a frightful pallor overspread her face.

"Tell me! Oh! tell me, Marguerite, have you ever before loved? Ah, pardon the question and answer it."

She made a supreme effort, recovered her self-possession and replied:

"No, not as you understand it."

"How?—not as I understand it? Ah! forgive me again, but your words increase my suffering."

"Oh! I have loved Nellie as a sister, her father and mother as parents, some acquaintances as friends, that is all."

She was answering these close questions! she was yielding to the fascination. Amid all her agony of conflicting emotions she was yielding.

"Marguerite! Marguerite! And this is true! You have never loved before!"

"It is true—yet what of that? for I know not even why I admit this! Oh! leave me, I am not myself. Hope nothing from what I have told you. I can never, never be your wife!" exclaimed Marguerite, with the half-suppressed and wild affright of one yielding to a terrible spell.

"But one word more. Is your hand free also, dearest Marguerite?"

"Yes, it is free; but what then? I have told you——"

"Then it is free no longer; for by the splendor of the heavens, it is mine. Marguerite, it is mine!" he exclaimed as he caught and pressed that white hand in his own.

Marguerite De Lancie's previsions had been prophetic. She had foreseen that an interview would be fatal to her resolution, and it proved fatal. Philip Helmstedt urged his suit with all the eloquence of passionate love, seconded by the dangerous advocate in Marguerite's heart, and he won it; and in an hour after, the pair that had met so inauspiciously, parted as betrothed lovers. Mr. Helmstedt went away in deep joy, and with a sense of triumph only held in check by his habitual dignity and self-control. And Marguerite remained in that scene of the betrothal, looking, not like a loving and happy affianced bride, but rather like a demented woman, with pale face and wild, affrighted eyes, strained upward as for help, and cold hands wrung together as in an appeal, and exclaiming under her breath:

"What have I done! Lord forgive me! Oh, Lord have pity on me!" And yet Marguerite De Lancie loved her betrothed with all her fiery soul. That love in a little while brought her some comfort in her strange distress.

"What's done is done," she said, in the tone of one who would nerve her soul to some endurance, and then she went to her room, smoothed her hair, dressed for the afternoon, and through all the remainder of the day moved about, the same brilliant, sparkling Marguerite as before.

In the evening the accepted suitor presented himself. And though he only mingled as before, in the train of Miss De Lancie, and acted in all respects with the greatest discretion, yet those particularly interested could read the subdued joy of his soul, and draw the proper inference.

That night, when Marguerite retired to her chamber, Nellie followed her, and casting herself at once into an armchair, she broke the subject by suddenly exclaiming: "Marguerite, I do believe you have been encouraging Ironsides!"

"Why do you think so—if I understand what you mean?"

"Oh, from his looks! He looks as bright as a candle in a dark lantern, and as happy as if he had just slain his enemy. I do fear you have given him hopes, Marguerite."

"And why fear it?"

"Oh, because, Marguerite, dear, I don't want you to have him!" said Nellie, with a show of great tenderness.

"Nonsense!"

"I do not believe you will, you see, but still I fear. Oh, Marguerite, he may be high-toned, magnanimous, and all that, but he is not tender, not gentle, not loving!"

"In a word—not a good nurse."

"No."

"Good! I do not want a nurse!"

"Ah! Marguerite, I am afraid of Philip Helmstedt. If you only knew how he treated his sister."

"His sister! I did not even know he had one."

"I dare say not; but he has. She is in the madhouse."

"In the madhouse!"

"Yes; I'll tell you all about it. It was before he went away the last time. His sister Agnes was then eighteen; they lived together. She was engaged to poor Hertford, the son of the notorious defaulter, who was no defaulter when that engagement was made. Agnes and Hertford were within a few days of their marriage when the father's embezzlements were discovered. Now poor young Hertford was not in the least implicated, yet as soon as his father's disgrace was made manifest, Philip Helmstedt, as the guardian of his sister, broke off the marriage."

"He could have done no otherwise," said Marguerite.

"In spite of her pledged word? In spite of her prayers and tears, and distracted grief?"

"He could have done no otherwise," repeated Marguerite, though her face grew very pale.

"That was not all. The lovers met, arranged a flight, and were about to escape, when Philip Helmstedt discovered them. He insulted the young man, struck him with his riding whip across the face, and bore his fainting sister home. The next day the two men met in a duel."

"They could have done no otherwise. It was the bloody code of honor!" reiterated Marguerite, yet her very lips were white, as she leaned forward against the top of Nellie's chair.

"Hertford lost his right arm, and Agnes lost—her reason!"

"My God!"

"Yes; 'a plague o' honor,' I say."

"Dear Nellie, leave me now; my head aches, and I am tired."

Nellie, accustomed to such abrupt dismissions, kissed her friend and retired.

"Honor, honor, honor," repeated Marguerite, when left alone. "Oh, Moloch of civilization, when will you be surfeited?"

The next morning Philip Helmstedt called, sent up his card to Miss De Lancie, and was not denied her presence.

"Show the gentleman into the music-room, and say that I will see him there, John," was the direction given by Miss De Lancie, who soon descended thither.

Mr. Helmstedt arose to meet her, and wondered at her pale, worn look.

"I hope you are in good health this morning, dear Marguerite," he said, offering to salute her. But she waved him off, saying:

"No! I am ill! And I come to you, this morning, Philip Helmstedt, to implore you to restore the promise wrenched from me yesterday," she said, and sunk, pallid and exhausted, upon the nearest chair.

A start and an attitude of astounded amazement was his only reply. A pause of a moment ensued, and Marguerite repeated:

"Will you be so generous as to give me back my plighted faith, Philip Helmstedt?"

"Marguerite! has nature balanced her glorious gift to you with a measure of insanity?" he inquired, at length, but without abatement of his astonishment.

"I sometimes think so. I do mad things occasionally. And the maddest thing I ever did, save one, was to give you that pledge yesterday."

"Thank you, fairest lady."

"And I ask you now to give it back to me."

"For what reason?"

"I can give you none!"

"No reason for your strange request?"

"None!"

"Then I assure you, my dearest Marguerite, that I am not mad."

"Indeed, you are upon one subject, if you did but know it. Once more, will you enfranchise my hand?"

"Do I look as if I would, lady of mine?"

"No! no! you do not! You never will! very well! be the consequences on your own head."

"Amen. I pray for no better."

"Heaven pity me!"

"My dearest, most capricious love! I do not know the motive of your strangest conduct; it may be that you only try the strength of my affection—try it, Marguerite! you will find it bear the test—but I do know, that if I doubted the truth of yours, I should disengage your hand at once."

There followed words of passionate entreaty on her part, met by earnest deprecation and unshaken firmness on his; but the spell was over her, and the scene ended as it had done the day previous; Philip was the victor, and the engagement was riveted, if possible, more firmly than before. Again Philip departed rejoicing; Marguerite, almost raving.

Yet Marguerite loved no less strongly and truly than did Philip.

Later in that forenoon, before going out, Nellie went into Marguerite's chamber, where she found her friend extended on her bed, so still and pale that she drew near in alarm and laid her hand upon her brow; it was beaded with a cold sweat.

"Marguerite! Marguerite! what is the matter? You are really ill."

"I am blue," said Marguerite.

"Blue! that you are literally—hands and face, too."

"Yes, I have got an ague," said Marguerite, shuddering, "but I will not be coddled! There."

In vain, Nellie, with a great show of solicitude, urged her services. Marguerite would receive none of them, and ended, as usual, by ordering Nellie out of the room.

In a few days the engagement between Mr. Helmstedt and Miss De Lancie was made known to the intimate friends of the parties. The marriage was appointed to take place early in the ensuing winter. Then the Richmond party dispersed—Colonel and Mrs. Houston went down to their plantation in Northumberland County; Philip Helmstedt proceeded to his island estates on the coast, to prepare his long-deserted home for the reception of his bride. And, lastly, Marguerite, after a hurried visit of inspection to

Plover's Point, went "gypsying," as she called it, for the whole summer and autumn. Upon this occasion, her mysterious absence was longer than usual. And when at last she rejoined her friends, her beautiful face betrayed the ravages of some strange, deep bitter sorrow.

Upon the following Christmas, once more, and for the last time, a merry party was assembled at Compton Hall. Among the guests were Nellie and her husband, on a visit to their parents. Marguerite De Lancie and Philip were also present. And there, under the auspices of Colonel and Mrs. Compton, they were united in marriage. By Marguerite's expressed will, the wedding was very quiet, and almost private. And immediately afterward the Christmas party broke up.

And Philip Helmstedt, instead of accompanying the Comptons and Houstons to Richmond, or starting upon a bridal tour, took his idolized wife to himself alone, and conveyed her to his bleak and lonely sea-girt home, where the wild waters lashed the shores both day and night, and the roar of the waves was ever heard.

CHAPTER V
THE EXCESS OF GLORY OBSCURED

"Muse, Grace, and Woman—in herself

All moods of mind contrasting—

The tenderest wail of human woe,

The scorn like lightning blasting;

Mirth sparkling like a diamond shower

From lips of lifelong sadness,

Clear picturings of majestic thought

Upon a ground of madness;

And over all romance and song

A magic lustre throwing,

And laureled Celie at her side

Her storied pages showing."

—Varied From Whittier.

How the wind raves, this bitter night, around that bleak, sea-girt, snow-covered island! how the waters roar as they break upon the beach! Not a star is out. Above, black, scudding clouds sail, like ships, across the dark ocean of ether—below, ships fly, like clouds, before the wind, across the troubled waters; thus sky and ocean seem to mingle in the fierce chaos of night and storm.

But that massive old stone mansion fronting the sea, and looking so like a fortification on the island, recks little of the storm that howls around it—a square, black block against the sky—a denser, more defined shadow in the midst of shadows, it looks, scarcely relieved by the tall, stately, Lombardy poplars that wave before the blast around it—a steady light, from a lower window the center of the front, streams in a line far out across garden, field, and beach, to the sea. Ay! little recks the strong house, built to brave just such weather, and little recks the beautiful woman, safely sheltered in the warmest, most luxurious room, of the wild wind and waves that rage so near its thick walls.

Let us leave the storm without and enter that nook. Look! this room had been furnished with direct regard to Marguerite's comfort, and though showing nothing like the splendor of modern parlors, it was comfortable and luxurious, as comfort and luxury were understood at that time and place; a costly French historic paper, representing the story of the Argonaunt sailors, adorned the walls; a rich, deep-wooded, square Turkey carpet covered the floor to within a foot of the chair-boards; heavy, dark crimson damask curtains, upheld by a gilded oar, fell in voluminous folds from the one deep bay window in front of the room; high-backed, richly-carved and crimson cushioned chairs were ranged against the walls; a curiously wrought cabinet stood in the recess on the right of the tall mantelpiece, and a grand piano in that on the left; oddly shaped and highly polished mahogany or black walnut stands and tables stood in corners or at side walls under hanging mirrors and old paintings; a fine sea view hung above the mantelpiece, and a pair of bronze candelabras, in the shape of anchors, adorned each end; choice books, vases, statuettes and bijouterie were scattered about; but the charm of the room was the crimson-curtained bay window, with its semi-circular sofa, and the beautiful harp and the music-stand that was a full-sized statue of St. Cecelia holding a scroll, which served as a rest for the paper. This recess had been fitted up by Philip Helmstedt in fond memory of the draperied bay window in the music-room at Colonel Compton's town house, where he had first breathed his love to Marguerite's ear.

The bridal pair, whose honeymoon in three months had not waned, were sitting on a short sofa, drawn up on the right of the fire. They were a very handsome couple and formed a fine picture as they sat—Philip, with his grandly-proportioned and graceful form, perfect Roman profile, stately head and short, curled, black hair and beard and high-bred air— Marguerite, in her superb beauty, which neither negligence nor overdress could mar—Marguerite sometimes so disdainful of the aid of ornament, was very simply clothed in a plain robe of fine, soft, crimson cloth, about the close bodice of which dropped here and there a stray ringlet from the rich mass of her slightly disheveled, but most beautiful hair. Her warm, inspiring face was glowing with life, and her deep, dark eyes were full of light. Some little graceful trifle of embroidery gave her slender, tapering fingers a fair excuse to move, while she listened to the voice of Philip reading "Childe Harold." But after all there was little sewing and little reading done. Marguerite's soul-lit eyes were oftener raised to Philip's face than lowered over her work; and Philip better loved the poetry in Marguerite's smile than the beauty of the canto before him. They had, in the very lavish redundance of life and consciousness of mutual self-sufficiency, left the gay and multitudinous city to retire to this secluded spot, this outpost of the continent, to be for a while all in all to each other; and three months of total isolation from the world had passed, and as yet they had not begun to be weary of each other's exclusive society. In truth, with their richly-endowed natures and boundless mutual resources, they could not soon exhaust the novelty of their wedded bliss. No lightest, softest cloud had as yet passed over the face of their honeymoon. If Mr. Helmstedt's despotic character occasionally betrayed itself, even toward his queenly bride, Marguerite, in her profound, self-abnegating, devoted love, with almost a saintly enthusiasm, quickly availed herself of the opportunity to prove how much deep joy is felt in silently, quietly, even secretly, laying our will at the feet of one we most delight to honor. And if Marguerite's beautiful face sometimes darkened with a strange gloom and terror, it was always in the few hours of Mr. Helmstedt's absence, and thus might easily be explained; for be it known to the reader that there was no way of communication between their island and the outside world except by boats, and the waters this windy season were always rough. If Mr. Helmstedt sometimes reflected upon the scenes of their stormy courtship, and wondered at the strange conduct of his beloved, he was half inclined to ascribe it all to a sort of melodramatic coquetry or caprice, or perhaps fanaticism in regard to the foolish pledge of celibacy once made between Miss De Lancie and Miss Compton, of which he had heard; it is true he thought that Marguerite was not a woman to act from either of these motives, but he was too happy in the possession of his bride to consider the matter deeply now, and it could be laid aside for future reference. Marguerite never reviewed the subject. Their life was now as profoundly still as it was deeply satisfied. They had no neighbors and no company whatever. "Buzzard's Bluff," Colonel Houston's place, was situated about five miles from them, up the Northumberland coast, but the colonel and his family were on a visit to the Comptons, in Richmond, and were not expected home for a month to come. Thus their days were very quiet.

How did they occupy their time? In reading, in writing, in music, in walking, riding, sailing, and, most of all, in endless conversations that permeated all other employments. Their island of three hundred acres scarcely afforded space enough for the long rides and drives they liked to take together; but on such few halcyon days as sometimes bless our winters, they would cross with their horses by the ferryboat to the Northumberland coast, and spend a day or half a day exploring the forest; sometimes, while the birding season lasted, a mounted groom; with fowling pieces and ammunition, would be ordered to attend, and upon these occasions a gay emulation as to which should bag the most game would engage their minds; at other times, alone and unattended, they rode long miles into the interior of the country, or down the coast to Buzzard's Bluff, to take a look at Nellie's home, or up the coast some twenty miles to spend a night at Marguerite's maiden home, Plover's Point. From the latter place Marguerite had brought her old nurse, Aunt Hapzibah, whom she promoted to the post of housekeeper at the island, and the daughter of the latter, Hildreth, who had long been her confidential maid, and the son, Forrest, whom she retained as her own especial messenger. And frequently when

"The air was still and the water still,"

or nearly so, the wedded pair would enter a rowboat and let it drift down the current, or guide it in and out among the scattering clusters of inlets that diversified the coast, where Mr. Helmstedt took a deep interest in pointing out to Marguerite vestiges of the former occupancy or visitings of those fierce buccaneers of the bay isles, that made so hideous the days and nights of the early settlers of Maryland, and from whom scandal said Philip Helmstedt himself had descended. Returning from these expeditions, they would pass the long, winter evenings as they were passing this one when I present them again to the reader, that is, in reading, work, or its semblance, conversation and music, when Marguerite would awaken the sleeping spirit of her harp to accompany her own rich, deep and soul-thrilling voice, in some sacred aria of Handel, or love song of Mozart, or simple, touching ballad of our own mother tongue. But Marguerite's improvisations were over. Upon this evening in question, Philip Helmstedt threw aside his book, and after gazing long and earnestly at his bride, as though he would absorb into his being the whole beautiful creature at his side, he said:

"Take your guitar, dear Marguerite, and give me some music—invest yourself in music, it is your natural atmosphere," and rising, he went to a table and brought thence the instrument, a rare and priceless one, imported from Spain, and laid it upon Marguerite's lap. She received it smilingly, and after tuning its chords, commenced and sung, in the original, one of

Camoens' exquisite Portuguese romaunts. He thanked her with a warm caress when she had finished, and, taking the guitar from her hand, said:

"You never improvise now, my Corinne! You never have done so since our union. Has inspiration fled?"

"I do not know—my gift of song was always an involuntary power—coming suddenly, vanishing unexpectedly. No, I never improvise now—the reason is, I think, that the soul never can set strongly in but one direction at a time."

"And that direction?"

She turned to him with a glance and a smile that fully answered his question.

"I am too happy to improvise, Philip," she said, dropping her beautiful head on his bosom, as he passed his arm around her, bent down and buried his face on the rich and fragrant tresses of her hair.

I present them to you in their wedded joy this evening, because it was the very last happy evening of their united lives. Even then a step was fast approaching, destined to bring discord, doubt, suspicion, and all the wretched catalogue of misery that follow in their train. While Marguerite's head still rested lovingly on Philip's bosom, and his fingers still threaded the lustrous black ringlets of her hair, while gazing down delightedly upon her perfect face, a sound was heard through the wind, that peculiar, heavy, swashing sound of a ferryboat striking the beach, followed by a quick, crunching step, breaking into the crusted snow and through the brushwood toward the house.

"It is my messenger from the post office—now for news of Nellie!" said Marguerite.

Philip looked slightly vexed.

"'Nellie!'—how you love Mrs. Houston, Marguerite! I do not understand such intimate female friendships."

"Doubtless you don't! It is owing to the slight circumstance of your being a man," said Marguerite, gayly, compensating for her light words by the passionate kiss she left on his brow as she went from his side to meet the messenger—ah! the ill-omened messenger that had entered the house and was hastening toward the parlor.

"Any letters, Forrest?" she eagerly inquired, as the boy came in.

"Only one, madam, for you," replied the man, delivering the missive.

"From Nellie, I judge!" she exclaimed, confidently, as she took it; but on seeing the postmark and superscription, she suddenly caught her breath, suppressing a sharp cry, and sank upon a chair.

Mr. Helmstedt, who had just turned and walked to the window to look out upon the wild weather, did not see this agitation.

Marguerite broke the seal and read; fear, grief and cruel remorse storming in her darkened and convulsed countenance.

Philip Helmstedt, having satisfied himself that the wind was increasing in force, and that vessels would be lost before morning, now turned and walked toward his wife.

She heard his step, oh! what a supreme effort of the soul was that—an effort in which years of life are lost—with which she commanded her grief and terror to retire, her heart to be still, her face to be calm, her tones to be steady, and her whole aspect to be cheerful and disengaged as her husband joined her.

"Your letter was not from Mrs. Houston, love? I am almost sorry—that is, I am sorry for your disappointment as a man half jealous of 'Nellie's' share in your heart can be," he said.

Marguerite smiled archly at this badinage, but did not otherwise reply.

"Well, then, if not from Nellie, I hope you heard good news from some other dear friend."

"As if I had scores of other dear friends!—but be at ease, thou jealous Spaniard, for Nellie is almost your only rival."

"I would not have even one," replied Mr. Helmstedt; but his eyes were fixed while he spoke upon the letter, held lightly, carelessly in Marguerite's hand, and that interested him as everything connected with her always did; and yet concerning which, that chivalrous regard to courtesy that ever distinguished him, except in moments of ungovernable passion, restrained him from inquiring.

Marguerite saw this, and, lightly wringing the paper in her fingers, said:

"It is from an acquaintance—I have so many—perhaps it would amuse you to look it over."

"Thank you, dear Marguerite," replied Mr. Helmstedt, extending his hand to take it.

She had not expected this—she had offered believing he would decline it, as he certainly would have done had he been less deeply interested in all that concerned her.

"By the way, no! I fear I ought not to let you see it, Philip! It is from an acquaintance who has made me the depository of her confidence—I must not abuse it even to you. You would not ask it, Philip?"

"Assuredly not, except, inasmuch as I wish to share every thought and feeling of yours, my beloved! Do you know that this desire makes me jealous even of your silence and your reveries? And I would enter even into them! Nothing less would content me."

"Then be contented, Philip, for you are the soul of all my reveries; you fill my heart, as I am sure I do yours." Then casting the letter into the fire, lightly, as a thing of no account, she went and took up her guitar and began strumming its strings and humming another Portuguese song; then, laying that aside again, she rang the bell and ordered tea.

"We will have it served here, Philip," she said; "it is so bleak in the dining-room."

Forrest, who had meanwhile doffed his overcoat and warmed himself, answered the summons and received the necessary directions. He drew out a table, then went and presently returned with Hildreth, bringing the service of delicate white china, thin and transparent as the finest shells, and richly-chased silver, more costly from its rare workmanship than for its precious metal; and then the light bread and tea cakes, *chef-d'œuvres* of Aunt Hapsy's culinary skill; and the rich, West India sweetmeats with which Philip, for want of a housekeeper to prepare domestic ones before Marguerite's arrival, had stocked the closets. When the "hissing urn" was placed upon the table, Forrest and Hildreth retired, leaving their mistress and master alone; for Mr. Helmstedt loved with Marguerite to linger over his elegant and luxurious little tea table, toasting, idling, and conversing at ease with her, free from the presence of others. And seldom had Marguerite been more beautiful, brilliant, witty, and fascinating than upon this evening, when she had but him to please; and his occasional ringing laughter testified her happy power to move to healthful mirth even that grave, saturnine nature.

An hour of trifling with the delicate viands on the table, amid jest and low-toned silvery laughter, and then the bell was rung and the service removed.

"And now—the spirit comes, and I will give you a song—an improvisation! Quick, give me the guitar—for I must seize the fancy as it flies—for it is fading even now like a vanishing sail on the horizon."

"The guitar? The harp is your instrument of improvisation."

"No! the guitar; I know what I am saying," and, receiving it from the hands of her husband, she sat down, and while an arch smile hovered under the black fringes of her half-closed eyelids, and about the corners of her slightly parted lips, she began strumming a queer prelude, and then, like a demented minstrel, struck up one of the oddest inventions in the shape of a ballad that was ever sung out of Bedlam.

Philip listened with undisguised astonishment and irrepressible mirth, which presently broke bounds in a ringing peal of laughter. Marguerite paused and waited until his cachinnations should be over, with a gravity that almost provoked him to a fresh peal, but he restrained himself, as he wished the ballad to go on, and Marguerite recommenced and continued uninterrupted through about twenty stanzas, each more extravagant than the other, until the last one set Philip off again in a convulsion of laughter.

"Thalia," he said; "Thalia as well as Melpomene."

"This is the very first comic piece I have ever attempted—the first time that the laughing muse has visited me," said Marguerite, laying down her guitar, and approaching the side of her husband.

"And I alone have heard it! So I would have it, Marguerite. I almost detest that any other should enjoy your gifts and accomplishments."

"Egotist!" she exclaimed, but with the fond, worshiping tone and manner, wherewith she might have said, "Idol!"

"So you like my music, Philip?"

"How can you ask, my love? Your music delights me, as all you ever say and do always must."

"I have heard that ever when the lute and voice of an *improvvisatrice* has chained her master, she has the dear privilege of asking a boon that he may not deny her," said Marguerite, in the same light, jesting tone, under which it was impossible to detect a substratum of deep, terrible earnestness.

"How? What do you say, my love?"

"My voice and stringed instrument have pleased my master, and I would crave of him a boon."

"Dearest love! do not use such a phrase, even in the wantonness of your sport."

"What is, then, Mr. Helmstedt but Marguerite's master?"

"Her own faithful lover, husband, servant, all in one; and my lady knows she has but to speak and her will is law," said Philip, gallantly.

"Away with such tinsel flattery. In 'grand gravity,' as my dear father used to say, I am no longer my own, but yours—I cannot come or go, change my residence, sell or purchase property, make a contract or prosecute an offender, or do anything else that a free woman would do, without your sanction. You are my master—my owner."

Was this possible? her master? the master of this proud and gifted woman, who ever before had looked and stepped, and spoken like a sovereign queen? Yes, it is true; he knew it before, but now from her own glowing lips it came, bringing a new, strong, thrilling, and most delicious sense of possession and realization, and his eye traveled delightedly over the enchanting face and form of his beautiful wife, as his heart repeated, "She speaks but truth—she, with all her wondrous dower of beauty and genius and learning is solely mine—my own, own! I wish the prerogative were even greater. I would have the power of life and death over this glorious creature, that were I about myself to die, I could slay her lest another should ever possess her;" but his lips spoke otherwise.

"Dear love," he said, drawing her up to him, "we all know that the one-sided statute, a barbarous remnant of the dark ages, invests a husband with certain very harsh powers; but it is almost a dead letter. Who in this enlightened age thinks of acting upon it? Never reproach me with a bad law I had no hand in making, sweet love."

"'Reproach' you, Philip!" she whispered, yielding herself to his caress; "no! if the law were a hundredfold stricter, investing you with power over your Marguerite a hundredfold greater, she would not complain of it; for it cannot give so much as her heart gives you ever and ever! Should it clothe you with the power of life and death over her, it would be no more than your power now, for the sword could not kill more surely, Philip, than your possible unkindness would. No! were the statutes a thousand times more arbitrary, and your own nature more despotic, they nor you could exact never so much as my heart pours freely out to you, ever and ever."

He answered only by folding her closer to his bosom, and then said:

"But the boon, Marguerite; or rather the command, my lady, what is it?"

"Philip," she said, raising her head from his bosom, and fixing her eyes on his face, "Philip, I want—heavens! how the storm raves!—do you hear it, Philip?"

"Yes, love, do not mind it; it cannot enter."

"But the ships, the ships at sea."

"Do not think of them, love; we cannot help them; what is beyond remedy is beyond regret."

"True, that is very true! what is beyond remedy is beyond regret," said Marguerite, meditatively.

"But the 'boon,' as you call it, the command, as I regard it—what is it, Marguerite?"

"Philip, I am about to ask from you a great proof of your confidence in me," she said, fixing her eyes earnestly, pleadingly upon his face.

"A proof of my confidence in you, Marguerite?" he repeated, slowly, and then, after a thoughtful pause, he added, "Does it need proof then? Marguerite, I know not how much the humbling sense of dishonor would crush me, could I cease for one single hour to confide in you—in you, the sacred depository of my family honor, and all my best and purest interests— you, whom it were desecration, in any respect, to doubt. Lady, for the love of heaven, consult your own dignity and mine before demanding a proof of that which should be above proof and immeasurably beyond the possibility of question."

"You take this matter very seriously, Philip," said Marguerite, with a troubled brow.

"Because it is a very serious matter, love—but the boon; what is it, lady? I am almost ready to promise beforehand that it is granted, though I might suffer the fate of Ninus for my rashness. Come, the boon, name it! only for heaven's sake ask it not as proof of confidence."

"And yet it must necessarily be such, nor can you help it, my lord," said Marguerite, smiling with assumed gayety.

"Well, well! let's hear and judge of that."

Marguerite still hesitated, then she spoke to the point.

"I beg you will permit me to leave you for a month."

"To leave me for a month!" exclaimed Philip Helmstedt, astonishment, vexation, and wonder struggling in his face, "that is asking a boon with a bitter vengeance. In the name of heaven where do you wish to go? To your friend Nellie, perchance?"

"I wish to go away unquestioned, unattended and unfollowed."

"But, Marguerite," he stammered, "but this is the maddest proposition."

"For one month—only for one month, Philip, of unfettered action and unquestioned motives. I wish the door of my delightsome cage opened, that I may fly abroad and feel myself once more a free agent in God's boundless creation. One month of irresponsible liberty, and then I render myself back to my sweet bondage and my dear master. I love both too well, too well, to remain away long," said Marguerite, caressing him with a fascinating blending of passion with playfulness, that at another time must have wiled the will from his heart, and the heart from his bosom. Now, to this proposition, he was adamant.

"And when do you propose to start?" he asked.

"To-morrow, if you will permit me."

"Had you not better defer it a week, or ten days—until the first of April, for instance: all-fools'-day would be a 'marvellous proper' one for you to go, and me to speed you on such an expedition."

Marguerite laughed strangely.

"Will you allow me to ask you one question, my love? Where do you wish to go?"

"Gipsying."

"Gipsying?"

"'Aye, my good lord.'"

"Oh, yes; I remember! Marguerite, let me tell you seriously that I cannot consent to your wish."

"You do not mean to say that you refuse to let me go?" exclaimed Marguerite, all her assumed lightness vanishing in fear.

"Let us understand each other. You desire my consent that you shall leave home for one month, without explaining whither or wherefore you go?"

"Yes."

"Then most assuredly I cannot sanction any thing of the sort."

"Philip, I implore you."

"Marguerite, you reduce me to the alternative of doubting your sincerity or your sanity!"

"Philip, I am sane, and I am deeply in earnest! Ah! Philip, by our love, I do entreat you grant me this boon—to leave your house for a month's absence, unquestioned by you! Extend the aegis of your sanction over my absence that none other may dare to question it."

"Assuredly none shall dare to question the conduct of Mrs. Helmstedt, because I shall take care that her acts are above criticism. As to my sanction of your absence, Marguerite, you have had my answer," said Mr. Helmstedt, walking away in severe displeasure and throwing himself into a chair.

There was silence in the room for a few minutes, during which the howling of the storm without rose fearfully on the ear. Then Marguerite, the proud and beautiful, went and sank down at his feet, clasped his knees and bowed her stately head upon them, crying:

"Philip, I pray you, look at me here!"

"Mrs. Helmstedt, for your own dignity, leave this attitude," he said, taking her hands and trying to force her to rise.

"No, no, no, not until you listen to me, Philip! Oh, Philip, look down and see who it is that kneels here! petitioning for a span of freedom. One who three short months ago was mistress of much land and many slaves, 'queen o'er herself,' could go unchecked and come unquestioned, was accustomed to granting, not to asking boons, until her marriage."

"Do you regret the sacrifice?"

"Regret it! How can you ask the question? If my possessions and privileges had been multiplied a thousand fold, they should have been, as I am now, all your own, to do your will with! No! I only referred to it to move you to generosity!"

"Marguerite! I cannot tolerate to see you in that attitude one instant longer," said Mr. Helmstedt, taking her hands and forcing her to rise and sit by his side, "Now let us talk reasonably about this matter. Tell me, your husband, who has the right to know, why and where you wish to go, and I promise you that you shall go unquestioned and unblamed of all."

"Oh, God, if I might!" escaped the lips of Marguerite, but she speedily controlled herself and said, "Philip, if you had secret business that concerned others, and that peremptorily called you from home to attend to it, would you not feel justified in leaving without even satisfying your wife's curiosity as to why and where you went, if you could not do it without disclosing to her the affairs of others!"

"No—decidedly no! from my wife I have no secrets. I, who trusted her with my peace and honor, trust her also with all lesser matters; and to leave home for a month's absence without informing her whither and wherefore I should go—Why, Marguerite, I hope you never really deemed me capable of offering you such an offence."

"Oh, God!—and yet you could do so, unquestioned and unblamed, as many men do!"

"I could, but would not."

"While I—would but cannot. Well, that is the difference between us."

"Certainly, Marguerite, there is a difference between what would be fitting to—a profane man to a sacred woman—there is a 'divinity that hedges' the latter, through which she cannot break but to lose her glory."

"But in my girlhood I had unmeasured, irresponsible liberty. None dared to cavil at my actions."

"Perhaps so, for maidens are all Dianas. Besides, she who went 'gypsying,' year after year, could compromise only herself; now her eccentricities, charming as they are, might involve the honor of a most honorable family."

"Descendants of a pirate at best," said Marguerite's memory; but her heart rejected the change of her mind, and replied instead, "My husband, my dear, dear husband, my lord, idolized even now in his implacability;" her lips spoke nothing.

"Much was permissible and even graceful in Miss De Lancie, that could not be tolerated in Mrs. Helmstedt," continued Philip.

"A great accession of dignity and importance certainly," sneered Marguerite's sarcastic intellect. "Away! I am his wife! his loving wife," replied her worshiping heart; but her lips spoke not.

"You do not answer me, Marguerite."

"I was listening, beloved."

"And you see this subject as I do?"

"Certainly, certainly, and the way you put it leaves me no hope but in your generosity. Ah, Philip, be more generous than ever man was before. Ask me no questions, but let me go forth upon my errand, and cover my absence with the shield of your authority that none may venture to cavil."

"Confide in me and I will do it. I promise you, in advance, not knowing of what nature that confidence may be."

"Oh, Heaven, if—I cannot. Alas! Philip, I cannot!"

"Why?"

"The affair concerns others."

"There are no others whose interest and claims can conflict with those of your husband."

"I—have a—friend—in deadly peril—I would go to—the assistance of my friend."

"How confused—nay, great Heaven, how guilty you look! Marguerite, who is that friend? Where is he, or she? What is the nature of the peril? What connection have you with her or him? Why must you go secretly? Answer these questions before asking my consent."

"Ah, if I dared! if I dared!" she exclaimed, thrown partly off her guard by agitation, and looking, gazing intently in his face; "but no, I cannot— oh! I cannot!—that sarcastic incredulity, that fierce, blazing scorn—I cannot dare it! Guilty? You even now said I looked, Philip! I am not guilty! The Lord knoweth it well—not guilty, but most unfortunate—most wretched! Philip, your unhappy wife is an honorable woman!"

"She thinks it necessary, however, to assure me of that which should be above question. Unhappy? Why are you unhappy? Marguerite, how you torture me."

"Philip, for the last time I pray you, I beseech you, grant my wish. Do not deny me, Philip; do not! Life, more than life, sanity hangs upon your answer! Philip, will you sanction my going?"

"Most assuredly not, Marguerite."

"Oh, Heaven! how can you be so inflexible, Philip? I asked for a month—a fortnight might do—Philip; let me go for a fortnight!"

"No."

"For a week then, Philip; for a week! Oh, I do implore you—I, who never asked a favor before! Let me go but for a week!"

"Not for a week—not for a day! under the circumstances in which you wish to go," said Mr. Helmstedt, with stern inflexibility.

Again Marguerite threw herself at her husband's feet, clasping his knees, and lifting a deathly brow bedewed with the sweat of a great agony, and eyes strained outward in mortal prayer, she pleaded as a mother might plead for a child's life. In vain, for Mr. Helmstedt grew obdurate in proportion to the earnestness of her prayers, and at last arose and strode away, and stood with folded arms at the window, looking out upon the stormy weather, while she remained writhing on the spot where late she had kneeled.

So passed half an hour, during which no sound was heard but the fierce moaning, wailing, and howling of the wind, and the detonating roar and thunder of the waves as they broke upon the beach; during which Marguerite remained upon the carpet, with her face buried in the cushions of the sofa, writhing silently, or occasionally uttering a low moan like one in great pain; and Philip Helmstedt stood reflecting bitterly upon what had just passed. To have seen that proud, beautiful and gifted creature, that regal woman, one of nature's and society's queens, "le Marguerite des Marguerites!" His wife, so bowed down, crushed, humiliated, was a bitter experience to a man of his haughty, scornful, sarcastic nature; passionately as he had loved her, proud as he had been to possess her, now that she was discrowned and fallen, her value was greatly lessened in his estimation. For not her glorious beauty had fascinated his senses, or her wonderful genius had charmed his mind, or her high social position tempted his ambition, so much as her native queenliness had flattered the inordinate pride of his character. He did not care to possess a woman who was only beautiful, amiable or intellectual, or even all these combined; but to conquer and possess this grand creature with the signet of royalty impressed upon brow and breast—this was a triumph of which Lucifer himself might have been proud. But now this queen was discrowned, fallen, fallen into a miserable, weeping, pleading woman, no longer worthy of his rule, for it could bring no delight to his arrogant temper to subjugate weakness and humility, but only strength and pride equal to his own. And what was it that had suddenly stricken Marguerite down from her pride of place and cast her quivering at his feet? What was it that she concealed from him? While vexing himself with these thoughts, he heard through all the roar of the storm a low, shuddering sigh, a muffled rustling of drapery and a soft step, and turned to see that his wife had risen to leave the room.

"One moment, if you please, Marguerite," he said, approaching her. She looked around, still so beautiful, but oh! how changed within a few hours. Was this Richmond's magnificent Marguerite, queen of beauty and of song, whom he had proudly carried off from all competitors? She, looking so subdued, so pale, with a pallor heightened by the contrast of the crimson dress she wore, and the lustrous purplish hair that fell, uncurled and waving in disheveled locks, down each side her white cheeks and over her bosom.

"I wish to talk with you, if you please, Marguerite."

She bent her head and silently gave him her hand, and suffered him to lead her back toward the fire, where he placed her on the sofa, and then, standing at the opposite corner of the hearth, and resting his elbow on the mantelpiece, he spoke.

"Marguerite, there is much that must be cleared up before there can ever more be peace between us."

"Question me; it is your right, Philip," she said, in a subdued tone, steadying her trembling frame in a sitting posture on the sofa.

"Recline, Marguerite; repose yourself while we converse," he said, for deeply displeased as he was, it moved his heart to see her sitting there so white and gaunt.

She took him at his word and sank down with her elbow on the piled-up cushions, and her fingers run up through her lustrous tresses supporting her head, and repeated.

"Question me, Philip, it is your right!"

"I must go far back. The scene of this evening has awakened other recollections, not important by themselves, but foreboding, threatening, in connection with what has occurred to-night. I allude in the first place to those yearly migrations of yours that so puzzled your friends; will you now explain them to me?"

"Philip, ask to take the living, beating heart from my bosom and you shall do it—but I cannot give you the explanation you desire," she answered, in a mournful tone.

"You cannot!" he repeated, growing white and speaking through his closed teeth.

"I cannot, alas! Philip, it concerns another."

"Another! Man or woman?"

"Neith—oh, Heaven, Philip, I cannot tell you!"

"Very well," he said, but there was that in his tone and manner that made his simple exclamation more alarming than the bitterest reproaches and threats could have been.

"Philip! Philip! these things occurred before our engagement, and you heard of them. Forgive me for reminding you that you might have requested an explanation of them, and if refused, you might have withdrawn."

"No, Marguerite! I am amazed to hear you say so. I had no right then to question your course of conduct; it would have been an unpardonable insult to you to have done so; moreover, I thoroughly confided in the honor of a woman whom I found at the head of the best society, respected, flattered, followed, courted, as you were. I never could have foreseen that such a woman would bring into our married life an embarrassing mystery, which I beg her now to elucidate."

"Yet it is a pity, oh! what a pity that you had not asked this elucidation a year since!" exclaimed Marguerite, in a voice of anguish.

"Why? Would you then have given it to me?"

"Alas! no, for my power to do so was no greater then than now. But then, at least, on my refusal to confide this affair (that concerns others, Philip) to you, you might have withdrawn from me—now, alas! it is too late."

"Perhaps not," remarked Mr. Helmstedt, in a calm, but significant tone.

"My God! what mean you, Philip?" exclaimed his wife, starting up from her recumbent position.

"To question you farther—that is all for the present."

She sank down again and covered her face with her hands. He continued.

"Recall, Marguerite, the day of our betrothal. There was a fierce anguish, a terrible conflict in your mind before you consented to become my wife; that scene has recurred to me again and again. Taken as a link in this chain of inexplicable circumstances connected with you, it becomes of serious importance. Will you explain the cause of your distress upon the occasion referred to?"

A groan was her only answer, while her head remained buried in the cushions of the sofa.

"So! you will not even clear up that matter?"

"Not 'will not,' but cannot, Philip, cannot!"

"Very well," he said, again, in a tone that entered her heart like a sword, and made her start up once more and gaze upon him, exclaiming:

"Oh, Philip, be merciful! I mean be just! Remember, on the day to which you allude, I warned you, warned you faithfully of much misery that might result from our union; and even before that—oh! remember, Philip, how sedulously I avoided you—how I persevered in trying to keep off the—I had nearly said—catastrophe of our engagement."

"Say it then! nay, you have said it! add that I followed and persecuted you with my suit until I wrested from you a reluctant consent, and that I must now bear the consequences!"

"No, no, no, I say not that, nor anything like it. No, Philip, my beloved, my idolized, I am not charging you; Heaven forbid! I am put upon my defense, you know, and earnestly desire to be clear before my judge. Listen then, Philip, to this much of a confession. When I first met you I felt your influence over me. Take this to your heart, Philip, as a shield against doubt of me—you are the first and last and only man I ever loved, if love be the word for that all-pervading power that gives me over body, soul and spirit to your possession. As I said when I first met you, I felt your influence. Day by day this spell increased, and I knew that you were my fate! Yet I tried to battle it off, but even at the great distance I kept I still felt your power growing, Philip, and I knew, I knew that that power would be irresistible! I had resolved never to marry, because, yes! I confess I had a secret (concerning others, you know, Philip), that I could not confide to any other, even to you; therefore I fled your presence—therefore when you overtook and confronted me I warned you faithfully, you know with how little effect! heart and soul I was yours, Philip! you knew it and took possession. And now we are united, Philip, God be thanked, for with all the misery it may bring me, Philip, I am still less wretched than I should be apart from you. And such, I believe, is the case with you. You are happier now, even with the cloud between us, than you would be if severed from me! Ah, Philip, is there any misfortune so great as separation to those whose lives are bound up in each other? Is not the cloudiest union more endurable than dreary severance?"

"That depends, Marguerite!—there is another link in this dark chain that I would have explained—the letter you received this evening."

"The letter—oh, God! have mercy on me," she cried, in a half smothered voice.

"Yes, the letter!" repeated Mr. Helmstedt, coolly, with his eyes still fixed steadily upon her pallid countenance that could scarcely bear his gaze.

"Oh! I told you—that it—was from an acquaintance—who—confided to me some of her troubles—which—was intended for no other eye but mine. Yes! that was what I told you, Philip," said Marguerite, confused, yet struggling almost successfully for self-control.

"Yes, I know you did, and doubtless told me truly so far as you spoke; but your manner was not truthful, Marguerite. You affected to treat that letter lightly, yet you took care to destroy it; you talked, jested, laughed with unprecedented gayety; your manner completely deceived me, though as I look at it from my present view it was a little overdone. You sang and played, and became Thalia, Allegra, 'for this night only,' and when the point toward which all this acting tended, came, and you made your desire known to me, you affected to put it as a playful test of my confidence, a caprice; but when you found your bagatelle treated seriously, and your desire steadily and gravely refused, Marguerite, your acting all was over. And now I demand an explanation of your conduct, for, Marguerite, deception will be henceforth fruitless forever!"

"Deception!"

"Yes, madam, that was the word I used, purposely and with a full appreciation of the meaning," said Mr. Helmstedt, sternly.

"Deception! Heaven and earth! deception charged by you upon me!" she exclaimed, and then sank down, covering her face with her hands and whispering to her own heart, "I am right—I am right, he must never be told—he would never be just."

"I know that the charge I have made is a dishonoring one, madam, but its dishonor consists in its truth. I requested you to explain that letter; and I await your reply."

"Thus far, Philip, I will explain: that—yes!—that letter was—a connecting link in the chain of circumstances you spoke of—it brought me news of—that one's peril of which I told you, and made me, still leaves me, how anxious to go to—that one's help. Could you but trust me?"

"Which I cannot now do, which I can never again entirely do. The woman who could practice upon me as you have done this evening, can never more be fully trusted! Still, if you can satisfactorily account for your strange conduct, we may yet go on together with some measure of mutual regard and comfort; which is, I suppose, all that, after the novelty of the honeymoon is past, ordinarily falls to the lot of married people. The glamour, dotage, infatuation, that deceived us into believing that our wedded love was something richer, rarer, diviner than that of other mortals like us, is forever gone! And the utmost that I venture to hope now, Mrs. Helmstedt, is that your speedy explanation may prove that, with this mystery, you have not brought dishonor on the family you have entered."

"Dishonor!" cried Marguerite, dropping her hands, that until now had covered her face, and gazing wildly at her husband.

"Aye, madam, dishonor!"

"Great Heaven! had another but yourself made that charge!" she exclaimed, in a voice deep and smothered with intense emotion.

"The deception of which you stand convicted is in itself dishonor, and no very great way from deeper dishonor! You need not look so shocked, madam, (though that may be acting also.) Come, exculpate yourself!" he said, fiercely, giving vent to the storm of jealous fury that had been gathering for hours in his breast.

But his wife gazed upon him with the look of one thunder-stricken, as she replied:

"Oh, doubtless, Mr. Helmstedt, you have the right to do what you will with your own, even to the extremity of thus degrading her."

"No sarcasms, if you please, madam; they ill become your present ambiguous position. Rather clear yourself. Come, do it; for if I find that you have brought shame— —"

"Philip!"

Without regarding her indignant interruption, he went on:

"Upon the honorable name you bear—by the living Lord that hears me! I will take justice in my own hands and—kill you!"

She had continued to gaze upon him with her great, dark eyes, standing forth like burning stars until the last terrible words fell from his lips—when, dropping her eyelids, her face relaxed into a most dubious and mournful smile, as she said:

"That were an easier feat than you imagine, Philip. The heart burns too fiercely in this breast to burn long. Your words add fuel to the flame. But in this implied charge upon your wife, the injustice that you do her, is nothing compared to the great wrong you inflict upon your own honor."

"Once more—will you clear yourself before me?"

"No."

"What! 'No?'"

"No! Alas! why multiply words, when all is contained in that monosyllable?"

"What is the meaning of this, madam?"

"That your three-months wife, even while acknowledging your right to command her, disobeys you, because she must, Philip! she must! but even in so doing, she submits herself to you to meet uncomplainingly all consequences—yes, to say short, they are natural and just! Philip, you have my final answer. Do your will! I am yours!"

And saying this, she arose, and with a manner full of loving submission, went to his side, laid her hand lightly upon his arm and looked up into his face.

But he shook that hand off as if it had been a viper; and when she replaced it, and again looked pleadingly up into his face, he took her by the arm and whirled her off toward the sofa, where she dropped amid the cushions, and then with a fierce, half-arrested oath, he flung himself out of the room.

"I cannot blame him: no one could. Oh, God," she cried, sinking down and burying her head amid the cushions. Quickly with sudden energy she arose, and went to the window and looked out; the sky was still darker with clouds than with night; but the wind had ceased and the sea was quiet. She returned toward the fireplace and rang the bell, which was speedily answered by Forrest.

Forrest, the son of her old nurse, Aunt Hapsy, was a tall, stalwart, jet-black negro of some fifty years of age, faithfully and devotedly attached to his mistress, and whose favorite vanity it was to boast that—Laws! niggers! he had toted Miss Marget about in his arms, of'en an' of'en when she was no more'n so high, holding his broad black palm about two feet from the ground.

"How is the weather, Forrest?" inquired Mrs. Helmstedt, who was now at the cabinet, that I have mentioned as standing to the right of the fireplace, and writing rapidly.

"Bad 'nough, Miss Marget, ma'am, I 'sures you."

"The wind has stopped."

"O'ny to catch his breaf, Miss Marget, ma'am. He'll 'mence 'gain strong'n ever—you'll hear—'cause ef he didn't stop at de tide comin' in, dis ebenen, he ain't gwine stop till it do go out to-morrow morn'n."

Mrs. Helmstedt had finished writing, folded, closed and directed a letter, which she now brought to her messenger.

"Forrest, I don't wish you to endanger your life by venturing to cross to the shore in a gale, but I wish this letter posted in time to go out in the mail at six o'clock to-morrow morning, and so you may take charge of it now; and if the wind should go down at any time to-night, you can carry it to the post office."

"Miss Marget, ma'am, it goes. I ain't gwine to ask no win' no leave to take your letter to de pos'—when you wants it go it goes," said the faithful creature, putting the letter carefully into his breast pocket.

"Any oder orders, Miss Marget, ma'am?"

"No, only take care of yourself."

Forrest bowed reverently and went out, softly closing the door behind him.

Marguerite went and sat down on the sofa, and drew a little workstand toward her, on which she rested both elbows, while she dropped her forehead upon the palms of her hands. She had scarcely sat down, when Philip Helmstedt, as from second thought, re-entered the room, from which, indeed, he had scarcely been absent ten minutes. Marguerite dropped her hands and looked up with an expression of welcome in her face; Mr. Helmstedt did not glance toward her, but went to the cabinet—the upper portion of which was a bookcase—selected a volume, and came and drew a chair to the corner of the fireplace opposite to Marguerite's sofa, sat down and seemed to read, but really studied Marguerite's countenance; and she felt that influence, though now, while her head rested upon one arm leaned on the stand, her eyes were never lifted from the floor. So passed some twenty minutes.

Eleven o'clock struck. They were in the habit of taking some light refreshments at this hour, before retiring for the night. And now the door opened and Hildreth entered, bringing a waiter, upon which stood two silver baskets, containing oranges and Malaga grapes, which she brought and placed upon the stand before her mistress, and then retired.

Mr. Helmstedt threw down his book, drew his chair to the stand, and took up and peeled an orange, which he placed upon a plate with a bunch of grapes, and offered to Marguerite.

She looked up to see what promise there might be in this act, ready, anxious to meet any advance half-way; but she saw in his stern brow and averted eyes, no hope of present reconciliation, and understood that this form of courtesy sprang only from the habitual good breeding, that ever, save when passion threw him off his guard, governed all his actions. She received the plate with a faint smile and a "thank you," and made a pretense of eating by shredding the orange and picking to pieces the bunch of grapes; while Mr. Helmstedt, on his part, made no pretense whatever, but having served Marguerite, retired to his chair and book. She looked after him, her heart full to breaking, and presently rising she rang for her maid, and retired.

Hildreth, the confidential maid of Mrs. Helmstedt, was a good-looking, comfortable, matronly woman, over forty years of age, very much like her brother Forrest in the largeness of her form, and the shining darkness of her skin, as well as in her devoted attachment to her mistress. She was a widow, and the mother of four stalwart boys, who were engaged upon the fisheries belonging to the island. For the rest, Hildreth was an uncharitable moralist, and a strict disciplinarian, visiting the sins of the fathers upon the children in her bitter intolerance of mulattoes. Hildreth affected grave Quaker colors for her gowns, and snow-white, cotton cloth for her turbans, neck-handkerchiefs, and aprons. Can you see her now? her large form clad in gray linsey, a white handkerchief folded across her bosom and tied down under the white apron, and her jet-black, self-satisfied face surmounted by the white turban? Hildreth was not the most refined and delicate of natures, and consequently her faithful affection for her mistress was sometimes troublesome from its intrusiveness. This evening, in attending Mrs. Helmstedt to her room, she saw at once the signs of misery on her face, and became exacting in her sympathy.

Was her mistress sick? had she a headache? would she bathe her feet? would she have a cup of tea? what could she do for her? And when Mrs. Helmstedt gave her to understand that silence and darkness, solitude and rest were all she required, Hildreth so conscientiously interpreted her wishes that she closed every shutter, drew down every blind, and lowered every curtain of the windows, to keep out the sound of the wind and sea; turned the damper to keep the stove from "roaring," stopped the clock to keep it from "ticking," ejected a pet kitten to keep it from "purring," closed the curtains around her lady's bed, and having thus, as far as human power could, secured profound silence and deep darkness, she quietly withdrew, without even moving the air with a "good-night."

There is no fanaticism like the fanaticism of love, whether it exists in the bosom of a cloistered nun, wrapped in visions of her Divine Bridegroom, or in that of a devoted wife, a faithful slave, or a poor dog who stretches himself across the grave of his master and dies. That love, that self-abnegating love, that even in this busy, struggling, proud, sensual world, where a cool heart, with a clear head and elastic conscience, are the elements of success, still lives in obscure places and humble bosoms; that love that, often misunderstood, neglected, scorned, martyred, still burns till death, burns beyond—to what does it tend? To that spirit world where all good affections, all beautiful dreams, and divine aspirations shall be proved to have been prophecies, shall be abundantly realized.

Such thoughts as these did not pass through the simple mind of Hildreth, any more than they would have passed through the brain of poor Tray, looking wistfully in his master's thoughtful face, as she went down to the parlor, and, curtseying respectfully, told her master that she feared Mrs. Helmstedt was very ill. That gentleman gave Hildreth to understand that she might release herself of responsibility, as he should attend to the matter.

No sleep visited the eyes of Marguerite that night. It was after midnight when Philip entered her chamber, and went to rest without speaking to her.

And from this evening, for many days, this pair, occupying the same chamber, meeting at the same table, scarcely exchanged a glance or word. Yet in every possible manner, Marguerite studied the comfort and anticipated the wishes of her husband, who, on his part, now that the first frenzy of his anger was over, did not fail in courtesy toward her, cold, freezing, as that courtesy might be. Often Marguerite's heart yearned to break through this cold reserve; but it was impossible to do so. Not the black armor of the Black Prince was blacker, harder, colder, more impassable and repellent, than the atmosphere of frozen self-retention in which Mr. Helmstedt encased himself.

By her conduct, on that fatal evening, his love and pride had been deeply, almost mortally wounded. A storm of contending astonishment, indignation, wonder, and conjecture had been raised in his bosom. The East, West, North and South, as it were, of opposite passions and emotions had been brought together in fierce conflict. His glory in Marguerite's queenly nature had been met by humiliating doubt of her, and his passionate love by anger that might settle into hate. And now that the first chaotic violence of this tempest of warring thoughts and feelings had subsided, he resumed his habitual self-control and dignified courtesy, and determined to seek light upon the dark subject that had occasioned the first estrangement between himself and his beloved wife. He felt fully justified, even by his own nice code of honor, in watching Marguerite closely. Alas! all he discovered in her was a deeply-seated sorrow, not to be consoled, an intense anxiety difficult to conceal, an extreme restlessness impossible to govern; and through all a tender solicitude and affectionate deference toward himself, that was perhaps the greatest trial to his dignity and firmness. For, notwithstanding her fault, and his just anger, even he, with his stern, uncompromising temper, found it difficult to live side by side with that beautiful, impassioned, and fascinating woman, whom he ardently loved, without becoming unconditionally reconciled to her.

She, with the fine instinct of her nature, saw this, and knew that but for the pride and scorn that forbade him to make the first advance, they might become reconciled. She, proud as Juno toward all else, had no pride toward those she loved, least of all toward him. Therefore, one morning, when they had breakfasted as usual, without exchanging a word, and Mr. Helmstedt had risen and taken his hat to leave the room, Marguerite got up and slowly, hesitatingly, even bashfully, followed him into the passageway, and, stealing to his side, softly and meekly laid her hand and dropped her face upon his arm, and murmured:

"Philip! I cannot bear this longer, dearest! my heart feels cold, and lone, and houseless; take me back to my home in your heart, Philip."

There could have been nothing more alluring to him than this submission of that proud, beautiful woman, and her whole action was so full of grace, tenderness, and passion that his firmness gave way before it. His arms glided around her waist, and his lips sought hers silently, ere they murmured:

"Come, then to your home in this bosom, beloved, where there is an aching void, until you fill it."

And so a sweet, but superficial peace was sealed between the husband and wife—so sweet that it was like a new bridal, so superficial that the slightest friction might break it. No more for them on earth would life be what it had been. A secret lay between them that Marguerite was determined to conceal, and Philip had resolved to discover; and though he would not again compromise his position toward her by demanding an explanation sure to be refused, he did not for an hour relax his vigilance and his endeavors to find a clew to her mystery. He attended the post office, and left orders that letters for his family should be delivered into no other hands but his own. He watched Marguerite's deportment, noting her fits of deep and mournful abstraction, her sudden starts, her sleepless nights and cheerless days, and failing health, and more than all, her distracting, maddening manner toward himself, alternating like sunshine and darkness, passionate love, and deep and fearful remorse as inexplicable as it was irradicable.

Not another week of quiet domestic happiness, such as other people have, was it henceforth their fate to know. Yet why should this have been? Mutually loving and loved as devotedly as ever was a wedded pair, blessed with the full possession of every good that nature and fortune can combine to bestow, with youth, health, beauty, genius, riches, honor—why should their wedded life be thus clouded? Why should she be moody, silent, fitful often, all but wretched and despairing? Often even emitting the wild gleam, like heat-lightning from her dark and splendid eyes, of what might be incipient insanity?

One evening, like the night described in the beginning of this chapter (for stormy nights were now frequent), when the wind howled around the island and the waves lashed its shores, Marguerite reclined upon the semi-circular sofa within the recess of the bay window, and looked out upon the night as she had often looked before. No light gleamed from the window where the lady sat alone, gazing out upon the dark and angry waste of waters; that stormy scene without was in unison with the fierce, tempestuous emotions within her own heart—that friendly veil of darkness was a rest to her, who, weary of her ill-worn mask of smiles, would lay it aside for a while. Twice had Forrest entered to bring lights, and twice had been directed to withdraw, the last dismissal being accompanied with an injunction not to come again until he should hear the bell. And so Marguerite sat alone in darkness, her eyes and her soul roving out into the wild night over the troubled bosom of the ever-complaining sea. She sat until the sound of a boat pushed up upon the sand, accompanied by the hearty tones and outspringing steps of the oarsmen, and followed by one resonant, commanding voice, and firm, authoritative tread, caused her heart to leap, her cheek to flush, her eye to glow and her whole dark countenance to light up as she recognized the approach of her husband. She sprang up and rang.

"Lamps and wood, Forrest," she said. But before the servant could obey the order, Philip Helmstedt's eager step crossed the threshold, and the next instant his arms were around her and her head on his bosom. They had been separated only for a day, and yet, notwithstanding all that had passed and all that yet remained unexplained between them, theirs was a lover's meeting. Is any one surprised at this, or inclined to take it as a sign of returning confidence and harmony, and a prognostic of future happiness to this pair? Let them not be deceived! It was but the warmth of a passion more uncertain than the sunshine of an April day.

"Sitting in darkness again, my own Marguerite? Why do you do so?" said Philip, with tender reproach.

"Why should I not?" returned Marguerite, smilingly.

"Because it will make you melancholy, this bleak and dreary scene."

"No, indeed, it will not. It is a grand scene. Come, look out and see."

"Thank you, love; I have had enough of it for one evening; and I rather wonder at your taste for it."

"Ah! it suits me—it suits me, this savage coast and weather! Rave on, winds! thunder on, sea! my heart beats time to the fierce music of your voices. 'Deep calleth unto deep'—deep soul to deep sea!"

"Marguerite!"

"Well?"

"What is the matter with you?"

"Nothing: only I like this howling chaos of wind and water!"

"You are in one of your dark moods."

"Could I be bright and you away?"

"Flatterer! I am here now. And here are the lights. And now I have a letter for you."

"A letter! Oh! give it quickly," cried Marguerite, thrown off her guard.

"Why, how hasty you are."

"True; I am daily expecting a letter from Nellie, and I do begin to think that I have nerves. And now, to discipline these excitable nerves, I will not look at the letter until after tea."

"Pooh, my love, I should much rather you would read it now and get it off your mind," said Philip Helmstedt, placing her in a chair beside the little stand, and setting a lamp upon it, before he put the letter in her hand.

He watched her narrowly, and saw her lips grow white as she read the postmark and superscription, saw the trembling of her fingers as she broke the seal, and heard the half-smothered exclamation of joy as she glanced at the contents; and then she quickly folded the letter, and was about to put it into her pocket when he spoke.

"Stay!"

"Well!"

"That letter was not from Mrs. Houston."

"No; you were aware of that; you saw the postmark."

"Yes, Marguerite; and I could have seen the contents had I chosen it, and would, under all the circumstances, have been justified in so doing; but I would not break your seal, Marguerite. Now, however, that I have delivered the letter, and you have read it, I claim the right to know its contents."

Marguerite held the letter close against her bosom, while she gazed upon him in astonishment and expectation, not to say dread.

"With your leave, my lady," he said, approaching her; and, throwing one arm around her shoulders, held her fast, while he drew the letter from her relaxing fingers. She watched him while he looked again at the postmark "New York," which told next to nothing, and then opened and read the contents—three words, without either date or signature, "All is well!" that was all.

He looked up at her. And her low, deep, melodious laughter—that delicious laughter that charmed like music all who heard it, but that now sounded wild and strange, answered his look.

"Your correspondent has been well tutored, madam."

"Why, of course," she said, still laughing; but presently growing serious, she added: "Philip, would to God I could confide to you this matter. It is the one pain of my life that I cannot. The time may come, Philip, when I may be able to do so—but not now."

"Marguerite, it is but fair to tell you that I shall take every possible means to discover your secret; and if I find that it reflects discredit on you, by Heaven——"

"Hush! for the sake of mercy, no rash vows. Why should it reflect discredit upon any? Why should mystery be always in thought linked with guilt? Philip, I am free from reproach!"

"But, great Heavens! that it should be necessary to assure me of this! I wonder that your brow is not crimsoned with the thought that it is so."

"Ah, Philip Helmstedt, it is your own suspicious nature, your want of charity and faith that makes it so," said Marguerite.

"Life has—the world has—deprived me of charity and faith, and taught me suspicion—a lesson that I have not unlearned in your company, Mrs. Helmstedt."

"Philip, dear Philip, still hope and trust in me; it may be that I shall not wholly disappoint you," she replied.

But Mr. Helmstedt answered only by a scornful smile; and, having too much pride to continue a controversy, that for the present, at least, must only end in defeat, fell into silent and resentful gloom and sullenness.

The harmony and happiness of their island home was broken up; the seclusion once so delightful was now insufferable; his presence on the estate was not essentially necessary; and, therefore, after some reflection, Philip Helmstedt determined to go to Richmond for a month or six weeks.

When he announced this intention to his wife, requesting her to be ready to accompany him in a week, Marguerite received the news with indifference and promised to comply.

It was near the first of April when they reached Richmond. They had secured apartments at the — — House, where they were quickly sought by

Colonel Compton and Mrs. Houston, who came to press upon them, for the term of their stay in Richmond, the hospitalities of the colonel's mansion.

Marguerite would willingly have left the hotel for the more genial atmosphere of her friend's house; but she waited the will of Mr. Helmstedt, who had an especial aversion to become the recipient of private entertainment for any length of time, and, therefore, on the part of himself and wife, courteously declined that friendly invitation, promising at the same time to dine with them at an early day.

The colonel and his daughter finished their call and returned home disappointed; Nellie with her instinctive dislike to Mr. Helmstedt much augmented.

The fashionable season was over, or so nearly so, that, to electrify society into new life, it required just such an event as the reappearance of its late idol as a bride, and Mrs. De Lancie Helmstedt (for by the will of her father, his sole child and heiress was obliged to retain her patronymic with her married name).

Numerous calls were made upon the newly-wedded pair, and many parties were given in their honor.

Marguerite was still the reigning queen of beauty, song, and fashion, with a difference—there was a deeper glow upon her cheeks and lips, a wilder fire in her eyes, and in her songs a dashing recklessness alternating with a depth of pathos that "from rival eyes unwilling tears could summon." Those who envied her wondrous charms did not hesitate to apply to her such terms as "eccentric," and even "partially deranged." While her very best friends, including Nellie Houston, thought that, during her three months' retirement on Helmstedts Island, Marguerite had

> "Suffered a sea change
> Into something wild and strange."

No more of those mysterious letters had come to her, at least among those forwarded from their home post office, and nothing had transpired to revive the memory of the exciting events on the island. But Mr. Helmstedt, although he disdained to renew the topic, had not in the least degree relaxed his vigilant watchfulness and persevering endeavors to gain knowledge of Marguerite's secret; vainly, for not the slightest event occurred to throw light upon that dark subject. Marguerite was not less tender and devoted in private than brilliant and fascinating in public; and, despite his bounded confidence, he could not choose but passionately love the beautiful and alluring woman, who, with one reservation, so amply satisfied his love and pride.

Their month's visit drew to a close, when Mr. Helmstedt accepted an invitation to a dinner given to Thomas Jefferson, in honor of his arrival at the capital. Upon the day of the entertainment, he left Marguerite at four o'clock. And as the wine-drinking, toasting, and speech-making continued long after the cloth was removed, it was very late in the evening before the company broke up and he was permitted to return to his hotel.

On entering first his private parlor, which was lighted up, he missed Marguerite, who, with her sleepless temperament, usually kept very late hours, and whom, upon the rare occasions of his absence from her in the evening, he usually, when he returned, found still sitting up reading while she awaited him. Upon glancing round the empty room, a vague anxiety seized him and he hurried into the adjoining chamber, which he found dark, and called in a low, distinct tone:

"Marguerite! Marguerite!"

But instead of her sweet voice in answer, came a silent, dreary sense of vacancy and solitude. He hurried back into the parlor, snatched up one of the two lighted lamps that stood upon the mantelpiece, and hastened into the chamber, to find it indeed void of the presence he sought. An impulse to ring and inquire when Mrs. Helmstedt had gone out was instantly arrested by his habitual caution. A terrible presentiment, that he thought scarcely justified by the circumstances, disturbed him. He remembered that she could not have gone to any place of amusement, for she never entered such scenes unaccompanied by himself; besides, she had distinctly informed him that preparations for departure would keep her busy in her room all the evening. He looked narrowly around the chamber; the bed had not been disturbed, the clothes closets and bureaus were empty, and the trunks packed and strapped; but one, a small trunk belonging to Marguerite, was gone. The same moment that he discovered this fact, his eyes fell upon a note lying on the dressing-bureau. He snatched it up: it was directed in Marguerite's hand to himself. He tore it open, and with a deadly pale cheek and darkly-lowering brow, read as follows:

Our Private Parlor, — — House, 6 P.M.

My Beloved Husband: A holy duty calls me from you for a few days, but it is with a bleeding heart and foreboding mind that I go. Well do I know, Philip, all that I dare in thus leaving without your sanction. But equally well am I aware, from what has already passed, that that sanction never could have been obtained. I pray you to forgive the manner of my going, an extremity to which your former inflexibility has driven me; and I even venture further to pray that, even now, you will extend the shield of your authority over my absence, as your own excellent judgment must convince you will be best. Philip, dearest, you will make no stir, cause no talk—you will not even pursue me, for, though you might follow me to New York, yet in that great thoroughfare you would lose trace of me. But you will, as I earnestly pray you to do, await, at home, the coming of your most unhappy but devoted

Marguerite.

It would be impossible to describe the storm of outraged love and pride, of rage, grief, and jealousy that warred in Philip Helmstedt's bosom.

"Yes! by the eternal that hears me, I will wait her coming—and then! then!" he muttered within himself as he cast the letter into the fire. All night long, like a chafed lion in his cell, he paced the narrow limits of his lonely apartments, giving ill vent to the fierceness of his passions in half-muttered threats and curses, the deeper for suppression. But when morning broke, and the world was astir, he realized that he had to meet it, and his course was taken. His emotions were repressed and his brow was cleared; he rang for his servant, made a careful toilet, and at his usual hour, and with his usual appearance and manner, descended to the breakfast table.

"I hope Mrs. Helmstedt is not indisposed this morning," said a lady opposite, when she observed the vacant chair at his side.

"Thank you, madam; Mrs. Helmstedt is perfectly well. She left for New York last evening," replied Mr. Helmstedt, with his habitual, dignified courtesy. And this story went the rounds of the table, then of the hotel, and then of the city, and though it excited surprise, proved in the end satisfactory.

Later in the day he took leave of his friends. And by the next morning's packet he sailed for the island, which he reached at the end of the week. And once in his own little, isolated kingdom, he said:

"Yes, I will await you here, and then, Marguerite! then!"

CHAPTER VI
THE WIFE'S RETURN

"She had moved to the echoing sounds of fame—

Silently, silently died her name;

Silently melted her life away

As ye have seen a rich flower decay,

Or a lamp that hath swiftly burned expire,

Or a bright stream shrink from a summer fire."

Nearly maddened between the deeply suppressed, conflicting passions of wounded love, outraged pride, gloomy jealousy, fierce anger, and burning desire of revenge, Philip Helmstedt's impetuous spirit would have devoured the time between his arrival at the island and Marguerite's expected return. Now feeling, through the magic power of memory and imagination, the wondrous magnetism of her personality, and praying for her arrival only that all else might be forgotten in the rapture of their meeting—then, with all the force of his excessive pride and scorn, sternly spurning that desire as most unworthy. Now torturing himself with sinister speculations as to where she might be? what doing? with whom tarrying? Then feeling intensely, as resentfully, his indubitable right to know, and longing for her return that he might make her feel the power of the man whose affection and whose authority had been equally slighted and despised. And through all these moods of love and jealousy still invoking, ever invoking, with a breathless, burning impatience that would have consumed and shriveled up the intervening days—the hour of her return; for still he doted on her with a fatuity that neither possession nor time had power to sate, nor pride nor anger force to destroy—nay, that these agencies only goaded into frenzy. Strong man that he was, she possessed him like a fever, a madness, a shrouding fire! he could not deliver himself from the fascination of her individuality. Was she a modern Lamia, a serpent woman who held him, another Lexius, in her fatal toils? So it sometimes seemed to him as he walked moodily up and down the long piazza before the house, looking out upon the sea. At all events she held him! very well, let it be so, since he held her so surely, and she should feel it! Oh! for the hour of her return! All day he paced the long piazza or walked down to the beach, spyglass in hand, to look out for the packet that should bear her to the isle. But packet after packet sailed by, and day succeeded day until a month had passed, and still Marguerite came not. And day by day Philip Helmstedt grew darker, thinner, and gloomier. Sleep forsook his bed, and appetite his board; it often happened that by night his pillow was not pressed, and by day his meals were left untasted.

Speculation was rife among the servants of the household. All understood that something was wrong in the family. The Helmstedt servants took the part of their master, while the De Lancie negroes advocated the cause of their mistress. It was a very great trial to poor old Aunt Hapzibah, the housekeeper, to find her best efforts unavailing to make her master comfortable in the absence of her mistress. Every one likes to be appreciated; and no one more than an old family cook whose glory lies in her art; and so it proved too much for the philosophy of the old woman, who had taken much pride in letting "Marse Fillup see that eberyting went on as riglar as dough Miss Marget was home hersef" — to see her best endeavors unnoticed and her most *recherché* dishes untasted. And so—partly for her own relief, and partly for the edification of her underlings in the kitchen, she frequently held forth upon the state of affairs in something like the following style:

"De Lord bress de day an' hour as ever I toted mysef inter dis here house! De Lord men' it I pray! Wonner what Marse Fillup Hempseed mean a-scornin' my bes' cook dishes? Better not keep on a-'spisin' de Lord's good wittles—'deed hadn' he if he is Marse Fillup Hempseed! Come to want bread if he does—'deed will he! Set him up! What he 'spect? Sen' him young ducks an' green peas? down dey comes ontotch! Try him wid lily white weal an' spinnidge? down it come ontaste! Sen' up spring chicken an' sparrowgrass? all de same! I gwine stop of it now, I tell you good! 'deed is I. I ain't gwine be fool long o' Marse Fillup Hemps'd's funnelly nonsense no longer! I gwine sen' him up middlin' and greens, or mutton an' turnups— you hear me good, don't you?"

"I wonder what does ail master?" remarked Hildreth.

"I know what ail him well 'nough! I know de reason why he won't eat his wittles!"

"What is it, den?"

"He can't eat anyt'ing else case he's—eatin' his own heart! An' it makes men mad—that sort o' eatin' does!"

"My Lors!" ejaculated Hildreth, in real or affected horror.

"Eatin' his own heart," continued old Hapzibah—"eatin' his own heart, wid his black eagle head an' hook nose poke down in his buzzum a-chawin' an' a-chawin'! Always a-chawin' an' a-chawin'! Walkin' up an' down de peeazzy a-chawin' an' a-chawin'. Stan'in' up to his screwtaw, 'tendin' to write, but only a-chawin' an' a-chawin'. Settin' down at de table, a-chawin' an' a-chawin'—not my good wittles, mine you, but his own heart—always his own heart. He better stop of it, too. It won't 'gest, nor likewise 'gree wid him, nor udderwise fetch Miss Marget home one minit 'fore she thinks proper for to come."

"Well, den, ennyways, t'ink it 'pears mon'ous strange your Miss Marget don't come home ef our Marse Fillup wants her to come," here put in old Neptune, one of the Helmstedt negroes.

"Set him up wid it," indignantly broke in Aunt Hapzibah—"set you an' your marse bofe up wid it. Who de sarpent! he? or you either? I reckon my Miss Marget allers went an' come when ebber she thought proper, 'fore ebber she saw de hook nose o' Marse Fillup Hempseed, of any his low-life saut water niggers either. Not as I tends for to hurt your feelin's, Nep; you can't help bein' of an' antibberous creetur like a lan' tarrapin or a water dog, as 'longs to nyther to'ther nor which, nor likewise to hit you in de teef wid your marster, who is a right 'spectable, 'sponsible, 'greeable gemplemun, ef he'd leave off a-hookin' of his crook nose inter his buzzum an' a-chawin' his own heart; which he'd better, too, or it'll run him rampin' mad!—you see, chillun, you see!"

One afternoon, during the last week in May, Philip Helmstedt, as usual, walked up and down the beach in front of his mansion house. With his arms folded and his head bowed upon his chest, in deep thought, he paced with measured steps up and down the sands. Occasionally he stopped, drew a small spyglass from his pocket, placed it at his eye, and swept the sea to the horizon.

Before him, miles away to the westward, lay the western shore of Maryland and Virginia, cloven and divided by the broad and bay-like mouth of the Potomac—with Point Lookout on the north and Point Rodgers on the south. Beyond this cleft coast the western horizon was black with storm clouds. A freshening gale was rising and rushing over the surface of the water, rippling its waves, and making a deep, low, thrilling murmur, as if Nature, the *improvvisatrice*, swept the chords of her grand harp in a prelude to some sublime performance. Occasionally flocks of sea fowl, sailing slowly, lighted upon the island or the shores. All signs indicated an approaching storm. Philip Helmstedt stood, telescope in hand, traversing the now dark and angry waste of waters. Far, far away up the distant Potomac, like a white speck upon the black waters, came a vessel driven before the wind, reeling against the tide, yet gallantly holding her course and hugging the Maryland coast. Marguerite might be in that packet (as, indeed, she might have been in any passing packet for the last month), and Philip Helmstedt watched its course with great interest. Nearing the mouth of the river, the packet veered away to avoid the strong current around Point Lookout, and, still struggling between wind and tide, steered for the middle of the channel. Soon she was clear of the eddies and out into the open bay, with her head turned southward. Then it was that Philip observed a boat put out from her side. A convincing presentiment assured him that Marguerite had arrived. The gale was now high and the sea rough; and that little boat, in which he felt sure that she was seated, would have but a doubtful chance between winds and waves. Dread for Marguerite's safety, with the eagle instinct to swoop upon and seize his coveted prey, combined to instigate Philip Helmstedt to speedy action. He threw down the spyglass and hastened along the beach until he came to the boathouse, where he unfastened a skiff, threw himself into it and pushed off from the shore. A more skillful sailor than Philip Helmstedt never handled an oar—a gift inherited from all his seafaring forefathers and perfected by years of practice. He pushed the boat on amid heaving waves and flashing brine, heedless of the blinding spray dashed into his face, until he drew sufficiently near the other boat to see that it was manned by two oarsmen, and then to recognize Marguerite as its passenger. And in another moment the boats were side by side. Philip Helmstedt was standing resting on his oar, and Marguerite had risen with one low-toned exclamation of joy.

"Oh! Mr. Helmstedt, this is very kind; thank you—thank you."

He did not reply by word or look.

The wind was so high, the water so rough, and the skiffs so light that they were every instant striking together, rebounding off, and in imminent danger of being whirled in the waves and lost.

"Quick, men; shift Mrs. Helmstedt's baggage into this boat," commanded Mr. Helmstedt, as with averted eyes he coldly took Marguerite's hand and assisted her to enter his skiff. The two men hastily transferred the little traveling trunk that comprised Marguerite's whole baggage—and then, with a respectful leave-taking, laid to their oars and pulled rapidly to overtake the vessel.

Philip and Marguerite were left alone. Without addressing her, he turned the head of the skiff and rowed for the island. The first flush of pleasure had died from Marguerite's face, leaving her very pale—with a pallor that was heightened by the nunlike character of her costume, which consisted simply of a gown, mantle and hood, all of black silk. For some moments Marguerite fixed her large, mournful eyes upon the face of her husband, vainly trying to catch his eyes, that remained smoldering under their heavy lids. Then she suddenly spoke to him.

"Philip! will you not forgive me?"

The thrilling, passionate, tearful voice, for once, seemed not to affect him. He made no answer. She gazed imploringly upon his face—and saw, and shuddered to see that an ashen paleness had overspread his cheek, while his eyes remained rooted to the bottom of the boat.

"Philip! oh! Heaven—speak to me, Philip!" she cried, in a voice of anguish, laying her hand and dropping her sobbing face upon his knee.

The effect was terrible. Spurning her from him, he sprang to his feet, nearly capsizing the skiff, that rocked fearfully under them, and exclaimed:

"I do not know where you find courage to lift your eyes to my face, madam, or address me! Where have you been? Come, trifling is over between us! Explain, exculpate yourself from suspicion! or these waters shall engulf at once your sin and my dishonor!"

"Philip! Philip!" she cried, in a voice of thrilling misery.

"Explain! explain! or in another moment God have mercy on your soul!" he exclaimed, drawing in the oar, planting its end heavily on the prow of the skiff, in such a manner that by leaning his weight upon it he could capsize the boat—standing there, glaring upon her.

"Philip! Philip! for the Saviour's sake, sit down," she cried, wringing her pale fingers in an ecstasy of terror.

"Coward! coward! coward! you fear death, and do not fear me nor shame!" said Philip Helmstedt, his eyes burning upon her with a consuming scorn that seemed to dry up her very heart's blood. "Once more, and for the last time, madam, will you explain?"

"Philip! mercy!"

"Commend yourself to the mercy of Heaven! I have none!" cried Philip Helmstedt, about to throw his whole weight upon the oar to upset the boat, when Marguerite, with a shriek, sprung up and clasped his knees, exclaiming:

"Mercy! Philip! it is not my life I beg at your hands; it were not worth the prayer! but another innocent life, Philip, spare your child," and fainted at his feet.

The boat, shaken by this violent scene, was rocking fearfully, and he had much ado to steady it, while Marguerite lay in a dead heap at his feet. The frenzy of his anger was passing for the present. The announcement that she had just made to him, her swoon and her perfect helplessness, as well as that majestic beauty, against the influence of which he had been struggling through all this scene, combined to sway his frantic purpose. He stood like a man awakened from a nightmare, recovered from a fever, come to himself. After cautiously trimming the boat, and letting it drift until it had spent the violence of the impetus, he took up the oar, turned its head, and rowed swiftly toward the island. Pushing the skiff up upon the sand, he got out and fastened it, and then went to lift Marguerite, who, on being raised, sighed and opened her eyes, and said, a little wildly and incoherently:

"You will never be troubled by any more letters, Philip."

"Ah?"

"No! and I will never leave you again, Philip."

"I intend that you never shall have the opportunity, my—Marguerite."

She had, with his assistance, risen to her feet, and, leaning on his arm, she suffered herself to be led up the slope toward the house. The whole sky was now overcast and blackened. The wind so buffeted them that Marguerite could scarcely stand, much less walk against it. Philip had to keep his arm around her shoulders, and busy himself with her veil and mantle, that were continually blown and flapped into her face and around her head. By the time they had reached the house, and dispatched Forrest to put the boat away and bring the trunk home, the storm had burst.

All night the tempest raged. Marguerite, in the midst of all her private trouble, was sleepless with anxiety for the fate of the little vessel she had left. But for Philip, a navy might have been engulfed, and he remained unconcerned by anything aside from his own domestic wrong. The next morning the terrible devastation of the storm was revealed in the torn forests, prostrate fences and ruined crops. Early Marguerite, with her spyglass, was on the lookout at the balcony of her chamber window, that was immediately over the bay window of the parlor, and commanded a magnificent sea view. And soon she had the relief of seeing the poor little bark safely sheltered in Wicomia inlet. With a sigh of gratitude, Marguerite turned from that instance of salvation to face her own doubtful, if not dangerous, prospect. Philip Helmstedt, since bringing her safely to the house, had not noticed her by word or look. He remained silent, reserved, and gloomy—in a mood that she dreaded to interrupt, lest she should again rouse him to some repetition of his fury on the boat; but in every gentle and submissive way she sought to soothe, accepting all his scornful repulses with the patience of one offending where she loved, yet unable to do otherwise, and solicitous to atone. It was difficult to resist the pleading eyes and voice of this magnetic woman, yet they were resisted.

In this constrained and painful manner a week passed, and brought the first of June, when Colonel Houston and his family came down to their seat at Buzzard's Bluff. Mr. and Mrs. Helmstedt were seated at their cold, *tête-à-tête* breakfast table when Nellie's messenger, Lemuel, came in with a note announcing her arrival at home, and begging her dearest Marguerite, as the sky was so beautiful and the water so calm, to come at once and spend the day with her.

The mournful face of Marguerite lighted up with a transient smile; passing the note across the table to Mr. Helmstedt, she said:

"I will go," and then rang the bell and directed Forrest, who answered it, to conduct the messenger into the kitchen, give him breakfast, and then get the boat *Nereide* ready to take her to Buzzard's Bluff. The man bowed and was about to leave the room, when Mr. Helmstedt looked up from his note and said, "Stop!"

Forrest paused, hat in hand, waiting in respectful silence for his master's speech. After a moment, Mr. Helmstedt said:

"No matter, another time will do; hasten to obey your mistress now."

The two men then withdrew, and Mr. Helmstedt turned to his wife, and said:

"Upon second thoughts, I would not countermand your order, madam, or humble you in the presence of your servants. But you cannot leave this island, Mrs. Helmstedt."

"Dear Philip—Mr. Helmstedt! what mean you?"

"That you are a prisoner! That you have been such since your last landing! and that you shall remain such—if it be for fifty years—do you hear?—until you choose to clear up the doubt that rests upon your conduct!"

"Mr. Helmstedt, you do not mean this!" exclaimed the lady, rising excitedly from her seat.

"Not?—look, Marguerite!" he replied, rising, and following her to the window, where she stood with her large, mournful eyes now wildly glancing from the bright, glad waters without to the darkened room and the stern visaged man within. "Look, Marguerite! This island is a mile long, by a quarter of a mile wide—with many thousand acres, with deep, shady woods and pleasant springs and streams and breezy beaches—almost room, variety and pleasure enough for a home. Your house is, besides, comfortable, and your servants capable and attentive. I say your house and servants, for here you shall be a queen if you like——"

"A captive queen—less happy than a free scullion!"

"A captive by your own contumacy, lady. And, mark me, I have shown you the limit of your range—this island—attempt to pass it and your freedom of motion, now bounded only by the sea, shall be contracted within the walls of this house, and so the space shall narrow around you, Marguerite, until——"

"Six feet by two will suffice me!"

"Aye! until then, if need be!"

"Mr. Helmstedt, you cannot mean this—you are a gentleman!"

"Or was; but never a fool, or a tool, lady! God knows—Satan knows how strongly and exclusively I have loved—still love! but you have placed me in a false and humiliating position, where I must take care of your honor and mine as best I may. You cannot imagine that I can permit you to fly off, year after year, whither, with whom, to whom, for what purpose I know not, and you refuse to tell! You left me no other alternative, Marguerite but to repudiate——"

"Oh! no, no! sweet Heaven, not that! You love me, Philip Helmstedt! I know you do. You could kill, but could not banish me! I could die, but could not leave you, Philip!" interrupted his wife, with an outbreak of agony that started cold drops of dew from her forehead.

"Compose yourself. I know that we are tied together (not so much by church and state as by something inherent in the souls of both) for weal or woe, blessing or cursing, heaven or hell—who can say? But assuredly tied together for time and for eternity!"

"God be thanked for that, at worst!" exclaimed Marguerite, fervently. "Anything—anything but the death to live, of absence from you, Philip! Oh, why did you use that murderous word?"

"You left me no other alternative than to repudiate——"

"Ah!" cried Marguerite, as if again the word had pierced her heart.

"Or—I was about to say—restrain you. I cannot repudiate—I must restrain you. You, yourself, must see the propriety of the measure."

"But, Philip, my husband, do you mean to say that I may not even visit Mrs. Houston?"

"I mean to say that until you satisfactorily explain your late escapade, you shall not leave the island for any purpose whatever."

"Not even to visit Nellie?"

"Not even to visit Mrs. Houston."

"Philip, she will expect me; she will come and invite me to her house; what shall I say to my bosom friend in explanation? or, keeping silence, what shall I leave her to think?"

"Say what you please to Mrs. Houston; tell her the truth, or decline to explain the motives of your seclusion to her—even as you have refused to exhibit the purpose of your journeys to me. You can do these things, Mrs. Helmstedt."

"Oh, Heaven! but the retort is natural. What will Colonel Compton think or say?"

"Refer Colonel Compton to me for an elucidation. I am always ready, Marguerite, to answer for my course of conduct, though I may seldom recognize the right of any man to question it."

"I could even plead for an exception in favor of my little Nellie but that I know your inflexible will, Philip."

"It is scarcely more so than your own; but now, do you forget that there is an answer to be written to Mrs. Houston?"

"Ah, yes," said Marguerite, going to the escritoire that we have already named, and hastily writing a few words.

> "Dearest Nellie:—I am not well and cannot go to you; waive ceremony, beloved, and come to your Marguerite."

Meanwhile Mr. Helmstedt rang for Mrs. Houston's messenger, who, he was informed, had gone down to the beach to assist Forrest in rigging the *Nereide*.

"We will walk down to the beach and send him home," said Mr. Helmstedt, taking his straw hat and turning toward Marguerite. She arose to join him, and they walked out together across the front piazza, down the steps, and down the terraced garden, through the orchard and the timothy field, and, finally, to the sanded beach, where they found the two negroes rigging the boat.

"Mrs. Helmstedt will not go, Forrest, so that you may leave the bark. Lemuel, you will take this note to your mistress, and say that we shall be glad to see the family here."

Marguerite had not been down on the sands since the stormy evening of her arrival, and now she noticed, with astonishment, that of all the little fleet of some half-dozen boats of all sizes that were usually moored within the boathouse but a single one, the little *Nereide*, remained; and she saw that drawn into the house, the door of which was chained and locked and the key delivered up to Mr. Helmstedt. When this was done and the men had gone, Marguerite turned to her husband for an explanation.

"Why, where are all the boats, Mr. Helmstedt?"

"Sold, given away, broken up, dispersed—all except this one, which will serve the necessities of myself and men."

"But why, Philip?"

"Can you not surmise? You are a prisoner—it is no jest, Marguerite—a prisoner! and we do not leave the means of escape near such. I am not playing with you, Marguerite! You fled me once, and maddened me almost to the verge of murder and suicide."

"I know it. Oh, Heaven forgive me!"

"And you must have no opportunity for repeating that experiment. Your restraint is a real one, as you will find."

She turned upon him a look so full of love, resignation and devotion, as she held out both her hands and said:

"Well, I accept the restraint, Philip. I accept it. Oh, my dear husband, how much more merciful than that other alternative of separation! for your Marguerite tells you, Philip, that, would it come without sin, she would rather take death from your hands than banishment. The one great terror of her life, Philip, is of losing you by death or separation; she could not survive the loss, Philip, for her very life lives in your bosom. How can a widow live? Your Marguerite could not breathe without you; while with you, from you she could accept anything—anything. Since you do not banish her, do your will with her; you have the right; she is your own."

A few more words sighed out upon his bosom, to which he at last had drawn her, and then, lifting her head, she murmured:

"And listen, dearest husband; give yourself no care or anxiety for the safe custody of your prisoner, for she will not try to escape. It is your command, dearest Philip, that binds me to the narrow limits of this island, as no other earthly power could do. You know me, Philip; you know that, were I in duress against my will, I would free myself; I would escape, were it only to heaven or to hades! Your bond, Philip, is not on this mortal frame, but on my heart, soul, spirit, and I should feel its restricting power were all nature else beckoning me over the limits you have prescribed, and all opportunities favorable to the transgression."

"You love me so; you say your life lives within mine, and I believe it does, for you inhabit me, you possess me, nor can I unhouse you, incendiary as you are—and yet you will not give me your confidence—will not justify yourself before me—while I, on my part, may not abate one jot or tittle of your restraint until you do."

"I do not arraign you even in my thoughts, love; so far from that, I accept you for my judge; I submit to your sentence. There is this dark cloud settled on my bowed head, love (would it rested only on my own), and some day it may be lifted. In the meantime, since you do not exile me, do your royal will unquestioned with your own, my king. Ah, Philip! we are not angels, you and I; and we may never find heaven in this world or the next; but, such as we are, even with this cloud between us, we love each other; on this earth we cannot part; and even in the next we must be saved or lost—together."

"Marguerite, tell me, is there a hope that, one day, this mystery may be cleared up?"

"Philip, dearest, yes; a faint hope that I scarcely dare to entertain."

During all this time she had been standing within his circling arm, with her face upon his shoulder, and her soft, fragrant ringlets flowing past his cheek. Now, as she lifted her head, her wild, mournful eyes fell upon a distant sail skimming rapidly over the surface of the sparkling water, from the direction of Buzzard's Bluff.

"Nellie is coming, dear husband," she said, "but she shall know that it is my own pleasure to stay home, as it truly is since you will it."

"No concealment for my sake, Marguerite. I tell you, I will answer for what I do. Kiss me now, thou cleaving madness, before that boat comes."

On bounded the little sailboat over the flashing water, and presently drew so near that Nellie, in her green hood, could be recognized. And in a few more minutes the little boat touched the beach, and Nellie, with her two boys, as she called her stepsons, jumped ashore and ran to greet Marguerite and Mr. Helmstedt.

"And here are my boys, whom you have never seen before, Marguerite. Ralph, speak to Mrs. Helmstedt. Franky, that's not the way to make a bow, sir, pulling a lock of your hair; you must have learned that from Black Lem. Ralph does not do so; he's a gentleman," said the young stepmother.

Marguerite, who had embraced Nellie with great affection, received her stepsons with kindness. And Mr. Helmstedt, who had welcomed the party with much cordiality, now led the way up to the house.

This was Mrs. Houston's first visit to Mrs. De Lancie Helmstedt's new home, and she was full of curiosity and observation.

"How rich the land is, Marguerite! I declare the isle is green down to the very water's edge in most places—and so well timbered. And the house, too; how substantial and comfortable its strong, gray walls look. I like that bay window with the round balcony over it, to the right of the entrance; such an unusual thing in this part of the country."

"Yes, my husband had it built just before he brought me home; the bay window abuts from my own parlor, and is arranged in memory of that 'celebrated' bay window of your father's library and music-room. The round balcony above it opens from my chamber, which is just over the parlor; both the window below and the balcony above command a magnificent western view of the bay and the opposite shore of Maryland and Virginia, divided by the mouth of the Potomac; you shall see for yourself to-day."

"And yet it must be lonesome here for you, Marguerite. I do not understand how one like you, who have led so brilliant a life in the midst of the world, can bear to live here. Why, I can scarcely endure Buzzard's Bluff, although it is a fine old place, on the mainland, with neighbors all around."

"'My mind to me a kingdom is:

Such perfect joy I find therein,'"

murmured Marguerite, with an ambiguous smile.

The day passed agreeably to all. Mrs. Houston had a budget of city news and gossip to open and deliver; and, by the time this was done, dinner was announced; and, when that meal was over, Mrs. Houston reminded her hostess of her promise to show her through the house.

Nellie was unhesitating in her commendations of Marguerite's chamber.

"Rose-colored window curtains and bed hangings and lounge covers, by all that's delightful. Why, Marguerite, you have everything in civilized style in this savage part of the world!" Then they passed out of the chamber upon the balcony, and stood admiring the wide expanse of blue water, dotted here and there with islets, and the far distant coast, split just opposite by the river, and varied up and down by frequent headlands and inlets. Marguerite placed a spyglass in her friend's hand.

"I declare, Marguerite, this island lies along due east of the mouth of the Potomac. Why, I can see the pines on Point Lookout and Point Rogers with the naked eye—and, with the aid of the glass, I do think I can see so far up the river as your place, Plover's Point."

"That is fancy, my dear; Plover's Point is fifteen miles up the river."

As the air was calm and the water smooth, with the promise of continuing so for the night at least, and as there was a full moon, Mrs. Houston felt safe in remaining to tea.

When she was ready to go home, and before she left the chamber, where she had put on her outer garments, she tried to persuade Marguerite not only to come very soon to Buzzard's Bluff, but to fix the day when she might expect her.

"You will excuse me for some time yet, dearest Nellie. The truth is that I arrived at home the day of the last storm; in crossing in a boat from the schooner to the island, the wind was high and the water very rough, and I received a terrible fright—was within an inch of being lost, in fact; I have not entered a boat since—have not the least idea that I shall be able to do so for a long time," said Mrs. Helmstedt, evasively.

"Why, not even when the sea is as calm as it is this beautiful night?"

"I fear not—the sea is proverbially treacherous."

"Why, you do not mean to say that, rather than venture on the water, you will confine yourself to this island all your life?"

"I know not, indeed; life is uncertain—mine may be very short."

"Why, Marguerite, how unlike yourself you are at this moment. What! Marguerite—my heroic Marguerite—she who 'held the blast in scorn,' growing nervous, fearing storms, doubting still water even, thinking of death? Whew! there must be some noteworthy reason for this metamorphosis! Say, is it so, my dearest Mrs. Helmstedt?" inquired Nellie, with a smile, half archness, half love.

For an answer Marguerite kissed her tenderly, when Nellie said:

"Well, well! I shall visit you frequently, Marguerite, whether you come to see me or not, for no change has come over your little Nellie, whom you know you can treat as you please—slight her, flout her, affront her, and she is still your little Nellie. Now, please to lend me a shawl, for the air on the bay is too cool at night to make my black silk scarf comfortable, and I'll go."

Mr. and Mrs. Helmstedt walked down to the beach with Nellie and her boys, saw them enter the boat, which quickly left the beach, and, with the dipping oars raising sparkles of light in its course, glided buoyantly over the moonlit water toward the distant point of Buzzard's Bluff.

Philip Helmstedt and Marguerite were left alone on the beach.

Philip stood with folded arms and moody brow, gloomily watching the vanishing boat.

But Marguerite was watching him.

He turned and looked at her, saying, in a troubled voice:

"Marguerite, you are the warden of your own liberty. You can speak, if you choose, the words that will free you from restraint. Why will you not do it? You punish me even more than yourself by the obstinate silence that makes you a prisoner."

"Philip, it is not as you think. I cannot speak those words to which you allude; but, Philip, beloved, I can and do accept your fiat. Let it rest so, dearest, until, perhaps, a day may come when I may be clear before you."

"The air is too chill for you; come to the house," said Mr. Helmstedt, and, without making any comment upon her words, he gave Marguerite his arm and led her home.

From that day forward, by tacit consent, they never alluded to the subject that gave both so much uneasiness. And life passed calmly and monotonously at the island.

Mrs. Houston made herself merry in talking to her mother, who was on a visit to Buzzard's Bluff, of Marguerite's nervousness and its probable cause. And both mother and daughter waived ceremony and often visited the island, where they were always received with warm welcome both by Mr. and Mrs. Helmstedt. And not the faintest suspicion that there was any cause of disagreement between their friends ever approached the minds of either the Houstons or the Comptons. They saw the deep attachment that existed between Philip and Marguerite, and believed them to be very happy. It is true that Mrs. Helmstedt's palpable ill-health was a subject of frequent comment on the part of Mrs. Houston, as well as of serious anxiety to Mrs. Compton.

"I fear that Marguerite will not live; I fear that she will die as her mother died," said the elder lady.

"I can scarcely believe that such a glorious creature should die; nor do I believe it. But she does remind me of that rich, bright, tropical flower that I bought at the conservatory in Richmond and brought down to Buzzard's Bluff. It did not fade or bleach in our bleak air but dropped its head, wilted and died, as brilliant in death as in life. Marguerite lived out her glorious life in Richmond among worshiping friends—but now! And yet Philip Helmstedt loves her devotedly, loves her almost to death, as my little stepson, Franky, vows he loves me," said Nellie.

"'To death!' there is some love like the blessed vivifying sunshine, such as the colonel's affection for you, Nellie; and some love like the destroying fire, such as Philip Helmstedt's passion for Marguerite. And I do not know that she is one whit behind him in the infatuation," replied her mother.

One morning Mrs. Houston brought a new visitor to see the beautiful recluse of Helmstedt's Island, the Rev. Mr. Wellworth, the pastor of Rockbridge parish, on the Northumberland shore, a gentleman who, from his elevated moral and intellectual character, was an invaluable acquisition to their limited circle.

Mr. Wellworth expressed a hope that Mrs. Helmstedt would come to church, and also that she would call on Mrs. Wellworth, who would be very happy to see her.

But Marguerite excused herself by saying that her health and spirits were fluctuating and uncertain, and that she never left home, although she would, at all times, be very much pleased to receive Mr. and Mrs. Wellworth, who, she hoped, would do her the signal favor to waive etiquette and come as often as they could make it convenient or agreeable.

Readily admitting the validity of these excuses, the pastor took the lady at her word, and soon brought his wife to visit her.

And, excepting the family at Buzzard's Bluff, this amiable pair were the only acquaintances Mrs. Helmstedt possessed in the neighborhood.

Thus calmly and monotonously passed life on and around the island; its passage marked that year by only two important events.

The first was the retirement of Colonel Compton from political life (dismissed the public service by the new President, Thomas Jefferson), followed by the breaking up of his establishment at Richmond and the removal to Northumberland County, where the colonel and his wife took up their abode with their daughter and son-in-law at Buzzard's Bluff. This event broke off the intimate connection between them and the bustling world they had left, though for a few weeks of every winter Nellie went to visit her friends in the city, and for a month or two, every summer, received and entertained them at Buzzard's Bluff. Nellie declared that without this variety she should go melancholy mad; and at the same time wondered how Marguerite—the beautiful and brilliant Marguerite—would endure the isolation and monotony of her life on the island.

The other important occurrence was the accouchement of Mrs. Helmstedt, that took place early in October, when she became the mother of a lovely little girl. The sex of this child was a serious disappointment to

Mr. Helmstedt, who had quite set his heart upon a son and heir, and who could scarcely conceal his vexation from the penetrating, beseeching eyes of his unhappy wife.

Mrs. Compton came and passed six weeks with the invalid, nursing her with the same maternal care that, in like circumstances, she would have bestowed upon her own daughter Nellie, and often repeating, cheerfully:

"When Marguerite gets well we shall have her out among us again," or other hopeful words to the same effect.

But Marguerite was never again quite well. Brighter and brighter, month after month, burned in her sunken cheeks and mournful eyes the secret fire that was consuming her frame.

CHAPTER VII
THE VISITOR

"Speak, speak, thou fearful guest!"

—Longfellow.

"I could a tale unfold whose lightest word
Would harrow up thy blood!"

—Shakespeare.

Spiritually speaking, there is no such thing as time or space, as measured by numbers. For often moments in our experience drag themselves painfully on into indefinitely protracted duration, and sometimes years pass in a dream, "as a tale that is told."

Life passed monotonously to all on Helmstedt's Island; but most monotonously to her who might not leave its shores. Every one else among its inhabitants often varied the scene by going upon the mainland on either side of the bay. Mr. Helmstedt went off almost every morning, not infrequently remaining out all day to dine at Colonel Houston's, Mr. Wellworth's, or some other friend's house. The domestic and out-servants relieved each other in turn, that they might go to church on Sundays or visit their friends on the shore. Only Marguerite never upon any account left the island. The Houstons and the Comptons would expostulate with her, and talk to Mr. Helmstedt, alike in vain.

"Indeed I cannot leave the island, dear friends," would Marguerite say, without assigning any reason why she would not.

"Mrs. Helmstedt does not choose to leave home; it is her will to confine herself to the island, and her will is a very dominant one, as you know," would be Mr. Helmstedt's explanation.

"I declare it is a monomania! Marguerite is a riddle. Here some years ago she used to run away from us all, and be absent six or seven months, without deigning to inform us either where or why she went; now she chooses to confine herself within the limits of her island home, without giving us any reason for the eccentricity. But I suppose, indeed, that it is all occasioned by the state of her nerves," would be Nellie's comment upon all this.

Meanwhile Mrs. Helmstedt passed her time in superintending her house and servants, all of which was faultlessly managed; in rearing her child; and in attending, as only a devoted wife can attend, to the personal comforts of her husband during the day, and in entertaining him and any chance visitor with her harp or voice or varied conversation in the evening. Those days upon which Mr. Helmstedt was absent were the longest and heaviest of all to the recluse—but her greatest comforts were her child, her occupations and the contemplation of the glorious scenery around her.

She could never weary of the "infinite variety" of the sea. Some days, in fine, weather, when the sky was clear, the air calm and the water smooth, the bay spread out a vast level mirror, framed far away by green shores and reflecting the firmament from a bosom pure and peaceable as heaven. Other days, when the winds were rising and the waves heaving, the whole sky lowered down upon the sea, the wild waters leaped to meet it, and clouds and waves were mingled together in dreadful chaos, like two opposing armies in mortal conflict. Some nights the whole grand expanse of the bay was changed into an ocean of fluid silver, with shores of diamond light, by the shining of the full moon down upon the clear water and glittering, white sandy beach. Other nights, when there was no moon, the dark, transparent waters reflected clearly the deep blue firmament, brilliantly studded with stars. And between these extreme phases, under foul or fair days, or dark or bright nights, there was every variety and shade of change.

When the weather and her engagements permitted, Mrs. Helmstedt, attended only by her faithful Newfoundlander, Fidelle, passed much time in walking up and down the sandy beach, looking far out upon the free waters, or using her spyglass to observe some distant passing ship and its crew. She made the most of the space allotted to her. The isle, a mile long by a quarter broad, was about two miles and a half round. Often, to afford herself the longest walk, she started from some given spot, and, following the beach, made the circuit of the island—a long and varied walk for a stranger, but monotonous to her who had no other, and who from her earliest infancy had been a natural rambler. She who through childhood and youth had delighted to wander out among the wild scenes of nature, and lose herself amid the pathless woods, or to spring upon her favorite steed and fly over hill and vale, miles and miles away; or jump into a boat propelled by her own single hand, and explore the coast, with its frequent points and headlands, creeks and inlets, felt most severely and bitterly this constraint upon her motions. She never complained, in word, or even in look; she accepted the suffering and hid it deep in her heart with her secret sorrow. Both preyed upon her health of mind and body. Daily her form grew thinner and the fire in her cheeks and eye brighter and fiercer.

Philip Helmstedt observed all this with pain and dread. Yet his pride and firmness would not permit him to yield one tittle.

"This is a conflict between our wills, Marguerite," he said, "and one in which you should at once, as you must sooner or later, yield."

"I will when I can, Philip."

"You must, for you are very weary of this island."

"I have not said so."

"You are very obstinate, Mrs. Helmstedt."

"I am very unhappy in offending you—that is a greater sorrow to me than my restraint."

"They are the same in fact. Remember, Marguerite, that you are your own custodian, and know how to get your liberty. Speak and you are free!"

"Would, indeed, that I might utter the words you wish to hear, Philip Helmstedt. Alas, I cannot!"

"Will not, you mean. Very well, Marguerite, then remember that you choose this confinement to the island."

She bowed her head in proud though sad acquiescence, saying:

"Be it so! I accept your version of the affair, Philip. I choose this confinement on the island."

Mrs. Helmstedt's immense wealth was for the present not only of no use, but of vexation to her; it was troublesome to manage, on account of her various estates being in places distant, or of difficult access, and some four or five times in the course of each year it became necessary for Mr. Helmstedt to make a journey of three or four weeks for the settlement of accounts.

These absences were so trying to the secluded woman, who had no companion but her husband, and could scarcely bear to lose him for a day, that she suggested to Mr. Helmstedt that they should avail themselves of the first favorable opportunity to dispose of Eagle Flight, her mountain farm, and of her house on Loudoun street, in Winchester. Whereupon Mr. Helmstedt, who desired nothing better, immediately advertised the property for sale, and soon found purchasers. When the transfer was made and price paid, Mr. Helmstedt consulted his wife in regard to the disposition of the purchase money.

"Invest it in your own name, and in any way you see fit, dear Philip," she said.

And he probably took her at her word, for the subject was never renewed between them.

Plover's Point, her most valuable estate, being but fifteen miles up the river, on the Virginia side, was so readily accessible that it had been permitted to remain under cultivation, in the hands of an overseer, subject to the occasional supervision of the master. But at last an opportunity was presented of selling the place for a very liberal price, and Mr. Helmstedt made known the fact to his wife. But Marguerite declined to dispose of Plover's Point upon any terms whatever.

"It was my mother's ancestral home, and my own birthplace, dearest Philip. As my mother left it to me, I wish to leave it to my daughter."

"As you please," said her husband, and dropped the subject.

A few days after that he came to her with an inquiry whether she would be willing to give a lease of the property for a term of years, and, glad to be able to meet his wishes at any point, Mrs. Helmstedt at once agreed to the proposition.

The new tenant of Plover's Point was Dr. Hartley, with his wife, son and daughter. They were a great accession to the neighborhood, for, though fifteen miles up the river, they were, in that spacious district, considered neighbors. The Houstons, Comptons and Wellworths called upon them, as also did Mr. Helmstedt, who apologized for the non-appearance of his wife, saying that Mrs. Helmstedt suffered in health and spirits and never left her home, and expressed a hope that they would dispense with form and visit her there. And this, at last, Dr. and Mrs. Hartley decided to do, and, after having once made the acquaintance of Marguerite, they felt powerfully attracted to pursue it.

About this time, five years from the birth of her daughter, Marguerite became the mother of an infant son, who merely opened his eyes upon this world to close them immediately in death.

The loss of the babe was a severe disappointment to Mr. Helmstedt, and, for that reason, a heavier sorrow to Marguerite. Her health was now so enfeebled that her physician, Dr. Hartley, earnestly advised a change of air and scene, and his advice was warmly seconded by her friends at Buzzard's Bluff.

This consultation took place in the presence of Marguerite, who smiled proudly and mournfully.

Her husband answered:

"It shall be just as Mrs. Helmstedt decides; but as she has confined herself exclusively to her home, against the wishes and advice of all her friends, for more than five years, I greatly fear that she will not be induced, by anybody, to leave it."

Mrs. Houston replied:

"Think of it, Dr. Hartley. Mrs. Helmstedt has not set foot off this island for nearly six years! Enough in itself to ruin her health and spirits."

"Quite enough, indeed," said the kind-hearted physician, adding, "I hope, Mr. Helmstedt, that you will be able to persuade your wife to leave here for a time."

"I shall endeavor to do so," gravely answered that gentleman.

And when the visitors had all departed, and Mr. Helmstedt was alone with his wife, he took her white, transparent hand, and gazing mournfully into her emaciated, but still brilliantly beautiful face, said:

"Marguerite, will you have mercy on yourself? Will you save your life? Will you, in a word, make the revelation I require as your only possible ransom, so that I may take you where you may recover your health? Will you, Marguerite?"

She shook her head in sorrowful pride.

"Have you so mistaken me after all these years, Philip? And do you think that the revelation I could not make for your dear sake six years ago I can make now for my own? No, Philip, no."

And again, for a time, the harassing subject was dropped.

Mrs. Helmstedt had one dear consolation; a lone angel was ever at her side, her little daughter "Margaret," as her Anglo-Saxon father preferred to write the name. As the lady's health temporarily rallied, her sweetest employment was that of educating this child.

Margaret had inherited little of her mother's transcendent beauty and genius; but the shadow of that mother's woe lay lingering in her eyes—those large, soft, dark eyes, so full of earnest tenderness. Through the dreariest seasons in all the long and dreary years of her confinement—those desolate seasons when Mr. Helmstedt was varying the scene of his life at Baltimore, Annapolis, or some other point to which business or inclination called him; and Nellie was enjoying the society of her friends in Richmond, and Marguerite was left for weary weeks and months, companionless on the island, this loving child was her sweetest comforter. And little Margaret, with her premature and thoughtful sympathy, better liked to linger near her sad-browed mother, than even to leave the isle; but sweet as was this companionship, Mrs. Helmstedt, with a mother's unselfish affection, was solicitous that Margaret should enjoy the company of friends of her own age, and frequently sent her, under the charge of Ralph or Franky Houston, to pass a day at Rockbridge parsonage with Grace Wellworth, the clergyman's child, or a week at Plover's Point with Clare Hartley, the doctor's daughter; and still more frequently she invited one or both of those little girls to spend a few days on the island.

But at length there came a time, when Margaret was about twelve years of age, that she lost the society of her young friends. Grace Wellworth and Clare Hartley were sent up together to Richmond, under the charge of Colonel and Mrs. Houston, who were going thither on a visit, to enter a first-class boarding school, and thus Margaret was left companionless; and for a little while suffered a depression of spirits, strange and sad in one so young.

Mrs. Helmstedt saw this with alarm, and dreaded the farther effect of isolation and solitude upon her loving and sensitive child.

"She must not suffer through my fate. Dear as she is, she must leave me. The sins of her parents shall not be visited upon her innocent head," said Marguerite to herself. (Alas! Mrs. Helmstedt, how could you prevent the action of that natural and certain consequence?) And that same day, being in her own special parlor, of the bay window, with Mr. Helmstedt, she said:

"Do you not think, Philip, that it would be best to send our daughter to Richmond, to be educated with her friends, Grace and Clare?"

"By no means, Marguerite; the plan is not to be thought of for a moment," answered Mr. Helmstedt, who did not love his child with one tithe of the affection he bestowed upon his wife—notwithstanding that through pride and obstinacy he still kept the latter a sort of prisoner of honor—and who, knowing how dear to her was the society of her little girl, would not let the interest of Margaret conflict for an instant with the happiness of her mother.

"But our child has attained an age now when she needs the companionship of her equals, as much as she wants teachers."

"Marguerite! there is not in this wide world a teacher, man or woman, so, in all respects, and for all reasons, competent to educate your daughter as yourself. You delight, also, in the occupation of instructing her; therefore, she shall not leave you."

"But her isolation—her loneliness? Her evident depression of spirits?"

"She feels the loss of her companions, as she must feel it for some days, after which she will get over it. For the rest, a child abroad with nature as she is, cannot suffer from loneliness; and even if she did, her sufferings would be less than nothing compared with what you would feel in losing her for years."

"I pray you do not consider me in this affair."

"Cease, dear Marguerite; the child is better with you, and shall not leave you," said Mr. Helmstedt.

And as little Margaret entered at the same moment to take her music lesson, the subject was dropped, and Mr. Helmstedt left the room.

But Marguerite did not yield the point. After giving her young daughter her lesson on the harp, and while sitting exhausted on her sofa, she suddenly said:

"My dear, you miss Grace and Clare very much, don't you?"

"Yes, dear mother."

"Wouldn't you like to go to Richmond and enter the same school they are in?" she inquired, pushing aside the dark clustering curls from the child's fair forehead, and looking wistfully into her face, which was suddenly shadowed by a cloud of grief or fear. "Say, would you not, my Margaret?"

The little red lip quivered, and the dark eyes melted into tears; but she answered by asking, softly:

"Do you want me to go, mamma?"

"I think, perhaps, it might be best that you should do so, my love."

"Well, then, I will go," she said, meekly, struggling to govern her feelings, and then, losing all self-control, she burst into a fit of irrepressible weeping; in the midst of which her father re-entered the room, and learning the cause of her emotion, said:

"Cease crying this moment, Madge. You shall not leave your mother."

"But—sir, mamma prefers that I should go," said the little girl, quickly swallowing her sobs and wiping her eyes, for she feared even more than she loved her father, though she loved him very much.

"Your mother prefers that you should go, only because she sees you look sad, and fears that you feel lonesome here without companions of your own age."

"Oh, but—I should be more lonesome at Richmond, away from my dear mamma," said the little maiden, with a look of amazement, that her mother should, for a moment, think otherwise.

"Of course you would; so then let the matter rest. Mrs. Helmstedt, are you at length satisfied?"

Marguerite bowed and smiled to her husband, and then turned upon her daughter a look of ineffable tenderness, while forming the secret resolution that her own devoted love and care should compensate to the maiden for the absence alike of teachers and companions.

And well she kept her silent promise. No princess ever had an instructress at once so accomplished, so competent and zealous as this little island rustic possessed in her gifted and devoted mother. And from this day also, whether for her beloved mother's sake, she shook off her sadness, or whether a happy reaction had taken place, Margaret did not appear to suffer in the least degree from the loneliness so dreaded for her. As other more favored children learn to walk by nature, so this lonely island maiden learned to ride on horseback, to row a skiff, and to work a little sailboat. And daily, after her lessons were over, she would, in her free, unquestioned way, run down to the beach, get into her little boat and row around the isle, or if the wind was fresh and not too high plant her slender mast and hoist her sail.

Ralph Houston was at this time at Harvard University, but Franky was at home, preparing for college, under the direction of the Rev. Mr. Wellworth, whom he attended in his library three times a week. And Franky came often to the island to see his young neighbor, Margaret, and in his affectionate zeal would have been Grace, Clare, the city of Richmond and himself, all in one, for her sweet sake. While at home in the evenings, he carved "cornelian" rings and bodkins out of broken tortoiseshell combs, and "ivory" needle-cases and paper-folders out of boiled mutton bones for her; and she wore and used them because they were Franky's work. And if he had pocket money, as he generally had, for he was a great favorite with his stepmother, who liberally supplied him, he was sure to send it by the first opportunity to the city to buy the newest book, picture or music for Margaret, who, whether the present were good, bad or indifferent of its kind, read the book, framed the picture or learned the music, because it was the gift of Franky. As time passed Mr. Houston observed this growing friendship with delight, and prophesied the future union of the youth and maiden—a provision at which Franky would blush scarlet between boyish shame and joy. Other interested parties took cognizance of this state of affairs. Mr. Helmstedt, whenever he gave himself the trouble to think of his daughter's future, viewed this prospect without dissatisfaction, which was, perhaps, the highest degree of approbation of which his sombre nature was now capable. And Mrs. Helmstedt also, conscious of the precarious hold of her feverish spirit upon her frail body, found great comfort in the contemplation of Franky's clear mind and affectionate heart, cheerful temper and strong attachment to her child. But if Margaret loved Franky it was "at second best," and as much for the sake of one far away as for his own. There is no accounting for the waywardness of the passions and affections, and if the truth must here be told, Margaret in her secret heart better liked the dark, earnest, thoughtful man, Ralph, who was twelve years her senior, and whom she never saw more than twice a year, than this fair, gay, gentle youth who was her almost daily companion. And no one suspected this secret, which was but dimly revealed to the young maiden's self.

But at length the passage of time brought the day when Margaret was to lose Franky also. Ralph Houston had graduated at Harvard, and was coming home for a visit previous to going out to make the grand tour. And Franky, now fully prepared to enter college, was to take his brother's vacated rooms at the university. Nellie Houston had appropriated all her available funds in fitting out Franky for his new life, purchasing delicacies and luxuries in the way of fine and costly wearing apparel and elegant toilet apparatus, such as his father's prudence or economy would have denied him; for never did a mother dote upon an only son with a fonder affection than did Nellie on her fair stepson, her "pretty boy," as she called him, even after he was twenty years of age. Many of the presents she had purchased for her "boy," such as a rich watch and chain, a costly seal ring, a heavily chased gold pencil case with a ruby setting, richly embroidered velvet fatigue cap and slippers, a handsome dressing gown, Paris kid gloves, linen cambric handkerchiefs, perfumery, scented soaps, etc.—articles, some of them, only fit for a lady's toilet, she had smuggled into his trunks, unknown to his father; but some things accidentally fell under the observation of the colonel, who stared in astonishment.

"Why, what upon the face of the earth, Nellie, do you think Frank wants with this gimcrack?" he said, raising the lid of an elegant inlaid dressing case.

"He will want it at his morning exercises," said Nellie.

"Ah, it is you who are making a dandy of that boy! I shall, by and by, expect to hear, as the highest praise that can be bestowed upon him, that he is 'ladylike.'"

"Well, sir, your gallantry will not deny that is very high praise."

"Humph! yes! about as high as it would be to call a lady 'manly.'"

"Well, why shouldn't that be high praise also? Why should not a man, with all his manliness, possess the delicate tastes of a woman? And why should not a woman, with all her womanliness, possess the courage and fortitude of a man? My Franky shall have lace shirt frills and collars and cuffs, if he likes; and I, if there's to be a war with England, as they say, will go and "'list for a sojer,' if I like," said Nellie, petulantly.

"Ha, ha, ha! You will certainly have an opportunity, my dear," said the colonel; then, growing serious, "for a war can no longer be staved off."

In addition to her other efforts to please her "boy," Nellie determined upon giving him a farewell party, the first party ever given in the neighborhood. It was difficult in that sparse district to "drum up" enough young people to form a single quadrille. Grace Wellworth and Clare Hartley were at home for the Easter holidays. Grace had brought a schoolmate with her, and Clare had an elder brother, John; and these four were invited. Mr. and Mrs. Helmstedt and their daughter were, of course, bidden; Nellie herself carried the invitation, with the view of teazing Marguerite into accepting it.

"Now, Marguerite, you must be sure to come, it will do you good. You can come over early in the afternoon, so as to get a good rest before it is time to dress, and when all is over you can stay all night, you know. Marguerite, do come. Mr. Helmstedt, lay your commands on her, make her come, bring her," said Nellie, playfully appealing to the master of the house.

"If Mrs. Helmstedt had placed the slightest value upon her husband's wishes, not to use so obnoxious a word as commands, madam, she would not have confined herself to the island thus long," said that gentleman.

"You will please to excuse me, dear Nellie. Mr. Helmstedt and Margaret will go with pleasure, but for myself, I cannot leave home."

"You only think so, Marguerite. I declare it is a monomania that your friends ought not to put up with," said Nellie, impatiently. But her words were as vain then as they had been for many years past.

She went home to make arrangements for her *fête*, and Marguerite busied herself in preparing her daughter's costume for the occasion. Margaret was delighted at the prospect of going to a party, a thing that she had heard of and read of, but never witnessed. At length the all-important day arrived. Mr. Helmstedt said that he should attend his daughter to Buzzard's Bluff, but that afterward he should have to leave her there and go to a political meeting at Heathville, so that she must prepare herself to stay all night with her friends, as he should not be able to return for her until morning.

"But then mamma will be alone all night," said Margaret, uneasily.

"Never think of me, sweet girl; I shall sleep," replied her mother.

Early in the afternoon Forrest received orders to get the *Nereide* ready to take his master and young mistress across to the Bluff. And Mrs. Helmstedt, with affectionate care, dressed her daughter. Never had Margaret been in full dress before. Her attire was rather delicate than rich, and consisted of a lace robe over a rose-colored silk skirt, and a wreath of white and red rosebuds in her hair. Her white kid gloves and white satin shoes were wrapped up to be put on when she should reach the Bluff.

When all was ready Marguerite walked down with her husband and daughter to the beach to see them off. As they reached the sands a pleasant object met their view. It was a fairylike boat, of elegant form, artistically painted, of a shaded gray on the outside and white, flushed with rose-color, on the inside; and bore upon its prow, in silver characters, *The Pearl Shell*.

"And here is the pearl," said Franky Houston, who had just leaped on shore, going to Margaret and taking her hand, "will you allow me to put her in it, Mr. Helmstedt?"

"Certainly, Franky, since you were so kind as to come. Your dainty 'shell' is also somewhat cleaner and more suitable to her dress than our working-day boat."

"How do you do, Mrs. Helmstedt? Come, Margaret," said the youth.

"Stop, Franky, I must bid mamma good-by first," replied the maiden, going up to her mother. "Sweet mamma! you will not be lonesome?"

"No—no, my love, I shall go to sleep—good-evening," said Mrs. Helmstedt, throwing over her daughter's head and shoulders a fleecy white shawl, to protect her from the sea breeze.

"Come, Margaret," pleaded her companion.

"Yes, yes, I am coming, Franky. Mamma, dearest mamma! I do so dislike to leave you alone to-night—it seems so cruel. We are all going but you. Everybody on the island, black and white, can go abroad but you. Mamma, why is it? Why do you never leave the island, dearest mamma?" inquired Margaret, fixing her earnest, tender eyes wistfully upon her mother's face.

"Because I do not will to do so, my dear; there, go and enjoy yourself, love. See, your father and Forrest are already in the other boat, and Franky is waiting to put my pearl in his shell. Good-night, sweet!" said Mrs. Helmstedt, kissing her daughter, with a smile so bright that it cheered the maiden, and sent her tripping to join her companion.

The *Nereide*, containing Mr. Helmstedt and his man, had already left the shore. Franky handed Margaret into the dainty boat, that was so perfectly clean as not to endanger the spotless purity of her gala dress. When she was seated, and Franky had taken his place at the oars and pushed a little way from the shore, he said:

"This boat is yours, you know, dear Margaret; my parting gift; I had it built on purpose, and painted it myself, and named it for you. 'Margaret,' you know, means 'pearl,' and this boat that carries you is a pearl shell; I colored it as near like one as I could. I should like to have the pleasure of rowing you about in it, but"—with a deep sigh—"I can't! However, you will not want attention, Margaret, for my brother Ralph will be home, where I am sure he will stay; for they say that we are on the eve of war with England, in which case it will not be expedient for him to go to Europe—so, of course, he will stay home, and equally, of course, if he is a great Don, he will supply my place to you, Margaret! You have not answered one word that I have said to you—why, what is the matter?"

Margaret, with her thoughts and affections still lingering with her mother left behind, had turned to give her a last look, and in doing so had started and grown pale to see her still standing there, her black dress strongly marked against the drear, white beach, alone, desolate, in an attitude and with an expression of utter despair. Margaret had never before surprised that look of heartbroken hopelessness upon her mother's well-guarded countenance, and now having seen it, she never afterward in life forgot it.

"You do not speak, Margaret; you do not like my boat?"

"Oh, indeed I do, Franky! And you are very kind; but I am thinking of mamma; I am afraid she will be lonesome to-night, and, indeed, I wish to return to her."

"Nonsense, my dear Margaret. She would send you off again; besides, what would your father say?"

"But do, then, look at her, Franky, where she stands alone."

The youth turned around; but Mrs. Helmstedt saw them watching her, smiled her bright, delusive smile, waved them adieu, and turned away.

Margaret sighed.

And Franky pulled rapidly for the Bluff, which they reached just after sunset.

"Is not that a fine sight, Margaret?" asked her companion, as they left the boat and climbed the bluff, pointing to the illuminated front of the mansion that cast a long stream of red light across the darkening water.

"Yes," said Margaret, absently; for she saw in her "mind's eye," not the twenty festive lights before her, but her mother's solitary figure left behind on the beach.

They soon arrived at the house, where the young girl was met by Mrs. Houston, who conducted her to the dressing-room, where Grace Wellworth, Clare Hartley, and half a dozen other young ladies were arranging their toilets. Very enthusiastic was the greeting between Margaret and her young friends, whom she had not met since their return.

"Why, what exquisite taste is displayed in your toilet, Madge, you little rustic; one would think a city milliner had arranged it—who dressed you?" inquired Clare Hartley.

"A more delicate hand—my dearest mamma," said Margaret, her thoughts again reverting to the mournful figure left standing alone on the beach.

When they were all ready, they descended to the dancing-room—two large parlors thrown into one, brilliantly lighted, and half filled with a company of young, middle-aged and elderly persons, for there was not youth enough in that neighborhood to make a considerable assembly of themselves. A temporary platform at one end of the room accommodated four sable musicians, with a large and small violin, a tambourine and banjo, which they were tuning up with great zeal.

Franky "opened the ball" by leading Margaret out; other couples instantly followed, and the dancing commenced, but through the liveliest strains of the music Margaret heard only her lonely mother's fond "good-night," and with flying feet and beaming smiles around her, saw only her mother's solitary figure and mournful brow.

Ah! Marguerite Helmstedt! How could you presume to say: "The sins of her parents shall not be visited upon this child."

About nine o'clock the supper was served, and, while the company were crowding in to the supper table, Margaret called Franky aside and said:

"Franky, the moonlight is bright upon the water; if you love me, dear Franky, take me home to mamma."

"Why, you do astound me, dear Margaret! What would the company say? Mother would never let you go."

"I must steal away unobserved, for, Franky, I am sick to return to mamma. Something draws me so strongly that I must and will go, even, if need be, alone—do you understand?"

"I understand, dear Madge, that you inherit firmness from both sides of your house, and that it is of very little use to oppose your will; therefore, Margaret, I am at your orders."

"Thank you, dear Franky—now go and see that the boat is ready, while I run and put on my other shoes and shawl. We can go away quite unobserved, and when you return you can make my apologies and adieus to Mrs. Houston."

Franky obeyed her.

And ten minutes after the youth and maiden were in *The Pearl Shell*, skimming over the moonlit waters toward the isle.

Meanwhile Mrs. Helmstedt, when she had waved adieu to the young people on their way to the party and turned from them, did not go immediately home, but rambled up toward the north end of the island, and here she walked up and down the sands, watching absently the monotonous in-coming of the tide, or the leap and dip of the fish, or the slow sailing of some laggard water fowl through the evening air. As far as her eye could reach not a sail was visible in any direction; land and water was a scene of unbroken solitude for hours while she walked there. The sunset threw into deep shadow the long line of the opposite western shore, the sky grew dark, and still the sad recluse pursued her lonely monotonous walk. After awhile the full moon rose and changed the darkened bay into a sea of fluid silver, and shining full against the blackened western shore, changed it into a line of diamond light. Then Marguerite was aware of a sail making down the bay and bearing full upon the island. There was no reason for the feeling, but the approach of this packet filled the lady's mind with a strange anxiety, alike impossible to explain or expel. The vessel anchored near the isle and sent out a boat, manned by two sailors, and containing a third person, apparently a passenger.

The boat rowed rapidly toward the very spot upon which the lady stood watching. In five minutes it touched the sands, and the passenger, a gentleman of about fifty years of age, stepped ashore, and, walking up to Marguerite, bowed respectfully and inquired:

"Will you be so good as to inform me, madam, whether Mrs. Helmstedt is at present at home."

But as the stranger approached, Marguerite had grown pale, and now, leaning against a pine tree for support, exclaimed in a faint tone:

"My God, has it come at last?"

"I fear, madam, that I have alarmed you by my sudden approach; reassure yourself, dear lady!" said the visitor, politely.

But Marguerite, dropping her hands from before her agonized countenance, exclaimed:

"Braunton! am I so changed, then, that you do not know me? I am Marguerite Helmstedt, whom you seek. But in the name of Heaven, then, what fatality has brought you here?"

"A fatality indeed, madam," answered the stranger, in a sad tone.

"Come up to the house! by a merciful chance I am alone this evening," said the lady, struggling to sustain herself against the agony of mind that was written in characters of iron on her corrugated brow. The stranger gave her his arm as an indispensable support, and the two proceeded toward the mansion.

CHAPTER VIII
LOVE, WAR AND BETROTHAL

"Her mother smiled upon her bed,

As at its side we knelt to wed,

And the bride rose from her knee;

And she kissed the lips of her mother dead

Or ever she kissed me."

—E. B. Browning.

None ever knew what passed between Mrs. Helmstedt and the gray-haired stranger who was closeted with her, in her favorite parlor, for several hours, that evening. No one was in the house, in fact, at the time, except the lady, her venerable guest, and her two confidential servants, Hildreth and Forrest, who had, of late years, grown into the habit of silence in regard to everything concerning their unhappy mistress. Once in the wane of that evening, Forrest rapped at the door for orders, and had caught a glimpse of his mistress's blanched and haggard face, as she directed him to retire and wait until he should hear her bell. And after waiting in the dining-room opposite, for some hours, Forrest heard the departure of the visitor, but listened in vain for Mrs. Helmstedt's bell.

Meanwhile, *The Pearl Shell*, containing Margaret and Franky, glided swiftly over the moonlit waters. As they neared the island, they saw another boat, containing a pair of oarsmen and a single passenger, push off from the beach and row rapidly toward a schooner, anchored some quarter of a mile off. But as it was not an unusual occurrence for passing vessels to send out boats to the isle for water, wood or provisions, purchased from the negroes, the sight of this one leaving its shores occasioned no remark.

"Now row swiftly home, dear Franky, or they will wonder what has become of us," said Margaret, as soon as she had sprung upon the shore. But Franky refused to leave her until at least he had seen her safely housed. So he took her hand, and they ran on up the sandy barren, through the long timothy field, through the orchard, and through the garden, until they reached the front piazza, where Margaret insisted upon dismissing her boy lover, who reluctantly left her.

And Margaret ran into the hall door, and thence into her mother's favorite parlor, on the threshold of which she stood appalled!

The two wax candles upon the mantelpiece were burning dimly, and their pale light fell ominously upon the figure of Mrs. Helmstedt, sitting on the short sofa, with her hands clasped rigidly together on her lap, her eyes fixed and strained outward, and her face blanched and frozen as if the hand of death had just passed over it.

One instant Margaret stood panic-stricken, and the next she was at her mother's side, speaking to her, kissing her, stroking her forehead, and trying to unclasp and rub her rigidly-locked hands. For some minutes these efforts were all in vain; and then a deep shuddering sigh, that shook her whole form like the passage of an inward storm, dissolved the spell that had bound her, and she grew conscious of the presence of her child.

"Mamma, what shall I bring you? I had better call Hildreth," said Margaret, softly stealing away. But the hand that she had been rubbing now closed on hers with a tight, restraining clasp, and a deep, hollow, cavernous voice, that she scarcely recognized as her mother's answered:

"No—no—call no one, my child—stay with me."

Margaret dropped upon the sofa, beside her mother, with a look of mute wonder and devoted love, and seemed to await her further commands.

"My child," spoke the same hollow, cavernous, awful voice, "speak to no living soul of what you have seen to-night."

"I will not, dear mamma; but tell me what I can do for you."

"Nothing, nothing, Margaret."

"Can I not help you somehow?"

"I am beyond help, Margaret."

"Mother, mother, trust in your loving child, the child of your heart, who would give you back her life if she could give you happiness with it, mother," murmured Margaret, most tenderly, as she caressed and fondled the rigid form of that dark, sorrowful woman—"trust in your loving child, mother, your child that heard your heart calling her to-night over the moonlit waters, and through all the music and laughter came hurrying to your side."

"Ah! so you did, my love, so you did; and I, so absorbed in my own thoughts, did not even ask you whence you came, or how, or why."

"Franky brought me at my earnest request. Now trust in me, dear mother, trust in your faithful child."

"If ever I be driven to lay the burden of my grief upon any human heart, Margaret, it must be on yours—only on yours! for little Margaret, in my life, I have loved many and worshiped one, but I fully trust only you."

"Trust me ever, mother! trust me fully, trust me even unto death; for I would be faithful unto death," said the maiden, earnestly, fervently, solemnly.

"I know it, and I do trust you perfectly. Yet not now, not just now, need I shift this weight from my heart to yours—'tis enough that one living heart should bear that burthen at a time. I may leave it to you as a legacy, my Margaret."

"A legacy—a legacy—oh! mother, what mean you?" inquired the maiden, as the sudden paleness of a deadly terror overspread her sweet face.

"Nothing, nothing, my dove, that should alarm you. It is the order of nature, is it not, that parents should die before their children? But who talks of dying now? Your soft touches, my child, have given me new life and strength. Lend me your arm; I will retire."

"Let me sleep with you to-night, dear mother," pleaded the maiden, from whose earnest face the paleness of fear had not yet vanished.

An affectionate pressure of the hand was her only answer. And Margaret assisted Mrs. Helmstedt to gain her chamber. That night, in her prayers, Margaret earnestly thanked God that she had been led to come home so opportunely to her lonely mother's help.

And from that night the close union between the mother and daughter seemed even more firmly cemented.

The next day Mr. Helmstedt returned. He had spent the night at Heathville, and called in the morning at Buzzard's Bluff for Margaret, and hearing that she had grown anxious upon account of her mother left alone on the island, and had returned, he simply approved the step and dropped the subject.

Later in the same week, Franky Houston, boy as he was, took a tearful leave of Margaret, turning back many times to assure her that Ralph, when he came, would not leave her to mope in loneliness, but would certainly, to the best of his ability, supply his (Franky's) place. And so the candid, open-hearted boy left.

And Margaret, who had grown to understand how dear she was to Franky, felt her heart stricken with compunction to know how glad she was that his place would soon be supplied by Ralph.

Grace Wellworth and Clare Hartley had also returned to their city school. And "Island Mag" was left again companionless.

Not for a long time.

With the warm days of early summer came Ralph Houston, as he said, for a short visit home, before he should sail for Europe to make the grand tour.

But this month of June, 1812, was a month big with the fate of nations as well as of individuals. The bitter disputes between the young Republic and the "Mother Country," like all family quarrels, did not tend toward reconciliation, but on the contrary, month by month, and year by year, had grown more acrid and exasperating, until at length a war could no longer be warded off, and thus, without the least preparation, either military or naval, Congress on the eighteenth of June, 1812, declared war against Great Britain. Never had Young America before, and never since, taken so rash and impetuous a step. Never had an unfortunate country plunged headlong into an unequal and perilous war under more forbidding circumstances; with two formidable antagonists, and without either army or navy in readiness to meet them. Yet no sooner had the tocsin sounded through the land, than "the spirit of '76" was aroused, and an army arose. Simultaneously, all over the country, volunteer companies were formed and marched toward the principal points of gathering.

Among the first who started into action at the country's call, was Philip Helmstedt, who set about raising a company of volunteers in his own neighborhood, and at his own expense. This enterprise took him frequently from home, and kept him absent for many days at a time. At last, about the middle of July, he had formed and equipped his troop of one hundred men, and was prepared to march them to obtain his commission from Mr. Madison.

Mrs. Helmstedt had watched his preparations for departure with the mournful resignation of one whom sorrow had accustomed to submission. He was to join his men at Belleview, and take one of the larger packets bound up the Potomac River to the capital.

On the morning of his departure, Mrs. Helmstedt had risen early to superintend the final arrangements for his comfort. And they breakfasted alone at an early hour. Their child had not left her chamber, her father having taken leave of her on the evening previous. When breakfast was over, and the servants had withdrawn from the room by their master's order, Mr. Helmstedt approached his wife, and seating himself beside her on the sofa, said:

"Marguerite! we are about to part. God knows for how long. It may be years before we meet, if, indeed, we ever meet again, Marguerite!"

"I know how long it will be—until we meet in the spirit world!" thought Mrs. Helmstedt; but she spoke not, only looked lovingly, mournfully in the face of her departing husband.

"Marguerite, shall not this painful feud of years come to an end between us?"

"There is not, there never has been, there never can be a feud between us, dearest Philip. It was my bitter misfortune not to be able to comply with your just requirements. In view of that, you fixed my fate and I accepted it. There is no feud, dearest husband."

"Marguerite, I cannot endure the thought of leaving you for so long a time, restricted to the narrow confines of this island, and yet I cannot do otherwise unless——"

"Dearest Philip, I have grown accustomed to confinement on this island, and do not——" She paused abruptly.

"Marguerite, you were about to say that you do not care about it; but you never uttered an untruth in your life, and could not be betrayed into doing so now. Marguerite, you do care; you care bitterly about the restraint that is placed upon your motions. Dear Marguerite, you know the conditions of peace and freedom. Will you not, even at this late day, accept them?"

"Oh, Mr. Helmstedt, had it been possible for me to have accepted these conditions, I should have done so, not for my own advantage, but for your satisfaction, thirteen years ago! Since that time nothing has happened to render the impossible possible."

"Then I am to understand, Marguerite, that you still hold out in your resistance?" said Mr. Helmstedt, more gloomily than angrily.

She did not reply at first, except by a steady, mute, appealing look from her dark, mournful eyes. But as Mr. Helmstedt still looked for a reply, she said:

"Dear Philip, as you remarked, we are just about to part, and Heaven only knows if ever we shall meet again on earth. Let us not have hard feelings toward each other."

"Good-by Marguerite," he said, suddenly rising and taking his hat and gloves.

"Good-by—not yet. Philip turn: let me look at you!" She clung tightly to the hand he had given her, and held him fast while she fixed a long, deep gaze upon his face—a gaze so strange, so wistful, so embarrassing, that Mr. Helmstedt cut it short by saying, gently:

"Farewell, dearest! let me be gone."

"Not yet! oh, not yet! a moment more!" her bosom swelled and heaved, her lips quivered, but no tear dimmed her brilliant, feverish eyes, that were still fixed in a riveting gaze upon his face.

Mr. Helmstedt felt himself strongly moved.

"Marguerite, why Marguerite, dearest, this is not like you! You are in soul a Spartan woman! You will receive my parting kiss now and bid me go," he said, and opened his arms and pressed her to his heart a moment and then with another whispered, "Farewell," released her.

"God bless you, Philip Helmstedt," she said.

The next instant he was gone. She watched him from the door, where he was joined by his groom and valet, down to the beach and into the boat; and then she went upstairs to the balcony over the bay window and watched the boat out of sight.

"There! That is the last! I shall never see his face again," she murmured, in heartbroken tones, and might have cast herself upon the ground in her desolation, but that two gentle arms were wound about her, and a loving voice said,

"Dearest mother."

No more than just that—so little, yet so much.

"He is gone, Margaret, your father is gone," said Mrs. Helmstedt, passing her arm over the head of the maiden and drawing it down to her bosom—"he is gone—gone!"

"I know it, dear mother, I know it; but so also is every good and true American gone, on the same path."

"True, my dove, true," said Mrs. Helmstedt; but she did not say, what farther she felt to be true, namely, that from her he had gone forever.

That afternoon following the departure, Ralph Houston, with affectionate thoughtfulness, came over to cheer the lonely ladies.

He had accompanied Mr. Helmstedt from the Bluff to Belleview, and witnessed the embarkation of himself and his company, on board the schooner *Kingfisher*, bound for Alexandria and Washington, and after thus seeing them off, he had ridden back as fast as possible, and crossed to the isle. Mr. Houston spent the evening, planned some amusement for the next afternoon, and took leave.

Ten days of weary waiting passed, and then Mrs. Helmstedt received a letter from her husband, announcing that they had reached Washington; that he had received a captain's commission; had reported himself and his company ready for service; and that they were then waiting orders.

"Has my father any idea where he will be sent, mamma?" inquired Margaret, after this letter had been read aloud.

"No, my dear; at least he has hinted so; we must wait to hear."

Ten, fifteen, twenty more anxious days passed, heavily, and then came a second letter from Mr., now Captain, Helmstedt, postmarked New York, and bringing the intelligence that upon the next day succeeding the writing of the first letter, he had received orders to depart immediately with his troops to join General Van Rennselaer on the Canadian frontier; that the suddenness of the departure and the rapidity of the journey had prevented him, until now, from writing a line home; but that they were now delayed in New York, for a day or two, waiting for a reinforcement from the State militia.

This was the last letter that Mrs. Helmstedt received for many months; but she sent on and ordered the principal Northern papers, that she might be kept advised of the progress of the campaign.

Alas! little but continuous disaster signalized this opening of the war; repeated rebuffs, varied by small successes, and climaxing in the defeat of

Hull, and the loss of Detroit, with all Michigan territory. These calamities, while they shocked, aroused the temperate blood of all those laggards at home, who, until now, had looked on philosophically, while others went forth to fight.

Colonel Houston applied for orders, and old Colonel Compton sat in his leathern armchair, and swore at the gouty limb that unfitted him for service. At length the news of the disastrous defeat of Van Rennselaer, on the fourth of October, followed by his resignation of the command reached them. And when General Smythe, of Virginia, was appointed to fill his post, Colonel Houston received orders to join the latter, and proceed with him to the Northern frontier.

Ralph Houston was most anxious to enter upon the service; but at the earnest entreaty of his father, reluctantly consented to remain, for awhile, at the Bluff, for the protection of the family left behind.

Mrs. Houston accompanied her husband as far as Buffalo, where she remained to be in easy reach of him.

At the Bluff were left old Colonel and Mrs. Compton ("a comfortable couple," who were always, and especially now, in their quiet old age, company enough for each other), and Ralph Houston as a caretaker.

At the lonely isle were left Mrs. Helmstedt and her daughter. And very desolate would the lady have been, only for the presence of her "dove." Very monotonously passed the winter days on the sea-girt isle. No visitors came, and the mail, bringing newspapers and an occasional letter from Captain Helmstedt, Mrs. Houston, or Franky, arrived only once a week; and not always then. But for the frequent society of Ralph Houston, who was almost an inmate of the family, the dreary life would have been almost insupportable to the mother and child. While they sat at needlework in Mrs. Helmstedt's private room, he read to them through all the forenoon; or, if the sun was warm and the air balmy, as often happens in our Southern winters, he invited them out to walk over the isle; or when, in addition to warm sun and balmy air, there was still water, he prepared the little *Pearl Shell*, the gift of Franky to Margaret, and took the maiden across to the Bluff to visit the old people there. But as no persuasion would ever induce Mrs. Helmstedt to join them in these water trips, they were at last relinquished, or at least very seldom indulged in.

"Dear Margaret, I think your mother has a natural antipathy to water, has she not?" asked Ralph Houston, one day, of the girl.

"No, it is to leaving the isle; if my dear mamma was a Catholic, I should think she had taken a vow never to leave Helmstedt's Isle. As it is, I am at a loss to know why she ever remains here, Mr. Houston."

"I never remember to have seen her off the isle, since she came here. There must be a cause for her seclusion greater than any that appears," thought Ralph Houston, as he handed Margaret into the little skiff, and threw his glance up to the house, where from the balcony of her chamber window Mrs. Helmstedt watched their departure from the shore. For this was upon one of those very rare occasions when they took a little water trip, leaving the lady alone on the isle. As he glanced up, Ralph thought Mrs. Helmstedt's thin face more sunken, and her eyes more brilliant, than he had ever noticed them before; and for the first time the thought that death, speedy death, was awaiting that once glorious woman, smote him to the heart. They were not out long; even Mr. Houston now no longer pleaded with Margaret to remain out upon the water to see the wintry sunset; but followed her first hint to return. The winter evenings at the isle were pleasant with Ralph Houston for a guest. He read to the mother and daughter, while they sewed or sketched; and sometimes the three formed a little concert among themselves, Mrs. Helmstedt playing on the harp, Margaret on the piano, and Ralph Houston on the flute; and sometimes, that is to say, once a week, or seldomer, the mail came in, bringing its keen excitement; it always reached the isle on the evening of Saturday, when Ralph Houston was sure to remain to hear the latest news of the absent. Always there were newspapers, bringing fresh and startling news from the Canadian frontier, the Indian settlements, or from the ocean, where our infant navy, like young Hercules in his cradle, was strangling the serpents of wrong and oppression, and winning more glorious laurels than were lost upon the land. Sometimes, there came intelligence of a disastrous loss on the Northern frontier—sometimes, of a glorious victory at sea; but whether were the news of triumph or defeat, it ever roused Ralph Houston's blood almost beyond the power of his control. He chafed and fretted like Marmion in Tantallon Hold.

"A most unworthy task, dear Margaret, to be left at home to take care of two old people, who do not need either my company or protection, while the struggling country cries aloud for every man capable of bearing arms to come to her help! A most unworthy post is mine!"

They were standing alone within the bay window of the parlor, on Sunday morning, after having read in the papers, that had come the evening before, of the repulse of Smythe at Niagara.

Ralph spoke as bitterly as he felt, the enforced inaction of his life.

"A most unmanly part to play!"

"'They also serve who only stand and wait,'" said Margaret, gently.

His stern face softened instantly, and he looked on her with a smile, full of deep tenderness and beauty, as he answered:

"True, sweet Margaret, yet, nevertheless, the only circumstance that renders this standing and waiting endurable is—do you know what, dear maiden? Your sweet society, and the thought that I may be useful in making the days pass less heavily to you and to her who is dearer to you."

A swift, burning blush crimsoned the neck and face of the young girl. And just at this juncture Mrs. Helmstedt entered the room. Always her first glance was directed in search of her daughter; and now, she started and pressed her hand to her heart, at the tableau that was presented to her. Within the crimson-draped recess of the bay window the pair were standing. Ralph stood, resting one elbow upon the frame of the harp, and clasping Margaret's hand, and bending over her half-averted and deeply-blushing face. Both were too absorbed in their own emotions to perceive her gentle entrance, and she stood for a minute, unobserved, gazing upon them. To Mrs. Helmstedt, her young daughter, had, up to this hour, seemed an unconscious child, and now she stood revealed to her a young maiden, awakening to the consciousness of loving and being loved. Yet though this revelation was unexpected, it was not quite unacceptable. More than in any other man, Mrs. Helmstedt confided in Ralph Houston for the wisdom, goodness and power, inherent in his soul, and including in themselves every other virtue. And, after a few years, should she live to pass them, and should he have the patience and constancy to wait—with less reluctance than to any other man, would she entrust the life-happiness of her only and cherished daughter, to the charge of Ralph Houston. All this passed, in an instant, through the mind of the mother, as she crossed the room and bade them "Good-morning."

Margaret started; the blush deepened on her face. But Mr. Houston, still holding her hand, and leading her from the recess, greeted Mrs. Helmstedt affectionately, and said, frankly, as one who would not conceal his disposition:

"I was just telling Margaret that nothing but her sweet society, and the hope of being useful to herself and her mother, could reconcile me, at this time, to the unworthy inactivity of my life."

"We should indeed be very badly off without you, Mr. Houston; but I do not see what compensation for a dull life you can find in the company of a little island rustic."

"'A little island rustic,' my dear lady. I have lived in the great world where there are more false jewels than real ones, and I know how to prize a real pearl that I find amid the sea!"

"Do not waste poetry on my little girl, Ralph Houston."

"Again! 'little girl!' Well, I suppose she is a little girl, scarce fourteen years of age, just in her dawn of existence! Yet the dawn is very beautiful! and we, who are up early enough, love to watch it warm and brighten to the perfect day," he said, bending a grave, sweet look upon the downcast face of Margaret.

To break up this conversation and relieve her little daughter's embarrassment, Mrs. Helmstedt touched the bell and ordered breakfast to be served directly in that parlor; and it was speedily brought thither.

Spring at length opened, and the recluse family of the island were once more in communication with the outside world.

Old Colonel and Mrs. Compton paid a visit of a day and night to Mrs. Helmstedt, and again, although they knew it to be a mere form, renewed their oft-repeated entreaties that their hostess would return their visit.

The Wellworths came and spent a couple of days, and carried off Margaret to pass a week at the parsonage. And during the absence of the young girl, it should be observed, that Ralph Houston did not slacken in the least degree his visits to the island, and his friendly attentions to the solitary lady there.

Soon after Margaret returned home, the doctor and Mrs. Hartley came to the isle to spend a day, and when they departed took the maiden with them to Plover's Point to spend a fortnight. Truth to tell, the young girl did not like to leave her mother; but Mrs. Helmstedt, ever fearful of the effect of too much isolation and solitude upon the sensitive nature of her daughter, firmly insisted upon her going.

Ralph Houston was ubiquitous. He did not fail in daily visits to the island, and yet two or three times a week he contrived to be twenty miles up the river at Plover's Point. There are no secrets in a country neighborhood. The attachment of Ralph Houston, the heir of Buzzard's Bluff, to the little island maiden was no secret, though a great mystery to all.

"What can a man of twenty-five see in a child of fourteen?" asked one gossip.

"Money," quoth the other—"money; Miss Helmstedt is the richest heiress in the whole South, as she will inherit both her mother's and her father's large property."

"Humph! I guess Mr. Houston will have to wait a long time for that property; Mr. and Mrs. Helmstedt look as if they might be the elder brother and sister, rather than the parents of Miss Helmstedt."

"It is true they are a very youthful-looking and handsome pair; but at last their daughter will inherit their property, if she lives; and meantime, when she marries, no doubt her parents will dower her handsomely; and that is what Mr. Houston knows. Ah! he sees what's what, and takes time by the forelock, and wins her heart before any one else dreams of laying siege to it."

"But her parents will never permit her to marry so young."

"Of course not; but what matter to Mr. Houston, if he can secure her heart and her promise. He understands perfectly well what he is doing."

Thus, with their usual perspicacity and charity, the *quidnuncs* of the county settled the matter.

Meantime the news from the Canadian frontier was of the most disheartening character. The defeat and capture of General Winchester, at Frenchtown, was followed speedily by that of Generals Greene and Clay at Fort Meigs, and Generals Winder and Chandler at Burlington Heights.

Colonel Houston had been dangerously wounded, and after lying ill two months in camp, was sent home to recuperate. He arrived at the Bluff, in charge of Nellie, who had grown to be quite a campaigner, and attended by his faithful servant, Lemuel. Nellie could not leave her wounded soldier, but she dispatched a note announcing her arrival, and explaining her position to Mrs. Helmstedt, and praying that lady to come to her at once without ceremony.

This was perhaps the severest trial to which Mrs. Helmstedt's fidelity had been put. She did not hesitate a moment, however; but wrote a reply, pleading to be excused, upon the score of her shattered health. This answer of course displeased little Mrs. Houston, who, in a few days, just as soon as she could leave her invalid, went over to the island with the intention of relieving her heart by upbraiding her cold friend. But as soon as she met

Mrs. Helmstedt and saw her changed face, Nellie burst into tears, and cast her arms about Marguerite's neck, and had no word of reproach for the suffering woman.

As Colonel Houston recovered from the fatigue of his journey, and convalesced under the genial influences of his quiet home and native air, Nellie often left him to spend a day with Mrs. Helmstedt. And as often as otherwise she found Ralph Houston there before her.

"That is right, Ralph," she one day said, approvingly, "I shall be sure to tell Franky, when I write, what care you take of his little sweetheart."

"Sweetheart?" repeated Ralph, with a grave, displeased look.

"Yes, sweetheart, or ladylove, if you like it better. Didn't you know that my Franky and little Margaret were cut out for each other?"

"Really, no, nor do I know it now."

"Well, I inform you; so don't go too far, my fine fellow."

Ralph was silent. These remarks affected him despite his reason, and raised into importance many trifling incidents until now unnoticed, such as the raillery of Margaret upon the subject of Franky by Dr. Hartley; the favorite keepsakes of Margaret, all gifts of Franky; and finally, the frequent correspondence between the young collegian and the island maiden. Then Frank was handsome, gay, near the age of the young girl, and had been her intimate companion for years. All this looked very illy ominous to the hopes of Ralph, but he generously resolved to investigate the case, and if he found an incipient attachment existing between the youth and maiden, to withdraw at once from the rivalship, at whatever cost to his own feelings. This conversation with Mrs. Houston had occurred one Saturday afternoon, as he was taking that lady from Helmstedt's Island to the Bluff. So anxious became Ralph Houston upon this subject, that after seeing his stepmother safe home, he turned about and rowed swiftly to the island, and entered the parlor just as Mrs. Helmstedt had received the weekly mail.

"I felt sure you would return and join us in discussing the news brought by this post; and it is glorious, at last. This paper contains an account of the repulse of Proctor from before Fort Stevenson, by the gallant Croghan! Do read it," said Mrs. Helmstedt, passing the paper to Mr. Houston.

"And here I am yet!" impatiently exclaimed Ralph, as he took the paper and sat down to assure himself of the contents. But frequently, in the course of his perusal, he glanced over the edge of the sheet at Margaret, who sat absorbed in the letter she was reading—now smiling, now looking grave, and anon with eyes swimming in tears.

"Yes, it was a brilliant action, and Lieutenant Croghan is a true hero," he said, as he finished the perusal and laid the paper aside. But his eyes were fixed on the maiden. Mrs. Helmstedt noticed this and said:

"Margaret has a pleasant letter from Franky." Ralph visibly changed color.

"Read it, my child."

"You read it, Mr. Houston; dear Franky!" exclaimed the girl, half smiling, half weeping, as she gave the letter to Ralph. Mr. Houston felt that he must peruse it. It was a frank, gay, affectionate letter, written as freely as a boy might write to his sister, yet much more warmly than any boy would be apt so to write. Mr. Houston could gather nothing definite from its contents. It certainly was not the letter of a young, diffident, uncertain lover, but it might mean either an intimate, youthful friendship or an understood betrothal. Upon the whole, Ralph felt disheartened; but resolved to see farther before resigning his hopes. He arose to take leave, and declining the friendly invitation of Mrs. Helmstedt, that he should spend the night on the isle, departed.

The next morning Ralph had some conversation with his father, the result of which was the consent of Colonel Houston that he should depart, as a volunteer, to serve under General Browne.

The same day Mr. Houston went over to the island to apprise his friends there of his intended departure. Mrs. Helmstedt was not surprised or displeased, but on the contrary, cordially approved his resolution. But Margaret, no adept at concealment, betrayed so much deep and keen distress, that Mr. Houston's lately entertained ideas of an attachment between herself and Frank were all shaken. And he determined, ere the day should be over, to satisfy himself upon that point. In the course of his visit he contrived to say, aside to Mrs. Helmstedt:

"Pray, grant me a confidential interview of a few moments."

"Margaret, my child, go down to the quarters and see if Uncle Ben is any better to-day, and if he wants anything from the house; and if he does, have it got and sent to him. One of our gardeners is ill, Mr. Houston. Now then, how can I serve you?" she asked, when her daughter had left the room.

"Mrs. Helmstedt, what I have to say relates to the fair creature who has just left us. You will place confidence in me when I assure you that, with the exception of those few impulsive words uttered the other morning, and afterward repeated to you, I have never said anything to your young daughter of the subject that lies nearest my heart; because, in fact, it is an affair belonging to the future, and I did not wish to be premature."

"You were quite right, Ralph. It is time enough three or four years hence for any one to think of addressing Margaret."

"Assuredly. But yet, as I deeply appreciate and devotedly love this young maiden, it behooves me to have some security that I am not freighting with my whole life's happiness some untenable bark in which it may go to the bottom."

"And what precisely do you mean by that, Mr. Houston?"

"In a word, I have gathered from the conversation of my fair stepmother, and from other corroborating circumstances, that there exists a sort of Paul and Virginia affection between my younger brother Frank and Margaret Helmstedt."

"Permit me to assure you that testimony and circumstances have deceived you. It is not so. Of Frank I cannot speak advisedly; but, as far as her sentiments toward him are concerned, Margaret is heart whole."

"Are you sure of this?" asked Ralph, with a deep joy lighting up his dark and earnest countenance.

"Absolutely certain of it."

"Then, Mrs. Helmstedt, since this is so, and as I am about to depart for a long and dangerous service, will you permit me to speak to your daughter upon this subject?"

The lady hesitated.

"Understand me, if you please Mrs. Helmstedt. I know that, even under the most auspicious circumstances, the marriage must be delayed for years, and under any circumstances shall wait your fullest concurrence; for my pearl once secured to my affections I can wait. Nor do I wish now to bind her by any pledge to me, but leaving her entirely free, I desire only to pledge myself to her, that I may write to her as freely and confidentially as to my betrothed. You can trust me to that extent, Mrs. Helmstedt?"

"I can trust you fully to any extent, Ralph Houston. It is not lack of confidence in you. But you understand that I must not sanction your addresses to my daughter without consulting her father. Taking for granted that your inclinations are approved by your family, I advise you to get Colonel Houston to write to Captain Helmstedt upon this subject. That is the proper course to pursue, and in the meantime I beg you to delay speaking of this matter to Margaret until you have heard from her father."

"I will obey you, certainly, Mrs. Helmstedt, although — —"

"The formality is a bore, you mean. Well, I know you think so, and yet it must be borne."

Mr. Houston arose to leave.

"Will you not wait to see Margaret?"

"I think not now, Mrs. Helmstedt, for if she should wear the sweet, pale face she wore just now, I should have some trouble to keep my promise. Good-morning, madam."

The "inclinations" of Ralph Houston were highly approved by his father, who sat down the same day and wrote to Captain Helmstedt, asking the hand of Margaret in betrothal to his son, and stating that a mere betrothal was all that was necessary to satisfy the young people for some years.

A weary fortnight passed before there could arrive any answer to this letter. At last, however, it came. Captain Helmstedt, with the stately politeness of his nature, acknowledged the compliment paid to his daughter; expressed the highest consideration for the suitor and his family; did not as a general thing approve of early betrothals or long engagements; thought this, however, to be an exceptional case; and concluded by referring the matter exclusively to the maiden's mother, in whose excellent judgment and maternal affection he expressed the highest confidence.

"There, you may look upon this as the sanction of your addresses; for, of course, I suppose there will be no difficulty raised by Mrs. Helmstedt," said Colonel Houston, as he placed the letter in the hands of son.

"Oh, no, sir! in fact, Mrs. Helmstedt has given me to understand as much."

"What is all that about?" inquired Nellie, who did not happen to be *au fait* to these transactions.

Colonel Houston explained.

"And Margaret will engage herself to you, Ralph, who are ten or twelve years older than she is? And Mrs. Helmstedt will sanction that engagement? Well, well, well."

"Why, what is the matter?" asked Colonel Houston.

"This world! this world! I did not think that Margaret was so light and fickle, or that her mother was so—governed by worldly motives."

"Pray tell me what you mean?" asked Ralph Houston, uneasily.

"Why, the whole county knew Margaret and my Franky were like a pair of young turtle doves. Everybody remarked it, and said they were born for each other! Shame on you, Ralph Houston, to offer to supplant your younger brother in his absence; and shame on that wanton girl and her worldly mother to allow you to do it!"

"Nellie, come, come, this will not do," said Colonel Houston.

"But I know what it means," Nellie continued impetuously, "they know you are the eldest son and heir according to our barbarous law of primogeniture, which, I thank Heaven, Mr. Jefferson is about to get repealed, and they think that you will have nearly all your father's estate, while poor Franky will have little or nothing; but I'll see! All that I have any control over shall go to swell the portion of my Franky, until we shall see if he shall not be a little richer than his fortunate elder brother. Oh, the unprincipled creatures."

"Cornelia!" exclaimed Colonel Houston, severely.

Ralph's face flushed for an instant, and then, controlling himself, he answered, with his usual moderation:

"You are in error, fair little mother; I neither could, nor would supplant any man, least of all my brother; no such attachment as that to which you allude exists, or has existed; I have ascertained that fact."

But Nellie angrily averted her head without deigning to reply. And Ralph, although he had so positively repudiated all belief in the groundless assertions of his stepmother, nevertheless felt a deep uneasiness impossible to dislodge. A single seed of distrust had been sown in his heart, where it was destined to germinate and to be fostered into strong and bitter growth.

In the midst of this conversation the family were interrupted by the entrance of Jessie Bell—as she was familiarly and jocosely called, Jezebel—

Mrs. Houston's maid, who reported a messenger from the island waiting without.

"Let him come in here," said Colonel Houston; and the next moment Uncle Ben entered with a face so gray and corrugated that Mrs. Houston and Ralph became alarmed, and simultaneously exclaimed:

"Why, old man! what is the matter?"

"Marster in heaven knows, ma'am! but I think my mistess is dying!"

"Dying!"

Every member of the family were now upon their feet, exclaiming and questioning in a chaos of surprise, grief, and dismay.

"Yes, ma'am, very suddint! No, sir, dere was no good come of it, as we dem knew. Yes, Marse Ralph, sir, Miss Marget is with her ma, an' very much 'stress," said the old man, answering right and left to the storm of questions that was hailed upon him.

"I'll tell you all I know 'bout it, Marse Colonel Houston, sir, if de ladies'll hush an' listen a minute. See, las' night I fotch de mail home 's usual. Der was a letter from our marster as pleased our mistress very much. I never seen her in sitch sperrits—she, nor Miss Marget! We sarvints, we all noticed it, and said how something was gwine happen. Same way dis mornin', Miss Marget and her mother both in sitch sperrits at the breakfas' table. After breakfas' dey went out long o' me in de garden, to 'rect me 'bout transplantin' some late flowers, and we were all busy, when all of a suddint mistress give a short, low scream, and when we all looked up, there stood mistress as white as a lily, pressing her hand to her heart and staring straight before her. We glanced roun' to see what scared she; and it was a little, old, leaky boat with one oar, and a young man in a shabby uniform, like a runaway sojer, just stepping from it onto the beach. He came up while mistress stood there pale as death and pressing her hand on her heart; and he tetched his cap sort o' half impident and half sorrowful. Mistess raised her hand for a minit as if to check him, and then she beckoned him to follow her, and went on to the house. Miss Marget looked oneasy, an' I didn't know what to make of it. More'n two hours passed, and then the young man came out, walking fast, with his head down, and passed right by without seeing us, and got into his leaky boat, and pushed off as if the old inemy was arter him.

"Miss Marget ran in the house to her mother. But in two minutes we heard her screaming like she was mad, and we all about the place rushed into the house, and up the stairs, into mistess' chamber. And there we saw our mistress, lying on the floor, like one stone dead, and Miss Marget wringing her hands and crying, and trying to raise her. We were all scared almost to death, for there, besides, was the cabinet, where the plate and jewelry is kept, all open; and we made sure that that 'serter had robbed and frightened mistress into this swoon. Forrest went arter the doctor; and Hildreth and Aunt Hapzibah put her to bed, and tried every way to fetch her round. But when she come to herself, she fell into convulsions; and when that was over, she sunk into the same swoon. Then Aunt Hapsy sent me, pos' haste, arter Miss Nellie an' Mr. Ralph. An' here I is, an' dat's all."

Nellie, who looked very pale and anxious, now touched the bell, and summoned Jezebel to bring her scarf, bonnet and gloves, while Mr. Houston went out to order the boat got ready to take them to the island.

And in less than a quarter of an hour Mrs. Houston and Ralph, forgetful of their late feud in their common cause of anxiety, were seated side by side in the boat, that, propelled by six stalwart negro oarsmen, glided with directness and rapidity toward the island. As soon as the boat touched the beach Nellie sprang out, and without waiting an instant for Ralph, hurried to the house.

"In her own bedroom, Mrs. Houston," was the mournful reply of Hildreth to that lady's hasty question.

Nellie hastened upstairs and entered the chamber of sickness and death. Coming out of the brilliant light into the half-darkened room, Nellie at first saw only Dr. Hartley standing at the foot of the bed; as she advanced she found Margaret, pale, but still and self-collected, at the head. Nellie's haste and anxiety sunk into awe as she saw, extended on the bed, the ruin of the once beautiful Marguerite De Lancie. All her late displeasure was forgotten or repented as she gazed upon that form and face so magnificent even in wreck. The pillows had been withdrawn to give her easier breathing, and her superb head lay low; the lace nightcap had been removed to give coolness to her throbbing temples, and her rich, purplish-black tresses, unbound, rolled in mournful splendor down each side of her pallid, sunken face, and flowed along upon the white counterpane; her eyes were half closed in that fearful state that is not sleep or waking, and that Nellie at first sight believed to be death.

Mrs. Houston turned an appealing glance to the physician, who bent forward and murmured in an almost inaudible tone:

"She is easier than she has been since her attack, madam. She has been resting thus for" (the doctor took out and consulted his watch) "twenty-five minutes."

"But what, then, is the nature of her illness?"

"An acute attack of her old disease, brought on apparently by some great shock."

"Is she in imminent danger?"

"Hush—sh!" said the physician, glancing toward his patient. Nellie followed that glance, and saw that Mrs. Helmstedt's eyes were open, and that she was attending to their conversation.

"Oh, Marguerite! dear Marguerite! what is this?" cried Mrs. Houston, bending over her friend and dropping tears and kisses on her deathlike brow.

"Nothing unusual, Nellie; only the 'one event' that 'happeneth to all;' only death. Though in truth, it is inconvenient to die just now, Nellie; this morning I had no reason to expect the messenger; and to say truth, I was in no respect ready."

"Marguerite! dear Marguerite! let me send for the minister," said Nellie, wringing her hands and dropping fast tears.

"No; what good can the minister do me, think you? No, Nellie; that is not what I meant. If I have lived all my days for the pride of life and the affections of the flesh, at least I will not mock God now with the offer of a heart that these idols have ground to dust. As I have lived, will I die, without adding fear and self-deception to the catalogue of my follies." Mrs. Helmstedt spoke faintly and at intervals, and now she paused longer than usual, and, gathering breath, resumed:

"But since this summons has found me unready, in other respects which may be remedied, I must use the hours left for action. Nellie, Nellie; this is no time for useless tears," she added, seeing Mrs. Houston weeping vehemently; "you must aid me. Dr. Hartley, will you grant me a few moments alone with my friend?"

"Not unless you both promise that your interview is not to be exciting or exhausting."

"We promise, doctor, that on the contrary, it shall be soothing. Margaret, my child, attend the doctor down into the parlor, and see that refreshments are placed before him."

Pale and still and self-governed, the young maiden followed the physician from the chamber. And the friends were left alone.

"Colonel Houston got a letter from my husband yesterday?" inquired Mrs. Helmstedt.

"He got it this morning, dear Marguerite."

"I received one from my husband last night; he spoke of one mailed at the same time to Colonel Houston; he consents to the betrothal of Margaret to Ralph, or rather, he refers the matter to me, which amounts to the same thing. Nellie, I have but a few hours to live; before I die I wish to place the hand of my child in that of Ralph in solemn betrothal; and, when I rest in the grave, you will take my orphan child as your daughter home, and comfort her until her father, to whom Dr. Hartley has written, arrives. Oh, Nellie, be kind to my dove!"

"Indeed I will! Oh, indeed I will, though I was disappointed for Franky! I will love her as tenderly as if she were my own. Don't doubt me. You know I have always been a good stepmother?"

"An excellent one, dear Nellie."

"And don't you know, then, how tenderly I should cherish your orphan child? I have two sons; but no daughter; I should take Margaret to my heart as a much-desired daughter," said Nellie, earnestly, and at that moment, in that mood, she sincerely meant all she said.

"Thank you, dear Nellie. Margaret will, at the age of eighteen, inherit the greater portion of my patrimony, including Plover's Point, which has been secured to her. This will make her independent. Upon the demise of her father—long and happily may he yet live—she will come into the possession of one of the largest fortunes in the South. Ralph's expectations, I know, are nearly equal; therefore, deny her no indulgence, no wish of her heart that wealth can satisfy; for Margaret is not selfish or exacting, and will make no unreasonable demands. But how I twaddle. Have the soul of kindness toward my orphan girl, and that will teach you what to do."

"Don't doubt me, Marguerite. I will swear to you if you require it," said Nellie, who believed herself to be as constant as she was fervent.

"It is enough! Is Ralph here?"

"Yes, dearest Marguerite."

"Let him be called at once."

Nellie flew to do her friend's bidding, and swiftly returned with Mr. Houston.

"Draw near, dearest Ralph; look in my face; but do not look so shocked; you read what is before me, and what I wish you to do; you have seen my husband's letter to your father; there is another, which came yesterday to me; Margaret will show it to you; go to her, dearest Ralph; she has read her father's letter, and is prepared to hear what you have to say; go to her now, for I would join your hands before sunset; do not leave her again until I leave her; and then take her with you to your parents' home to await her father's coming. And oh! Ralph! as you hope for the blessing of God at your greatest need, comfort your orphan bride, as only you can comfort her."

"As God hears me!" said Ralph Houston, reverently, dropping upon one knee, and bending his noble head over the wan hand the lady had extended to him.

"Go to her now, Ralph, for I would join your hands before sunset."

Ralph pressed the wasted fingers to his lips, arose and went out, in search of Margaret.

He found the maiden alone in her mother's favorite parlor. Dr. Hartley had gone out to send messengers for Mr. Wellworth and Colonel Houston to come immediately to the island, if they wished to see Mrs. Helmstedt once more in life. And Margaret had thrown herself down upon the sofa in solitude, to give way to the torrent of grief that she had so heroically suppressed in the sickroom of her mother.

Ralph Houston entered the sacred precincts of her filial grief as reverently as he had left the death-chamber of her mother. He closed the door softly, advanced and knelt an instant to press a pure kiss upon her tearful face; then rising, he lifted her tenderly, from the sofa, and gathered her to his bosom.

"Permit me, dearest," he said, "for henceforth your sorrows are also mine."

What farther he said is sacred between those two hearts.

The day waned—the shadows of evening gathered over the earth, and the shadows of death over the chamber.

Mr. Wellworth and Colonel Houston arrived about the same time.

The clergyman was immediately shown up into the chamber of Mrs. Helmstedt. She was sinking rapidly. He went gravely to her side, expressing sorrow for her illness, and anxiety to hear how she felt. And finding from her answers that she still retained full possession of her brilliant intellect, he drew a chair, sat down, and entered upon religious topics.

But Mrs. Helmstedt smiled mournfully, and stopped him, saying:

"Too late, good friend, too late; I would that I had had your Christian faith imprinted upon my heart while it was soft enough to receive the impression—it might have made me happier at this hour; but it is too late, and it does not matter!"

"Not matter! that you have no faith! Oh! Mrs. Helmstedt, my child, is it possible that with all your splendor of intellectual endowments you lack faith!"

Marguerite smiled more mournfully than before. "I believe in God, because I see Him in His glorious works; I believe in Christ as a wonder that once existed on this earth; but—as for a future state of rewards and punishments—as for our immortality, I tell you, despite all the gifts of intellect with which you credit me, and my extensive reading, observation and experience, at this hour I know not where in the next I shall be; or whether with the stopping of this beating brain, and the cooling of this burning heart, thought and affection will cease to exist; or if they will be transferred to another form and sphere. I know nothing."

"God have mercy on you!" prayed the good minister, who would then and there have sought to inspire the "saving faith," but that the dying woman silenced him.

"Too late, dear friend, too late; the short time left me must be given, not to selfish thoughts on my own uncertain future, but to the welfare of those I am about to leave. Will you please to ring the bell?"

The minister complied.

Mrs. Houston forestalled every servant by hastening to answer the summons.

"Dear Nellie, bring Ralph and Margaret to me, and ask your husband and the doctor to attend. And let lights be brought, Nellie; it is growing dusky here, or else my sight is failing, and I would see the face of my child plainly."

Nellie stopped an instant to press a kiss upon the clammy brow of her friend, and then hastened to do her bidding.

A few minutes after, the door opened, and Ralph Houston entered, reverently supporting the pale but self-controlled maiden on his arm, and accompanied by his father, stepmother, and the doctor.

They approached the bed, and grouped themselves around it. On the right side stood Ralph, Margaret, and Mr. Wellworth; on the left, Colonel and Mrs. Houston and Dr. Hartley.

The dying woman turned her dark eyes from one group to the other, and then spoke.

"We sent for you, Mr. Wellworth, to join the hands of this young pair— not in marriage, for which one of them is much too youthful; but in a solemn betrothal, that shall possess all the sanctity, if not the legal force of marriage. Will you do this?"

"I will do everything in my power to serve Mrs. Helmstedt or her family," said the clergyman.

"Margaret, my love, draw this ring from my finger, and hand it to Mr. Wellworth, who will give it to Ralph," said Mrs. Helmstedt, holding out her thin, transparent hand, from the fourth finger of which Margaret drew the plain gold circlet, her mother's wedding ring, and passed it to the minister, who put it in the hand of Ralph Houston. Then the dying woman turned her solemn eyes upon Mr. Houston, and in a voice thrilling with the depth and strength of a mother's deathless love, said:

"Ralph Houston, you promise here, in the awful presence of God— of the living, and of the dying—to love and respect this maiden, as your destined wife, and to wed her when she shall have attained a suitable age?"

Ralph passed his arm protectingly around the half-sinking form of Margaret, and answered, slowly and solemnly:

"In the presence of God, and of her mother, I promise to love, and honor and serve, my affianced bride, Margaret, until such time as she shall bestow her hand in full marriage on me, and thenceforth forever. So help me God and all good angels."

"Amen. Now place the ring upon her finger."

Ralph Houston obeyed; and then Mrs. Helmstedt beckoned them to draw nearer, and taking the hand of Margaret, she placed it in that of Ralph, saying, solemnly:

"Ralph Houston, I bestow upon you my heart's precious child—my dove, as you have heard me call her. Oh, be tender with her! And may God so love and bless you, as you shall love and bless the dove that is to nestle in your home."

"Amen!" in turn said Ralph.

And still holding their hands together, Mrs. Helmstedt—skeptic for herself, believer for her child—called on Mr. Wellworth to seal and bless this betrothal with prayer and benediction.

At the signal of the minister, all knelt. And while Mrs. Helmstedt still held together the hands of the young couple, Mr. Wellworth reverently lifted his voice and prayed God's blessing upon the living and the dying.

They all arose from their knees, and Mrs. Helmstedt pressed those joined hands to her lips before she released them. She was very much exhausted, and turning to the doctor, whispered, in a voice nearly extinct through faintness:

"Doctor, I must live an hour longer—one hour longer, doctor—is there no potential drug that will keep life in this frame for an hour?"

"You may live many hours, or even days—nay, you may even recover, dear lady—for while there is life there is hope. Now, you are only exhausted, and this will restore you," said the physician, pouring out a cordial, and placing it to her lips.

"Thank you; yes, this is reviving!" answered Mrs. Helmstedt, drawing one deep, free breath.

"And now you must lie still and rest."

"I will—soon. Dear friends," she continued, addressing the group around the bed, "you will please withdraw now and leave me alone with my child. Go you also, dear Ralph, and leave Margaret with me. You will have her all to yourself soon. Well, then, kiss me before you go," she added, seeing Ralph Houston hesitated. He bent down and pressed a reverential kiss upon her cold forehead, and a loving one upon her fading lips, and then arose and silently followed the others from the room.

And the mother and child were left alone.

The room seemed changed and darkened. The shadow of some "coming event" other than death hung over them.

Mrs. Helmstedt lay with her hands folded in what seemed prayer; but was only deep thought.

Margaret stood affectionately waiting her wishes.

Neither spoke for a few minutes.

Then Mrs. Helmstedt said, in a changed and solemn voice, whose sound caused Margaret's heart to thrill with strange dread:

"Come hither, my dove."

"I am here, sweet, dear mother," replied the girl, striving to repress her grief.

The lady opened her eyes.

"Come sit upon the bed beside me—sit so that I can see your face—give me your hand."

Margaret obeyed, silently praying to God to give her strength to repress the flood of tears that were ready to gush forth.

"Little Margaret, for, though you are an affianced bride, you are still my little Margaret," said the lady, closing her fingers upon the soft hand and gazing fondly into the dark, true, tender eyes of the maiden, "little Margaret, some time ago, when your loving heart led you to leave a festive scene to rejoin your lonely mother, and you surprised me prostrated with grief and dismay, you implored me to confide my sorrows to your faithful heart; and I told you that if ever I was driven to trust the terrible secret of my life to mortal man or woman, it should be to my loving, loyal child—only to her. You remember?"

"Oh, yes—yes, mamma!"

"That time has come, my dove! I have a precious trust to bequeath as a legacy to some one; it is a secret that has been the grief and bane and terror of my life; a secret that lies as yet between my soul and God; yet must I not go hence and leave no clew to its discovery.

"Little daughter—as I said once before—I love many; I worship one; I trust only you; for of all the people I have known, loved, and respected, you are the most true-hearted, I think also the wisest. Dear child, I will not bind you by any promise to keep the secret about to be entrusted to your charge, for I feel sure that for my sake you will keep it."

"Through life and unto death, mamma; the rack should not wring it from me; may God so keep my soul as I shall keep your secret, mother."

"Nay, nay, there is a contingency, my child, under which you might reveal it; and it is to provide for this possible contingency that I feel constrained to leave this secret with you."

"I will be faithful, dearest mother."

"I know it, my dove!—sit closer now and listen. But stop—first go and see if the door is closed."

"It is closed, dear mother."

"Ah, but go and lock it, my child."

Margaret complied.

"It is fast now, dear mother."

"Come then and sit upon the bed where you were before, so that I can see your sweet face; give me your dear hand again—there!—now listen."

CHAPTER IX
FALLING ASLEEP

"Oh, Mother Earth, upon thy lap

Thy weary ones receiving,

And o'er them, silent as a dream,

Thy grassy mantle weaving,

Fold softly in thy long embrace,

That heart so worn and broken,

And cool its pulse of fire beneath

Thy shadows old and oaken!"

—Whittier.

Meanwhile, the friends assembled downstairs, in Mrs. Helmstedt's parlor, waited anxiously for her summons.

Presently, the bell rang, and Nellie Houston sprang up quickly to answer it. And soon after she left, Margaret appeared, but with a face so changed, so aghast, that all who beheld it were stricken with fear and wonder. It wore no expression of grief, or terror, or anxiety—it looked as if all these emotions were impossible to it, henceforth—it looked awed and appalled, as though some tremendous revelation of sin or suffering, or both, had fallen like a thunderbolt upon that young brow, and stricken childhood from it at once and forever.

Ralph Houston, who was waiting for her appearance, sprang up to meet her, and, alarmed at her expression of countenance, hastened toward her, exclaiming:

"Margaret, Margaret! what is it?"

But, with a gesture of almost awful solemnity, she waved him away, and, silent as a visitant from the grave, passed through and left the room.

Ralph gazed after her in consternation, and then turned upon his father a look of mute inquiry.

The colonel gravely shook his head, and remained silent.

Margaret did not return.

Some hours subsequent to this, near midnight, were assembled, in the chamber of death, old Colonel and Mrs. Compton, the Houstons, Dr. Hartley and Mr. Wellworth—all the family and friends, in fact, except Margaret. She had not made her appearance since. With that look of annihilated youth, she had passed through the parlor, and gone out. All wondered at her absence from the dying bed of her idolized mother; but none expressed an opinion upon the subject.

The chamber was dimly lighted by a shaded lamp that stood upon the hearth, and, reversing the natural course of light, threw the shadows, in strange, fantastic shapes, to the ceiling. It projected the shadow of Mr. Wellworth, who stood at Mrs. Helmstedt's feet, up over the bed, until it looked like the form of some dark spirit, swooping down to snatch the soul of the dying.

Mrs. Helmstedt lay on her back, with her head quite low, and her hands wandering gently over the white quilt, as if in search of some other clasping hands—sometimes murmuring softly to herself in calm delirium, and occasionally opening her eyes and looking around cognizantly, as though recognizing all who were present, and missing one who was not.

Nellie stood at her right hand, often bending anxiously over her.

Another hour passed; and still Marguerite Helmstedt lay in a state of gentle, whispering delirium, varied with brief lucid intervals. Was it in the former or the latter of these conditions that she breathed the name of her mother, then of her father, then of Nellie?

At the sound of her own name, Mrs. Houston bent to listen to her words.

"Nellie, dearest," she murmured, very softly, "when prisoners die, their bodies are given up to their friends, are they not?"

"Yes, surely, dearest Marguerite, when they have friends to claim their bodies," answered the lady, greatly wondering at the strange direction the dying woman's delirium had now taken.

"And if they have not friends, then they are buried in the prison grounds, are they not?" continued Mrs. Helmstedt.

"Of course, I suppose so, dear Marguerite."

"But, Nellie, I have friends to claim my body, after death, have I not?"

"What do you say, dearest?" inquired Mrs. Houston, bending closer down, for the voice of the dying was nearly extinct.

"I say, Nellie, dear, when my spirit flees, it would not leave this poor, racked frame behind in the prison. Claim my body, Nellie, and bury it anywhere! anywhere! out of this prison!"

"Yes, dearest Marguerite; be content; I will do it," answered Mrs. Houston, soothingly, as she would have spoken to a maniac.

"What does she say?" asked old Mrs. Compton.

"Oh, nothing to any purpose, mother. She is wandering dreadfully in her mind," whispered the unsuspicious Nellie. As if calmed by her friend's promise, Mrs. Helmstedt lay perfectly quiet for a few moments, and then her fair, thin hand went wandering over the quilt, as if to clasp that other loving hand, and not meeting it, she opened her large, dark eyes, turning them about the dusky room, as if in search of some one; then she raised and fixed them, with a wild gaze, upon that sinister shadow that swooped over her head.

At this moment, the door was quietly opened, and Margaret entered. Her face had again changed. It now wore the look of one who had, in this short space of time, suffered, struggled and overcome—of one who had gazed steadily in the face of some appalling trial, and nerved her heart to meet it—the look, in short, of a martyr who had conquered the fear of torture and of death, and was prepared to offer up her life. But from this night, through all time, Margaret's face never resumed its youthful character of simplicity and freedom.

On coming into the room, her eyes were at once turned toward her mother, and the first object that met their glance was the large, starry eyes fixed, as if magnetized, upon the swooping shadow on the ceiling.

Margaret went at once to the fireplace and removed the lamp from the hearth to the mantelpiece, and placed an alabaster shade over it, thus reducing the spectres, and bringing the unnatural relations of shadow and substance into harmony again. Then she went softly to her mother's side and slipped her hand into that wandering hand, that now closed fondly and contentedly upon it. The clasp of her child's slender fingers seemed to recall the wandering senses of Mrs. Helmstedt. Her dark eyes softened from their fixed and fiery gaze, as she turned then on her loving child, murmuring:

"Margaret! my little Margaret!"

And presently she said: "It is time you were at rest, dear friends. Bid me good-night. Margaret will lie down here by me. And we will sleep."

No one seemed inclined to comply with this proposition, until Mrs. Helmstedt, looking annoyed, Dr. Hartley beckoned Margaret, who left her mother's side for an instant, to hear what he had to say.

"My dear child, I myself am of the opinion that we had all best retire from the room. Shall you be afraid to stay here and watch alone?"

"Oh, no, doctor, no!"

"'But not alone art thou, if One above doth guide thee on thy way.' Very well; return to your watch, my child, and be sure, upon the least sign of change, to call me quietly. I shall stay in the next room."

"Yes, doctor," said Margaret, going softly back to her place.

"Come, friends, I think we had better retire and leave this child with her mother," said the doctor.

"Bid me good-night first," said Mrs. Helmstedt, as they all prepared to withdraw.

They all drew near her bed—Mrs. Houston nearest.

"You last, Nellie, you last, dear Nellie," said Mrs. Helmstedt, as Mrs. Houston stooped to receive her kiss.

One by one they bade her good-night, and left the room. Mrs. Houston, by request, lingered longer.

"Come closer, Nellie—closer still—bend down," whispered Mrs. Helmstedt, "I have one last favor to ask of you, dear Nellie. A trifle, yet I implore it. A foolish one, perhaps; for little may reck the soul, even if it survive, where or how the cast-off body lies. But do not lay me here, Nellie! Lay me at the feet of my father and mother, under the old trees at Plover's Point. Do you promise me?"

"Yes, yes, dearest Margaret," faltered Nellie, through her gushing tears.

"Now kiss me and go to bed. Good-night."

Mrs. Houston left the room, and the mother and child were once more alone together.

"Are you sleepy, little Margaret?"

"No, dearest mamma."

"I am, and so ought you to be, my dove. Come, loosen your wrapper; lie down on the bed beside me, and I will pat your little shoulder softly, until we both fall to sleep, as we used to do long ago, Margaret," said Mrs. Helmstedt, speaking with a playfulness strange and incomprehensible to her child, who, though her heart seemed almost breaking, and though these tender words and acts weakened and unnerved her, prepared to comply. Once more she lay down by her mother's side, and felt the gentle hand upon her neck, and the cooing voice in her ear, as that dying mother sought, as heretofore, to soothe her child to sleep.

Let us draw the curtain and leave them so.

The friends, dismissed from Mrs. Helmstedt's deathbed, reassembled in the parlor. The doctor lingered there for a moment to take some little refreshment previous to resuming his watch in the spare room above.

"What do you think of her now, doctor?" inquired Mrs. Compton.

"I think, madam, that the quieter she remains the longer her life will last. She will live through the night probably—through the morrow possibly."

The night indeed was far spent. No one thought of retiring to rest. The doctor took a lamp and a book, and went softly upstairs to sit and watch in the room adjoining Mrs. Helmstedt's. And the party who were left below gathered around the little wood fire that, even at this season, the chilly nights on the bleak island rendered necessary.

Amid the distress and confusion that had reigned throughout the house since the mistress' illness, no usual household duty, save only the getting of meals and the making of beds, had been attended to. Among other neglected matters, the window shutters had remained open all night. So that the first faint dawn of morning was plainly visible through the windows.

As soon as it was daylight the sad party separated—old Mrs. Compton going about to take upon herself, for the better comfort of the family, the supervision of domestic affairs, and Nellie stealing softly on tiptoe up to the death-chamber. Nevertheless, the watchful old physician heard, and came to speak to her at his own door.

"How has she passed the night, doctor?"

"In perfect repose, as far as I can judge."

Nellie stole noiselessly into the room, softly took away the night lamp that was still burning, then gently opened a window to admit the fresh morning air, and finally went up to the bedside to gaze upon the mother and child. It was a touching picture. Both were sleeping. The shadows of death had crept more darkly still over Mrs. Helmstedt's beautiful face, but she seemed to rest quietly, with one hand laid over Margaret's shoulder, in a protecting, soothing manner. Margaret's face had the troubled look of one who had been overcome by sleep, in the midst, and despite of great sorrow. As Nellie gazed, Mrs. Helmstedt, with the sensitiveness of the dying, perceived her presence, and opened her eyes.

"How are you, dear Marguerite?" inquired Nellie.

Her lips moved, and Nellie stopped to catch the faint murmur that came from them.

"Hush—sh! don't wake her. It took so long to get her to sleep—and sleep is such a blessing."

"Sleep is such a blessing!" These were the last words of Marguerite Helmstedt. Saying them, her eyes turned with unutterable love upon the little form sleeping beside her, and her hand essayed again its soothing part, but that dying hand was too feeble, and it slipped, powerless, from its work.

Margaret, at the same moment, opened her eyes, with that distressed, perplexed expression wherewith we first awake after a great sorrow. But in an instant all was remembered. Her mother dying since yesterday! Simultaneously with this anguish of recovered memory came that strange power of self-control, with which this young creature was so greatly endowed.

"How are you, sweet mother?" she asked, calmly.

The lips of the dying woman fluttered and faintly smiled, but no audible sound issued thence. Her powers of speech had failed. Margaret grew deadly pale.

"Do not be alarmed, and do not worry her with questions. She is very much exhausted. The doctor will give her a cordial presently," said the pitying Nellie, seeking to conceal the terrible truth. But had she looked for an instant into that pale, resolute face she would not have feared any unseemly outburst of sorrow on the part of that young girl.

Nellie, assisted by Margaret, placed Mrs. Helmstedt in an easier position and arranged the bed drapery. Then, while old Mrs. Compton and Dr. Hartley paid a visit to the room, she took Margaret downstairs and constrained her to take a cup of coffee, that she might be able to attend upon her mother through the day, Nellie said. And upon this adjuration, Margaret forced herself to take some refreshment.

After that the young girl resumed her watch, and never again left her dying mother.

As yesterday passed, so passed this day, except that Mrs. Helmstedt was sinking faster. As yesterday, so to-day, she lay quietly, in a gentle, murmuring delirium, not one word of which was audible, but which flowed on in a continuous stream of inarticulate music. Her life waned with the day. Late in the afternoon, during a lucid interval, she signed her wish that all might depart from the room and leave her alone with her child.

And they went.

And as upon the night preceding, so upon this afternoon, at a sign from Mrs. Helmstedt, Margaret lay down beside her, as if consenting to take some rest. At another sign she drew her mother's powerless hand over her own shoulder. And then, with a sigh of content, Mrs. Helmstedt closed her eyes as if to sleep.

The day was dying. The sun was sinking low on the horizon. In the parlor below the friends of the family were watching its slow but sure descent, and mentally comparing it with the steady decline of life in one above, and mournfully wondering whether she could live to see another sunrise.

In the recess of the beloved bay window Mrs. Helmstedt's forsaken harp still stood in mournful splendor. The level beams of the setting sun, now shining through this window, touched the harp, drawing from its burnished frame responsive rays, "in lines of golden light." A moment thus stood the harp in a blaze of quivering glory, and then, as a sheaf that is gathered up, the rays were all withdrawn, and the sun sunk below the horizon. Simultaneously, as if some awful hand had swept its strings, each chord of that harp in swift succession snapped, in a long, wild, wailing diapason of melody, that died in silence with the dying sun, as though all music, light and life went out together, forever. All arose to their feet and looked into each other's faces, in awe-stricken silence. And the same instant a sudden, prolonged, despairing shriek rang through the house.

"It is Margaret! Something has happened!" exclaimed Ralph Houston, breaking the spell.

All immediately hurried upstairs with prophetic intimations of what had occurred.

They were right.

Marguerite Helmstedt was dead, and her daughter was distracted!

With matchless heroism Margaret had maintained her self-control until now; but the grief restrained for her idolized mother's sake now broke all bounds—and raged, a wild, wild storm of sorrow. Who shall dare to approach her with words of comfort? Who, indeed, can console her? Not one of you, well-meaning friends; for you never sounded the depths of woe like hers. Not you, young lover; for in the passionate idolatry of her grief, she feels that to listen to your voice, beloved as it is, would, at this hour, be sacrilege to the presence of the dead. Not even you, holy, eloquent minister of God. Seek not to soothe her sorrow, any one of you. It were vain, and worse than vain. It was a mockery. Can you breathe the breath of life again into the cold bosom of the dead mother that lies in yonder chamber? Can you cause that stilled heart to beat? those closed eyes to open? those silent lips to speak and murmur softly, "My little Margaret, my dove?" In a word, can you raise the dead to life? If not, then go, and trouble her not with your commonplaces. Before the image of an only child, just orphaned of her mother, that merely human comforter who best comprehends her sorrow would stand the most confounded—dumb. Leave her to God. Only He who wounds can heal.

That afternoon, late as it was, Dr. Hartley set off for his home, to commence preparations for the burial; as, in accordance with Mrs. Helmstedt's directions, she was to be laid beside her father and mother, in her ancestral resting-ground at Plover's Point.

It was long before Margaret could be forced to leave her mother's chamber, and then no one knew what to do with a child so lost in woe, until, at last, her old nurse, Hildreth, without venturing a single word of consolation, just lifted and bore her away from them all—bore her up to an old quiet attic, a sort of "chamber of desolation," where she sat down and held her—still never breathing a word—only making of her own embracing arms a physical support for the fainting form, and her affectionate bosom a pillow for the weeping head. And so she held her for hours while she moaned and wept.

"Oh, mother, come back to me! I cannot bear it—I cannot! Oh, God, have mercy! Send her back to me! Thou canst do all things, dear God—send her back!" And sometimes: "Oh, mother! do you hear me? are you near me? where are you? Oh, take me with you! take me with you! I am your child, your heart's child! I cannot live without you, I cannot! Oh, my mother, call me after you—call me, mother! Don't you hear me—don't you hear your child? Oh, mother, can't you answer me—can't you answer your child? Oh, no—you cannot—you cannot! and I am growing crazy!" And other wild words like these; to all of which old Hildreth listened without making any expostulation, uttering any rebuke, or offering any vain words of comfort. At last, when exhausted nature succumbed to a deep and trance-like sleep, old Hildreth carried her down and tenderly undressed and put her to bed, and sat watching hours while she slept.

The next morning, when Margaret opened her eyes, her grief awoke afresh. She wished to fly immediately to the side of her mother. But this was strictly forbidden. At last, partly because she had already shed such floods of tears, and partly because she made almost superhuman efforts to control herself, she restrained the outward expression of her grief, and went to Mrs. Houston and said:

"Let me see my mother. If you do not, I shall die. But if you do, I will be very quiet, I will not make a moan, nor shed a tear, nor utter a single complaint. Consider—when the coffin is once closed I shall never—never see her face or hold her hand again! Even now I can never more hear her voice or meet her eyes; but I can look upon her face, and hold her hands, and kiss her; but in a little while I cannot even do that. Consider then how precious, how priceless is every moment of a time so short; and let me go."

Margaret spoke with so much self-control and forced calmness that her words and manner were strangely formal. And Mrs. Houston, deceived by them, consented to her wish.

And Margaret went down to the favorite parlor, where Mrs. Helmstedt was laid out. The shutters were all closed to darken the room; but the windows were up to ventilate it; and the breeze blowing through the Venetian blinds of the bay window played upon the broken harp, making a fitful moaning in strange harmony with the scene. Margaret reverently lifted the covering from the face of the dead, and pressed kiss after kiss upon the cold brow and lips. And then she took her seat by the side of her dead mother, and never left her again for a moment while she lay in that room.

The third day from that, being Saturday, the funeral took place. As it was to be a boat funeral, all the neighbors of the adjacent shores and islands sent or brought their boats. A large company assembled at the house. The religious services were performed in the parlor where the body had been first laid out.

After which the procession formed and moved down to the beach, where about fifty boats were moored. Not a single sail among them—all were large or small rowboats. The oars were all muffled, and the oarsmen wore badges of mourning on their sleeves.

The island boat, the *Nereide*, had had her sails and masts all taken away, and had been painted white, and furnished with a canopy of black velvet raised on four poles. The twelve oarsmen seated in it were clothed in deep mourning. Into this boat the coffin was reverently lowered. This was the signal for the embarkation of every one else. In twenty minutes every boat was ready to fall into the procession that was beginning to form. The boat containing the Rev. Mr. Wellworth and Dr. Hartley led the van. Then followed the *Nereide*, with its sacred freight. Behind that came *The Pearl Shell*, containing the orphaned girl, Mrs. Houston and Ralph.

After them came a skiff bearing Colonel and Mrs. Compton and Colonel Houston. Other boats, occupied by friends and acquaintances, and others still, filled with old family servants, followed in slow succession to the number of fifty boats or more.

Slowly and silently the long procession moved across the waters. It formed a spectacle solemn and impressive, as it was strange and picturesque.

The sun was near its setting when this funeral train reached Plover's Point, an abrupt headland crowned with ancient forest trees, that nearly hid from sight the old graystone dwelling-house. On the west side of this bluff, under the shadows of great elms and oaks of a hundred years' growth, the family resting place lay. Here the boats landed. The coffin was reverently lifted out. The foot procession formed and walked slowly up the hill. And just as the latest rays of the setting sun were flecking all the green foliage with gold, they gathered around her last bed, that had been opened under the shade of a mighty oak. There they lay her down to rest—

> "There, where with living ear and eye
> She heard Potomac's flowing,
> And through her tall, ancestral trees
> Saw Autumn's sunset glowing,
> She sleeps, still looking to the West,
> Beneath the dark wood shadow,
> As if she still would see the sun
> Sink down on wave and meadow."

CHAPTER X
THE ORPHAN BRIDE

"Come, Margaret, come, my child, it is time to go home," said Mrs. Houston, gently trying to raise the orphan from her kneeling posture by the grave—"come, dear Margaret."

"Oh, I cannot! Oh, I cannot! Not yet! Not so soon!"

"My love, the boat is waiting and the rest of our friends are gone."

"Oh, I cannot go so soon! I cannot hurry away and leave her here alone."

"But, Margaret, it is late, and we have far to go."

"Go then, dear Mrs. Houston, and leave me here with her. I cannot forsake her so soon. Dr. Hartley will let me stay at his house a few days to be near her, I know."

"As long as you like, my dearest child! as if it were your own house—as it is—and as if you were my own child," said the kind-hearted physician, laying his hand as in benediction upon the bowed head of the kneeling girl.

"But, my child, think of Ralph! You have not spoken of him since—since your hands were united. Consider now a little the feeling of Ralph, who loves you so entirely," whispered Mrs. Houston, stooping and caressing her, and thinking that all good purposes must be served in drawing the orphan girl from the last sleeping place of her mother.

"Oh, I cannot! I cannot! I cannot think of any living! I can think only of her! of her! my mother! Oh, my mother!"

"What! not think of Ralph, who loves you so devotedly?"

"Not now! Oh, I cannot now! I should be most unworthy of any love if I could turn from her grave, so soon, to meet it! Mr. Houston knows that," she passionately cried.

"I do, my Margaret! I feel and understand it all. I would not seek to draw you from this place; but I would remain and mourn with you," said

Ralph Houston, in a low and reverential tone, but not so low that the good doctor did not overhear it, for he hastened to urge:

"Remain with her, then, Mr. Houston! there is no reason why you should not, and every reason why you should."

And so said Mrs. Houston, and so said all friends.

"But what says my Margaret?" inquired Ralph Houston, stooping and speaking gently.

"No, Mr. Houston, do not stay, please; leave me here alone with her—let her have me all to herself, for a little while," whispered Margaret. And Ralph arose up, thanked Dr. Hartley, and declined his hospitality.

"Good-by, then, dear Margaret! I shall come to you in a day or two."

"Good-by, Mrs. Houston."

"But you must not call me Mrs. Houston now, my child. You must call me mother. I have no other daughter, and you have no other mother now. Besides, you are my daughter-in-law, you know. So you must call me mother. Say—will you not?"

"Oh, I cannot! I cannot, Mrs. Houston! You are my mother's friend, and I love you very dearly; but I cannot give you her dear title. I had but one mother in this world—in all eternity we can have but one; to call another person so, however near and dear, would be vain and false; excuse me, Mrs. Houston," said the girl, gravely.

"As you please then, dear. You will get over these morbid feelings. Good-night, God bless you," said Mrs. Houston, stooping and pressing a kiss upon the brow of her adopted daughter.

When every one else was gone, the old doctor lingered near Margaret.

"Will you come now, my child?" he asked, gently.

"Presently, dear doctor. Please go and leave me here a little while alone with her."

"If I do, will you come in before the dew begins to fall?"

"Yes, indeed I will."

The doctor walked away through the woods in the direction of the house. Let us also leave the orphan to her sacred grief, nor inquire whether she spent the next hour in weeping or in prayer. The doctor kept on to the house and told his daughter Clare to prepare the best bedchamber for the accommodation of her friend Margaret.

And before the dew fell, true to her promise, Margaret came in.

Clare took charge of her. If ever there existed a perfectly sound mind in a perfectly sound body, that body and mind was Clare Hartley's. She was "a queen of noble nature's crowning." She was a fine, tall, well-developed girl, with a fresh and ruddy complexion, hair as black as the black eagle's crest, and eyes as bright and strong as his glance when sailing toward the sun; with a cheerful smile, and a pleasant, elastic voice. She took charge of Margaret, and in her wise, strong, loving way, ministered to all her needs— knowing when to speak to her, and better still, when to be silent—when to wait upon her, and best of all, when to leave her alone. And Margaret was by her own desire very much left alone.

Every morning she stole from the house, and went down through the woods to sit beside her mother's grave. For the first few days, the hours passed there were spent in inconsolable grief. Then after a week she would sit there quietly, tearlessly, in pensive thought.

In the second week of her stay, Mrs. Houston came and brought her clothing from the island, and with it a large packet of linen cut out and partly sewed. This was a set of shirts that Margaret and her mother had been making up for her father the very day that Mrs. Helmstedt had been struck with her death sickness.

"I thought that if she could be interested in any of her former occupations, her spirits might sooner rally," said Mrs. Houston to Clare. And afterward, in delivering the parcel to Margaret, she said:

"You know, your father will be home soon, my dear, and will want these to take back to camp with him. Will you not try to finish them all in time?"

"Oh, yes! give them to me! how could I forget them. She was so anxious they should be done," said Margaret, with an eagerness strangely at variance with her earnest, mournful countenance.

In unrolling the packet, she came upon the shirt-ruffles that she knew her mother had been hemming. There were the very last stitches she had set. There was the delicate needle just where she had stuck it when she left her sewing to go out into the garden that fatal morning. Margaret burst into tears and wept as if her heart would break, until she became exhausted. Then she reverently rolled up that relic, saying:

"I cannot finish this ruffle. I would not draw out the needle her fingers put there, for the world. I will keep this unchanged in remembrance of her."

"And when will you be willing to come home?" said Mrs. Houston.

"After my father comes and goes. I would rather stay here near her to meet him."

"And, when he goes, will you come?"

"Yes."

After dinner Mrs. Houston left Plover's Point.

Margaret remained, and, each morning after breakfast, took her little workbasket and walked through the woods down beside the grave, and sat sewing there all day.

One day while she sat thus a gentle footstep approached, a soft hand was laid upon her shoulder and a loving voice murmured her name.

Margaret looked up to see the mild old minister, Mr. Wellworth, standing near her.

"My child," he said, "why do you sit here day after day to give way to grief?"

"Oh, Mr. Wellworth, I do not sit here to give way to grief. I only sit here to be near her," pleaded Margaret.

"But, my child, do you know that you grieve as one without hope and without God in the world?"

Margaret did not answer; she had never in her life received any religious instruction, and scarcely understood the bearing of the minister's words.

"Shall I tell you, Margaret, of Him who came down from heaven to light up the darkness of the grave?"

Margaret raised her eyes in a mute, appealing glance to his face.

"Shall I speak of Him, Margaret? Of Him, of whom, when his friends had seen him dead and buried out of their sight, the angel of the sepulchre said, 'He is not here, but risen?'"

Still that uplifted, appealing gaze.

"Of Him, Margaret, who said, 'I am the resurrection and the life?'"

"Oh, yes! yes! tell me of Him! tell me something to relieve this dreadful sense of loss and death that is pressing all the life out of my heart," said Margaret, earnestly.

The old man took the seat beside her, held her hand in his own, and for the first time opened to her vision the spiritual views of life, death and immortality—of man, Christ and God.

Sorrow softens and never sears the heart of childhood and youth. Sorrow had made very tender and impressible the heart of the orphan; its soil was in a good state for the reception of the good seed.

To hear of God the Father, of Christ the Saviour, of the Holy Ghost the Comforter—was to her thirsting and fainting spirit the very water of life.

She followed where her pastor led—she sought the Saviour and found Him not far off. Here Margaret received her first deep religious impressions—impressions that not all the stormy waves that dashed over her after-life were able to efface. In religion she found her greatest, her sweetest, her only all-sufficient comfort. So it was in following the strong attractions of her spirit that Margaret gradually advanced until she became a fervent Christian.

It was on Monday of the third week of Margaret's visit that, just at sunset, Mr. Helmstedt arrived at Plover's Point. And, reader, if you had been, however justly, angry with Philip Helmstedt, you must still have forgiven him that day, before the woe that was stamped upon his brow.

His innocent daughter's tempestuous sobs and tears had been healthful and refreshing compared to the silent, dry, acrid, burning and consuming grief that preyed upon the heart and conscience of this stricken and remorseful man. Scarcely waiting to return the greeting of the doctor and his family, Mr. Helmstedt, in a deep, husky voice, whispered to his daughter:

"Come, Margaret, show me where they have laid her."

She arose and went before, he following, through the deep woods, down beside the grassy grave.

"Here is her resting place, my father."

"Go and leave me here, my girl."

"But, my father——"

"Obey me, Margaret."

She reluctantly withdrew, and left the proud mourner, who could not brook that even his child should look upon his bitter, sombre, remorseful grief.

"I have killed her, I have killed her!" he groaned in the spirit. "I have killed her as surely as if my dirk's point had reached her breast! I crushed that strong, high heart under the iron heel of my pride! I have killed her! I have killed her! I have killed her in her glorious prime, ere yet one silver thread had mingled with her ebon locks! And I! What am I now? Ah, pride! Ah, devil pride! do you laugh now to see to what you have driven me? Do you laugh to see that I have done to death the noblest creature that ever stepped upon this earth? Yes, laugh, pride! laugh Satan! for that is your other name."

Oh! terrible is grief when it is mixed with remorse, and more terrible are both when without hope—without God! They become despair—they may become—madness!

It was late that evening when Mr. Helmstedt rejoined the family in the drawing-room of Plover's Point. And his sombre, reserved manner repelled those kind friends who would otherwise have sought means to console him.

The next day Mrs. Houston came to make another effort to recover her adopted daughter.

Mr. Helmstedt met the bosom friend of his late wife with deep yet well-controlled emotion.

He begged for a private interview, and, in the conversation that ensued, apologized for the necessity, and questioned her closely as to the details of his wife's last illness.

Mrs. Houston told him that Marguerite's health had steadily declined, and that the proximate cause of her death was a trifle—the intrusion of a fugitive British soldier whom she had relieved and dismissed; but whose strange or rude behavior was supposed to have alarmed her and accelerated and aggravated an attack of the heart to which she had of late grown subject, and which, in this instance, proved fatal.

"An attack of the heart—yes, yes—that which is the most strained the soonest breaks," said Philip Helmstedt to himself, with a pang of remorse.

Again and again begging pardon for his persistence, he inquired concerning the last scenes of her life, hoping to hear some last charge or message from her to himself. There was none, or, at least, none trusted to

Mrs. Houston's delivery. Ah! Philip Helmstedt, could you imagine that the last words of your dying wife to her absent husband could be confided to any messenger less sacred than her child and yours, when she was at hand to take charge of it?

The same morning, when Mr. Helmstedt walked through the woods down to the grave, he found his daughter Margaret sitting sewing by the grassy mound. She arose as her father approached, and stood waiting to retire at his bidding.

"No, no, my child! you need not go now. Sit down here by me." And Philip Helmstedt took his seat and motioned Margaret to place herself by his side.

"Now tell me about your mother, Margaret," he said.

The poor girl controlled her feelings and obeyed—related how, for months past, her mother's life had steadily waned, how at shorter and still shorter intervals those dreadful heart spasms had occurred—how—though the narrator did not then know why—she had put her house in order—how anxiously, feverishly she had looked and longed for his return, until that fatal day when a sudden attack of the heart had terminated her existence.

"But her last hours! her last hours, Margaret?"

"They were tranquil, my father. I spent the last night alone with her— she talked to me of you. She bade me give you these farewell kisses from her. She bade me tell you that her last love and thoughts were all yours— and to beg you, with my arms around your neck and my head on your bosom, to comfort yourself by loving her little, bereaved daughter," said the child, scarcely able to refrain from sobbing.

"And I will, my Margaret! I will be faithful to the charge," replied the proud man, more nearly humbled than he had ever before been in his life.

"I passed the last two hours of her life alone with her. She died with her head on my bosom, her hand over my shoulder. Her last sigh—I seem to feel it now—was breathed on my forehead and through my hair."

"Oh, Heaven! But yourself, my Margaret. What were her directions in regard to your future?"

"She had received your letter, dear father, intrusting her with the sole disposal of your daughter's hand. And being so near dissolution, she sent for Mr. Houston and joined our hands in betrothal at her deathbed. Then she wished that after she had departed her orphan girl should go home with Mr. Houston to wait your will and disposition, my father."

Mr. Helmstedt turned and looked upon his youthful daughter. He had scarcely looked at her since his return. Although he had met her with affection and kissed her with tenderness, so absorbed had he been in his bitter, remorseful grief, that he scarcely fixed his eyes upon her, or noticed that in his two years' absence she had grown from childhood into womanhood. But now, when without hesitating bashfulness, when with serious self-possession, she spoke of her betrothal, he turned and gazed upon her.

She was looking so grave and womanly in her deep mourning robe, her plainly banded hair and her thoughtful, earnest, fervent countenance, whence youthful lightness seemed banished forever. There was a profounder depth of thought and feeling under that young face than her great sorrow alone could have produced—as though strange suffering and severe reflection, searching trial, and terrible struggle, and the knowledge, experience and wisdom that they bring, had prematurely come upon that young soul.

Her father contemplated her countenance with an increasing wonder and interest. His voice, in addressing her, unconsciously assumed a tone of respect; and when in rising to leave the spot he offered her his arm, the deferential courtesy of the gentleman blended in his manner with the tender affection of the father. And afterward, in the presence of others, he always called her, or spoke of her, as Miss Helmstedt, an example which all others were, of course, expected to follow.

The next day Mr. Helmstedt departed for the island. Margaret was anxious to accompany her father thither, but he declined her offer, expressing his desire and necessity to be alone. He went to the island, to the scene of his high-spirited, broken-hearted wife's long, half-voluntary, half-enforced confinement; he went to indulge in solitude his bitter, remorseful grief.

He remained there a fortnight, inhabiting the vacant rooms, wandering about amid the deserted scenes, once so full, so insinct, so alive with Marguerite De Lancie's bright, animating and inspiring presence—now only haunted by her memory. He seemed to derive a strange, morose satisfaction in thus torturing his own conscience-stricken soul.

Once, from Marguerite's favorite parlor, were heard the sounds of deep, convulsive weeping and sobbing; and old Hapzibah, who was the listener upon this occasion, fearing discovery, hurried away in no less astonishment than consternation. And this was the only instance in the whole course of his existence upon which Mr. Helmstedt was ever suspected of such unbending.

At the end of a fortnight, having appointed an overseer to take charge of the island plantation, Mr. Helmstedt returned to Plover's Point.

This was on a Saturday.

The next day, Sunday, his young daughter Margaret formally united with the Protestant Episcopal Church, over which Mr. Wellworth had charge, and received her first communion from his venerable hands.

And on Monday morning Mr. Helmstedt conveyed his daughter to Buzzard's Bluff, where he placed her in charge of her prospective mother-in-law. The same day, calling Margaret into an unoccupied parlor, he said to her:

"My dear, since you are to remain here under the guardianship of your future relatives, and as you are, though so youthful, a girl of unusual discretion, and an affianced bride, I wish to place your maintenance here upon the most liberal and independent footing. I have set apart the rents of Plover's Point, which is, indeed, your own property, to your support. The rents of the house, farm and fisheries amount, in all, to twelve hundred dollars a year. Enough for your incidental expenses, Margaret?"

"Oh, amply, amply, my dear father."

"I have requested Dr. Hartley to pay this over to you quarterly. In addition to this, you will certainly need a maid of your own, my dear; and it will also be more convenient for you to have a messenger of your own, for there will be times when you may wish to send a letter to the post office, or a note to some of your young friends, or even an errand to the village shops, when you may not like to call upon the servants of the family. I have, therefore, consulted Mrs. Houston, and with her concurrence have directed Hildreth and Forrest to come over and remain here in your service."

"Are they willing to come, dear father?"

"What has that to do with it, my dear? But since you ask, I will inform you they are very anxious to be near you."

"I thank you earnestly, my dear father."

"Forrest will bring over your riding horse and your own little sailboat."

"I thank you, sir."

"And here, Margaret, it will be two months before the first quarter's rent is due on Plover's Point, and you may need funds. Take this, my dear." And he placed in her hand a pocketbook containing a check for five hundred dollars, and also several bank notes of smaller value. Margaret, who did not as yet know what the book contained, received it in the same meek, thankful spirit.

"And now let us rejoin Mrs. Houston and Ralph, who thinks it unkind that I should thus, on the last day of our stay, keep his promised bride away from him."

The next morning Mr. Helmstedt and Ralph Houston took leave of their friends and departed together for the Northern seat of war.

Margaret bore her trials with a fortitude and resignation wonderful when found in one so young. The recent and sudden decease of her idolized mother, the departure of her father and her lover to meet the toils, privations, and dangers of a desperate war, and above all, the undivided responsibility of a dread secret—a fatal secret, weighing upon her bosom—were enough, combined, to crush the spirit of any human being less firm, patient, and courageous than this young creature; and even such as she was, the burden oppressed, overshadowed, and subdued her soul to a seriousness almost falling to gloom.

Mrs. Houston, to do that superficial little lady justice, applied herself with more earnestness than any one would have given her credit for possessing, to the delicate and difficult task of consoling the orphan. And her advantages for doing this were excellent.

Buzzard's Bluff was a fine, pleasant, cheerful residence. It was, in fact, a high, grassy, rolling hill, rising gradually from the water's edge, and, far behind, crowned with the dense primitive forest.

Upon the brow of this green hill, against the background of the green forest, stood the white dwelling-house, fronting the water. It was a large brick edifice covered with white stucco, relieved by many green Venetian window-blinds, and presenting a very gay and bright aspect. Its style of architecture was very simple, being that in which ninety-nine out of a hundred of the better sort of country houses in that neighborhood were then built. The mansion consisted of a square central edifice, of two stories, with a wide hall running through the middle of each story from front to back, and having four spacious rooms on each floor. This main edifice was continued by a long back building.

And it was flanked on the right by a tasteful wing, having a peaked roof with a gable-end front, one large, double window below, and a fanlight above. There were also side windows and a side door opening into a flower garden. The whole wing, walls, windows, and roof, was completely covered with creeping vines, cape jessamine, clematis, honeysuckles, running roses, etc., that gave portions of the mansion the appearance of a beautiful summer house. This contained two large rooms, divided by a short passage, and had been given up entirely to the use of Ralph. The front room, with the large seaward window, he had occupied as a private sitting, reading, writing and lounging parlor; the back room was his sleeping chamber. A staircase in the short dividing passage led up into the room in the roof, lighted by two opposite gable fanlights, where he stowed his guns, game-bags, fishing tackle, etc.

Now, during the month that Margaret had passed at the Point, Ralph had gradually removed his personal effects from this wing, had caused both parlor and chamber to be newly papered, painted, and furnished, and then expressed his wish that upon his departure for the Northern frontier the whole wing, as the most separated, beautiful and desirable portion of the establishment, might be given up to the exclusive use of his affianced bride.

Mrs. Houston consented, with the proviso that he should not vacate the rooms until the hour of his departure for camp.

Accordingly, the first evening of Margaret's arrival she had been accommodated with a pleasant chamber on the second-floor front of the main building.

But on Tuesday morning, after Mr. Helmstedt and Ralph Houston had departed, Mrs. Houston and her maids went busily to work and refreshed the two pretty rooms of the wing, hanging white lace curtains to the windows, white lace valances to the toilet table and tester, etc., and transfiguring the neatly-kept bachelor's apartments into a lady's charming little boudoir and bedchamber.

When all was arranged, even to the fresh flowers in the white vases upon the front room mantelpiece, and the choice books from Mrs. Houston's own private library upon the center table, the busy little lady, in her eagerness to surprise and please, hurried away to seek Margaret and introduce her to her delightful apartments. She tripped swiftly and softly up the stairs, and into the room, where she surprised Margaret, quite absorbed in some work at her writing-desk.

"Oh, you are busy! Whom are you writing to, my dear?" she inquired eagerly, hastening to the side of the girl and looking over her shoulder.

She meant nothing, or next to nothing—it was her heedless, impulsive way. She was in a hurry, and did not stop to remember that the question was rude, even when Margaret, with a sudden blush, reversed her sheet of paper, and, keeping her hand pressed down upon it, arose in agitation.

"Why, how startled you are, my dear! How nervous you must be! I ought not to have come upon you so suddenly. But to whom are you writing, my dear?"

"To—a—correspondent, Mrs. Houston."

"Why, just look there now! See what a good hand I am at guessing, for I even judged as much! But who is your correspondent then, my dear?"

"A—friend! Mrs. Houston."

"Good, again! I had imagined so, since you have no enemies, my child. But who then is this friend, you little rustic? You have not even acquaintances to write letters to, much less friends, unless it is Franky! Ah, by the way, don't write to Franky, Margaret! He could not bear it now."

Margaret made no comment, and Mrs. Houston, growing uneasy upon the subject of Franky, said:

"I hope you are not writing to Franky, Margaret!"

"No, Mrs. Houston, I am not."

"If not to Franky, to whom then? It cannot be to your father or Ralph, for they have just left you. Come! this is getting interesting! Who is your correspondent, little one? Your old duenna insists upon knowing."

Margaret turned pale, but remained silent.

"Dear me, how mysterious you are! My curiosity is growing irresistible! Who is it?"

Margaret suddenly burst into tears.

This brought the heedless little lady to her senses. She hastened to soothe and apologize.

"Why, Margaret, my dear child! Why, Margaret! Dear me, how sorry I am! I am very sorry, Margaret! What a thoughtless chatterbox I am of my age! But then I was only teazing you to rouse you a little, my dear! I did not mean to hurt you! And then I had such a pleasant surprise for you. Forgive me."

Margaret slipped her left hand into Mrs. Houston's (her right was still pressed upon the letter), and said:

"Forgive me. It is I who am nervous and irritable and require sufferance. You are very, very kind to me in all things, and I feel it."

The little lady stooped and kissed her, saying:

"Such words are absurd between you and me, Maggie. Come, I will leave you now to finish your letter, and return to you by and by."

And then she left the room, thinking within herself: "The sensitive little creature! Who would have thought my heedless words would have distressed her so? I did not care about knowing to whom the letter was written, I am sure. But, by the way, to whom could she have been writing? And, now I reflect, it was very strange that she should have been so exceedingly distressed by my questionings! It never occurred to me before, but it really was rather mysterious! I must try to find out what it all means! I ought to do so! I am her guardian, her mother-in-law. I am responsible for her to her father and to her betrothed husband."

Meanwhile Margaret Helmstedt had started up, closed the door and turned the key, and clasping her pale face between her hands, began pacing the floor and exclaiming at intervals:

"Oh, Heaven of heavens, how nearly all had been lost! Oh, I am unfit, I am unfit for this dreadful trust! To think I should have set down to write to him, and left the door unfastened! Farewell to liberty and frankness! I am given over to bonds, to vigilance and secretiveness forever! Oh, mother! my mother! I will be true to you! Oh, our Father who art in heaven, help me to be firm and wise and true!"

She came back at last, and sat down to her writing-desk, and finished her letter. Then opening her pocketbook, she took out the check for five hundred dollars, drawn by her father, in her favor, on a Baltimore bank, inclosed it in the letter, sealed and directed it, and placed it in the sanctity of her bosom.

Then folding her arms upon her writing-desk, she dropped her head upon them, and in that attitude of dejection remained until the ringing of the supper bell aroused her.

Colonel Houston, who was waiting for her in the hall, received her with his old-school courtesy, drew her hand within his arm and led her out upon the lawn, where, under the shade of a gigantic chestnut tree, the tea table was set—its snowy drapery and glistening service making a pleasant contrast to the vivid green verdure of the lawn upon which it stood. Old Colonel and Mrs. Compton and Nellie formed a pleasing group around the table. Colonel Houston handed Margaret to her place, and took his own seat.

"My dear, I am going to send Lemuel to Heathville to-morrow, and if you like to leave your letter with me, I will give it to him to put in the post office," said Mrs. Houston.

"I thank you, Mrs. Houston," said Margaret.

"Ah! that is what kept you in your room all the afternoon, my dear. You were writing a letter; whom were you writing to, my child?" said old Mrs. Compton.

"Pray excuse me," said Margaret, embarrassed.

This answer surprised the family group, who had, however, the tact to withdraw their attention and change the subject.

After tea, an hour or two was spent upon the pleasant lawn, strolling through the groves, or down to the silvery beach, and watching the monotonous motion of the sea, the occasional leap and plunge of the fish, the solitary flight of a laggard water fowl, and perhaps the distant appearance of a sail.

At last, when the full moon was high in the heavens, the family returned to the house.

Mrs. Houston took Margaret's arm, and saying:

"I have a little surprise for you, my love," led her into the pretty wing appropriated to her.

The rooms were illumined by a shaded alabaster lamp that diffused a sort of tender moonlight tone over the bright carpet and chairs and sofa covers, and the marble-topped tables, and white lace window curtains of the boudoir, and fell softly upon the pure white draperies of the sleeping-room beyond.

Hildreth, in her neat, sober gown of gray stuff, and her apron, neckhandkerchief and turban of white linen, stood in attendance.

Margaret had not seen her faithful nurse for a month—that is, not since her mother's decease—and now she sprang to greet her, scarcely able to refrain from bursting into tears.

Mrs. Houston interfered.

"Now, my dear Margaret, here are your apartments—a sweet little boudoir and chamber, I flatter myself, as can be found in Maryland—connected with the house, yet entirely separate and private. And here are your servants; Hildreth will occupy the room in the roof above, and Forrest has a quarter in the grove there, within easy sound of your bell. Your boat is secure in the boathouse below, and your horse is in the best stall in the stable."

"I thank you, dear Mrs. Houston."

"I understand, also, that your father has assigned you a very liberal income. Consequently, my dear, you are in all things as independent as a little queen in her palace. Consider also, dear Margaret, that it is a great accession of happiness to us all to have you here, and we should wish to have as much of your company as possible. Therefore, when you are inclined to society, come among us; at all other times, you can retire to this, your castle. And at all times and seasons our house and servants are at your orders, Margaret; for you know that as the bride of our eldest son and heir, you are in some sort our Princess of Wales," she concluded, playfully.

"I thank you, dear Mrs. Houston," again said the young girl. Her thoughts were too gravely preoccupied to give much attention to the prattle of the lady.

"And by the way, Margaret, where is your letter, my dear? I shall dispatch Lemuel early in the morning."

"You are very considerate, Mrs. Houston, but I do not purpose to send it by Lemuel."

"As you please, my dear. Good-night," she said, kissing the maiden with sincere affection, notwithstanding that, as she left the room, her baffled curiosity induced her to murmur:

"There is some ill mystery, that I am constrained to discover, connected with that letter."

Miss Helmstedt, left to herself, directed Hildreth to secure the doors communicating with the main building, and then go and call Forrest to her presence.

"I shall not tax you much, Forrest," she said, "though to-night I have to require rather an arduous service of you."

"Nothing is hard that I do for you, Miss Margaret," replied Forrest.

"Listen then—to-night, after you are sure that all the family are retired, and there is no possibility of your being observed, take my horse from the stable, and ride, as for your life, to Belleview, and put this carefully in the post office," she said, drawing the letter from her bosom and placing it in the hand of Forrest.

The old man looked at her wistfully, uneasily, drew a deep sigh, bowed reverently, put the letter in his pocket, and, at a sign from his mistress, left the room.

But that night at eleven o'clock, Nellie, watching from her window, saw Miss Helmstedt's messenger ride away over the hills through the moonlight.

CHAPTER XI
THE MYSTERIOUS CORRESPONDENT

"You, sir! I want to see you! Come hither!" said Mrs. Houston, as she stood upon the back piazza, early the next morning, and beckoned Forrest to her presence.

The old man bowed in his deferential manner, advanced and stood hat in hand before the little lady.

"Where did you go last night after we had all retired?"

Forrest bowed again, humbly and deprecatingly, but remained silent.

"Did you hear me speak to you?" inquired Mrs. Houston, impatiently.

The old man bowed once more very meekly, and answered:

"I went after no harm, mistress."

"Nor after any good, I'll venture to say!—but that is not the point, sir. I ask you where you went! and I intend to have an answer."

"I begs your pardon sincere, mistress, but mus' 'cline for to 'form you."

"You old villain! Do you dare to defy me here on my own premises? I'll see about this!" exclaimed the lady, in a voice more shrill than ladylike, as with a flushed face and excited air she turned into the house to summon Colonel Houston.

But she was intercepted by Margaret, who had heard the voice, and now came from her own apartment and stood before her.

"Stay, Mrs. Houston, I sent Forrest away on an errand, last night, and if he declined to inform you whither he went, it was from no disrespect to you; but from fidelity to me. I had enjoined him not to speak to any one of his errand," she said, in a voice and manner so respectful as to take away everything offensive from her words.

"You did! Now then where did you send him, Margaret? I am your guardian, and I have a right to know."

"You must forgive me, Mrs. Houston, if I decline to inform you," replied the maiden, firmly, though still very respectfully.

"I know, however. It was to mail that letter."

"You must draw your own conclusions, dear madam."

"I know it was to mail that letter! And I will put on my bonnet and drive over to the post office, and demand of the postmaster to whom the letter mailed last night by the negro Forrest was directed! There's not so many letters go to that little office but what he will be able to recollect!" exclaimed Mrs. Houston, angrily.

"Oh, God!"

The words breathed forth possessed so much of prayerful woe that the little lady half started, and turned back to see Margaret grow pale and sink upon the corner of the hall settee.

Mrs. Houston hesitated between her curiosity and anger on the one hand, and her pity on the other. Finally she made a compromise. Coming to Margaret's side, she said:

"Maggie, I am treated abominably, standing as I do in your mother's place toward you, and being as I am your guardian—abominably! Now I am sure I do not wish to pry into your correspondence, unless it is an improper one."

"Mrs. Houston, my mother's daughter could not have an improper correspondence, as you should be the first to feel assured."

"Yet, Margaret, as it appears to me, if this correspondence were proper, you would not be so solicitous to conceal it from me."

It occurred to Margaret to reply, "Mrs. Houston, suppose that I were writing sentimental letters to a female friend, which might not be really wrong, yet which I should not like to expose to your ridicule, would I not, in such a case, even though it were a proper correspondence, be solicitous to conceal it from you?"—but her exact truthfulness prevented her from putting this supposititious case, and as she did not in any other manner reply, Mrs. Houston continued:

"So you see, Margaret, that you force me to investigate this matter, and I shall, therefore, immediately after breakfast, proceed to the village to make inquiries at the post office." And having announced this resolution, the lady, still struggling with her feelings of displeasure, left the hall.

Margaret withdrew to her own sitting-room, and threw herself upon her knees to pray. Soon rising she touched the bell and summoned Forrest.

The old man came in looking very sorrowful.

"How did it become known that you left the premises last night, Forrest?"

"Somebody must o' 'spicioned me, chile, an' been on de watch."

"Yes! yes! I see now! that was it; but, Forrest, this is what I called you to say: In future, whenever Mrs. Houston asks you a question about your services to your mistress, refer her to me."

"Yes, Miss Marget."

"You may go now."

"Pardon, Miss Marget; I wants to say somefin as'll set your min' at ease 'bout dat letter."

"Ah, yes, you mailed it?"

"True for you, Miss Marget; but listen; de pos' office was shet up. So I jes drap de letter inter de letter-box. Same minit der was two colored boys an' a white man drap as many as five or six letters in long o' mine. So even ef de pos'masser could o' see me t'rough de winder, which he couldn't, how he gwine know which letter 'mong de half-dozen I drap in?"

"True! true! true! Oh, that was very providential! Oh, thank Heaven!" exclaimed Margaret, fervently clasping her hands.

The old man bowed and retired.

After breakfast, Mrs. Houston, without explaining the motive of her journey to any one, ordered her carriage, and drove to the village as upon a shopping excursion.

Now you have not known Mrs. Nellie Houston thus long without discovering that with some good qualities, she was, in some respects, a very silly woman. She drove up to the post office, and by her indiscreet questions respecting "a certain letter mailed the night before by Forrest, the messenger of her ward, Miss Helmstedt," set the weak-headed young postmaster to wondering, conjecturing and speculating. And when she found that he could give her no satisfaction in respect of the letter, she made matters worse by directing him to detain any letters sent there by her ward, Miss Helmstedt, unless such letters happened to be directed to a Helmstedt or a

Houston, who were the only correspondents of Miss Helmstedt recognized by her family.

The postmaster thereupon informed Mrs. Houston, that if she wished to interfere with the correspondence of her ward, she must do so at her own discretion, and necessarily before they should be sent to his office, as he had no authority to detain letters sent thither to be mailed, and might even be subjected to prosecution for so doing.

Mrs. Houston went away baffled and angered, and also totally unconscious of the serious mischief she had set on foot.

To an idle and shallow young man she had spoken indiscreetly of the young maiden whose orphanage she had promised to cherish and defend, exposing her actions to suspicion and her character to speculation. She had left the spotless name of Margaret Helmstedt a theme of low village gossip.

And thus having done as much evil as any foolish woman could well do in an hour, she entered her carriage, and with the solemn conviction of having discharged her duty, drove home to the Bluff.

"God defend me, only, from my friends, for of my enemies I can myself take care," prayed one who seemed to have known this world right well.

From that day Margaret Helmstedt, whenever she had occasion to write a letter, took care to turn the key of her room door; and whenever she had occasion to mail one, took equal precaution to give it, unperceived, into the hands of Forrest, with directions that he should drop it into the letter-box at a moment when he should see other letters, from other sources, going in. Poor girl! she was slowly acquiring an art hateful to her soul. And one also that did not avail her greatly. For notwithstanding all her precautions, the report crept about that Miss Helmstedt had a secret correspondent, very much disapproved of by her friends. And in course of time also, the name of this correspondent transpired. And this is the manner in which it happened. Young Simpson, the postmaster, to whom Mrs. Houston had so imprudently given a portion of her confidence, found his curiosity piqued to discover who this forbidden correspondent might be, and after weeks of patient waiting, convinced himself that the letters addressed in a fair Italian hand to a certain person were those dropped into the box by Miss Helmstedt's messenger, old Forrest. A few more observations confirmed this conviction. Then wishing to gain consequence in the eyes of Mrs. Houston, he availed himself of the first opportunity presented by the presence of that lady at the office to inform her of the discovery he had made.

"You are sure that is the name?" inquired the lady, in surprise.

"Yes, madam, that is the name, in a regular slanting hand. I always find a letter bearing that name in the box the moment after that old man has been seen about here, and never at any other time."

"Very well; I thank you for your information; but mind! pray do not speak of this matter to any one but myself; for I would not like to have this subject discussed in town," said Mrs. Houston.

"Oh, certainly not, madam! You may rely on me," replied the young man, who, in half an hour afterward, laughed over the whole affair with a companion, both making very merry over the idea that the wealthy heiress, Miss Helmstedt, should be engaged to one lover and in private correspondence with another.

And so the ball set in motion by Nellie's indiscretion rolled finely, never wanting a helping hand to propel it on its course; and gathered as it rolled. The rumor changed its form: the gossip became slander. And every one in the county, with the exception of Miss Helmstedt and her friends, "knew" that young lady was in "secret" correspondence with a low, disreputable sailor, whose acquaintance she had formed in some inexplicable manner, and the discovery of whose surreptitious visits to the island had been the proximate cause of her mother's death.

Could Mrs. Houston have imagined half the evil that must accrue from her own imprudent conversation, she would have been touched with compunction; as it was, hearing nothing whatever of this injurious calumny, the guilty reveled in the rewards of "an approving conscience." She kept her discovery of the mysterious name to herself; hinting to no one, least of all to Margaret, the extent of her knowledge upon this subject. And in order to throw the girl off her guard, she was careful never to resume the subject of the letters.

And the plan succeeded so far that Margaret continued, at intervals of three or four weeks, to send off those mysterious letters, and thus the scandal grew and strengthened. That upon such slight grounds the good name of an innocent girl should have been assailed may astonish those unacquainted with the peculiar character of a neighborhood where the conduct of woman is governed by the most stringent conventionalism, and where such stringency is made necessary by the existing fact, that the slightest eccentricity of conduct, however innocent, or even meritorious it may be, is made the ground of the gravest animadversions.

Mrs. Houston, unconscious, as I said, of the rumors abroad, and biding her time for farther discoveries, treated Margaret with great kindness. Nellie had always, of all things, desired a daughter of her own. In her attached stepchild, Franky, she felt that she had quite a son of her own, and in Margaret she would have been pleased to possess the coveted daughter. As well as her capricious temper would allow her to do so, she sought to conduct herself as a mother toward the orphan girl; at times overwhelming her with flippant caresses and puerile attentions, which she might have mistaken for "the sweet, small courtesies of life," but which were very distasteful and unwelcome to one of Margaret Helmstedt's profound, earnest, impassioned soul, and mournful life experiences.

The malaria of slander that filled all the air without must necessarily at last penetrate the precincts of home.

One day, a miserable, dark, drizzling day, near the last of November, Mr. Wellworth presented himself at the Bluff, and requested to see Mrs. Houston alone.

Nellie obeyed the summons, and went to receive the pastoral call in the front parlor across the hall from Margaret's wing.

On entering the room she was struck at once by the unusually grave and even troubled look of the minister.

He arose and greeted her, handed a chair, and when she was seated resumed his own.

And then, after a little conversation, opened the subject of his visit.

"Mrs. Houston it is my very painful duty to advise you of the existence of certain rumors in regard to your amiable ward that I know to be as false as they are injurious, but with which I am equally certain you should be made acquainted."

Nellie was really amazed—so unconscious was she of the effect of her own mischief-making. She drew out her perfumed pocket handkerchief to have it ready, and then inquired:

"To what purpose should I be informed of false, injurious rumors, sir? I know nothing of the rumors to which you refer."

"I verily believe you, madam. But you should be made acquainted with them, as, in the event of their having been occasioned by any little act of thoughtlessness on the part of Miss Helmstedt, you may counsel that young lady and put a stop to this gossiping."

"I do entreat you, sir, to speak plainly."

"You must pardon me then, madam, if I take you at your word. It is currently reported, then, that Miss Helmstedt is in secret correspondence, 'secret' no longer, with a person of low and disreputable character, a waterman, skipper, or something of the sort, whose acquaintance she formed in her mother's lifetime and during her father's absence, while she lived almost alone, on her native island. Now, of course, I know this rumor to be essentially false and calumnious; but I know also how delicate is the bloom on a young girl's fair name, and how easily a careless handling will smirch it. Some thoughtless, perhaps some praiseworthy act on the part of this young creature—such as the sending of charitable donations through the post office, or something of the sort—may have given rise to this rumor, which should at once be met and put down by her friends. But I advise you, my dear madam, to speak to Miss Helmstedt and ascertain what ground, if any, however slight, there may be for this injurious rumor."

For all answer, Mrs. Houston put her handkerchief to her face and began to weep.

"No, no, my dear Mrs. Houston, don't take this too much to heart! these things must be firmly confronted and dealt with—not wept over."

"Oh, sir! good sir! you don't know! you don't know! It is too true! Margaret gives me a world of anxiety."

"Madam! you shock me! What is it you say?"

"Oh! sir, I am glad you came this morning! I have been wanting to ask your advice for a long time; but I did not like to. It is too true! Margaret is very imprudent!"

"Dear Heaven, madam! do you tell me that you knew of this report, and that it is not unfounded?"

"Oh! no, sir, I knew nothing of the report, as I told you before! I knew that Margaret was very, very imprudent, and gave me excessive uneasiness, but I did not dream that she had compromised herself to such an extent! Oh, never!" exclaimed Nellie, still and always unsuspicious of her own great share in creating the evil.

"You said that you had thought of asking my counsel. If you please to explain, my dear Mrs. Houston, you shall have the benefit of the best counsel my poor ability will furnish."

"Oh! Heavens, sir! girls are not what they used to be when I was young—though I am scarcely middle-aged now—but they are not."

"And Miss Helmstedt?"

"Oh, sir! Margaret is indeed in correspondence with some unknown man, whose very name I never heard in all my life before! She does all she can to keep the affair secret, and she thinks she keeps it so; but poor thing, having very little art, she cannot succeed in concealing the fact that she sends off these mysterious letters about once a month."

"And do you not expostulate with her?" inquired the deeply-shocked minister.

"Oh, I did at first, sir, but I made no more impression upon her than if she had been a marble statue of Firmness. She would not tell me who her correspondent was, where he was, what he was, what was the nature of the acquaintance between them; in short, she would tell me nothing about him."

"And can neither Colonel nor Mrs. Compton, nor your husband, impress her with the impropriety of this proceeding?"

"Oh, sir, they know nothing about it. No one in this house knows anything about Margaret's conduct but myself. And the rumor you have just brought me has never reached them, I am sure."

"Suppose you let me talk with my young friend. She means well, I am sure."

"Well, sir, you shall have the opportunity you desire. But—excuse me for quoting for your benefit a homely adage—'Trot sire, trot dam, and the colt will never pace!' Margaret Helmstedt takes stubbornness from both parents, and may be supposed to have a double allowance," said Mrs. Houston, putting her hand to the bell cord.

A servant appeared.

"Let Miss Helmstedt know that Mr. Wellworth desires to see her," said Mrs. Houston.

The messenger withdrew, and soon returned with the answer that Miss Helmstedt would be glad to receive Mr. Wellworth in her own sitting-room.

"Will you accompany me hither then, Mrs. Houston?"

"No, I think not, sir. I fancy Miss Helmstedt prefers a private interview with her pastor. And I believe also that such a one would afford the best opportunity for your counseling Margaret."

"Then you will excuse me, madam?"

"Certainly; and await here the issue of your visit," said Mrs. Houston.

With a bow, the clergyman left the room, crossed the hall, and rapped at the door of Miss Helmstedt's parlor.

It was opened by Hildreth, who stood in her starched puritanical costume, curtseying while the pastor entered the pretty boudoir.

Margaret, still clothed in deep mourning, with her black hair plainly banded each side of her pale, clear, thoughtful face, sat in her low sewing-chair, engaged in plain needlework. She quietly laid it aside, and, with a warm smile of welcome, arose to meet her minister.

"You are looking better than when I saw you last, my child," said the good pastor, pressing her hand, and mistaking the transient glow of pleasure for the permanent bloom of health.

"I am quite well, thank you, dear Mr. Wellworth! and you?"

"Always well, my child, thank Heaven."

"And dearest Grace? I have not seen her so long."

"Ah! she has even too good health, if possible! it makes her wild. We have to keep her at home to tame her."

"But see—I am housekeeping here to myself, almost. My dear father has placed my maintenance upon the most lavish footing, and Mrs. Houston has given to his requests in regard to me the most liberal interpretation. See! I have, like a little princess, an establishment of my own. This wing of the house, a maid and messenger, a boat and horse; and my dear father has even written to have the carriage brought from the island for my use, so that I may be able to visit or send for my friends at pleasure," said Margaret, with a transient feeling of girlish delight in her independence.

"Yes, my child, I see; and I know that, in addition to this, you have an ample income. These are all great and unusual privileges for a young girl like yourself, not past childhood," said Mr. Wellworth, very gravely.

"Oh! I know they are. I know, too, that these favors are lavished upon me in compassion for—to console me for—as if anything could make me cease to regret——" Here faltering, and finding herself on the verge of tears, Margaret paused, made an effort, controlled herself and resumed: "It is done in kindness toward her child; and I accept it all in the same spirit."

"It is accorded in consideration of your grave and important position, my dear girl—do you never think of it? Young as you are, you are the affianced wife of the heir of this house."

Again a transient flush of bashful joy chased the melancholy from Margaret's face. Blushing, she dropped her eyes and remained silent.

"You think sometimes of your position, Margaret?" asked the clergyman, who, for his purpose, wished to lead and fix her mind upon this subject— "you remember sometimes that you are Ralph Houston's promised wife?"

For an instant she lifted her dark eyelashes, darting one swift, shy, but most eloquent glance deep into his face, then, dropping them, crimsoned even to the edges of her black hair, and still continued silent.

"Ah! I see you do. I see you do. But do you know my dear, that something of the same discreet exclusiveness, reserve, circumspection, is demanded of a betrothed maiden as of a wife?" inquired the clergyman, solemnly.

Again her beautiful dark eyes were raised, in that quick, and quickly-withdrawn, penetrating, earnest, fervid, impassioned glance, that said, more eloquently than words would have spoken, "All that you demand for him, and more, a millionfold, will my own heart, daily, hourly yield!" and then the blush deepened on her cheek, and she remained dumb.

"She, the promised wife, I mean, must not hold free conversation with gentlemen who are not her own near relatives; she must not correspond with them—she must not, in a word, do many things, which, though they might be perfectly innocent in a disengaged woman, would be very reprehensible in a betrothed maiden."

Margaret's color visibly fluctuated—her bosom perceptibly fluttered.

"Well, Margaret, what do you think of that which I have been telling you?"

"Oh! I know—I know you speak truly. I hope I know my duty and love to do it," she said, in an agitated, confused manner; "but let us talk of something else, dear Mr. Wellworth. Let us talk of my little, independent establishment here. When I spoke of the pleasant nature of my surroundings, it was to win your consent that dear Grace might come and be my guest for a week. She would be such a sweet comfort to me, and I could make her so happy here! If you will consent, I will send Forrest with the carriage for her to-morrow. Say, will you, dear Mr. Wellworth?"

"Perhaps; we will talk about that by and by. Margaret," he said, suddenly lowering his voice, "dismiss your woman, I wish to speak alone with you, my child."

"Hildreth, go, but remain in sound of my bell," said Miss Helmstedt.

As soon as Hildreth had left the room, Mr. Wellworth drew his chair beside the low seat of Margaret, took her hand, and would have held it while he spoke, but that she, who always shrank even from the fatherly familiarity of her pastor, very gently withdrew it, and respectfully inquired:

"What was it you wished to say to me, dear Mr. Wellworth?"

"A very serious matter, my dear child. Margaret, I have no art in circumnavigating a subject. I have been trying to approach gradually the subject of my visit to you this morning, and I have not succeeded. I am no nearer than when I first entered. I know not how to 'break' bad news ——"

"In a word, sir, has misfortune happened to any of my friends?" inquired Margaret, with a pale cheek, but with a strange, calm voice.

"No; that were more easily told than what I have to tell," said the minister, solemnly.

"Please go on then, sir, and let me know the worst at once."

"Then, my dear Margaret, I have been informed that you, a betrothed wife, have an intimate male correspondent, who is neither your father nor your affianced husband, and whose name and character, and relations with yourself, you decline to divulge?"

Margaret grew ashen pale, clasped her hands, compressed her lips, and remained silent.

"What have you to say to this charge, Margaret?"

There was a pause, while Mr. Wellworth gazed upon the maiden's steadfast, thoughtful face. She reasoned with herself; she struggled with herself. It occurred to her to say, "My correspondent is a gray-haired man, whom I have never set eyes upon." But immediately, she reflected. "No, this may put suspicion upon the true scent; I must say nothing."

"Well, Margaret, what have you to answer to this charge?"

"Nothing, sir."

"Nothing?"

"Nothing."

"You admit it, then?"

"I neither admit nor deny it!"

"Margaret, this will never do. Are you aware that you seriously imperil, nay, more, that you gravely compromise your good name?"

Her pale cheek grew paler than before, the tightly-clasped fingers trembled, the compressed lips sprang quivering apart, and then closed more firmly than ever. It had occurred to her to say: "But this correspondence is solely a business affair, with one of whom I have no personal knowledge whatever." But then came the reflection: "If I give them this explanation, this ever so slight clue, these worldly-wise people will follow it up until they unravel the whole mystery, and I shall have proved myself a cowardly traitor to her confidence. No, I must be dumb before my accusers!"

"You do not speak, Margaret."

"I have nothing to say, sir!"

"Ah, dear Heaven! I see that I must not 'prophesy smooth things' to you, my girl. I must not spare the truth! Listen, then, Miss Helmstedt: Your name has become a byword in the village shops! What now will you do?"

It was on her pallid lips to say: "I will trust in God;" but she said it only in her heart, adding: "I must not even insist upon my innocence; for if they believe me, they will be forced to find the right track to this scent."

"Margaret Helmstedt, why do you not answer me?"

"Because, sir, I have nothing to say."

"Nothing to say?"

"Nothing—nothing to say!"

"Listen to me, then. You seem to have some regard for your betrothed husband. You seem even to understand the duty you owe him! Think, I beg you, what must be the feelings of a proud and honorable man like Ralph Houston, on returning to this neighborhood and finding the name and fame of his affianced bride lightly canvassed?"

It was piteous to see how dark with woe her face became. Her hands were clenched until it seemed as though the blood must start from her finger nails; but not one word escaped her painfully-compressed lips.

"I ask you, Miss Helmstedt, when Ralph Houston returns to this neighborhood and hears what I and others have heard—what do you suppose he will do?"

"He will do his own good pleasure; and I—I shall submit," said the maiden, meekly bowing her head.

But then in an instant—even as though she had heard Ralph's voice in her ear—there was a change. Her beautiful head was raised, her color flushed brightly back, her dark eyes kindled, flashed, and she replied:

"He may hear, as you and others do, incredible things said of me; but he will not, as you and others do, believe them! And I only dread to think what his reply would be to any who should, in his presence, speak with levity of any woman he respects."

"Margaret, pause—bethink you! this is no idle gossip! It is slander, do you hear? It is the venomed serpent slander that has fixed its fangs upon your maiden name. I believe, of course, unjustly! but nothing except an open explanation will enable your friends to exculpate you and silence your calumniators. Will you not give them such a weapon?"

"I cannot," she breathed, in a low tone of returning despair.

"Reflect, girl. Ralph Houston, when he arrives, will surely hear these reports; for, in the country, nothing is forgotten. He may stand by you—I doubt not with his unfunded faith and chivalrous generosity that he will; but—will you, loving and honoring him, as I am sure you do, will you, with a blemished name, give your hand to him, a man of stainless honor?"

"No, no! oh, never, no!" came like a wail of woe from her lips, as her head sank down upon her bosom.

"Then, Margaret, give your friends the right to explain and clear your conduct."

She was incapable of reply, and so remained silent.

"You will not?"

She mournfully shook her head.

"Good-by, Margaret; God give you a better spirit. I must leave you now," said the old pastor. And he arose, laid his hand in silent prayer upon the stricken young head bent beneath him, then took up his broad-brimmed hat and quietly left the room.

As he came out, Mrs. Houston opened the front parlor door and invited him in there.

"Well, sir, what success?" she inquired, anxiously, as soon as they were both seated.

The good old man slowly shook his head.

"None whatever, madam."

"She still refuses to explain?"

"Ah, yes, madam!"

"In fact, it is just what I expected. I am not surprised. There never was such contumacious obstinacy. Dear me, what shall I do? What would you advise me to do?"

"Be patient, Mrs. Houston; and, above all things, avoid betraying to any others out of your own immediate family the anxiety that you reveal to me. 'It is written that a man's foes shall be those of his own household.' Unnatural and horrible as it sounds, every one who has lived, observed and reflected to any purpose, must have discovered that still more frequently a woman's foes are of such."

"Really and truly, Mr. Wellworth, that is a very strange speech of yours. I hope you do not suppose that any one in this house is the enemy of Margaret Helmstedt?"

"Assuredly not. I merely wished to entreat that you will not again speak of this correspondence in the village post office."

"But dear me, what then am I to do?"

"Leave matters just where they are for the present. There is nothing wrong in this, farther than that it has unfortunately been made the occasion of gossip; therefore, of course it must be perfectly cleared up for Margaret's own sake. But our interference at present evidently will not tend to precipitate a satisfactory denouement."

"Oh, how I wish her father or Ralph were home. I have a great mind to write to them!" exclaimed Nellie, who certainly was governed by an unconscious attraction toward mischief-making.

"My good lady, do nothing of the sort; it would be both useless and harmful."

"What, then, shall I do?" questioned Nellie, impatiently.

"Consult your husband."

"Consult Colonel Houston! You certainly can't know Colonel Houston. Why, well as he likes me, he would—bite my head off if I came to him with any tale of scandal," said Nellie, querulously.

"Then leave the matter to me for the present," said the minister, rising and taking his leave.

Meanwhile, Margaret Helmstedt had remained where the pastor had left her, with clenched hands and sunken head in the same attitude of fixed despair. Then, suddenly rising, with a low, long wail of woe, she threw herself on her knees before her mother's portrait, and raising both arms with open hands, as though offering up some oblation to that image, she cried:

"Oh, mother! mother! here is the first gift, a spotless name! freely renounced for thy sake! freely offered up to thee! Only look on me! love me, my mother! for I have loved thee more than all things—even than him, mother mine!"

Mrs. Houston, in her excited state of feeling, could not keep quiet. Even at the risk of being "flouted" or ridiculed, she went into the colonel's little study, which was the small room in the second story immediately over the front entrance, and sitting down beside him, solemnly entered upon the all-engrossing subject of her thoughts. The colonel listened, going through the successive stages of being surprised, amused and bored, and finally, when she ceased and waited for his comments, he just went on tickling his ear with the feathered end of his pen and smiled in silence.

"Now, then, colonel, what do you think of all this?"

"Why, that it must be all perfectly correct, my dear, and need not give you the slightest uneasiness. That our fair little daughter-in-law regularly writes and receives letters from a certain person, is of course a sufficient proof of the correctness of both correspondence and correspondent," said the colonel, gallantly.

"All that may be very true, and at the same time very indiscreet—think of what they say."

"Tah—tah, my love! never mind 'they say!' the only practical part of it is, that in the absence of Ralph, if I should happen to meet with 'they say' in man's form, I shall be at the trouble of chastising him, that's all!"

"Now, colonel! of all things, I do hope that you will not, at your age, do anything rash."

"Then, my pretty one, pray do not trouble me or yourself, and far less little Margaret, with this ridiculous wickedness," he said, drawing her head down to give her a parting kiss, and then good-humoredly putting her out of the study.

Colonel Houston, in his contempt of gossip, had unhappily treated the subject with more levity than it deserved. In such a neighborhood as this of which I write, calumny is not to be despised or lived down—it must be met and strangled; or it will be pampered and cherished until it grows a very "fire-mouthed dragon, horrible and bright."

In such a place events and sensations do not rapidly succeed each other, and a choice piece of scandal is long "rolled as a sweet morsel under the tongue." Margaret either ceased to write obnoxious letters, or else she changed her post office, but that circumstance did not change the subject of village gossip—it only furnished a new cause of conjecture. And this continued until near Christmas, when Frank Houston was expected home to spend the holidays, and a large party was invited to dinner and for the evening to meet him.

Frank arrived on Christmas eve, at night. He involuntarily betrayed some little agitation on first meeting Margaret; his emotion, slight as it was, and soon as it was conquered, was perceived by his fond stepmother, upon whom it produced the effect of reviving all her former feelings of suspicion and resentment toward Margaret, for having, as she supposed, trifled with his affections, and abandoned him in favor of his elder brother. And this resuscitated hostility was unconsciously increased by Frank, who, being alone with his stepmother later in the evening, said with a rueful attempt at smiling:

"So Ralph and my little Margo—mine no longer! are to be married. Well, when I went away I charged him with the care of my little love; and he has taken excellent care of her, that is all."

"You have been treated villainously, Franky! villainously, my poor boy! And I am grieved to death to think I had anything to do with it! only— what could I do at such a time as that, when her mother, my poor, dear, Marguerite, was dying?" said Nellie, half crying from the mixed motives of revived grief for the loss of her friend, and indignation at what she persisted in regarding as the wrongs of her favorite stepson.

"However, Franky, dear, I can tell you, if that will be any comfort to you, that I don't think you have lost a treasure in Margaret, for I doubt if she will be any more faithful to Ralph than she has been to you!"

"Fair little mamma, that is not generous or even just!" said Frank, in a tone of rebuke, tempered by affectionate playfulness. "Don't let's imitate the philosophical fox in the fable, nor call sour these most luscious of grapes hung far above my reach. Margaret owed me no faith. My aspiration gave me no claim upon her consideration. She is a noble girl, and 'blistered be my tongue' if ever it say otherwise. Henceforth, for me, she is my brother's wife, no more, nor less," said the young man, swallowing the sob that had risen in his throat and nearly choked him.

"Oh, my dear Franky! my very heart bleeds for you," said Nellie, with the tears streaming down her face; for if the little lady had one deep, sincere affection in the world, it was for her "pretty boy," as, to the young man's ludicrous annoyance, she still called him.

But Frank wiped her tears away and kissed her. And the next moment Nellie was talking gayly of the party she had invited to do honor to his return home.

This festival fixed for Christmas was intended to come off the next afternoon. There was to be a dinner followed by an evening party. As the family were still in mourning for Mrs. Helmstedt, dancing was prohibited; but the evening was laid off to be employed in tea-drinking, parlor games, cards, and conversation.

Mrs. Houston, as far as the contradictory nature of her sentiments would permit, took some pride in the beauty, wealth, and social importance of her "daughter" Margaret; and experienced quite a fashionable, mamma-like solicitude for her favorable appearance upon the evening in question. Therefore, without ever having had any altercation with the pensive and unwilling girl upon the subject of her toilet, Nellie, on the morning of Christmas day, entered Margaret's little boudoir, accompanied by Jessie Bell, bringing a packet.

Margaret, who sat by the fire quietly reading, looked up, smiled, and invited her visitor to be seated.

"I have not time to sit down, Maggie; all those cakes are to be frosted yet; the jellies are waiting to be poured into the moulds; the cream has yet to be seasoned and put in the freezers; flowers cut in the greenhouse for the vases; and I know not what else besides. Here, Christmas Day, of all days in the year, that I should be working harder than any slave," said the little lady.

"I had no idea that you were so busy. Pray let me and Hildreth assist you. We are both skillful, you know. Please always let me know when I or my servants can be of any use to you, Mrs. Houston," said Miss Helmstedt, laying aside her book and rising.

"Nonsense, my dear, I don't really need your services or I should call upon you. I came in to bring you a Christmas gift. Your foolish little mother-in-law, whom you refuse to call 'mamma,' has not forgotten you. Jessie, open that box."

The waiting-maid obeyed, and drew from it a rich black velvet evening dress, made with a low corsage and short sleeves, and both neck and sleevelets trimmed with point lace.

"There! there is your dress for this evening, my dear. How do you like it?" asked the little lady, holding up the dress in triumph.

"It is very beautiful, and I am very grateful to you, Mrs. Houston."

"'Mrs. Houston!' There it is again! You will not say 'mamma.' By-and-by, I suppose, you will expect me also to say 'Mrs. Houston,' and we, a mother and daughter-in-law, shall be formally 'Mrs. Houston-ing' each other. Well, let that pass—'sufficient unto the day,' etc. Now, about this dress. You do not, after all, look as if you half liked it? It is true, I know, that velvet is rather matronly to wear for a girl of fifteen; but then, when one is in mourning, the choice of material is not very extensive; and besides, for Christmas, velvet may not be very much out of place, even on a young person. But I am sorry you don't like it," concluded Nellie, regretfully dropping the dress that she had been holding up to exhibition.

"Oh, I do like it, very much, indeed. I should be very tasteless not to like it, and very thankless not to feel your kindness. The dress is as beautiful as can be—only too fine for me," said Margaret.

"Not the least so, my dear girl. Consider," replied the little lady, launching out into a strain of good-humored compliment upon her "daughter's" face and figure, riches, position, prospects, etc.

Margaret arrested the flow of flattery by quietly and gratefully accepting the dress. She would have preferred to wear, even upon the coming festive evening, the nunlike black bombazine, that, ever since her mother's death, had been her costume. But, in very truth, her mind was now too heavily oppressed with a private and unshared responsibility, to admit of her giving much thought to the subject of her toilet. Her neatness was habitual, mechanical; beyond the necessity of being neat, dress was to her a matter of indifference.

Nellie next took out a small morocco case.

"And here," she said, "is Colonel Houston's Christmas offering to his little daughter-in-law."

Margaret opened the casket, and found a beautiful necklace and bracelet of jet, set in gold.

"I will wear them to-night, and thank the kind donor in person," said Miss Helmstedt, putting it beside her book on the stand.

Mrs. Houston then bustled out of the room, leaving the young girl to her coveted quiet.

Late in the afternoon, the Christmas party began to assemble—a mixed company of about forty individuals, comprising old, middle-aged, and young persons of both sexes. The evening was spent, according to programme, in tea-drinking, parlor games, tableaux, cards and conversation, *i. e.*, gossip, *i. e.*, scandal.

Among all the gayly attired young persons present Margaret Helmstedt, in her mourning-dress, with her black hair plainly braided around her fair, broad forehead, was pronounced not only the most beautiful, but by far the most interesting; her beauty, her orphanage, her heiress-ship, her extreme youth, and her singular position as a betrothed bride in the house of her father-in-law, all invested with a prestige of strange interest this fair young creature.

But, ah! her very pre-eminence among her companions, instigated the envious to seize upon, and use against her, any circumstance that might be turned to her disadvantage. Whispers went around. Sidelong glances were cast upon her.

As a daughter of the house, she shook off her melancholy pre-occupation, and exerted herself to entertain the visitors.

But matrons, whose daughters she had thrown into the shade, could not forgive her for being "talked of," and received all her hospitable attentions with coldness. And the maidens who had been thus overshadowed took their revenge in curling their lips and tossing their heads, as she passed or smiled upon them.

Now Margaret Helmstedt was neither insensible, cold, nor dull; on the contrary, she was intelligent to perceive, sensitive to feel, and reflective to refer this persecution back to its cause. And though no one could have judged from her appearance how much she suffered under the infliction; for, through all the trying evening, she exhibited the same quiet courtesy and ladylike demeanour; the iron entered her soul.

Only when the festival was over, the guests departed, the lights put out, and she found herself at liberty to seek the privacy of her own chamber, she dropped exhausted beside her bed, and burying her face in the coverlid, sighed forth:

"Oh, mother! mother! Oh, mother! mother!"

The Christmas party had the effect of giving zest and impetus to the village gossip, of which Margaret was the favorite theme. It was scarcely in fallen human nature to have seen a girl of fifteen so exalted beyond what was considered common and proper to one of her age, and not to recollect and repeat all that could justly or unjustly be said to her disadvantage.

This newly-augmented slander resulted in an event very humiliating to the family at the Bluff.

Near the end of the Christmas holidays, Frank happened to be in the village upon some unimportant business. While loitering near a group of young men in one of the shops, he started on hearing the name of Margaret Helmstedt coupled with a light laugh. Frank's eyes flashed as he advanced toward the group. He listened for a moment, to ascertain which of their number had thus taken the name of Miss Helmstedt upon irreverent lips; and when the culprit discovered himself, by again opening his mouth upon the same forbidden theme, without another word spoken on any side, Frank silently and coolly walked up, collared, and drew him struggling out from the group, and using the riding wand he held in his hand, proceeded to inflict upon him summary chastisement. When he considered the young man sufficiently punished, he spurned him away, threw his own card in the midst of the group, inviting whomsoever should list to take it up (with the quarrel), mounted his horse and rode home.

He said nothing of what had occurred to any member of the family.

But about the middle of the afternoon, he received a visit from the deputy sheriff of the county, who bore a pressing invitation from a justice of the peace, that "Franklin Pembroke Houston, of said county," should appear before him to answer certain charges.

"Why, what is this?" inquired Colonel Houston, who was present when the warrant was served.

"Oh, nothing, nothing; only I heard a certain Craven Jenkins taking a lady's name in vain, and gave him a lesson on reverence; and now, I suppose, I shall have to pay for the luxury, that is all," replied Frank. And then, being further pressed, he explained the whole matter to his father.

"You did well, my boy, and just what I should have done in your place. Come! we will go to the village and settle up for this matter," said the colonel, as he prepared to accompany his son.

The affair ended, with Frank, in his being fined one hundred dollars, which he declared to be cheap for the good done.

But not so unimportant was the result to the hapless girl, whom every event, whether festive or otherwise, seemed to plunge more deeply into trouble.

When, after New Year, Franky went away, Mrs. Houston accompanied him to Belleview, whence he took the packet. And after parting with him, on her return through the village, she chanced to hear, for the first time, the affair of the horsewhipping, for which her Franky had been fined. Upon inquiry, she further learned the occasion of that chastisement. And her indignation against Margaret, as the cause, knew no bounds.

Happily, it was a long, cold ride back to the Bluff, and the sedative effect of time and frost had somewhat lowered the temperature of little Mrs. Houston's blood before she reached home.

Nevertheless, she went straight to Margaret's sanctum, and laying off her bonnet there, reproached her bitterly.

Margaret bore this injustice with "a great patience." That had, however, but little power to disarm the lady, whose resentment continued for weeks.

Drearily passed the time to the hapless girl—the long desolate months brightened by the rare days when she would receive a visit from one of her two friends, Grace or Clare, or else get letters from her father or Ralph Houston.

Toward the spring, the news from camp held out the prospect of Mr. Houston's possible return home. And to Ralph's arrival poor Margaret looked forward with more of dread than hope.

CHAPTER XII
THE DAUGHTER'S FIDELITY

"Still through each change of fortune strange,

Racked nerve and brain all burning,

Her loving faith to given trust

Knew never shade of turning."

More than fifteen months have elapsed since the close of the last chapter—months, replete with the destiny of nations as of individuals. First, the prospects of peace through the mediation of the Emperor of Russia, or by any other means, seemed indefinitely postponed. The desired return of the long-absent soldiers to their homes, was a distant and doubtful hope. The war continued to be prosecuted on both sides with unremitting animosity.

Cockburn was on the Chesapeake. Now I know not whether history has softened, or tradition exaggerated the fierceness, rapacity, and cruelty of this licensed pirate and his crew. History tells of quiet farmsteads razed to the ground and peaceful villages burned to ashes. Tradition speaks of individual instances of monstrous atrocity, that resulted in the madness or death of the innocent victim. But whatever may stand recorded in history, or be believed in distant regions, concerning the conduct of the British fleet in the Chesapeake—here on the scene of action, here along the shores and among the isles of the Bay, the memory of Rear Admiral Cockburn and his crew, is, justly or unjustly, loaded with almost preternatural abhorrence.

The villages of Havre de Grace, Frenchtown, Fredericktown, Georgetown and Hampton, and other unguarded hamlets, whose natural protectors were absent at the distant theatres of the war, were successively assaulted, sacked and burned, while their helpless inhabitants, consisting of old men, women and children, were put to the sword, hunted away or carried off. The massacre on Craney Island, with all its concomitant horrors of debauchery, madness and violence, had carried consternation into every heart. Marauding parties were frequently landed to lay waste defenceless farmsteads, whose masters were absent on the Northern frontier.

Still, as yet, nothing had occurred to alarm, for themselves, our friends in the neighborhood of Helmstedt's Island. The sail of the enemy had been more than once seen in the distance, but not even a single foraging party had landed to lay them under tribute. Thus it was considered quite safe by the neighbors to vary the monotony of their lives by forming a picnic party for Helmstedt's Island. The company consisted of the Houstons, the Wellworths, the Hartleys, and others. The time appointed for the festival was the first of August. The day proved cool for the season, and consequently pleasant for the occasion. The Wellworths came down to the bluff to join the Houstons, with whom, at sunrise, they set out for the island, where they were met by the Hartleys and other friends, and regaled by a sumptuous seaside breakfast, previously prepared to order by the island housekeeper, Aunt Hapzibah. After that repast, the company separated into groups, according to their "attractions." Of the elder portion, some formed quiet whist parties in the drawing-room, and others sat down for a cozy gossip on the vine-shaded piazza. Of the younger party, some entered boats and went crabbing, while others formed quadrilles and danced to the sound of the tambourine, the fiddle, and the banjo, wielded with enthusiasm by the hands and arms of three ecstatic sable musicians. Margaret Helmstedt and her chosen friends, Grace Wellworth and Clare Hartley, separated themselves from the company, and with their arms affectionately intertwined around each other's waists, wandered down to the beach with the purpose of making the whole circuit of her beloved island. Margaret has changed and matured in these fifteen months. She has become very beautiful, very much like what her mother had been, but with a profounder and more mournful style, "a beauty that makes sad the eye." Time, experience and sorrow have prematurely done their work upon her. She, but sixteen years of age, looks much older. She is dressed quite plainly, in a gown of black gauze striped with black satin, a fine lace inside handkerchief and cuffs, white kid gloves and black morocco gaiters. Her jet-black hair is parted over her broad brow, and rippling in a myriad of shining wavelets that would, if permitted, fall in a cloud of ringlets around her sweet, pale face, and throw into deeper shade the shadowy, mournful eyes. The white chip hat, plainly trimmed with white ribbons, hangs idly from her arm. Within the last year Margaret's position has not improved. It is true that the subject of the letters and the unknown correspondent or lover has been suffered to die out. Not even country gossips can, without new materials, keep a vague scandal alive year after year. And no such stimuli had been afforded them. Margaret, whether she had ceased to write, or had taken a more effectual manner of concealing her correspondence, seemed neither to receive nor send any more mysterious letters. But she had not regained, nor even sought to regain, the confidence, esteem, and affection of her family. An atmosphere of distrust, coldness, and reserve, surrounded, chilled, and depressed her spirit, yet could not destroy the deep enthusiasm of some hidden devotion that inspired her soul, and gave to her beautiful, pale face, the air of rapt religious enthusiasm seen on the pictured brows of saints and angels. Even now, upon this festive occasion, as she walks between her friends, the same deep, serious, earnest fervor glows under the surface of her eloquent countenance. They were imparting to her, as girls will, their girlish mysteries, and inviting her to a similar confidence. But Margaret was pre-occupied and abstracted, and though her replies were always affectionate, they were not always to the point.

At last the brown-eyed and gentle little Grace ventured to say:

"I tell you what, Margaret, it is said that there are two sorts of people in this world—those who love, and those who permit themselves to be loved. If so, then you belong to the latter class."

"Why do you think so, dear Grace?"

"Why?—here my arm has been around your waist, and it might better have been around the stem of an oak sapling! that at least would have nodded over me a little; but you, you walk on erect, silent, thoughtful, and when I speak to you of the flowers along our path, you speak of the clouds over our heads, or make an equally applicable response to my observation, which shows how much attention you pay to what I say."

"I beg your pardon, dear Grace."

"Of course you do, and of course I grant it, which will not prevent your offending in the same way the very next minute."

"Cease, chatterbox!" exclaimed Clare Hartley. "Remember that Miss Helmstedt has other subjects to occupy her mind to the exclusion of your mature ideas. She is engaged, you know. Her affianced is far away. Like that other 'Margaret, who in Lithgow's bower, all lonely sat and wept the weary hour,' she may be thinking of:—

"'The war against her native soil

Her lover's risk in battle broil.'

"Though after all, since they seem to be so quiet up there, I shouldn't wonder if she is only thinking of household linens, with a view to housekeeping. Let the 'plenishing' be on the most liberal scale, Margaret, for I and Grace intend to spend a great deal of time with you after you are married."

"And we are to be your bridesmaids, of course, are we not, dear Margaret?"

"Dear Grace, pray do not speak of any future event with such presumptuous assurance. My marriage may never take place," replied Margaret, with a mournful earnestness that she did not attempt to conceal or modify.

"Your marriage may never take place!" exclaimed both her companions, in consternation.

"I mean that life is full of vicissitudes; one or the other of us may die."

"How gravely you speak! You are certainly the daughter of Heraclitus, the crying philosopher. Why, Margaret——"

She was interrupted by a piercing shriek from Grace Wellworth, who, breaking suddenly from her companions, ran like Atalanta up toward the inland of the island. They looked up to ascertain the cause. With wild eyes and blanched faces they recognized the occasion of her terror and flight. Three boats had been silently pushed up on the sands a few yards below them, and were now discharging their crews, consisting of about twelve or more from each boat, or from thirty-five to forty British soldiers in all. One of these men had instantly perceived the flight of Grace, and moved by the mere animal instinct to pursue the flying, as the hound pursues the running hare, had cried out:

"Atalanta! Atalanta! By George, when a girl flies she invites pursuit," and ran after her.

"For the love of Heaven, let us not follow her example. Let us stand our ground. Let us speak to the commanding officer, and we will save ourselves and her from farther aggression," said Margaret, looking very firm, and not a shade paler than usual. Clare drew herself up with dignity and remained standing beside her friend.

The pursuer of Grace had now overtaken, caught and lifted the terrified and struggling girl, and laughing gayly the while, was bearing her back to the scene. No more dangerous spirit than that of wild fun and frolic seemed to inspire the merry captor.

"Release me! Release me, I command you, villain!" cried Grace, wild with indignation and fear, and struggling desperately to free herself.

"Ha! ha! ha! the little brown partridge! how fierce and strong, and spiteful it is! How it flutters and flaps, and beats!" exclaimed the soldier, holding his captive tighter.

"Let me go! Let me go, I say, poltroon!" cried the girl, wrestling madly with her captor.

"Kingdom come! what a wild bird it is!" exclaimed the latter, squeezing his prize maliciously.

"Put me down! Put me down, I order you, marauder! coward! brute!" resumed Grace, now maddened with rage and terror.

"George! What! It is not a wild partridge, but a young hawk that I've caught! What claws and beak it has! how it bites, and tears, and scratches! I must look out for my face, or, by George! the best-looking soldier in his majesty's service will be ruined!"

"You a soldier! Poltroon! Coward!"

"Whe-ew! the little creature can call hard names, too. Well, come! one kiss for a cheap ransom, and I let you go! What! Not one kiss? Very well; what is not freely yielded must be boldly rifled! What the deuce——" And despite her frenzied struggles the "ransom" was seized, and Grace, furious at the indignity, was set upon her feet.

"For shame, ensign! How dare you? Go directly and ask the young lady's pardon," said the commanding officer, who had just that instant reached the scene.

The delinquent addressed touched his hat to his superior officer and said:

"I beg yours, lieutenant. If the bird had not flown, the falcon would not have flown!" and repeating the gesture of subordination, he turned to obey. Going up and standing before Grace, who gave him a furious look, he took off his cap, revealing a very finely turned head, bowed profoundly, and said:

"Young lady, Ensign Dawson humbly begs your pardon; and all the more humbly, because, poor wretch! he cannot repent! nor even—hardened sinner that he is—promise never to do so again. For if ever the opportunity should offer, son of perdition that you know him to be! he would be sure to repeat the offense. Under such unpromising prospects, you will deign to stretch out the sceptre of grace, whose touch is pardon to the poor devil— William Dawson?"

"'William Dawson.'" The words were echoed by a low, thrilling, impassioned voice, that did not come from Grace, whose lovely countenance, as she listened to the ensign's apology, underwent the most ludicrous series of phases; rage, curiosity, admiration, pride—all struggled for the supremacy a moment, and then, shocked at detecting in herself the slightest indication of relenting toward such unpardonable and atrocious impudence, she turned and walked away in haughty silence. Lieutenant King stepped after her to offer a more suitable apology. At the same instant Clare Hartley left the side of her friend, and went to soothe her.

And thus Margaret Helmstedt and the young ensign were left alone, standing a few yards apart.

He stood watching with laughing eyes the retreating form of Grace.

But Margaret's face was a study. Her thrilling, passionate voice it was that had echoed his name at the instant of hearing it. When that name first struck her ear, she had started and clutched her breast with both hands, as one who had received a shot in the heart. And, since that moment, she had been standing transfixed, white and still, with burning gaze fixed upon the young soldier. Presently her steadfast gaze attracted the attention of the man, who raised his eyes to hers. The meeting of those mutual glances did not dissolve, but changed the spell under which she labored.

She moved, stretched out her arm, and without withdrawing her gaze, like a somnambulist or a mesmerized subject, as if irresistibly drawn on, in measured steps, with fixed eyes and extended arm, she walked toward him, laid her hand firmly upon his breast, and gazed wistfully into his face.

The young soldier laughed, drew himself up, threw out his chest, folded his arms, lifted his head, and so seemed defiantly to offer himself for criticism. And in truth he had no just reason to avoid inspection. He was very possibly just what he had laughingly described himself—the handsomest man in his majesty's service. He was one of the finest specimens of the Anglo Saxon race—in form somewhat above the medium height—broad-shouldered, deep-chested, round-limbed, with a full face, fair, roseate complexion, flaxen hair, merry blue eyes, straight nose, finely curved, red and smiling lips, white teeth, and an expression of countenance replete with blended frankness, firmness, and good-humor.

But no recognition of his manly beauty was in the steadfast, profound, and serious gaze with which Margaret—her hand still laid upon his breast—regarded him.

"William Dawson. Your name is William Dawson?" she said, speaking low and slowly.

"Yes, fair one! William Dawson, hitherto ensign in his majesty's — — company of — —, but henceforth your liege subject!" replied the young soldier, laughingly though in great surprise.

"William Dawson," she repeated, without removing her eyes.

"You have said it, lovely lady."

"William Dawson," she reiterated, as it were, unconsciously.

"At your service, beautiful Virginian! What can I do to prove my devotion? Blow up the Albion? desert my colors! swear allegiance to that warlike hero, President Madison? or, I have it! cut off Rear Admiral Cockburn's ears? for I think he is the favorite antipathy of your charming countrywomen! Tell me what unheard-of audacity I shall perpetrate to prove my devotion, and above all things, tell the worshiped name of her for whom I am pledging myself to do anything and everything!" said the young soldier, in the same tone of gay, but not disrespectful, raillery.

"I am Margaret Helmstedt," she replied, in a low and thrilling voice.

"Great Heaven!"

It was all he said. And there fell a pause and deep silence between them for some intense and vital moments, during which they gazed with unutterable emotions upon each other's face and form. She could not have been whiter than she had been from the first, so she remained without color and without voluntary motion, but shaken upon her feet as a statue by an earthquake. He at length grew as pale as she was, shuddered through all his frame, seized her hand, drew her closer, as one having authority, held her firmly while he fixed upon her blanched face a gaze as earnest, as searching, as thrilling as her own had been.

He broke the silence.

"Margaret Helmstedt! Margaret Helmstedt! I see you then at last! And now that I gaze upon your face—how like, great Heaven! to hers. Come— come! You must go with me. You must inform me of that which you alone have power to communicate. You must confirm to me that fact which I suspect, but do not know; or, rather, which I know, but cannot prove. Come, Margaret Helmstedt, come;" and, closing his hand cruelly upon hers, he drew her, blanched and unresisting, after him, into the covert of the wood, where they were quickly hidden.

There had been unsuspected witnesses to this strange scene. So absorbed in their mutual subject of interest had been the maiden and the soldier, that they had not perceived that the trio, consisting of Lieutenant King, Clare Hartley, and Grace Wellworth, who were going up toward the house, had been met by another party, consisting of Mrs. Compton, Mrs. Houston, and Parson Wellworth, who were coming down toward the beach, and that a pause and a parley was the consequence. Nellie Houston, who was at the same time a furious patriot and a fearful poltroon, on seeing the hated and dreaded "redcoat," had clenched her fist, and frowned defiance, even while she paled and trembled with terror. Mrs. Compton had remained composed. She had been an old campaigner of the long revolutionary struggle, and was not easily disconcerted by the sight of the British uniform. The old parson had put on his spectacles and taken sight. Seeing that the officer, cap in hand, walked quietly and inoffensively on, between the two girls, neither of whom betrayed the least uneasiness, he turned to the frightened and belligerent Nellie, and said: "Do not be alarmed, madam; he is an officer and a gentleman, and will, no doubt, conduct himself as such, and compel his men to the manners of men."

And the next moment, when they met, the officer made good the words of the preacher. Bowing profoundly, he explained that his party had landed on the island for the purpose of procuring a supply of fresh water and provisions.

Nellie flushed to her forehead, bit her lips till the blood came, and turned away in silence. She had no good-will for the British, and would not feign even civility.

Mrs. Compton satisfied the claims of conventional politeness by bowing coldly.

Mr. Wellworth took upon himself to be spokesman of his party, and responded:

"Sir, Major Helmstedt, the proprietor of this estate, is now absent with the American army, in the North—doing, no doubt, good service to his country, and good execution among your ranks. We, whom you find on the spot, are only members of a picnic party, consisting in all of about fifteen ladies, young and old, two half-grown boys, and four aged men. Your force, sir, looks to me to be nearly, or quite, forty fighting men. Resistance on our part would be in vain, else, Christian minister as I am, I might be tempted to refuse to give to our enemy drink, though he were athirst, or meat, though he hungered. The available provisions of the island, sir, are just now very limited in quantity. The fortunes of war have placed them at your disposition, sir. We are in your power. We therefore confide in your honor, as a gentleman and an officer, that in appropriating the articles in question, you will proceed with the quietness and courtesy due to the presence of ladies."

To this speech, which was more candid than conciliating, the lieutenant bowed, assuring the clergyman that "booty" and not "beauty," was the present object in request; that the former should be removed with the least possible disturbance to the latter; and counseling him to withdraw the ladies to the upper chambers of the mansion, while his men came on and took possession, for an hour or so, of the lower rooms.

While the clergyman and the lieutenant thus conversed, Nellie turned to the two girls, who had left the side of their escort, and said:

"Why, where is Margaret? Where have you left her?"

"Margaret! Oh! on the beach, or just above it. There she is now, talking with that saucy ensign!" exclaimed Grace Wellworth, in a tone of pique.

"No fear for our heroic Margaret! She is quite competent to the care of her own personal safety," retorted Clare Hartley.

"Yet I think it is very indiscreet in Margaret to remain behind conversing with that impudent young ensign!" cried Grace, petulantly, drawing the attention of the whole party to the unconscious subject of her animadversions. Clare looked on in astonishment. Nellie gazed in consternation. Mr. Wellworth stared like a lunatic. And Lieutenant King declared it as his experience that Ensign Dawson was "the devil among the girls." And before this group had recovered their self-possession, they saw the young couple disappear in the woods.

"Go after them! Fly to her rescue! She is carried off! Run, Mr. Wellworth," cried Nellie, in a paroxysm of terror, as soon as she had recovered from her amazement.

But Lieutenant King advised the lady to be calm, and the clergyman to mind his own affairs, adding that the young girl had accompanied the soldier quite voluntarily, and that he would warrant her, or any lady, safe from offense by Ensign Dawson.

"You would warrant him, after witnessing his behavior to me!" exclaimed Grace, in a half-suppressed whisper, which was, however, not so much smothered, but that its purport reached the ears of the officer, who answered, earnestly:

"Had you been in the woods alone with that youthful soldier, he would have respected your solitude, and helplessness; but you were amid your friends; you ran, unwittingly challenging pursuit, and hence—but I do not defend him; he was wrong, and I beg pardon in his behalf."

"What? what? what was that, Grace?" asked old Mr. Wellworth, in alarm.

"Nothing, father! only when I took fright and ran away, he gave chase, caught and brought me back to my party; that is all," replied Grace, suppressing the fact of the rifled kiss, and blushing deeply for its suppression.

"Mr. Wellworth, I really must insist upon your going in search of Margaret. This lieutenant indorses the ensign; but who indorses the lieutenant?" inquired Nellie.

Lieutenant King bowed "as if he had received a compliment."

And moved by this persistence on the part of Mrs. Houston, the old clergyman took the path leading down to the thicket.

"Madam," said Lieutenant King, "will you permit me to counsel you to proceed to the house, and withdraw your female friends to the privacy of the upper chambers. Myself and my men, who are not desirable company for ladies, will follow in about fifteen minutes. They will want refreshments. You will, therefore, be so kind as to leave the keys of the pantry, storehouse, cellars, etc., in charge of some male servant, with orders to wait upon me."

"Sir, because all our able men are with the army, and we are defenseless and in your power, you shall be obeyed. And for no other reason on the face of the earth!" exclaimed Nellie, flushing with anger, as she beckoned her companions, and took the way, successively, through the meadow, the orchard, and the garden, to the house. As they turned away, the British officer bowed with scrupulous politeness, and laughed within himself, as he muttered:

"You are a 'good-nater' little lady," and took the way to the beach to bring together his men.

Meanwhile, Nellie and her companions reached the mansion, and spread consternation among the company by announcing that a British force had landed on the island. With the recollection of Craney Island fresh in their minds, there was not an old lady there who did not expect to be put to the sword, or a young woman or boy who did not look to be carried off. But the calm courage of Clare Hartley, and the cool serenity of old Mrs. Compton, did much toward soothing their fears and restoring quiet. Mrs. Houston then explained that they were all to go upstairs and lock themselves in the chambers, while the soldiers bivouacked below.

Hapzibah was then called, and ordered to produce the keys.

"Well, I 'spose how der's no help for it, Miss Nellie; fur ef I don't guv um up, dem are white niggers bust open ebery singly door in the house," said Hapzibah.

"Yes, and set it on fire afterward, and throw you in to feed the flames!" was the comforting reply.

"I 'fies 'em for to do it—white herrin's!—who's afeard?—'sides which, I don't believe I'd blaze for 'em!"

"No; you'd blow up like a skin of gunpowder. But hand over the keys, and go call your brother, old Euripedes, to take charge of them and wait on the gentlemen. You'll have to come upstairs with the ladies."

"Me go hide 'long o' de ladies, jes' as ef I was feared o' dem white niggers! Me leabe my poor, ole, innocen' brudder 'lone, to be put upon by dem debbils! I like to see myself a doin' of it! I'd see ole Hempseed Island sunk inter de bottom o' de sea wid all aboard fust—dat's me. Yer all hear me good, don't yer?"

"They'll certainly throw you in the fire if you talk in that way," said Nellie, laughing, in despite of her secret fears and anxieties.

"I wouldn't burn to save dere precious libes! I'd see 'em all blasted fust! I'd see it good! Dat's me! But I begs yer pardon, Miss Nellie, chile! I doesn't mean no 'fence, nor likewise no disrespect to you, honey—'deed no! But yer see de werry sight 'o one 'o dem dere b'iled crabs makes me crawl all ober— an' de sight o' one o' dere scarlet-coats drives me ravin' mad as ef I war a she-bull!—dat's me! 'Cause yer see, chile, de werry fust time one o' dem dere debbils put his fut on ter de islan' he done fetch death an' 'struction long ob him! An' now dat debbil done gone an' fetch forty more debbils more worse nor hisself. An' I wish, I does, how I could bore a hole in de islan' an' sink it wid all aboard, I do—dat's me. An' now I'll go arter my brudder You-Rip."

"Stay a moment," said Mrs. Houston. "You can tell us—is there much wine and liquor in the cellar?—for if those wretches are permitted to drink themselves to madness, even the word of their commanding officer is no security for their good behavior!"

"Wine an' likker! No, thanks be to my 'Vine Marster dere ain't a singly drap to cool dere parchy tongues, no more'n dere is in Aberyham's buzzum! Marse Fillup done ship it all away to camp, for he an' Marse Wrath to treat dere brudder ossifers wid, to keep dere couridge when dey goes inter battle. Wish it was me goin'! I wouldn't 'quire no sich. 'Sides which, I'd shoot somefin harder at 'em nor grapeshot inter 'em, as dey talk so much about, which it stands to reason shootin' grapes is nuffin but chile's play, and can't hurt nobody, much less dem dere hardened b'iled crabs, 'less deys 'stilled into likker an' drank too much of, 'sides bein' a waste o' de fruit; which dey do say as how 'willful waste make woeful want.'"

"My goodness alive, Happy, how you do run on. You make my head go round and round like a water-wheel. Do go now and send Euripedes to me," said Mrs. Houston.

"I gwine," said Hapzibah, who took herself off.

And just then the gentlemen of the party, who had been out fishing at the opposite extremity of the island, and had been sent for, arrived upon the scene, and received the intelligence of the landing of the foraging party on the western shore of the island, and of their momentarily expected arrival at the house.

And now at last there was promptitude of action. The ladies and female servants were collected and hurried upstairs, with recommendations not only to lock, but to bolt and bar themselves within the innermost chambers. Old Hapzibah's age, fearlessness and tearful remonstrances obtained for her the questionable privilege of remaining out to stand by her "poor ole angel," as she lovingly termed her brother. Euripedes and herself were intrusted with the keys, and directions to wait upon the foragers. The four old gentlemen and the two boys then armed themselves, and took their stations in the upper hall to defend, if necessary, the approach to the ladies' place of retreat. These arrangements were scarcely concluded, before the foraging party entered the house. And then followed the feast, and succeeded the orgies!—and such orgies! It was providential that there was no liquor to be found, though every cellar, closet, cupboard and pantry was ransacked, in the vain hope of finding a hidden store. The hampers of the picnic party were rifled of their costly delicacies, and a few bottles of rare wine discovered, but this went only a little way among so many. You should have heard old Hapzibah's indignant account of their proceedings. She said that "Each red debbil among 'em 'haved as if he wer' 'sessed o' seben oder debbils more worser dan hissef!" That when they failed to find the wine, they drove her "poor, ole, innocen', sufferin' darlin' on afore 'em an' swore all de hair off'n his head—de poor, ole, timidy, saf'-hearted chile, as couldn' stan' nuffin o' dere debblish doin's"—that because she, Aunt Hapzibah, couldn't be here, and there, and everywhere at once, "de 'fernal white niggers got into her cabin an' stole her trunk o' berryin' close, which she meant to go arter 'em herself, an' git 'em back even ef she had to pull 'em out'n Admirable Cockburn's own claws! Dough ef he, Cockburn, was admirable, she should like to know, she should, who was 'bominable! That de low-life white herrin's was so 'fraid o' bein' p'isoned, dat dey made poor, ole Rip, poor, ole, sufferin', put-upon angel, drink out'n ebery thing, whedder it 'greed with him or not—an' eben 'pelled him to drink out'n ebery singly milk-pan in the dairyhouse, which eberybody knows he neber could 'bide milk eber since he was weaned, which allers made him dead sick to his stumick."

Finally, it was sunset before the marauders left the island, carrying off with them not only all the grain, but all the meat, fruit, and garden vegetables, and also all the poultry, and all the live stock with the exception of one old black ram, the patriarch of the flock, whom Hapzibah swore bitterly to carry to Cockburn, when she went after her trunk.

It was quite dark before it was considered safe to warrant the descent of the ladies from their retreat. Fortunately there would be a moon, or else the half-starved and thoroughly wearied picnickers must have rowed home in darkness. Now, therefore, they assembled on the porch, to talk over their misadventure, and wait for the rising of the moon. But suddenly some one asked:

"Where is Margaret Helmstedt, and——"

"Where is Margaret?" was echoed all around.

Nellie had hoped that she was safe in the charge of Mr. Wellworth. But Mr. Wellworth, who from wandering all over the island now joined the party, declared that he had been unable to find her, and that he had expected to hear of her among her friends present. And now, as the alarm spread, and exclamations of: "Where is Margaret?" "Where can she be?" "Is it possible she can have been carried off?" were passed in distress from one to another, and all began to separate to prosecute the search for her, a quiet low voice was heard from their midst, saying:

"I am here—be not uneasy!" and, ghostlike, Margaret Helmstedt stood among them! The sight of the maiden was an immediate and great relief, but:

"Are you quite safe, my child?" asked Mr. Wellworth.

"Quite!" responded Margaret, sinking upon a bench as if greatly exhausted.

"Where have you been?" asked Mrs. Houston sharply.

"Beyond the wa——" Her voice died away in silence; she had fainted.

"It is fatigue, and fright, and want of food," said old Mrs. Compton, going to the poor girl, raising her head, and supporting it on her lap.

"And those wretches have not left so much as a drop of wine to revive her, or even a candle to see her face by," exclaimed Nellie, who, whatever her cause of displeasure might be, was always moved by the sight of physical suffering, with which she could the more readily sympathize. But Dr. Hartley caused Margaret's head to be laid down again, and water to be dashed in her face; and by these simple means her recovery was soon effected.

As the moon was now rising, the company prepared themselves, and went down to the beach to get into their boats, which, they thanked Heaven, had not been carried off by the marauders. The trip back was decidedly the pleasantest part of the whole expedition. An hour's row over the moonlit waters brought them to the Bluff, where Nellie ordered supper to be immediately prepared for the whole famished party, who remained her guests that night, and only separated after breakfast the next morning.

When her last guest had departed, Mrs. Houston entered the private sitting-room of Margaret Helmstedt, whom she found quietly sitting beside her workstand, engaged in sewing.

Taking a seat close beside her, Mrs. Houston said:

"Margaret, I have come to request an explanation of your strange conduct of yesterday, which, let me assure you, has given your friends great pain, and even revived all the old gossip of which you were the subject. Margaret, I await your answer."

She looked up from her work, and fixing her dark eyes full upon the face of her catechiser, answered firmly though gently:

"Mrs. Houston, I have no explanation to make!"

The little lady flushed and bit her lip.

Margaret continued her needlework.

"Then I am to understand, Miss Helmstedt, that you consider it quite proper for a young lady to spend two or three hours alone in the woods with a soldier, who is not of her kindred?"

Margaret might have replied with truth, "No, Mrs. Houston, I do not consider that at all proper," but she chose, on the contrary, to remain silent.

"And you doubtless think, besides, that an affianced bride owes no consideration to her betrothed husband."

"So far from that, I feel that she owes the same as if the church and the state had already blessed and confirmed the engagement," answered Margaret.

"Which, in your case, it will never do, unless certain suspicious acts of yours are satisfactorily explained."

"Mrs. Houston, I do not understand you," said Margaret, flushing deeply.

"You do not seem to know that the honor of Ralph is committed to your keeping!"

"Mrs. Houston, the honor of no human being can possibly go out of his own keeping, or into that of another."

The lady still bit her lip in high displeasure; but a glance at the pale, pensive face, and mourning dress of the orphan girl, a sudden recollection of her dead mother, a reflection upon the inevitable misery that any real imprudence might bring upon that mother's only child, perhaps modified her resentment, for in a kinder tone she said:

"Margaret Helmstedt, you are on the brink of a frightful precipice! pause! confide to me the nature of the acquaintance subsisting between yourself and that strange young man, whom you had evidently known previous to your meeting yesterday morning. Is he the person to whom you wrote those mysterious letters? Is he the same whose visit to the island caused your poor mother such keen distress? Was it the dread of your continued intimacy, and possible union with such an unadmissible person, that constrained her to betroth you to Ralph, and consign you to my care? Speak, Margaret! It may be in my power to help and save you!"

Margaret trembled through all her frame, but answered firmly:

"Dear Mrs. Houston, I thank you for your kindness, but—I have nothing to say!"

"Margaret; I adjure you by the memory of your dead mother, speak! explain!"

She might have replied, "And in the name of my dear, mother, I repudiate your adjuration!" But fearing to give the slightest clue, or in the least degree to compromise the memory of her who slept beneath the old oak beside the waves, she answered:

"Even so adjured, I can only repeat, that I have no explanation to make, Mrs. Houston."

"Then I will delay no longer. I will write to Ralph!" exclaimed Mrs. Houston, indignantly rising and leaving the room.

"Oh! mother! mother!" The wailing voice of the girl was smothered in her spread hands, and in her thick, disheveled hair as she cast herself upon the floor.

Now whether Mrs. Houston really put her threat into immediate execution, is not known. What is certain, the increased coldness of all the family, even of the kind-hearted, liberal-minded Colonel Houston, so distressed the spirit of the orphan girl that she seldom sought their company, and at last met them only at meal times. A fortnight passed thus, during which the family at the Bluff received no company and paid no visits. Such long seasons of isolation, even in summer, were not unusual in that sparsely settled place, where the undertaking of a friendly visit was really a serious piece of business.

At the end of a fortnight, however, as the family were sitting at dinner, Mr. Wellworth suddenly and unannounced entered the room. His countenance betrayed that some unusual circumstance had brought him out. All arose to receive him. In the midst of the general shaking of hands, the colonel put the question that all longed to ask.

"What has happened, Mr. Wellworth?"

"Why, sir, a party of British soldiers landed this morning and attacked the parsonage!"

"Good Heaven! I hope no serious damage has been done?" exclaimed Colonel Houston, while all listened with intense interest for his answer.

"No, thank the Lord! There was, providentially, a wedding at the church, a poor man's, whose friends had all gathered to see him married. We armed ourselves with what we could catch up, and, being much the larger party, succeeded in beating off the assailants."

"I hope there was no bloodshed?" said the kind-hearted Mrs. Compton.

"None on our side to speak of. They left one of their party on the field— Dodson—Carson—Dawson—yes, that is his name, Dawson—the very fellow that was with the foragers who broke in upon our picnic party."

A low half-suppressed cry from Margaret, had greeted the name of the wounded man. But no one heard it but Mrs. Houston, who resented it by saying:

"And I hope, Mr. Wellworth, the wretch was dead!"

"He may be so by this time, madam," replied the minister, in a voice of grave rebuke; "the poor young man is severely wounded. We have put him to bed; my daughter Grace and her maid are taking care of him, and I am off for Dr. Hartley. I called just to beg you to have me put across the bay."

"Certainly," replied Colonel Houston, who immediately despatched his waiter to give orders for the boat to be made ready. And in fifteen minutes Mr. Wellworth had departed on his errand.

It was late in the evening when the clergyman returned with the physician, and both took their way to the parsonage. The next morning, when Dr. Hartley called at the Bluff on his way home, he reported the wound of the young ensign not so dangerous as had been represented. And, in short, in a few days the young man was convalescent. Before his full recovery, the British fleet had left this portion of the bay, and had gone down to the mouth of the Patuxent. The attack upon the parsonage was the last foray made by their troops in that neighborhood.

One morning, about the third week in August, the family at Buzzard's Bluff were cast into a state of consternation by an unprecedented event. Margaret Helmstedt did not appear at the breakfast table. After awaiting her coming for some time, Mrs. Houston sent to inquire for her, and learned that she was not to be found. Her maid was also missing. Her footman was next sought for in vain, and during the search it was discovered that her little sail, *The Pearl Shell* had also been taken away. And while the trouble of the family was still at its height, Mr. Wellworth was announced, and entered with intelligence that seemed, in Mrs. Houston's estimation, to throw light upon the mystery of Margaret's flight—namely, that his prisoner, the young British ensign, William Dawson, had broken his parole and fled.

CHAPTER XIII
PERSECUTION

"They said that guilt a shade had cast
Upon her youthful fame,
And scornful murmurs as she passed
Were mingled with her name.
In truth, it was a painful sight
As former friends went by
To see her trembling lip grow white
Beneath each altered eye."

—Mrs. Holmes.

To the surprise of all the family at the Bluff, Margaret Helmstedt, the third morning from her disappearance, returned to her guardian's house. Mrs. Houston took upon herself the ungenial task of meeting the delinquent.

"Well, miss, or rather, I beg your pardon, madam, permit me to congratulate you! though really I had not supposed you would have so soon honored my humble house with a visit," said Nellie, as she met her at the door.

"Mrs. Houston, I do not understand you: pray, let me pass," pleaded the girl, who looked pale, exhausted, and heartbroken.

"Pass, indeed! I would first know who it is that so glibly demands to pass. No, madam; your right to pass here is forfeited. I only wonder that you should present yourself. But I suppose that you have come for your effects; if so, inform me where they shall be sent, and I will have them forwarded."

Margaret leaned half fainting against the door frame, but notwithstanding her physical prostration and mental disturbance, she maintained her presence of mind.

"Mrs. Houston, you are mistaken. I bear no new name or new relation, as your words would seem to imply."

"Then, miss, so much the worse!" exclaimed Nellie, indignantly.

"I do not understand you," said Margaret, in amazement.

"You do! And I wonder more than ever that you should presume to present yourself before me!" retorted the lady, raising her voice.

"Mrs. Houston, my mother was your bosom friend. Do not insult her daughter," said Margaret, as the blood rushed to her face.

"You have dishonored your mother!" exclaimed Nellie, in a paroxysm of emotion between anger, awakened memory and grief.

"God knoweth!" replied the maiden, dropping her head and her clasped hands with a gesture of profound despair.

But the altercation had reached the ears of Colonel Houston, who now came out, saying:

"Nellie, my dear, this is not the way to meet this exigency. Good-morning, Miss Helmstedt, pray walk in and be seated. Nellie, she is but a young thing! If she has committed any grave fault, it carries its own bitter punishment, God knows. As for us, since she presents herself here again, we must continue to give her shelter and protection until the arrival of her father. Nay, Nellie, my dear, I say this must be done whatever her offences may be."

"You too! Oh, you too, Colonel Houston!" involuntarily exclaimed Margaret, clasping her hands.

"Miss Helmstedt, my child, I am not your judge. Make a confidante of my wife, she loved your mother. Go into your apartment, Margaret. Attend her, Mrs. Houston."

"Colonel Houston, I thank you! Mrs. Houston," she continued, in a faltering voice; "I returned here only—because—it was my appointed place of abode—the home selected for me by my parents and—Ralph."

"Never mind about Ralph now, my child," said the colonel, in a gentle tone, which nevertheless cut Margaret to the heart. She meekly bowed her head and passed on to her own apartments, followed by Mrs. Houston, who threw herself into a chair and immediately commenced a close catechism, which was interrupted in the midst by Margaret saying:

"Dear Mrs. Houston, not from any want of respect to you, and not in defiance of your authority, but from the direst necessity—Oh, what am I saying!" She stopped suddenly in great anguish and remained silent.

"Margaret Helmstedt, what mean you?" demanded Mrs. Houston, indignantly.

"Nothing! I mean nothing!"

"You mean to affront me!"

"No, Heaven knows!"

"How can you explain or defend your conduct?"

"In no manner!"

"And you expect us quietly to submit to your contumacy?"

"No! Do your will. I cannot blame you!"

"And Ralph?"

Like the rising of an inward light came a transient glow of faith from her beautiful face.

"Ralph will think no evil," she said, softly.

"Yet let me assure you, Miss Helmstedt, that though Ralph Houston's chivalric confidence in you may be unshaken; yet his father will never now consent to the continuance of his engagement with you. You heard what Colonel Houston said?"

"I heard," said Margaret, with gentle dignity.

"You heard? what then!"

"Mr. Houston is twenty-eight years of age, and his own master."

"And what follows, pray, from that?"

"That in this matter he will do as seems to him right!"

"And yourself?"

"I leave my destiny with the fullest faith where God, my parents and his parents placed it—in the hands of my betrothed husband."

"And he will abide by his engagement! I know his Quixotic temper! he will. But, Margaret Helmstedt, delicacy requires of you to retire from the contract."

Margaret smiled mournfully, and answered earnestly:

"Madam, God knoweth that there are higher principles of action than fantastic delicacy. I have no right to break my engagement with Ralph Houston. I will free him from his bond; but if he holds me to mine, why so be it; he is wiser than I am, and in the name of the Lord I am his affianced wife."

Nellie scarcely knew how to reply to this. She looked straight into the face of the girl as though she would read and expose her soul. Superficially that face was pale and still; the lips compressed; the eyes cast down until the close, long lashes lay penciled on the white cheeks; but, under all, a repressed glow of devotion, sorrow, firmness, fervor, made eloquent the beautiful countenance, as she sat there, with her hands clasped and unconsciously pressed to her bosom. Despite of the strong circumstantial evidence, Nellie could not look into that face and hold to her belief the owner's unworthiness. And the little woman grew more angry at the inconsistency and contradiction of her own thoughts and feelings. She ascribed this to Margaret's skill in influencing her. And out of her pause and study she broke forth impatiently:

"You are an artful girl, Margaret. I do not know where you get your duplicity, not from your mother, I know. No matter; thank Heaven, in a few days your father and Ralph will be here, and my responsibility over." And rising, angrily, she left the room, and left Margaret remaining in the same attitude of superficial calmness and suppressed excitement.

Nellie went to her own especial sitting-room, communicating by short passages with storeroom, pantry and kitchen, and where she transacted all her housekeeping business. She found her own maid, the pretty mulatress, with knitting in hand, as usual, in attendance.

"Go at once, Jessie, and call Miss Helmstedt's servants here."

The girl obeyed, and soon returned, accompanied by Hildreth and Forrest, who made their "reverence," and stood waiting the lady's pleasure.

"I suppose your mistress has given you orders to reply to no questions in regard to her absence!" asked Nellie, sharply.

"No, madam; Miss Marget did nothing of the sort," answered Forrest.

"Be careful of your manner, sir."

Forrest bowed.

"When did she leave the house?"

"Night afore last."

"With whom?"

"Me an' Hild'eth, madam."

"No others?"

"No, madam."

"Where did she go?"

"Up the river some ways to a landin' on to de Marylan' shore as I never was at afore."

"And what then?"

"She lef' me den, Hild'eth an' me, at a farmhouse where we landed, an' took a horse an' rode away. She was gone all day. Last night she come back, an' paid de bill, and took boat an' come straight home."

"Very well, that is all very well of you, Forrest, so far. You have told the truth, I suppose; but you have not told the whole truth, I know. Whom did she meet at that farmhouse? and who rode away with her when she went?"

"Not a singly soul did she meet, 'cept it was de fam'ly. An' not a singly soul did ride with her."

"You are lying!" exclaimed Nellie, who, in her anger, was very capable of using strong language to the servants.

"No! 'fore my 'Vine Marster in heaben, I'se tellin' of you de trufe, Miss Nellie."

"You are not! Your mistress has tutored you what to say."

The old man's face flushed darkly, as he answered:

"I ax your pardon very humble, Miss Nellie; but Miss Marget couldn't tutor no one to no false. An' on de contrairy wise she said to we den, my sister an' me, she said: 'Forrest and Hildreth, mind when you are questioned in regard to me tell the truf as jus' you know it.' Dat's all, Miss Nellie. 'Deed it is, madam. Miss Marget is high beyant tutorin' anybody to any false."

"There! you are not requested to indorse Miss Helmstedt. And very likely she did not take you into her counsels. Now, tell me the name of the place where you stopped?"

"I doesn't know it, Miss Nellie, madam."

"Well, then, the name of the people?"

"Dey call de old gemman Marse John, an' de ole lady Miss Mary. I didn' hear no other name."

"You are deceiving me!"

"No, 'fore my Heabenly Marster, madam."

"You are!" And here followed an altercation not very creditable to the dignity of Mrs. Colonel Houston, and which was, besides, quite fruitless, as the servant could give her no further satisfaction.

All that forenoon Margaret sat in her room, occupying her hands with some needlework in which her heart took little interest. She dreaded the dinner hour, in which she should have to face the assembled family. She would gladly have remained fasting in her room, for, indeed, her appetite was gone, but she wished to do nothing that could be construed into an act of resentment. So, when the bell rang, she arose with a sigh, bathed her face, smoothed her black tresses, added a little lace collar and locket brooch to her black silk dress, and passed out to the dining-room.

The whole family were already seated at the table; but Colonel Houston, who never failed in courtesy to the orphan girl, arose, as usual, and handed her to her seat. Her eyes were cast down, her cheeks were deeply flushed. She wore, poor girl, what seemed a look of conscious guilt, but it was the consciousness, not of guilt, but of being thought guilty. She could scarcely lift her heavy lids to meet and return the cold nods of recognition with which old Colonel and Mrs. Compton acknowledged her presence. The fervid devotion that had nerved her heart to meet Mrs. Houston's single attack was chilled before this table full of cold faces and averted eyes. She could not partake of the meal; she could scarcely sustain herself through the sitting; and at the end she escaped from the table as from a scene of torture.

"She is suffering very much; I will go and talk to her," said the really kind-hearted old Mrs. Compton.

"No, mother, do nothing of the sort. It would be altogether useless. You might wear out your lungs to no purpose. She is perfectly contumacious," said Mrs. Houston.

"Nellie, my dear, she is the child of your best friend."

"I know it," exclaimed the little lady, with the tears of grief and rage rushing to her eyes, "and that is what makes it so difficult to deal with her; for if she were any other than Marguerite De Lancie's daughter, I would turn her out of the house without more ado."

"My good mother, and my dear wife, listen to me. You are both right, in a measure. I think with you, Nellie, that since Miss Helmstedt persistently declines to explain her strange course, self-respect and dignity should hold us all henceforth silent upon this subject. And with you, Mrs. Compton, I think that regard to the memory of the mother should govern our conduct toward the child until we can resign her into the hands of her father. The trial will be short. We may daily expect his arrival, and in the meantime we must avoid the obnoxious subject, and treat the young lady with the courtesy due solely to Marguerite De Lancie's daughter."

While this conversation was on the tapis, the door was thrown open, and the Rev. Mr. Wellworth announced. This worthy gentleman's arrival was, of late, the harbinger of startling news. The family had grown to expect it on seeing him. His appearance now corroborated their usual expectations. His manner was hurried, his face flushed, his expression angry.

"Good-day, friends! Has your fugitive returned?"

"Yes, why?" inquired three or four in a breath, rising from the table.

"Because mine has, that is all!" replied the old man, throwing down his hat and seating himself unceremoniously. "Yes, Ensign Dawson presented himself this morning at our house, looking as honest, as frank, and as innocent as that exemplary young man generally does. I inquired why he came, and how he dared present himself. He replied that he had been unavoidably detained, but that as soon as he was at liberty, he had returned to redeem his parole and save his honor. I told him that 'naught was never in danger,' but requested him to be more explicit. He declined, saying that he had explained to me that he had been detained, and had in the first moment of his liberty returned to give himself up, and that was enough for me to know."

"But, you asked him about the supposed companion of his flight?" inquired the indiscreet Nellie.

"Ay, and when I mentioned Margaret Helmstedt's name, his eyes flashed fire! he clapped his hand where his sword was not, and looked as if he would have run me through the body!"

"And gave you no satisfaction, I daresay?"

"None whatever—neither denying nor affirming anything."

"And what have you done with the villain? I hope you have locked him up in the cellar!" exclaimed the indignant Nellie.

"Not I, indeed; if I had, the case would have been hopeless."

"I—I do not understand you," said Nellie.

The clergyman looked all around the room, and then replied:

"There are no giddy young people here to repeat the story. I will tell you. Grace is a fool! All girls are, I believe! A scarlet coat with gilt ornaments inflames their imaginations—a wound melts their hearts! And our wounded prisoner, between his fine scarlet and gold coat and his broken rib—(well, you understand me!)—if I had locked him up in the cellar, or in the best bedroom, my girl would have straightway imagined me a tyrannical old despot, and my captive would have grown a hero in her eyes! No, I invited him to dinner, drank his health, played a game of backgammon with him, and afterward returned him his parole, and privately signified that he was at liberty to depart. And however my silly girl feels about it, she cannot say that I persecuted this 'poor wounded hussar.'"

"But, the d——l! you do not mean to say that this villain aspired to Grace also?" exclaimed Colonel Houston, in dismay.

"How can I tell? I do not know that he did aspire to Margaret, or that he didn't aspire to Grace! All I know is, that Grace behaved like a fool after his first departure and worse, if possible, after his second. But Margaret, you say, has returned?"

"She came back this morning."

"And what does the unfortunate girl say?"

"Like your prisoner, she refuses to affirm or deny anything."

"Mr. Wellworth," said Colonel Houston, "we have decided to speak no more upon the subject with Miss Helmstedt, but to leave matters as they are until the return of her father, who is daily expected."

"I think, under the circumstances, that that is as well," replied the old man. And soon after, he concluded his visit and departed.

And as the subject was no more mentioned to Margaret, she remained in ignorance of the visit of Mr. Wellworth.

And from this time Margaret Helmstedt kept her own apartments, except when forced to join the family at their meals. And upon these occasions, the silence of the ladies, and the half compassionate courtesy of Colonel Houston, wounded her heart more deeply than the most bitter reproaches could have done.

A week passed in this dreary manner, and still Major Helmstedt and Captain Houston had not returned, though they were as yet daily expected.

Margaret, lonely, desolate, craving companionship and sympathy, one day ordered her carriage and drove up to the parsonage to see Grace

Wellworth. She was shown into the little sitting-room where the parson's daughter sat sewing.

Grace arose to meet her friend with a constrained civility that cut Margaret to the heart. She could not associate her coldness with the calumnious reports afloat concerning herself, and therefore could not comprehend it.

But Margaret's heart yearned toward her friend; she could not bear to be at variance with her.

"My dearest Grace, what is the matter? have I unconsciously offended you in any way?" she inquired, gently, as she sat down beside the girl and laid her hand on her arm.

"Unconsciously! no, I think not! You are doubly a traitor, Margaret Helmstedt! Traitor to your betrothed and to your friend!" replied Miss Wellworth, bitterly.

"Grace! this from you!"

"Yes, this from me! of all others from me! The deeply injured have a right to complain and reproach."

"Oh, Grace! Grace! my friend!" exclaimed Margaret, wringing her hands.

But before another word was said, old Mr. Wellworth entered the room.

"Good-afternoon, Miss Helmstedt. Grace, my dear, go down to Dinah's quarter and give her her medicine, Miss Helmstedt will excuse you. One of our women has malaria fever, Miss Helmstedt."

"Indeed! I am sorry; but I have some skill in nursing: shall I not go with Grace?" inquired Margaret, as her friend arose to leave the room.

"No, young lady; I wish to have some conversation with you."

Grace sulkily departed, and Margaret meekly resumed her seat.

"Miss Helmstedt, my poor child, it is a very painful duty that I have now to perform. Since the decease of my wife, I have to watch with double vigilance over the welfare of my motherless daughter, and I should feel indebted to you, Margaret, if you would abstain from visiting Grace until some questions in regard to your course are satisfactorily answered."

Margaret's face grew gray with anguish as she arose to her feet, and clasping her hands, murmured:

"My God! my God! You do not think I could do anything that should separate me from the good of my own sex?"

"Margaret, unhappy child, that question is not for me to answer. I dare not judge you, but leave the matter to God above and to your father on earth."

"Farewell, Mr. Wellworth. I know the time will come when your kind nature will feel sorrow for having stricken a heart already so bruised and bleeding as this," she said, laying her hand upon her surcharged bosom; "but you are not to blame, so God bless you and farewell," she repeated, offering her hand.

The clergyman took and pressed it, and the tears sprang to his eyes as he answered:

"Margaret, the time has come, when I deeply regret the necessity of giving you pain. Alas! my child, 'the way of the transgressor is hard.' May God deliver your soul," and rising, he attended her to her carriage, placed her in it, and saying:

"God bless you!" closed the door and retired.

"Oh, mother! mother! Oh, mother! mother! behold the second gift—my only friendship! They are yours, mother! they are yours! only love me from heaven! for I love you beyond all on earth," cried Margaret, covering her sobbing face, and sinking back in the carriage.

Margaret returned home to her deserted and lonely rooms. No one came thither now; no one invited her thence. Darker lowered the clouds of fate over her devoted young head. Another weary week passed, and still the returning soldiers had not arrived. The Sabbath came—the first Sabbath in October.

Margaret had always found the sweetest consolation in the ordinances of religion. This, being the first Sabbath of the month, was sacrament Sunday. And never since her entrance into the church had Margaret missed the communion. And now, even in her deep distress, when she so bitterly needed the consolations of religion, it was with a subdued joy that she prepared to receive them. It was delightful autumn weather, and the whole family who were going would fill the family coach—so much had been intimated to Margaret through her attendants. Therefore she was obliged to order her own carriage. The lonely ride, under present circumstances, was far more endurable than the presence of the family would have been; and solitude and silence afforded her the opportunity for meditation that the occasion required.

She reached the church and left her carriage before the hour of service. The fine day had drawn an unusually large congregation together, and had kept them sauntering and gossiping out in the open air; but Margaret, as she smiled or nodded to one or another, met only scornful glances or averted heads. More than shocked, appalled and dismayed by this sort of reception, she hurried into the church and on to her pew.

Margaret had always, in preference to the Houstons' pew, occupied her own mother's, "to keep it warm," she had said, in affectionate explanation, to Mrs. Houston. Generally, Grace or Clare, or both, came and sat with her to keep her company. But to-day, as yet, neither of her friends had arrived, and she occupied her pew alone. As hers was one of those side pews in a line with the pulpit, her position commanded not only the preacher's, but the congregation's view. The preacher had not come. The congregation in the church was sparse, the large majority remaining in the yard. Yet, as Margaret's eyes casually roved over this thin assembly, she grew paler to notice how heads were put together, and whispers and sidelong glances were directed to herself. To escape this, and to find strength and comfort, she opened her pocket Bible and commenced reading.

Presently, the bell tolled; and the people came pouring in, filling their pews. About the time that all was quiet, the minister came in, followed at a little distance by his son and daughter, who passed into the parsonage pew, while he ascended into the pulpit, offered his preliminary private prayer, and then opening the book commenced the sublime ritual of worship.

"The Lord is in His holy temple. Let all the earth keep silence before Him."

These words, repeated Sunday after Sunday, never lost their sublime significance for Margaret. They ever impressed her solemnly, at once awing and elevating her soul. Now as they fell upon her ear, her sorrows and humiliations were, for the time, set aside. A hundred eyes might watch her, a hundred tongues malign her; but she neither heeded, nor even knew it. She knew she was alone—she could not help knowing this; Grace had passed her by; Clare had doubtless come, but not to her. She felt herself abandoned of human kind, but yet not alone, for "God was in His holy temple."

The opening exhortation, the hymn, the prayers, and the lessons for the day were all over, and the congregation knelt for the litany.

"From envy, hatred and malice, and all uncharitableness, good Lord deliver us."

These words had always slid easily over the tongue of Margaret, so foreign had these passions been to her life and experience; but now with what earnestness of heart they were repeated:

"That it may please Thee to forgive our enemies, persecutors and slanderers, and to turn their hearts."

Formal words once, repeated as by rote, now how full of significance to Margaret. "Oh, Father in Heaven," she added, "help me to ask this in all sincerity."

The litany was over, and the little bustle that ensued, of people rising from their knees, Margaret's pew door was opened, a warm hand clasped hers, and a cordial voice whispered in her ear:

"I am very late to-day, but 'better late than never,' even at church."

And Margaret, looking up, saw the bright face of Clare Hartley before her.

Poor Margaret, at this unexpected blessing, nearly burst into tears.

"Oh, Clare, have you heard? have you heard?" she eagerly whispered.

There was no time to say more; the services were recommenced, and the congregation attentive.

When the usual morning exercises were over, a portion of the congregation retired, while the other remained for the communion. Clare was not a communicant, but she stayed in the pew to wait for Margaret. Not with the first circle, nor yet with the second, but meekly with the third, Margaret approached the Lord's table. Mr. Wellworth administered the wine, and one of the deacons the bread. Margaret knelt near the center of the circle, so that about half the set were served before the minister came to her. And when he did, instead of putting the blessed chalice into her hand, he stooped and whispered:

"Miss Helmstedt, I would prefer to talk with you again before administering the sacrament to you."

This in face of the whole assembly. This at the altar. Had a thunderbolt fallen upon her head, she could scarcely have been more heavily stricken, more overwhelmed and stunned.

This, then, was the third offering; the comfort of the Christian sacraments was sacrificed. No earthly stay was left her now, but the regard of her stern father and the love of Ralph. Would they remain to her? For her father she could not decide. One who knew him best, and loved him most, had died because she dared not trust him with the secret of her life. But for Ralph! Ever at the thought of him, through her deeper distress, the great joy of faith arose, irradiating her soul and beaming from her countenance.

But now, alas! no thought, no feeling, but a sense of crushing shame possessed her. How she left that spot she never could have told! The first fact she knew was that Clare had left her pew to meet and join her; Clare's supporting arm was around her waist; Clare's encouraging voice was in her ears; Clare took her from the church and placed her in her carriage; and would have entered and sat beside her, but that Margaret, recovering her presence of mind, repulsed her, saying:

"No, Clare! no, beloved friend! it is almost well to have suffered so much to find a friend so loyal and true; but your girlish arm cannot singly sustain me. And you shall not compromise yourself for me. Leave me, brave girl; leave me to my fate!"

"Now may the Lord leave me when I do! No, please Heaven, Clare Hartley stands or falls with her friend!" exclaimed the noble girl, as she entered and seated herself beside Margaret. "Drive on, Forrest," she added, seeing Miss Helmstedt too much preoccupied to remember to give the order.

"My father was not at church to-day. So if you will send a messenger with a note from me to Dr. Hartley, I will remain with you, Margaret, until your father arrives."

"Oh, Clare! Clare! if you hurt yourself for me, I shall never forgive myself for allowing you to come."

"As if you could keep me away."

"Clare, do you know what they say of me?"

Clare shook her head, frowned, beat an impatient tattoo with her feet upon the mat, and answered:

"Know it! No; I do not! Do you suppose that I sit still and listen to any one slandering you? Do you imagine that any one would dare to slander you in my presence? I tell you, Margaret, that I should take the responsibility of expelling man or woman from my father's house who should dare to breathe a word against you."

"Oh, Clare! the circumstantial evidence against me is overwhelming!"

"What is circumstantial evidence, however strong, against your whole good and beautiful life?"

"You would never believe ill of me."

"Margaret—barring original sin, which I am required to believe in—I think I have a pure heart, a clear head, and strong eyes. I do not find so much evil in my own soul, as to be obliged to impute a part of it to another. I never confuse probabilities; and, lastly, I can tell an Agnes from a Calista at sight."

By this time the rapid drive had brought them home. Clare scribbled a hasty note, which Forrest conveyed to her father.

The Comptons and the Houstons were all communicants, and did not leave the church until all the services were over. They had been bitterly galled and humiliated by the repulse that Margaret Helmstedt, a member of their family, had received. On their way home, they discussed the propriety of immediately sending her off, with her servants, to Helmstedt's Island.

"Her father does not come; her conduct grows worse and worse; she has certainly forfeited all claims to our protection, and she compromises us every day," urged Nellie.

"I am not sure but that the isle would be the best and most secure retreat for her until the coming of her father; the servants there are faithful and reliable, and the place is not so very accessible to interlopers, now that the British have retired," said old Mrs. Compton.

Such being the opinion of the ladies of the family, upon a case immediately within their own province, Colonel Houston could say but little.

"Dear mother and fair wife, the matter rests with you at last; but for myself, I prefer that the girl should remain under our protection until the arrival of her father. I would place her nowhere, except in Major Helmstedt's own hands."

The ladies, however, decided that Margaret Helmstedt should, the next morning, be sent off to the isle. And the colonel reluctantly acquiesced. As for old Colonel Compton, from first to last he had not interfered, or even commented, except by a groan or a sigh.

Upon arriving at home, they were astonished to find Clare Hartley with Margaret. And when they were told that Forrest had been dispatched to

Plover's Point, with a note from Clare to inform her father of her whereabouts, Nellie prophesied that the messenger would bring back orders for Clare to return immediately. And she decided to say nothing to Margaret about the approaching exodus until after Clare's departure.

Mrs. Houston's prediction was verified. Forrest returned about sunset with a note from Dr. Hartley to his daughter, expressing surprise that she should have made this visit without consulting him, and commanding her, as it was too late for her to cross the bay that evening, to return, without fail, early the next morning.

Margaret gazed anxiously at Clare while the latter read her note.

"Well, Clare! well?" she asked, eagerly, as her friend folded the paper.

"Well, dear, as I left home without settling up some matters, I must run back for a few hours to-morrow morning; but I will be sure to come back and redeem my pledge of remaining near you until your father's arrival, dear Margaret; for every minute I see more clearly that you need some faithful friend at your side," replied Clare, who felt confident of being able to persuade her father to permit her return.

Clare slept with Margaret in her arms that night. And early the next morning—very early, to deprecate her father's displeasure, she entered Margaret's little *Pearl Shell*, and was taken by Forrest across the bay and up the river to Plover's Point.

She had scarcely disappeared from the house, before Mrs. Houston entered Miss Helmstedt's room.

Margaret was seated in her low sewing-chair with her elbow leaning on the little workstand beside her, her pale forehead bowed upon her open palm, and a small piece of needlework held laxly in the other hand lying idly upon her lap. Her eyes were hollow, her eyelashes drooping until they overshadowed cheeks that wore the extreme pallor of illness. Her whole aspect was one of mute despair.

The bustling entrance of Mrs. Houston was not perceived until the lady addressed her sharply:

"Miss Helmstedt, I have something to say to you."

Margaret started ever so slightly, and then quietly arose, handed her visitor a chair, and resumed her own seat, and after a little while her former attitude, her elbow resting on the stand, her head bowed upon her hand.

"Miss Helmstedt," said the lady, taking the offered seat with an air of importance, "we have decided that under present circumstances, it is better that you should leave the house at once with your servants, and retire to the isle. Your effects can be sent after you."

A little lower sank the bowed head—a little farther down slid the relaxed hand, that was the only external evidence of the new blow she had received. To have had her good name smirched with foul calumny; to have suffered the desertion of all her friends save one; to have been publicly turned from the communion table; all this had been bitter as the water of Marah! Still she had said to herself: "Though all in this house wound me with their frowns and none vouchsafe me a kind word or look, yet will I be patient and endure it until they come. My father and Ralph shall find me where they left me."

But now to be sent with dishonor from this home of shelter, where she awaited the coming of her father and her betrothed husband; and under such an overwhelming mass of circumstantial evidence against her as to justify in all men's eyes those who discarded her—this, indeed, was the bitterness of death!

Yet one word from her would have changed all. And now she was under no vow to withhold that word, for she recollected that her dying mother had said to her: "If ever, my little Margaret, your honor or happiness should be at stake through this charge with which I have burdened you, cast it off, give my secret to the wind!" And now a word that she was free to speak would lift her from the pit of ignominy and set her upon a mount of honor. It would bring the Comptons, the Houstons, the Wellworths and the whole company of her well-meaning, but mistaken friends to her feet. Old Mr. Wellworth would beg her pardon, Grace would weep upon her neck. The family here would lavish affection upon her. Nellie would busy herself in preparations for the approaching nuptials. The returning soldiers, instead of meeting disappointment and humiliation, would greet—the one his adored bride—the other his beloved daughter. And confidence, love and joy would follow.

But then a shadow of doubt would be cast upon that grave under the oaks by the river. And quickly as the temptation came, it was repulsed. The secret that Marguerite De Lancie had died to keep, her daughter would not divulge to be clear of blame. "No, mother, no, beautiful and gifted martyr, I can die with you, but I will never betray you! Come what will I will be silent." And compressing her sorrowful and bloodless lips and clasping her hands, Margaret "took up her burden of life again."

"Well, Miss Helmstedt, I am waiting here for any observation you may have to offer, I hope you will make no difficulty about the plan proposed."

"No, Mrs. Houston, I am ready to go."

"Then, Miss Helmstedt, you had better order your servants to pack up and prepare the boat. We wish you to leave this morning; for Colonel Houston, who intends to see you safe to the island, and charge the people there concerning you, has only this day at his disposal. To-morrow he goes to Washington, to meet Ralph and Frank, who, we learn by a letter received this morning, are on their way home."

This latter clause was an additional piece of cruelty, whether intentional or only thoughtless on the part of the speaker. Ralph so near home, and she dismissed in dishonor! Margaret felt it keenly; but she only inquired in a low and tremulous voice:

"And my father?"

"Your father, it appears, is still detained by business in New York. And now I will leave you to prepare for your removal."

Margaret rang for her servants, directed Hildreth to pack up her clothing, and Forrest to make ready the boat, for they were going back to the island.

Her faithful attendants heard in sorrowful dismay. They had acutely felt and deeply resented the indignities inflicted upon their young mistress.

An hour served for all necessary preparations, and then Margaret sent and reported herself ready to depart.

The family assembled in the hall to bid her good-by. When she took leave of them they all looked grave and troubled. Old Mrs. Compton kissed her on the cheek and prayed God to bless her. And the tears rushed to Colonel Houston's eyes when he offered his arm to the suffering girl, whose pale face looked so much paler in contrast with the mourning dress she still wore.

They left the house, entered the boat, and in due time reached Helmstedt's Island. Colonel Houston took her to the mansion, called the servants together, informed them that their master would be at home in a few days; and that their young mistress had come to prepare for his arrival, and to welcome him back to his house. That of course they would obey her in all things. This explanation of Margaret's presence was so probable and satisfactory, that her people had nothing to do but to express the great pleasure they felt in again receiving their young lady. In taking leave of Margaret, Colonel Houston was very deeply shaken. He could not say to her, "This act, Margaret, was the act of the women of my family, who, you know, hold of right the disposal of all such nice questions as these. I think they are wrong, but I cannot with propriety interfere." No, he could not denounce the doings of his own wife and mother, but he took the hand of the maiden and said:

"My dearest Margaret—my daughter, as I hoped once proudly to call you—if ever you should need a friend, in any strait, for any purpose, call on me. Will you, my dear girl?"

Miss Helmstedt remained silent, with her eyes cast down in bitter humiliation.

"Say, Margaret Helmstedt, my dear, will you do this?" earnestly pleaded Colonel Houston.

Margaret looked up. The faltering voice, and the tears on the old soldier's cheeks touched her heart.

"The bravest are ever the gentlest. God bless you, Colonel Houston. Yes, if ever poor Margaret Helmstedt needs a friend, she will call upon you," she said, holding out her hand.

The old man pressed it and hurried away.

The next morning Colonel Houston set out for Washington city to meet his son.

The reunion took place at the City Hotel.

Captain Houston was eager to proceed directly homeward; but a night's rest was necessary to the invalid soldier, and their departure was fixed for the next day. Ralph Houston's eagerness seemed not altogether one of joy; through the evening his manner was often abstracted and anxious.

When the party had at last separated for the night, Ralph left his own chamber and proceeded to that of his father. He found the veteran in bed, and much surprised at the unseasonable visit. Ralph threw himself into the easy-chair by his side, and opened the conversation by saying:

"I did not wish to speak before a third person, even when that person was my brother; but what then is this about Margaret? Mrs. Houston's letters drop strange, incomprehensible hints, and Margaret's little notes are constrained and sorrowful. Now, sir, what is the meaning of it all?"

"Ralph, it was to break the news to you that I came up hither to meet you," replied the colonel, solemnly.

"The news! Great Heaven, sir, what news can there be that needs such serious breaking? You told me that she was well!" exclaimed the captain, changing color, and rising in his anxiety.

"Ralph! Margaret Helmstedt is lost to you forever."

The soldier of a dozen battles dropped down into his chair as if felled, and covered his face with his hands.

"Ralph! be a man!"

A deep groan from the laboring bosom was the only response.

"Ralph! man! soldier! no faithless woman is worth such agony!"

He neither moved nor spoke; but remained with his face buried in his hands.

"Ralph! my son! my brave son! Ralph!" exclaimed the old man, rising in bed.

The captain put out his hand and gently pressed him back upon his pillow, saying in a calm, constrained voice:

"Lie still; do not disturb yourself; it is over. You said that she was lost to me, forever. She is married to another, then?"

"I wish to Heaven that I knew she was; but I only know that she ought to be."

"Tell me all!"

The voice was so hollow, so forced, so unnatural, that Colonel Houston could not under other circumstances have recognized it as his son's.

The old man commenced and related the circumstances as they were known to himself.

Captain Houston listened—his dreadful calmness as the story progressed, startled first into eager attention, then into a breathless straining for the end, and finally into astonishment and joy! And just as the story came to the point of Margaret's return from her mysterious trip, with the denial that she was married, he broke forth with:

"But you told me that she was lost to me forever! I see nothing to justify such an announcement!"

"Good Heaven, Ralph, you must be infatuated, man! But wait a moment." And taking up the thread of his narrative, he related how all Miss Helmstedt's friends, convinced of her guilt or folly, had deserted her.

At this part of the recital Ralph Houston's fine countenance darkened with sorrow, indignation and scorn.

"Poor dove!—but we can spare them. Go on, sir! go on!"

"Ralph, you make me anxious; but listen further." And the old man related how Margaret, presenting herself at the communion table, had, in the face of the whole congregation, been turned away.

Ralph Houston leaped upon his feet with a rebounding spring that shook the house, and stood, convulsed, livid, speechless, breathless with rage.

"Ralph! My God, you alarm me! Pray, pray govern yourself."

His breast labored, his face worked, his words came as if each syllable was uttered with agony: "Who—did—this?"

"Mr. Wellworth, once her friend!"

"An old man and a clergyman! God knoweth that shall not save him when I meet him."

"Ralph! Ralph! you are mad."

"And Margaret! How did she bear this? Oh! that I had been at her side. Oh, God, that I had been at her side!" exclaimed the captain, striding in rapid steps up and down the floor.

"She felt it, of course, very acutely."

"My dove! my poor, wounded dove! But you all comforted and sustained her, sir!"

"Ralph, we thought it best to send her home to the island."

"What!" exclaimed Captain Houston, pausing suddenly in his rapid walk.

"Yes, Ralph, we have sent her away home. We thought it best to do so," replied the colonel, generously suppressing the fact that it was altogether the women's work, against his own approval.

Ralph Houston had gone through all the stages of displeasure, indignation and fury. But he was past all that now! There are some wrongs so deep as to still the stormiest natures into a stern calm more to be feared than fury.

"What, do you tell me that in this hour of her bitterest need you have sent my promised bride from the protection of your roof?" he inquired, walking to the bedside, and speaking in a deep, calm, stern tone, from which all emotion seemed banished.

"Ralph, we deemed it proper to do so."

"Then hear me! Margaret Helmstedt shall be my wife within twenty-four hours; and, so help me God, at my utmost need, I will never cross the threshold of Buzzard's Bluff again!" exclaimed Captain Houston, striding from the room and banging the door behind him.

"Ralph! Ralph! my son, Ralph!" cried the colonel, starting up from the bed, throwing on his dressing-gown and following him through the passage. But Captain Houston had reached and locked himself in his own chamber, where he remained in obdurate silence.

The colonel went back to bed.

Ralph Houston, in his room, consulted the timepiece. It was eleven o'clock. He sat down to the table, drew writing materials before him, and wrote the following hasty note to his betrothed:

City Hotel, Washington, October 6, 1815.

> Margaret, My Beloved One:—Only this hour have I heard
> of your sorrows. Had I known them sooner, I would have
> come from the uttermost parts of the earth to your side. But
> be of good cheer, my own best love. Within twenty-four
> hours I shall be with you to claim your hand, and assume
> the precious privilege and sacred right of protecting you
> against the world for life and death and eternity.
>
> Yours,
>
> Ralph Houston.

"'It is written that for this cause shall a man leave father and mother and cleave to his wife.' I am glad of it. Let them go. For my poor, storm-beaten dove, she shall be safe in my bosom," said Ralph Houston, his heart burning with deep resentment against his family, and yearning with unutterable affection toward Margaret, as he sealed and directed the letter, and hastened with it to the office to save the midnight mail.

CHAPTER XIV
MARTYRDOM

"Mother, mother, up in heaven!

Stand upon the jasper sea

And be witness I have given

All the gifts required of me;

Hope that blessed me, bliss that crowned,

Love that left me with a wound,

Life itself that turned around."

—Mrs. Browning.

An evil fatality seemed to attend all events connected with Margaret Helmstedt. The letter mailed at midnight night, by being one minute too late for the post, was delayed a whole week, and until it could do no manner of good.

The little packet schooner, *Canvas Back*, Captain Miles Tawney, from Washington to Norfolk, on board which Ralph Houston, the next morning, embarked, when but thirty-six hours out got aground below Blackstone's Island, where she remained fast for a week.

And thus it unhappily chanced that Major Helmstedt, who reached Washington, on his way home, a few days after the departure of the Houstons from the city, and took passage in the first packet for Buzzard's Bluff, arrived thither the first of the returning soldiers.

Having no knowledge or suspicion of the important events that had occurred, he caused himself and his baggage to be landed upon the beach, below the mansion, in which he naturally expected to find his daughter dwelling in honor and security.

Leaving his trunks in charge of a loitering negro—whom he had found upon the sands, and who, to his hasty inquiries, had answered that all the family were well—he hurried up to the house.

He was met at the door by a servant, who, with ominous formality, ushered him into the parlor, and retreated to call his mistress.

Mrs. Houston soon entered, with a pale face, trembling frame, and a half-frightened, half-threatening aspect, that greatly surprised and perplexed Major Helmstedt, who however, arose with stately courtesy to receive and hand the lady to a chair.

After respectfully saluting and seating his hostess, he said:

"My daughter Margaret, madam—I hope she is well?"

"Well, I am sure I hope so, too; but Margaret is not with us!" replied the little lady, looking more frightened and more threatening than before.

"How, madam, Margaret not with you?" exclaimed Major Helmstedt, in astonishment, that was not free from alarm.

"No, sir. You must listen to me, major—it could not be helped," replied Nellie, who straightway began, and with a manner half-deprecating and half-defiant, related the story of Margaret's indiscretions, humiliations, and final expulsion.

Major Helmstedt listened with a mighty self-control. No muscle of his iron countenance moved. When she had concluded, he arose, with a cold and haughty manner.

"Slanders, madam—slanders all! I can say no more to a lady, however unworthy of the courtesy due to her sex. But I shall know how to call the men of her family to a strict account for this insult." And, throwing his hat upon his head, he strode from the room.

"Major Helmstedt—Major Helmstedt! Come back, sir. Don't go; you must please to listen to me," cried Nellie, running after him, the principle of fear now quite predominating over that of defiance.

But the outraged father, without deigning a word or look of reply, hurried onward toward the beach.

Nellie, in great alarm, dispatched a servant in haste after him, to beseech him, in her name, to return and stay to dinner—or, if he would not honor her so far, at least to accept the use of a carriage, or a boat, to convey him whithersoever he wished to go.

But Major Helmstedt, with arrogant scorn, repulsed all these offers. Throwing a half guinea to the negro to take temporary charge of his trunks, he strode on his way, following the windings of the waterside road for many miles, until late in the afternoon he reached Belleview, whence he intended to take a boat to the island.

His cause of indignation was reasonable, and his rage increased with time and reflection. That Margaret had been foully wronged by the Houstons he from his deepest convictions believed. That the charges brought against her had the slightest foundation in fact, he could not for a moment credit. All his own intimate knowledge of his pure-hearted child, from her earliest infancy to the day when he left her in Mrs. Houston's care, conclusively contradicted these calumnies. But that, for some reason or other, unconfessed, the Houstons wished to break off the contemplated alliance with his family he felt assured. And that his daughter's betrothed was in correspondence with Mrs. Houston, and in connivance with her plans, he had been left to believe, by the incoherence, if not by the intentional misrepresentations, of Nellie's statement. That they should wish, without just cause, to break the engagement with his daughter, was both dishonorable and dishonoring — that they should attempt this through such means, was scandalous and insulting to the last degree. That Ralph Houston should be either an active or a passive party to this plan, was an offense only to be satisfied by the blood of the offender. His pride in an old, untainted name, not less than his affection for his only daughter, was wounded to the very quick.

There seemed but one remedy — it was to be found only in "the bloody code," miscalled "of honor" — the code which required a man to wash out any real or fancied offense in the life-stream of the offender; the code which often made an honorable man responsible, with his life, for careless words uttered by the women of his family; that code which now enjoined Philip Helmstedt to seek the life of his daughter's betrothed, his intended son-in-law, his brother-in-arms. Nor was this all. The feeling that prompted Major Helmstedt was not only that of an affronted gentleman, who deems it necessary to defend in the duel his assailed manhood — it was much more — it was the blood-thirsty rage of a scornful and arrogant man, whose honor had been wounded in the most vulnerable place, through the only woman of his name, his one fair daughter, who had been by her betrothed and his family rejected, insulted, and expelled from their house, branded with indelible shame.

"Ralph Houston must die!"

He said it with remorseless resolution, with grim satisfaction, and in his heart devoted the souls of his purposed victim and all his family to the infernal deities.

In this evil mood, and in an evil hour, Major Helmstedt unhappily arrived at Belleview, and, still more unhappily, there met Ralph, who, in pursuance of his vow never to set foot upon Buzzard's Bluff again, had that morning landed at the village, with the intention there to engage a boat to take him to Helmstedt's Island, whither he was going to seek Margaret.

It was in the principal street of the village, and before the only hotel that they chanced to meet.

Ralph advanced with eager joy to greet his father-in-law.

But Major Helmstedt's mad and blind rage forestalled and rendered impossible all friendly words or explanations.

How he assailed and insulted Ralph Houston; how he hurled bitter scorn, taunt, and defiance in his teeth how in the presence of the gathering crowd, he charged falsehood, treachery, and cowardice upon him; how, to cap the climax of insult, the infuriate pulled off his glove and cast it sharply into the face of the young man; how, in short, he irremediably forced upon Ralph a quarrel, which the latter was, upon all accounts, most unwilling to take up, would be as painful, as needless, to detail at large.

Suffice it to say, that the circumstances of the case, and the public sentiment of the day considered, he left the young soldier, as a man of honor, no possible alternative but to accept his challenge.

"'Needs must when the devil drives;' and, as there is no honorable means of avoiding, I must meet this madman and receive his shot. I am not, however, obliged to return it. No code of honor can compel me to fire upon my Margaret's father," thought Ralph. Then aloud he said:

"Very well, sir; my brother Frank has doubtless by this time reached home, and will, with any friend whom you may appoint, arrange the terms of the meeting;" and, lifting his hat, Ralph Houston, "more in sorrow than in anger," turned away.

"There is no honorable way of escaping it, Frank, else be sure that I should not give him this meeting. As it is, I must receive his fire; but, so help me Heaven; nothing shall induce me to return it," said Captain Houston, as he talked over the matter with his brother that evening in the private parlor of the little inn at Belleview.

"Then, without a thought of defending yourself, you will stand up as a mark to be shot at by the best marksman in the country? You will be murdered! just simply murdered!" replied the younger man, in sorrow and disgust.

"There is no help for it, Frank. I must meet him, must receive his fire, and will not return it!"

"You will fall," said the youth, in a voice of despair.

"Probably. And if I do, Frank, go to my dearest Margaret and bear to her my last words. Tell her that I never so sinned against our mutual faith as for one instant to doubt her perfect purity; tell her that I was on my way to take her to my heart, to give her my name and to defend her against the world, when this fatal quarrel was forced upon me; tell her that I never fired upon her father, but that I died with her name upon my lips and her love within my heart. If I fall, as I probably shall, will you tell my widowed bride this?"

"I will! I will!" exclaimed Frank, in a voice of deep emotion.

Meanwhile the innocent and most unhappy cause of the impending duel had passed a miserable week on the solitary island, in dread anticipation of her father's and her lover's return, and with no one near her to breathe one hopeful, comforting, or sustaining word to her fainting heart.

It was late on the evening of the day of her father's arrival that she sat alone on the front piazza of her solitary dwelling, wrapped in despairing thought, yet with every nerve acute with involuntary vigilance, when, amid the low, musical semi-silence of the autumnal night, the sound of a boat, pushed gratingly up upon the gravelly beach, reached her listening ear.

And while she still watched and waited in breathless anxiety, she perceived by the clear starlight the tall figure of a man, dressed in the blue and buff uniform of an American officer, and in whose stature, air, and gait she recognized her father, approaching the house.

In joy, but still more in fear, she arose and hurried to meet him. But so terrible was the trouble of her mind and the agitation of her frame, that she could scarcely falter forth her inaudible words of welcome before she sank exhausted in his arms.

In silence the soldier lifted her up, noticing even then how very light was her wasted frame; in silence he kissed her cold lips, and bore her onward to the house, and into her mother's favorite parlor which was already lighted up, and where he placed her in an easy-chair. She sank back half fainting, while he stood and looked upon her, and saw how changed she was.

Her attenuated form, her emaciated face, with its cavernous eyes, hollow cheeks and temples, and pallid forehead, in fearful contrast with her flowing black locks and mourning dress, gave her the appearance of a girl in the very last stage of consumption. Yet this was the work only of calumny, persecution, and abandonment.

Some one should write a book on Unindicted Homicides.

While Major Helmstedt gazed in bitterness of heart upon this beautiful wreck of his fair, only daughter, she fixed her despairing eyes upon him, and said:

"My father, do you wonder to find me here!"

For answer, he stooped and kissed her forehead.

"Father, my heart bleeds for you. This is a sorrowful welcome home for the returning soldier."

"Trouble not yourself about me, my child. Your own wrongs are enough, and more than enough, to engage your thoughts. I know those wrongs, and, by the soul of your mother, they shall be terribly avenged!" said Major Helmstedt, in a low, deep, stern voice of relentless determination.

"Father, oh, God! what do you mean?" exclaimed Margaret, in alarm.

"I mean, my much injured child, that every tear they have caused you to shed, shall be balanced by a drop of heart's blood, though it should drain the veins of all who bear the name of Houston!"

"Oh, Heaven of heavens, my father!" cried Margaret, wringing her pale hands in the extremity of terror. Then suddenly catching the first hope that came, she said:

"But you cannot war upon women."

"Upon all men that bear the name of Houston, then! Yet did not they spare to war upon women—or rather worse, upon one poor, defenseless girl! Enough! they shall bitterly repay it!"

"But father! my father! it was not the men; they were ever kind to me. It was the women of the family, and even they were deceived by appearances," pleaded Margaret.

"It is you who are deceived! Mrs. Houston acted in concert with her husband and his son!"

"Ralph? never, never, my father. My life, my soul, upon Ralph's fidelity!" exclaimed Margaret, as a warm glow of loving faith flowed into and transfigured to angelic beauty her pale face.

"Miss Helmstedt, you are a fond and foolish girl, with all your sex's weak credulity. It is precisely Ralph Houston whom I shall hold to be the most responsible party in this affair!"

"Oh! my God!"

These words were wailed forth in such a tone of utter despair, and were accompanied by such a sudden blanching and sharpening of all her features, that Major Helmstedt in his turn became alarmed, and with what diplomacy he was master of, endeavored to modify the impression that he had given. But his palpable efforts only confirmed Margaret in her suspicion that he intended to challenge Ralph, and made her more wary and watchful to ascertain if this really were his purpose, so that, if possible, she might prevent this meeting. That the challenge had been already given she did not even suspect.

But from this moment the father and daughter were secretly arrayed against each other; he to conceal from her the impending duel; she to discover and prevent the meeting. And while he talked to her with a view of gradually doing away the impression that his first violent words had made upon her mind, she watched his countenance narrowly, keeping the while her own counsel. But it was not entirely the wish to conceal her own anguish of doubt and anxiety, but affectionate interest in him, that caused her at length to say:

"But, my dear father, you are just off a long, harassing journey; you are, indeed, greatly exhausted; your countenance is quite haggard; you are needing rest and refreshment. Let me go now and give the orders, while you occupy my sofa. Say, what shall I bring you, dear father?"

"Nothing, nothing, Margaret; I cannot——" began Major Helmstedt; but then suddenly reflecting, he said: "Yes, you may send me up a cup of coffee, and any trifle with it that may be at hand. No, I thank you, Margaret, you need not draw the sofa forward. I am going to my study, where I have letters to write. Send the refreshments thither. And send—let me see—yes! send Forrest to me."

"Very well, my dear father," replied the maiden, leaving the room. "'Letters to write!' 'letters to write!' and 'send Forrest.' So late at night, and just as he has returned home, oh, my soul!" she cried, within herself, as she went into the kitchen to give her orders.

When the tray was ready, Forrest was told to take it up to his master's study.

Margaret, after a little hesitation, drawn by her strong anxiety, followed, her light footsteps on the stairs and through the hall waking no echo. As she approached the door of her father's study, she heard the words:

"Forrest, take this case of pistols downstairs and thoroughly clean them; let no one see what you are about. Then have a boat—the soundest in the fleet—ready to take me to the landing below the burial ground, at Plover's Point. Do you prepare to go with me, and—listen farther. At about daybreak to-morrow, a gentleman will arrive hither. Be on the watch, and quietly bring him to this room. Have breakfast served for us here, and the boat ready for our departure when we rise from the table. And mind, execute all these orders in strict privacy, and breathe no word of their purport to any living creature. Do you understand?"

"I think I do, sir," replied the astonished negro, who imperfectly comprehended the affair.

Margaret knew all now. Her father had challenged her betrothed. The only two beings whom she loved supremely on this earth, were in a few hours hence to meet in mortal combat.

With a heart that seemed paralyzed within her suffocating bosom, she crept, reeling, to her own chamber, and with the habitual instinct of soliciting Divine counsel and assistance, she sank upon her knees beside the bed. But no petition escaped her icy lips, or even took the form of words in her paralyzed brain; her intellect seemed frozen with horror; and her only form of prayer was the eloquent, mute attitude, and the intense yearning of the suffering heart after the All Merciful's help and pity. She remained many minutes in this posture of silent prayer, before the power of reflection and of language returned to her, and even then her only cry was:

"Oh, God of pity, have mercy on them! Oh, God of strength, help and save!"

Then still looking to the Lord for guidance, she tried to think what was best to be done. It was now ten o'clock. Day would break at four. There were but six hours of a night to do all, if anything could be done. But what, indeed, could she do? Cut off by the bay from all the rest of the world, and with fifteen miles of water between herself and the nearest magistrate, what could the miserable maiden do to prevent this duel between her father and her lover? To a religious heart filled to overflowing with love and grief, and resolved upon risking everything for the safety of the beloved, almost all things are possible. Her first resolution was the nearly hopeless one of going to her father and beseeching him to abandon his purpose. And if that failed, she had in reverse a final, almost desperate determination. But there was not a moment to be lost.

Still mentally invoking Divine aid, she arose and went to the door of her father's study. It was closed; but turning the latch very softly, she entered unperceived.

Major Helmstedt sat at his table, so deeply absorbed in writing as not to be conscious of her presence, although his face was toward the door. That face was haggard with care, and those keen, strong eyes that followed the rapid gliding of his pen over the paper were strained with anxiety. So profound was his absorption in his work that the candles remained unsnuffed and burning with a murky and lurid light, and the cup of coffee on his table sat cold and untouched.

Margaret approached and looked over his shoulder.

It was his last will and testament that he was engaged in preparing.

The sight thrilled his daughter with a new horror. Meekly she crept to his side and softly laid her hand upon his shoulder, and gently murmured:

"Father, my dear father!"

He looked up suddenly, and in some confusion.

"What, Margo! not asleep yet, my girl? This is a late hour for young eyes to be open. And yet I am glad that you came to bid me good-night before retiring. It was affectionate of you, Margo," he said, laying down his pen, putting a blotter over his writing, and then drawing her to his side in a close embrace—"yes, it was affectionate of you, Margo; but ah, little one, no daughter loves as a true wife does. I have been thinking of your mother, dear."

"Think of her still, my father," replied the maiden, in a voice of thrilling solemnity.

Major Helmstedt's countenance changed, but, controlling himself, he pressed a kiss upon his daughter's brow, and said:

"Well, well, I will not keep you up. God bless you, my child, though I cannot. Good-night!" and with another kiss he would have dismissed her. But, softly laying her hand upon his right hand, she asked, in a voice thrilling with earnestness:

"Oh, my father, what is this that you are about to do?"

"Margaret, no prying into my private affairs—I will not suffer it!" exclaimed Major Helmstedt, in disturbed voice.

"My father, there is no need of prying; I know all! Providence, for His good purposes, has given the knowledge into my hands. Oh, did you think that He would permit this terrible thing to go on uninterruptedly to its bloody termination?"

"What mean you, girl?"

"Father, forgive me; but I overheard and understood your orders to Forrest."

"By my soul, Margaret, this is perfectly insufferable!" exclaimed Major Helmstedt, starting up, and then sinking back into his chair.

But softly and suddenly Margaret dropped at his feet, clasped his knees, and in a voice freighted with her heart's insupportable anguish, cried:

"Father! my father! hear me! hear me! hear your own lost Marguerite's heartbroken child, and do not make her orphaned and widowed in one hour!"

"Orphaned and widowed in one hour!"

"Yes, yes, and most cruelly so, by the mutual act of her father and her husband."

"By her father and husband?"

"Yes, yes. Am I not Ralph Houston's promised, sworn wife? Oh, my father!"

"Death, girl! You call yourself his promised wife; you pray me to stay my hand, nor avenge your wrongs, nor vindicate my own honor; you who have been calumniated, insulted, and expelled from his house?"

"Not by him, father! not with his knowledge or consent! Oh, never! never! My life, my soul, upon his stainless faith!"

"My daughter, rise and leave, I command you," said Major Helmstedt, giving his hand to assist her.

But she clung to his knees and groveled at his feet, crying:

"Father! father! pardon and hear me; hear me for my dead mother's sake! hear your Marguerite's orphan girl! do not make her a widow before she is a wife! My father, do not, oh, do not meet my betrothed in a duel! He was your oldest friend, your brother-in-arms, your promised son; he has stood by your side in many a well-fought battle; in camp and field you two have shared together the dangers and glories of the war. How can you meet as mortal foes? Crowned with victory, blessed with peace, you were both coming home—you to your only daughter, he to his promised bride—both to a devoted girl, who would have laid out her life to make your mutual fireside happy; but whose heart you are about to break! Oh, how can you do this most cruel deed? Oh! it is so horrible! so horrible, that you two should thus meet. Dueling is wicked, but this is worse than dueling! Murder is atrocious, but this is worse than murder! This is parricide! this is the meeting of a father and son, armed each against the other's life! A father and a son!"

"Son! no son or son-in-law of mine, if that is what you mean."

"Father, father, do not say so! He is the sworn husband of your only child. My hand, with your consent, was placed in his by my dying mother's hand. He clasped my fingers closely, promising never to forsake me! A promise made to the living in the presence of the dying! A promise that he has never retracted, and wishes never to retract. My soul's salvation upon Ralph Houston's honor!"

"Margaret Helmstedt! put the last seal to my mortification, and tell me that you love this man—this man whose family has spurned you!"

"I love him—for life, and death, and eternity!" she replied, in a tone vibrating with earnestness.

"You speak your own degradation, miserable girl."

"This is no time, Heaven knows, for the cowardice of girlish shame. Father, I love him! For three long years I have believed myself his destined wife. Long before our betrothal, as far back, or farther, perhaps, than memory reaches, I loved him, and knew that he loved me, and felt that in some strange way I belonged finally to him. Long, long before I ever heard of courtship, betrothal, or marriage, I felt in my deepest heart—and knew he felt it too—that Ralph was my final proprietor and prince, that I, at last and forever, was his own little Margaret—ay! as your Marguerite was yours, my father. And always and ever, in all the changes of our life, in joy and in sorrow, in presence and in absence, I seemed to repose sweetly in his heart as a little bird in its nest, loving him too quietly and securely to know how deeply and strongly. But oh, my father, it has remained for the anguish of this day to teach me how, above all creatures, I love my promised husband, even as my mother loved hers. The blow that reaches Ralph's heart would break my own. Father, I can conceive this globe upon which we live, with all its seas and continents, its mountains, plains and cities, its whole teeming life, collapsing and sinking out of sight through space, and yet myself continuing to live, somewhere, in some sphere of being; but, my father, I cannot conceive of Ralph's death and my own continued life, anywhere, as possible! for there, at that point, all sinks into darkness, chaos, annihilation! Swift madness or death would follow his loss! Oh, my father, say, is he not my husband? Oh, my father, will you make your child a widow, a widow by her father's hand?"

"Margaret, this is the very infatuation of passion!"

"Passion! Well, since grief and terror and despair have made my bosom so stormy, you may call it so! else never should my lifelong, quiet, contented attachment to Ralph be termed a passion, as if it were the feverish caprice of yesterday. But oh, Heaven! all this time you are not answering me. You do not promise that you will not meet him. Father, I cannot die of grief, else had I long since been lying beside your other Marguerite! But I feel that I may go mad, and that soon. Already reason reels with dwelling on this impending duel! with the thought that a few hours hence— —! Father, if you would not have your Marguerite's child go mad, curse the author of her being, and lay desperate hands upon her own life, forgo this duel! do not make her a widowed bride!"

"Wretched girl, it were better that you were dead, for come what may, Margaret, honor must be saved."

"Then you will kill him! My father will kill my husband!"

"Why do you harp upon this subject forever? Shall I not equally risk my own life?"

"No, no, no! he will never risk hurting a hair of your head. My life and soul upon it, he will fire into the air! I know and feel what he will do, here, deep in my heart. I know and feel what has been done. Father, you met him in your blind rage, you gave him no chance of explanation, but goaded and taunted, and drove him to the point of accepting your challenge. You will meet him, you will murder him! and I, oh, I shall go mad, and curse the father that gave me life, and him death!" she said, starting up and wildly traversing the floor.

"'Still waters run deep!' Who would have supposed this quiet maiden had inherited all Marguerite De Lancie's strength of feeling?" thought Major Helmstedt, as in a deep trouble he watched his daughter's distracted walk.

Suddenly, as that latent and final resolution, before mentioned, recurred to her mind, she paused, and came up to her father's side, and said:

"Father, this thing must go no farther!"

"What mean you, Margaret?"

"This duel must not take place."

"What absurdity—it must come off! Let all be lost so honor is saved!"

"Then listen well to me, my father," she said, in the long, deep, quiet tone of fixed determination; "this duel shall not take place!"

"Girl, you are mad. 'Shall not?'"

"Shall not, my father!"

"What preposterous absurdity! Who will prevent it?"

"I will!"

"You! Come, that is best of all. How do you propose to do it, fair daughter?"

"I shall lay the whole matter before the nearest magistrate!"

"Poor girl, if I did not pity you so deeply, I should smile at your folly. Why, Margaret, the nearest magistrate is fifteen miles off. It is now eleven o'clock at night, and the proposed meeting takes place at five in the morning!"

"Then the more reason for haste, my father, to save you from a crime. I will order a boat and depart immediately," said Margaret, going to the bell-rope and giving it a sudden peremptory pull.

"Oh, then I see that this will not do. You are desperate, you are dangerous, you must be restrained," said Major Helmstedt, rising and approaching his daughter.

"Father, what mean you now? You would not—you, a gentleman, an officer, would not lay violent hands on your daughter?" she said, shrinking away in amazement.

"In an exigency of this kind my daughter leaves me no alternative."

"No, no! You would not use force to hinder me in the discharge of a sacred duty?"

"Margaret, no more words. Come to your room," he said, taking her by the arm, and with gentle force conducting her to the door of her own chamber, in which he locked her securely.

Knowing resistance to be both vain and unbecoming, Margaret had, for the time, quietly submitted. She remained sitting motionless in the chair in which he had placed her, until she heard his retreating footsteps pause at the door of his study, and heard him enter and lock the door behind him.

Then she arose and stepped lightly over the carpeted floor, and looked from the front window out upon the night.

A dark, brilliant starlight night, with a fresh wind that swayed the branches of the trees.

Almost omnipotent is the religious heart; willing to sink all things for the salvation of the beloved.

The means of escape, and of preventing the duel, were quickly devised by her suggestive mind. Her chamber was on the second floor front. A grape vine of nearly twenty years' growth reached her window, and climbed up its side and over its top. The intertwined and knotted branches, thick as a man's wrist, and strong as a cable, presented a means of descent safe and easy as that of a staircase. And once free of the house, the course of the brave girl was clear.

There was no time to be lost. It was now half-past eleven o'clock. The household, except her father and the servant whom he had ordered to watch with him, was wrapped in sleep. Her father she knew to be deeply engaged in writing his will in the study. Forrest she supposed to be employed in cleaning the pistols in the back kitchen.

There was nothing then to interrupt her escape but the dogs, who before recognizing would surely break out upon her. But there was little to dread from that circumstance. The barking of the dogs was no unusual event of the night. Any noise in nature, the footstep of a negro walking out, the spring of a startled squirrel, the falling of a nut or a pine cone, was frequently enough to arouse their jealous vigilance, and provoke a canine concert. Only when the barking was very prolonged was attention usually aroused. Of this contingency there was no danger. They would probably break out in a furious onslaught, recognize her and be still.

But there was another serious difficulty. Margaret was very feeble; weeks of mental anguish, with the consequent loss of appetite and loss of sleep, had so exhausted her physical nature that not all the proverbial power of the mind over the body, the spirit over the flesh, could impart to her sufficient strength for an undertaking, that, in her stronger days, would have taxed her energies to the utmost. A restorative was absolutely necessary. A few drops of distilled lavender water—a favorite country cordial—gave her a fictitious strength.

Then tying on her black velvet hood, and her short black camlet riding cloak, she prepared to depart. First, she bolted the door on the inside that her father might not enter her room to ascertain her absence. Then she softly hoisted the window, and with perfect ease crossed the low sill and stepped upon the friendly vine, where she remained standing while she let down the window and closed the blinds.

Thus having restored everything to its usual order, she commenced her descent. Holding to the vines, stepping cautiously, and letting herself down slowly, she at length reached the ground safely.

Now for the dogs. But they were quiet. Their quick instincts were truer than her fears, and she passed on undisturbed.

How still and brilliant the starlight night. No sound but the sighing of the wind in the trees, and the trilling of the insects that wake at eve to chirp till day; and all distinctly, yet darkly visible, like a scene clearly drawn in Indian ink upon a gray ground.

She passed down through the garden, the orchard, and the stubble field to the beach, where her little sailboat, *The Pearl Shell*, lay.

For the trip that she contemplated of fifteen miles up the mouth of the river, a rowboat would have been far the safer. But Margaret was too weak for such prolonged labor as the management of the oar for two or three hours must necessitate. The sailboat would only require the trifling exertion of holding the tiller, and occasionally shifting the sails. Happily, the tide was in and just about to turn; the boat was, therefore, afloat, though chained to the boathouse, and so needed no exertion to push her off. Margaret went on board, untied the tiller, hoisted the sails, unlocked the chain and cast loose. She had but time to spring and seize the tiller before the wind filled the sails and the boat glided from the shore.

So far all had gone marvelously well. Let who would discover her escape now, she was safe from pursuit. Let who would follow, she could not be overtaken. Her boat was beyond measure the swiftest sailer of the island fleet. True, before this fresh wind the boat might capsize, especially as there was no one to manage it except herself, who to shift the sails must sometimes let go the tiller. But Margaret was without selfish, personal fear;

her purpose was high, and had been so far providentially favored; she would, therefore, believe in no accidents, but trust in God.

And what a strange scene was this, in which the solitary girl-mariner was out upon the lonely sea.

The broad canopy of heaven, of that deep, dark, intense blue of cloudless night, was thickly studded with myriads of stars, whose reflection in the mirror of the sea seemed other living stars disporting themselves amid the waves. Far away over the wide waters, darker lines upon the dark sea suggested the distant shores and headlands of the main. Straight before her flying boat, two black points, miles apart, indicated the entrance to the mouth of the Potomac River. She steered for the lower, or Smith's Point.

Under happier circumstances, the lonely night ride over the dark waters would have charmed the fancy of the fearless and adventurous girl. Now her only emotion was one of anxiety and haste. Taking Smith's Point for her "polar star," she gave all her sail to the wind. The boat flew over the water. I dare scarcely say in how marvelously short a time she reached this cape. This was the longest part of her voyage.

Hugging the Northumberland coast, she soon reached and doubled Plover's Point, and ran up into the little cove, the usual landing place, and pushed her boat upon the sands.

She next sprang out, secured the boat to a post, and began to climb the steep bank, that was thickly covered with a growth of pines, from which the place took its name.

Here danger of another and more appalling form threatened her. Fugitive slaves, than whom a more dangerous banditti can nowhere be found, were known to infest this coast, where by day they hid in caves and holes, and by night prowled about like wild beasts in search of food or prey. More than to meet the wildcat or the wolf, that were not yet banished from these woods, the maiden dreaded to encounter one of these famished and desperate human beasts! Lifting her heart in prayer to God for assistance, she passed courageously on her dark and dangerous way; starting at the sound of her own light footsteps upon some crackling, fallen branch, and holding her breath at the slight noise made by the moving of a rabbit or a bird in the foliage. At last she reached the summit of the wooded hill, and came out of the pine thicket on to the meadow. Then there was a fence to climb, a field to cross, and a gate to open before she reached the wooded lawn fronting the house. There the last peril, that of the watchdogs, awaited her. One mastiff barked furiously as she approached the gate; as she opened it, the whole pack broke in full cry upon her.

She paused and stood still, holding out one hand, and saying, gently:

"Why, Ponto! Why, Fido! What is the matter, good boys?"

The two foremost recognized and fawned upon her, and under their protection, as it were, she walked on through the excited pack, that, one by one, dropped gently under her influence, and walked quietly by her side.

So she reached the front of the house, passed up the piazza, and rang the bell. Peal upon peal she rung before she could make any one in that quiet house hear.

At last, however, an upper window was thrown up, and the voice of Dr. Hartley asked:

"Who's there?"

"It is I, Dr. Hartley. It is I, Margaret Helmstedt! come to you on a matter of life and death!"

"You! You, Margaret! You, at this hour! I am lost in wonder!"

"Oh, come down, quickly, quickly, or it will be too late!"

Evidently believing this to be an imminent necessity for his professional services, the doctor drew in his head, let down the window, hastily donned his apparel, and came down to admit his visitor.

Leading her into the sitting-room, he said:

"Now, my dear, who is ill? And what, in the name of all the saints, was the necessity of your coming out at this time of night with the messenger?"

"Dr. Hartley, look at me well. I came with no messenger. I left the island at midnight, and crossed the bay, and came up the river alone."

"Good Heaven, Miss Helmstedt! Margaret! what is it you tell me? What has happened?" he asked, terrified at the strange words and the ghastly looks of the girl.

"Dr. Hartley, my father has challenged Ralph Houston. They meet this morning, in the woods above the family burial ground. I escaped from the room in which my father had locked me, and came to give information to the authorities, that they may, if possible, stop this duel. What I desire particularly of your kindness is that you will go with me to Squire Johnson's, that I may lodge the necessary complaint. I regret to ask you to take this trouble; but I myself do not know the way to Squire Johnson's house."

"Margaret, my dear, I am exceedingly grieved to hear what you have told me. How did this happen? What was the occasion of it?"

"Oh, sir, spare me! in mercy spare me! There is, indeed, no time to tell you now. What we are to do should be done quickly. They meet very, very early this morning."

"Very well, Margaret. There is no necessity for your going to Squire Johnson's, for, indeed, you are too much exhausted for the ride. And I am now suffering too severely with rheumatism to bear the journey. But I will do better. I will put a servant on a swift horse, and dispatch a note that will bring Mr. Johnson hither. We can go hence to the dueling ground and prevent the meeting. Will not that be best?"

"So that we are in time—anything, sir."

Dr. Hartley then went out to rouse the boy whom he purposed to send, and after a few moments returned, and while the latter was saddling the horse, he wrote the note, so that in ten minutes the messenger was dispatched on his errand.

Day was now breaking, and the house servants were all astir. One of them came in to make the fire in the parlor fireplace, and Dr. Hartley gave orders for an early breakfast to be prepared for his weary guest.

Missing Clare from her customary morning haunts, Margaret ventured to inquire if she were in good health.

At the mention of his daughter's name, Dr. Hartley recollected now, for the first time, that there might be some good reason for treating his young visitor with rebuking coldness, and he answered, with distant politeness, that Clare had gone to pay her promised visit to her friends at Fort Warburton.

Margaret bore this change of manner in her host with her usual patient resignation. And when the cloth was laid, and breakfast was placed upon the table, and the doctor, with professional authority rather than with hospitable kindness, insisted that the exhausted girl should partake of some refreshment, she meekly complied, and forced herself to swallow a cup of coffee, though she could constrain nature no farther.

They had scarcely risen from the table, before the messenger returned with the news that Squire Johnson had left home for Washington City, and would be absent for several days.

"Oh, Heaven of heavens! What now can be done?" exclaimed Margaret, in anguish.

"Nothing can be done by compulsion, of course, but something may be accomplished by persuasion. I will go with you, Miss Helmstedt, to the ground, and use every friendly exertion to effect an adjustment of the difficulties between these antagonists," said Dr. Hartley.

"Oh, then, sir, let us hasten at once. No time is to be lost!" cried Margaret, in the very extremity of anxiety.

"It is but a short distance, Miss Helmstedt. Doubtless we shall be in full time," replied the doctor, buttoning up, his coat and taking down his hat from the peg.

Margaret had already, with trembling fingers, tied on her hood.

They immediately left the house.

"What time did you say they met, Miss Helmstedt?"

"I said, 'very early,' sir. Alas, I do not know the time to the hour. I fear, I fear—oh, let us hasten, sir."

"It is but five o'clock, Margaret, and the distance is short," said the doctor, beginning to pity her distress.

"Oh, God! perhaps it was at five they were to meet. Oh, hasten!"

Their way was first through the lawn, then through the stubble field, then into the copse wood that gradually merged in the thick forest behind the burial ground.

"Do you know the exact spot of the purposed meeting, Margaret?" inquired the doctor.

"Oh, no, sir, I do not. I only know that my father gave orders for the boat to be in readiness to take him (and his second, of course) to the beach below the burial ground at this point. Now, as the beach is narrow, and the burial ground too sacred a place for such a purpose, I thought of these woods above it."

"Exactly; and there is a natural opening, a sort of level glade, on the top of this wooded hill, that I think likely to be the place selected. We will push forward to that spot."

They hurried on. A walk of five minutes brought them to within the sound of voices, that convinced them that they were near the dueling ground.

A few more rapid steps led them to a small, level, open glade, on the summit of the wooded hill.

Oh, Heaven of heavens! What a sight to meet the eyes of a daughter and a promised wife!

The ground was already marked off. In the drawing of the lots it seemed that the best position had fallen to her father, for he stood with his back to the rising sun, which shone full into the face of Ralph, at the same time dazzling his eyes, and making him the fairest mark for the best marksman in the country.

At right angles with the principals stood the seconds, one of them having a handkerchief held in his hand, while the other prepared to give the word.

Margaret had not seen her betrothed for three years, and now, oh, agony insupportable, to meet him thus!

So absorbed were the duelists in the business upon which they met, and so quietly had she and her escort stolen upon the scene, that the antagonists had perceived no addition to their party, but went on with their bloody purpose.

At the very entrance of the newcomers upon the scene, the second of Major Helmstedt gave the word:

"One—two—three—fire!" Frank Houston dropped the handkerchief, Ralph fired into the air, and Margaret, springing forward, struck up the pistol of her father, so that it was discharged harmlessly into the upper branches of an old tree.

All this transpired in a single instant of time, so suddenly and unexpectedly, that until it was over no one knew what had happened.

Then followed a scene of confusion difficult or impossible to describe.

Major Helmstedt was the first to speak. Shaking Margaret's hand from his arm, he demanded, in a voice of concentrated rage:

"Miss Helmstedt, what is the meaning of this? How durst you come hither?"

Margaret, dropping upon her knees between the combatants and lifting up both arms, exclaimed:

"Oh, father! father! Oh, Ralph! Ralph! bury your bullets in this broken heart if you will, but do not point your weapons against each other!"

"Margaret, my beloved!" began Ralph Houston, springing to raise her, but before he could effect his purpose, Major Helmstedt had caught up his daughter, and with extended hands, exclaimed:

"Off, sir! How durst you? Touch her not! Address her not at your peril! Dr. Hartley, since you attended this self-willed girl hither, pray do me the favor to lead her from the scene. Gentlemen, seconds, I look to you to restore order, that the business of our meeting may proceed."

"Father, father!" cried Margaret, clasping his knees in an agony of prayer.

"Degenerate child, release me and begone! Dr. Hartley, will you relieve me of this girl?"

"Major Helmstedt, your daughter and myself came hither in the hope of mediating between yourself and your antagonist."

"Mediating! Sir, there is no such thing as mediation in a quarrel like this! Since you brought my daughter hither, will you take her off, sir, I ask you?" thundered Major Helmstedt, striving to unrivet the clinging arms of his child.

"Father, father! Hear me, hear me!" she cried.

"Peace, girl, I command you. Fool that you are, not to see that this is a mortal question, that can only be resolved in a death meeting between us. Girl, girl, girl! are you a Helmstedt? Do you know that the family of this man have made dishonoring charges upon you? Charges that, by the Heaven above, can be washed out only in life's blood? Take her away, Hartley."

"Father, father! Oh, God! the charges! the charges that they have made! they are true! they are true!" cried Margaret, clinging to his arms, while she hid her face upon his bosom.

Had a bombshell exploded in their midst, it could not have produced a severer or more painful shock.

Ralph Houston, after the first agonized start and shudder, drew nearer to her, and paused, pale as death, to listen further, if, perchance, he had heard aright.

All the others, after their first surprise, stood as if struck statue still.

Major Helmstedt remained nailed to the ground, a form of iron. Deep and unearthly was the sound of his voice, as, lifting the head of his daughter from his breast, he said:

"Miss Helmstedt, look me in the face!"

She raised her agonized eyes to his countenance.

All present looked and listened. No one thought by word or gesture of interfering between the father and daughter.

"Miss Helmstedt," he began, in the low, deep, stern tone of concentrated passion, "what was that which you said just now?"

"I said, my father, in effect, that you must not fight; that your cause is accurst; that the charges brought against me are—true!"

"You tell me that——"

"The charges brought against me are true!" she said, in a strange, ringing voice, every tone of which was audible to all present.

Had the fabled head of the Medusa, with all its fell powers, arisen before the assembled party, it could not have produced a more appalling effect. Each stood as if turned to stone by her words.

The father and daughter remained confronted like beings charged with the mortal and eternal destiny of each other. At length Margaret, unable to bear the scrutiny of his fixed gaze, dropped her head upon her bosom, buried her burning face in her hands, and turned away.

Then Major Helmstedt, keeping his eyes still fixed with a devouring gaze upon her, slowly raised, extended and dropped his hand heavily upon her shoulder, clutched, turned, and drew her up before him.

"Again! let fall your hands; raise your head; look me in the face, minion!"

She obeyed, dropping her hands, and lifting her face, crimsoned with blushes, to his merciless gaze.

"Repeat—for I can scarce believe the evidence of my own senses! The charges brought against you, by the Houstons, are——"

"True! They are true!" she replied, in a voice of utter despair.

"Then, for three years past, ever since your betrothal to Mr. Ralph Houston, you have been in secret correspondence with a strange young man, disapproved by your protectress?" asked Major Helmstedt, in a sepulchral tone.

"I have—I have!"

"And you have met this young man more than once in private?"

"Yes, yes!" she gasped, with a suffocating sob.

"On the day of the festival, and of the landing of the British upon our island, you passed several hours alone with this person in the woods?"

A deprecating wave of the hand and another sob was her only reply.

"Once, at least, you received this man in your private apartment at Buzzard's Bluff?"

A gesture of affirmation and of utter despondency was her answer.

"The night of that same visit, you secretly left the room of your protectors for an unexplained absence of several days, some of which were passed in the company of this person?"

For all reply, she raised and clasped her hands and dropped them down before her, and let her head fall upon her bosom with an action full of irremediable despair.

Her father's face was dark with anguish.

"Speak, minion!" he said, "these things must not be left to conjecture; they must be clearly understood. Speak! answer!"

"I did," she moaned, in an expiring voice, as her head sank lower upon her breast, and her form cowered under the weight of an overwhelming shame and sorrow.

And well she might. Here, in the presence of men, in the presence of her father and her lover, she was making admissions, the lightest one of which, unexplained, was sufficient to brand her woman's brow with ineffaceable and eternal dishonor!

Her lover's head had sunk upon his breast, and he stood with folded arms, set lips, downcast eyes and impassable brow, upon which none could read his thoughts.

Her father's face had grown darker and sterner, as he questioned and she answered, until now it was terrible to look upon.

A pause had followed her last words, and was broken at length by Major Helmstedt, who, in a voice, awful in the stillness and depth of suppressed passion, said:

"Wretched girl! why do you linger here? Begone! and never let me see you more!"

"Father, father! have mercy, have mercy on your poor child!" she exclaimed, clasping her hands and dropping at his feet.

"Minion! never dare to desecrate my name, or pollute my sight again. Begone!" he exclaimed, spurning her kneeling form and turning away.

"Oh, father, father! for the sweet love of the Saviour!" she cried, throwing her arms around his knees and clinging to him.

"Wretch! outcast! release me, avoid my presence, or I shall be driven to destroy you, wanton!" he thundered, giving way to fury, and shaking her as a viper from her clinging hold upon his feet; "wanton! courtez— —"

But ere that word of last reproach could be completed, swift as lightning she flew to his bosom, clung about his neck, placed her hand over his lips to arrest his further speech, and gazing intensely, fiercely into his eyes—into his soul, exclaimed:

"Father, do not finish your sentence. Unless you wish me to drop dead before you, do not. As you hope for salvation, never apply that name to—her daughter."

"Her daughter!" he retorted, violently, shaking her off, until she fell collapsed and exhausted at his feet—"her daughter! Changeling, no daughter of hers or of mine are you. She would disown and curse you from her grave! and— —"

"Oh, mother, mother! oh, mother, mother!" groaned the poor girl, writhing and groveling like a crushed worm on the ground.

"And I," he continued, heedless of her agony, as he stooped, clutched her arm, jerked her with a spring upon her feet, and held her tightly confronting him.

"I—there was a time when I was younger, that had any woman of my name or blood made the shameful confessions that you have made this day, I would have slain her on the instant with this, my right hand. But age somewhat cools the head, and now I only spurn you—thus!"

And tightening his grasp upon her shoulder, he whirled her off with such violence that she fell at several yards distant, stunned and insensible upon the ground.

Then, followed by his second, he strode haughtily from the place.

Dr. Hartley, who had remained standing in amazement through the latter part of this scene, now hurried to the assistance of the swooning girl.

But Ralph Houston, shaking off the dreadful apathy that had bound his faculties, hastened to intercept him. Kneeling beside the prostrate form, he lifted and placed it in an easier position. Then, turning to arrest the doctor's steps, he said:

"Before you come nearer to her, tell me this: What do you believe of her?"

"That she is a fallen girl," replied Dr. Hartley.

"Then, no nearer on your life and soul," said Ralph, lifting his hand to bar the doctor's further approach.

"What do you mean, Captain Houston?"

"That she still wears the betrothal ring I placed upon her finger. That I am, as yet, her affianced husband. And, by that name, I claim the right to protect her in this, her bitter extremity; to defend her bruised and broken heart from the wounds of unkind eyes! Had you had faith in her, charity for her, I should have accepted, with thanks, your help. As it is, you have none; do not let her awake to find a hostile countenance bending over her!"

"As you please, sir. But, remember, that if the assistance of a physician is absolutely required, my services, and my home also, await the needs of Marguerite De Lancie's daughter," said Dr. Hartley, turning to depart.

Frank also, at a sign from his brother, withdrew.

Ralph was alone with Margaret. He raised her light form, shuddering, amid all his deeper distress, to feel how light it was, and bore her down the wooded hill, to the great spreading oak, under which was the green mound of her mother's last sleeping place.

He laid her down so that her head rested on this mound as on a pillow, and then went to a spring near by to bring water, with which, kneeling, he bathed her face.

Long and assiduous efforts were required before she recovered from that mortal swoon.

When at length, with a deep and shuddering sigh, and a tremor that ran through all her frame, she opened her eyes, she found Ralph Houston kneeling by her side, bending with solicitous interest over her.

With only a dim and partial recollection of some great agony passed, she raised her eyes and stretched forth her arms, murmuring, in tender, pleading tones:

"Ralph, my friend, my savior, you do not believe me guilty? You know me so thoroughly; you always trusted me; you are sure that I am innocent?"

"Margaret," he said, in a voice of the deepest pain, "I pillowed your head here above your mother's bosom; had I not believed you guiltless of any deeper sin than inconstancy of affection, I should not have laid you in this sacred place."

"Inconstancy! Ralph?"

"Fear nothing, poor girl! it is not for me to judge or blame you. You were but a child when our betrothal took place; you could not have known your own heart; I was twelve years your senior, and I should have had more wisdom, justice, and generosity than to have bound the hand of a child of fourteen to that of a man of twenty-six. We have been separated for three years. You are now but seventeen, and I am in my thirtieth year. You have discovered your mistake, and I suffer a just punishment. It is natural."

"Oh, my God! my God! my cup overflows with bitterness!" moaned the poor maiden, in a voice almost inaudible from anguish.

"Compose yourself, dear Margaret. I do not reproach you in the least; I am here to serve you as I best may; to make you happy, if it be possible. And the first step to be taken is to restore to you your freedom."

"Oh, no! Oh, Lord of mercy, no! no! no!" she exclaimed, in an agony of prayer; and then, in sudden self-consciousness, she flushed all over her face and neck with maiden shame, and became suddenly silent.

"Dear Margaret," said Ralph, in a tone of infinite tenderness and compassion, "you have suffered so much that you are scarcely sane. You hardly know what you would have. Our betrothal must, of course, be annulled. You must be free to wed this lover of your choice. I hope that he is, in some measure, worthy of you; nay, since you love him, I must believe that he is so."

"Oh, Ralph, Ralph! Oh, Ralph, Ralph!" she cried, wringing her hands.

"Margaret, what is the meaning of this?"

"I have no lover except you. I never wronged you in thought, or word, or deed; never, never, never!"

"Dear Margaret, I have not charged you with wronging me."

"But I have no lover; do you hear, Ralph? I never have had one! I never should have so desecrated our sacred engagement."

"Poor Margaret, you are distracted! Much grief has made you mad! You no longer know what you say."

"Oh, I do, I do! never believe but I know every word that I speak. And I say that my heart has never wandered for an instant from its allegiance to yourself! And listen farther, Ralph," she said, sinking upon her knees beside that grave, and raising her hands and eyes to heaven with the most impressive solemnity, "listen while I swear this by the heart of her who sleeps beneath this sod, and by my hopes of meeting her in heaven! that he with whom my name has been so wrongfully connected was no lover of mine—could be no lover of mine!"

"Hold, Margaret! Do not forswear yourself even in a fit of partial derangement. Rise, and recall to yourself some circumstances that occurred immediately before you became insensible, and which, consequently, may have escaped your memory. Recollect, poor girl, the admissions you made to your father," said Ralph, taking her hand and gently constraining her to rise.

"Oh, Heaven! and you believe—you believe——"

"Your own confessions, Margaret, nothing more; for had an angel from heaven told the things of you that you have stated of yourself, I should not have believed him!"

"Oh, my mother! Oh, my God!" she cried, in a tone of such deep misery, that, through all his own trouble, Ralph deeply pitied and gently answered her.

"Be at ease. I do not reproach you, my child."

"But you believe. Oh, you believe——"

"Your own statement concerning yourself, dear Margaret; no more nor less."

"Believe no more. Not a hair's breadth more. Scarcely so much. And draw from that no inferences. On your soul, draw no inferences against me; for they would be most unjust. For I am yours; only yours; wholly yours. I have never, never had any purpose, wish, or thought at variance with your claims upon me."

"You must pardon me, Margaret, if I cannot reconcile your present statement with the admissions lately made to your father. Allow me to bring them to your memory."

"Oh, Heaven, have mercy on me!" she cried, covering her face.

"Remember, I do not reproach you with them; I only recall them to your mind. You have been in secret correspondence with this young man for three years past; you have given him private meetings; you have passed hours alone in the woods with him; you have received him in your chamber; you have been abroad for days in his company; you have confessed the truth of all this; and yet you declare that he is not, and cannot be a lover of yours. Margaret, Margaret, how can you expect me, for a moment, to credit the amazing inconsistency of your statements?"

While he spoke, she stood before him in an agony of confusion and distress, her form cowering; her face sunk upon her breast; her eyes shunning his gaze; her face, neck, and bosom crimsoned with fiery blushes; her hands writhed together; her whole aspect one of conscious guilt, convicted crime, and overwhelming shame.

The anguish stamped upon the brow of her lover was terrible to behold. Yet he governed his emotions, and compelled his voice to be steady in saying:

"Dear Margaret, if in any way you can reconcile these inconsistencies—speak!"

Speak. Ay, she might have done so. One word from her lips would have sufficed to lift the cloud of shame from her brow, and to crown her with an aureola of glory; would have averted the storm of calamity gathering darkly over her head, and restored her, a cherished daughter, to the protecting arms of her father; an honored maiden to the esteem of friends and companions; a beloved bride to the sheltering bosom of her bridegroom. A word would have done this; yet that word, which could have lifted the shadow from her own heart and life, must have bid it settle, dark and heavy, upon the grave of the dumb, defenseless dead beneath her feet. And the word remained unspoken.

"I can die for her; but I cannot betray her. I can live dishonored for her sake; but I cannot consign her memory to reproach," said the devoted daughter to her own bleeding and despairing heart.

"Margaret, can you explain the meaning of these letters, these meetings in the woods, on the river, in your own chamber?"

"Alas! I cannot. I can only endure," she moaned, in a voice replete with misery, as her head sunk lower upon her breast, and her form cowered nearer the ground, as if crushed by the insupportable weight of humiliation.

It was not in erring human wisdom to look upon her thus, to listen to her words, and not believe her a fallen angel!

And yet she was innocent. More than innocent. Devoted, heroic, holy.

But, notwithstanding this, and her secret consciousness of this, how could she—in her tender youth, with her maiden delicacy and sensitiveness to reproach—how could she stand in this baleful position, and not appear overwhelmed by guilt and shame?

There was a dread pause of some minutes, broken at length by Ralph, who said:

"Margaret, will you return me that betrothal ring?"

She answered:

"You placed it on my finger, Ralph! Will you also take it off? I was passive then; I will be passive now."

Ralph raised the pale hand in his own and tried to draw off the ring. But since, three years before, the token had been placed upon the little hand of the child, that hand had grown, and it was found impossible to draw the ring over the first joint.

Ralph Houston, unwilling to give her physical pain, resisted in his efforts, saying quietly, as he bowed and left her:

"The betrothal ring refuses to leave your finger, Margaret. Well, good-morning!"

A smile, holy with the light of faith, hope, and love, dawned within her soul and irradiated her brow. In a voice, solemn, thrilling with prophetic joy, she said:

"The ring remains with me! I hail it as the bow of promise! In this black tempest, the one shining star!"

CHAPTER XV
NIGHT AND ITS ONE STAR

Two years had elapsed since the disappearance of Margaret Helmstedt.

Major Helmstedt had caused secret investigations to be set on foot, that had resulted in demonstrating, beyond the shadow of a doubt, that Margaret Helmstedt and William Dawson had embarked as passengers on board the bark *Amphytrite*, bound from Norfolk to Liverpool. From the day upon which this fact was ascertained, Margaret's name was tacitly dropped by all her acquaintances.

It was about twelve months after the disappearance of Margaret that old Mr. Wellworth died, and his orphan daughter Grace found a refuge in the home of Nellie Houston.

Ralph Houston was then at home, considering himself quite released by circumstances from his rash vow of forsaking his father's house.

Grace, the weak-hearted little creature, permitted herself to mistake all Ralph's brotherly kindness for a warmer affection, and to fall incontinently in love with him.

When the clergyman's daughter had been their inmate for six months, Mrs. Houston astounded the young man by informing him that unless his intentions were serious, "he really should not go on so with the poor fatherless and motherless girl."

Captain Houston did not love Grace—but he rather liked her. He thought her very pretty, gentle, and winning; moreover, he believed her soft, pliable, elastic little heart capable of being broken!

Since Margaret was lost to him forever, perhaps he might as well as not make this pretty, engaging little creature his wife. The constant presence of Grace was an appeal to which he impulsively yielded. Then—the word spoken—there was no honorable retreat.

Christmas was the day appointed for the wedding. Clare Hartley consented to officiate as bridesmaid; Frank Houston agreed to act as groomsman, and Dr. Hartley offered to give the fatherless bride away.

The twenty-fifth day of December dawned clear and cold. The whole bridal company that had assembled the evening previous set out at the appointed hour for the church.

They reached the church a few minutes before nine o'clock. Dr. Simmons, the pastor, was already in attendance. The bridal party passed up the aisle and formed before the altar. Amid the solemn silence that ever precedes such rites the marriage ceremony commenced.

"Dearly beloved, we are gathered together here in the sight of God, and in the face of this company, to join together this man and this woman in holy matrimony; which is commended of Saint Paul to be honorable among all men; and therefore is not by any to be entered into unadvisedly or lightly; but reverently, discreetly, advisedly, soberly, and in the fear of God. Into this holy estate, these two persons present come now to be joined. If any man can show just cause why they may not be lawfully joined together, let him now speak, or else, hereafter, forever hold his peace— —"

Here the minister made the customary pause; and then, just as he was about to resume his reading, there was the sound of an opening door, and a clear, commanding voice, exclaiming:

"Stop, on your lives! The marriage must not proceed!"

At the same moment all eyes were turned in astonishment, to see a gentleman, with a veiled lady leaning on his arm, advancing toward the altar.

The minister laid down his book; the bridegroom turned, with a brow of stern inquiry, upon the intruder; the bride stood in trembling amazement. Colonel Houston alone had the presence of mind to demand, somewhat haughtily:

"Pray, sir, what is the meaning of this most offensive conduct? By what authority do you venture to interrupt these solemnities?"

The young stranger turned and bowed to the questioner, smiling good-humoredly as he answered:

"Faith, sir! by the authority conferred upon me by the ritual, which exhorts that any man who can show any cause why these two persons may not be united in matrimony, forthwith declare it. So adjured, I speak— happening to know two causes why these two persons may not be lawfully joined together. The fair bride has been for two years past my promised wife, and the gallant bridegroom's betrothal ring still encircles the finger of Margaret Helmstedt!"

"And who are you, sir, that ventures to take these words upon your lips?" now asked Ralph Houston, deeply shaken by the mention of his Margaret's name.

"I am," replied the young man, speaking slowly and distinctly, "William Daw, Earl of Falconridge, the half-brother of Margaret Helmstedt by the side of our mother, Marguerite De Lancie, who, previous to becoming the wife of Mr. Philip Helmstedt, had been the wife and the widow of Lord William Daw. Should my statement require confirmation," continued the young man, "it can be furnished by documents in my possession, and which I am prepared to submit to any person concerned." Bowing to the astounded party, he retraced his steps.

The silence of amazement bound all the hearers; nor was the spell broken until the young lady who leaned upon the arm of Lord Falconridge drew aside her veil, revealing the pale and lovely countenance of Margaret Helmstedt, and crossed over to the side of Major Helmstedt, saying:

"Father, the labor of my life is accomplished; my mother's name is clear forever!" and overpowered by excess of emotion, she sank fainting at the feet of her astonished parent.

"Margaret! my Margaret!" exclaimed Ralph Houston, forgetting everything else, and springing forward. Tenderly lifted in the arms of Ralph, Margaret was conveyed to the parsonage, and laid on the bed in the best chamber. Here efforts to restore her to consciousness were vainly pursued for a long time.

When at last a change came, returning life was scarcely less alarming than apparent death had been. For weeks she wandered in a most distressing delirium.

It was about this time that Major Helmstedt and Lord Falconridge had a long business conversation. The major, being perfectly assured in regard to his identity and his claims, delivered up into his lordship's hands such portion of his mother's estate as he would have legally inherited. After the transfer was made, Lord Falconridge executed an instrument, conveying the whole disputed property to his sister, Margaret Helmstedt, "and her heirs forever."

Not until Margaret was fully restored to health was the whole secret history of her mother's most unhappy life revealed. The facts, obtained at intervals, were, in brief, these:

Marguerite De Lancie, tempted by inordinate social ambition, had consented to a private marriage with Lord William Daw.

His lordship's tutor, the Rev. Mr. Murray, became a party to the plan, even to the extent of performing the marriage ceremony. His lordship's valet was the only witness. The certificate of marriage was left in the hands of the bride. The ceremony took place at Saratoga, in the month of July.

Two months after, early in September, Lord William Daw, summoned by his father to the bedside of his declining mother, sailed for England.

Marguerite received from him one letter, dated at sea, and in which he addressed her as his "beloved wife," and signed himself, boy-loverlike, her "adoring husband." This letter was directed to Lady William Daw, under cover to Marguerite De Lancie. It was the only one that he ever had the opportunity of writing to her. It arrived about the time that the wife first knew that she was also destined to become a mother.

In the January following the receipt of this letter, Marguerite went with the Comptons to the New Year's evening ball at the Executive Mansion. It was while standing up in a quadrille that she overheard two gentlemen speak of the wreck of the bark *Venture* off the coast of Cornwall, with the loss of all on board.

Marguerite fainted; and thence followed the terrible illness that brought her to the borders of death—of death, for which indeed she prayed and hoped; for what a wretched condition was hers! She, one of the most beautiful, accomplished, and high-spirited queens of society, found herself fated to become a mother, without the power of proving that she had ever possessed the right to the name of wife.

As soon as she was able to recollect, reflect, and act, she felt that the only hope of recognition as the widow of Lord William Daw rested with the family of the latter; and she determined to go secretly to England. She made her preparations and departed.

She reached London, where, overtaken by the pangs of maternity, she gave birth to a son, and immediately fell into a long and dangerous fever. Upon recovering, she sought the Yorkshire home of her father-in-law, and revealed to him her position.

Marguerite was prepared for doubt, difficulty, and delay, but not for the utter incredulity, scorn, and rejection, to which she was subjected by the arrogant Marquis of Eaglecliff. Marguerite exhibited the certificate of her marriage, and the sole letter her young husband had ever had the power to write to her, and pleaded for recognition.

Now the old marquis knew the handwriting of his son, and of his chaplain; but, feeling outraged by what he chose to consider artifice on the part of Marguerite, disobedience on that of William, and treachery on that of Mr. Murray, he contemptuously put aside the certificate as a forgery, and the letter, beginning "My beloved wife," as the mere nonsense of a boy-lover writing to his mistress.

Indignant and broken-hearted, Marguerite took her son and returned to her native country; put the boy out to nurse, and then sought her home in Virginia, to reflect, amid its quiet scenes, upon her future course.

Marguerite's confidential consultations with various eminent lawyers had resulted in no encouragement for her to seek legal redress; she determined to rear her boy in secrecy; and watch if, perchance, some opportunity for successfully pushing his claims should occur. Further, she resolved to remain unmarried, and to devote herself to the welfare of this unacknowledged son, so that, should all his rights of birth be finally denied, she could at last legally adopt him, and make him her sole heir. Somewhat quieted by this resolution, Marguerite De Lancie became once more the ascendant star of fashion. The greater part of each year she spent in the hamlet in the State of New York where she had placed her son at nurse, accounting for her long absences by the defiant answer, "I've been gypsying."

Thus three years slipped away, when at length Marguerite De Lancie met her fate in Philip Helmstedt, the only man whom she ever really loved.

The tale she durst not tell her lover, she insanely hoped might be successfully concealed, or safely confided to her husband. Ah, vain hope! Philip Helmstedt, to the last degree jealous and suspicious, was the worst man on the face of the earth to whom to confide her questionable story.

They were married; and for a time she was lost in the power that attracted, encircled, and swallowed up her whole fiery nature.

From this deep trance of bliss she was electrified by the receipt of a letter, advising her of the sudden and dangerous illness of the unowned child. Here was an exigency for which she was totally unprepared. She prayed

Philip Helmstedt to permit her to depart, for a season, unquestioned. This strange petition gave rise to the first misunderstanding between them. With the terrible scenes that followed the reader is already acquainted. She was not suffered to depart.

A subsequent letter informed her of the convalescence of her son.

A superficial peace, without confidence, ensued between herself and husband. They went to Richmond, where Marguerite, filled with grief, remorse, and terror, so distractedly overacted her part as queen of fashion, that she brought upon herself, from wondering friends, the suspicion of partial insanity.

It was at this time that she received a third letter, advising her of the nearly fatal relapse of her child.

Knowing from past experience how vain it would be to hope for Philip Helmstedt's consent to her unexpected absence, she secretly departed, to spend a few weeks with her suffering child. She reached the hamlet, nursed her boy through his illness, and then placed him to be reared and educated in the family of the poor village pastor, to whom, for his services as tutor, she offered a liberal salary.

The Rev. John Braunton was a man past middle age, of acute intellect, conscientious principles, and benevolent disposition. From his keen perceptive faculties it was impossible to hide the fact that the mysterious lady, who took such deep and painful interest in this child, was other than the boy's mother.

Having arranged a system of correspondence with the clergyman, and paid a half year's salary in advance, Marguerite Helmstedt departed for her Virginia home, full of intense anxiety as to the reception she would meet from her husband. We know what that reception was. Philip Helmstedt must have sacrificed her life to his jealous rage but that she was destined to be the mother of his child. He kept his wife from her son for fifteen years.

In the meantime Mr. Braunton, who regularly received his salary, wondered that he received no more visits from the guardian or mother of his pupil. As the years passed he expostulated by letter. Marguerite wept, but could not go.

Some time after this, Braunton suddenly appeared before her on the island to inform her that her boy, grown restive in his rustic residence, had run away from home. Nothing could be discovered in relation to the missing youth, and from this time Marguerite Helmstedt's health rapidly declined.

Once more Marguerite saw her son. In the spring of 1814 he suddenly appeared before her in the uniform of a British soldier—claimed her assistance, and adjured her to reveal to him his birth and parentage. His miserable mother evaded his question, besought him to return to the protection of Mr. Braunton, and, promising to write, or to see him again, dismissed him.

That visit was the deathblow from which Marguerite never recovered. She died, and, dying, bequeathed to her daughter the legacy of this secret.

Having vindicated her mother's honor, Margaret would now withhold the particulars of her own perseverance and self-denial in the cause of her brother. But her father and her lover were not to be thus put off. Little by little, they drew from the reluctant girl the story of her devotion to her mother's trust. The ample income, drawn from her mother's legacy of Plover's Point, had been regularly sent to Mr. Braunton, to be invested for the benefit of William Dawson; afterward a correspondence was opened with the young man.

When subsequently they happened to meet that day on Helmstedt Island, the young man sought to compel, from her lips, the story of his parentage; but Margaret refused to tell him anything, and spoke of her mother only as his patroness.

But when he begged to be shown her grave, Margaret consented. They took a boat and went up the river to the family burial ground at Plover's Point. They returned in the evening—the young soldier to rejoin his comrades—Margaret to rejoin her friends, and to meet suspicions which she had no power to quell.

It was some weeks after this when the famous attack upon the parsonage was made, and young William Dawson was taken prisoner. While upon his parole, an irresistible attraction drew him to seek Margaret. He visited her in her private apartment, entering and departing by the garden door. Nellie saw him depart. Margaret besought him to come no more. After that, he lingered near the house, and met her in her walks. The spies of Nellie Houston discovered and reported this interview. Yet again they met in the woods, where Margaret entreated him not to waylay her.

About that time also, Clare Hartley spoke in the presence of the young ensign of her own and Margaret Helmstedt's purposed visit to Fort Warburton. The visit was not made; but William Dawson, missing Margaret from her accustomed haunts, wandered off to the neighborhood of Fort

Warburton, where he was taken for a spy, and as such might have been hung, had he not bribed a messenger to carry a note to his sister, whom he now knew to be not at the fort. The messenger, in going away, was seen by Nellie, who naturally took him to be the young ensign. Margaret obeyed the peremptory summons, and the same night departed for Fort Warburton. With the terrible train of misfortunes that ensued, the reader is already acquainted.

Immediately after the prevented duel and the parting with her lover, Margaret sought her brother, and, taking the marriage certificate, and the letter of Lord William Daw, embarked with her brother for Liverpool.

On reaching England, she immediately sought the Marquis of Eaglecliff, and laid before him the claims of his grandson. At the first sight of the young man, the aged peer made an exclamation of surprise. So great was his likeness to the late Lord William Daw, that the marquis almost fancied he beheld again his long-lost son.

Legal steps were immediately taken to establish his identity and confirm his position. Law processes are proverbially slow. In all, it was about twelve months between the time that William Daw was acknowledged by his grandfather, and the time when his position as the legal heir of Eaglecliff was permanently established. And it was more than two years from the day upon which the brother and sister had sailed to England, to that upon which they so opportunely returned to America.

But little remains to be written. With spring, Margaret's beauty bloomed again.

In June Ralph Houston led his long-affianced bride to the altar. After an extended trip through New England, they took up their residence in the city of Richmond, where Ralph Houston had been appointed to a high official post.

Lord Falconridge remained through the winter, the guest of his sister and brother-in-law. Major Helmstedt, of course, took up his abode with his daughter and her husband.

Honest Frank Houston married Clare Hartley, with whom he lives very happily at Plover's Point.

I am sorry that I cannot present poor little Grace Wellworth as a countess, but, truth to tell, the young earl never resumed his addresses. So Grace, in fear of being an old maid, accepted the proposals soon afterward made to her by Mr. Simmons, the minister, to whom she makes a very exemplary wife.